A Game of Veils

EVA CHASE

THE ROYAL SPARES - BOOK 1

A Game of Veils

Book 1 in the Royal Spares series

First Digital Edition, 2024

Copyright © 2024 Eva Chase

Cover design: Sanja Balan (Sanja's Covers)

Map design: Fictive Designs

Ebook ISBN: 978-1-998752-90-4

Paperback ISBN: 978-1-998752-91-1

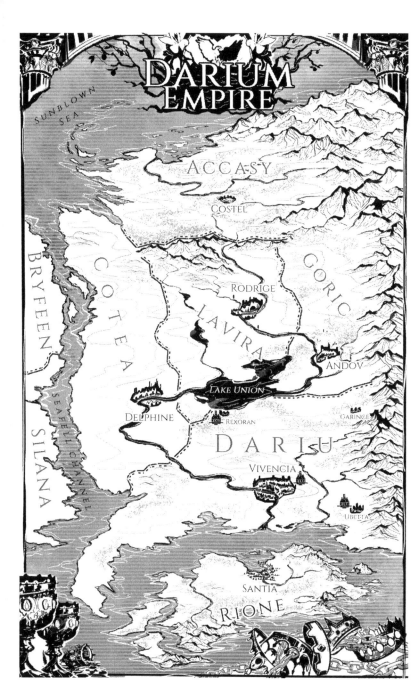

CHAPTER ONE

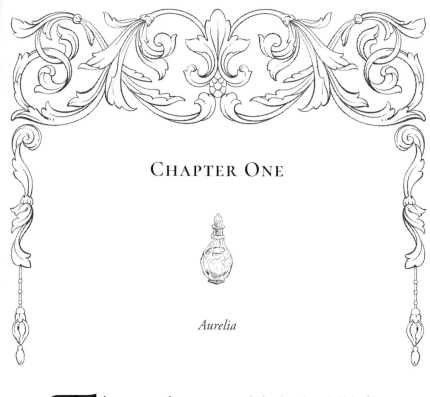

Aurelia

T he carriage has just crested the last low hill before the imperial capital when the spring breeze sours with the stink of rotting flesh.

Our driver exhales sharply and clucks at the horses to pick up the pace. My stomach knots.

The sight beyond the window can only be disturbing, but I need to face everything that lies ahead of me.

As I reach for the curtain, Cici makes a soft noise of protest where she's sitting on the opposite bench. When I tug at the fabric regardless, she simply closes her eyes.

At first, the narrow view shows only scattered farmhouses amid golden fields beneath the clear blue sky.

Then a post comes into view next to the road.

A corpse dangles, limp feet hovering over the ground, a head with blood-caked hair sagging. What skin I can see is purpled and torn by the beaks and teeth of scavengers.

The largest gouge was clearly made by a sword. Someone carved open this man's front from throat to groin to let his innards spill out in a gruesome display.

It's a reminder from Emperor Tarquin of what happens to those he believes threaten his empire.

Whatever the man's crimes, he wasn't alone in them. More posts stand in a row with his, each holding a body ripped apart in the same way.

The one beside him wears the remains of a dress. His wife? After her, another in trousers, and finally—

A form barely half the height of the others, tiny hands with mangled fingers, a crimson-splattered ribbon unraveling from pale hair.

I shut my own eyes then, clenching my hand against the urge to clamp it to my mouth. Willing down the surge of nausea that roils in my gut.

Cici won't judge me for my horror, but I'll be surrounded by those who will soon enough.

When I'm sure my arm won't shake, I tap three fingers to my forehead, heart, and belly in acknowledgment of the nine godlen who watch over us. Those lesser gods are the only divine power we can appeal to.

I finish the gesture of the divinities with a clasp of my hand over my sternum, where my skin beneath the bodice of my dress is branded with the sigil of the one godlen I specifically dedicated myself to.

Elox, I think in a silent prayer, *may their souls be at rest and let me bring healing to this place.*

Whatever that family did, I can't accept that a child deserved such brutal punishment.

The godlen of medicine and peace doesn't respond, but then, I've never met anyone the gods have spoken to directly. That isn't how they work.

A tendril of calm unfurls inside me as if in a gentle caress. My shoulders straighten in response.

I will not be shaken from my purpose.

When I open my eyes, the butchery beyond the window has passed behind us. The putrid stench is fading away.

Cici shoots me a tight smile, her sallow face looking slightly greenish. "His son could be different."

I allow myself what might be my last fully honest comment before the imperial palace swallows me and my maid up. "Let's hope so."

Should a woman be happier than this on her way to her wedding? In some ways, I am pleased.

I've spent twenty-one years standing on the sidelines, watching my country suffocate under the empire's thumb. Knowing it's my older sister who'll rule after our parents—as much as anyone in our family rules with the limited authority our conquerors allow us to keep—and that my primary value is in the loyalties my marriage can strengthen. All I could do was wait and find out what man I'd end up tied to.

For the first time, I'm contributing something to our kingdom, to my people. And it's more than I ever could have dreamed possible.

Somehow my parents arranged a betrothal to the most powerful bachelor in the continent: the heir to the entire empire.

Given Emperor Tarquin's reputation, agreeing to their proposition must have been an entirely strategic move on his part. He's tying my distant country more deeply into the empire, enforcing my parents' and my sister's loyalty for decades to come.

Gods only know what other factors motivated him to

accept the offer. This is a man who thinks stringing up mutilated children is a reasonable law enforcement tactic.

But his son, Marclinus, is a separate person. He isn't the one enforcing the laws… yet.

I'll keep an open mind. Find the best in the situation I've been presented with.

If the imperial heir will listen to me, I could give every citizen of Accasy a better future.

I fold my hands together on my lap, my thumb sliding over the rippled gold of the ring on my left forefinger. The impression rises up of Mother squeezing my hands when we stood in the castle courtyard just before I left.

You are wanted, she said, *and that is a kind of power. Don't let them strip away who you are. Trust in your gift.*

When she hugged me, the tremor that ran through her slim frame contradicted the confidence in her words.

The halt of the carriage tells me we've reached one of the gates into Dariu's massive capital city. When the driver produces his papers with their official seals and announces that he's escorting Princess Aurelia of Accasy, the guards wave us onward.

One aims a leering glance through the window as the wheels rattle by. I pretend I'm too distracted by the looming buildings to notice.

I've heard that over a hundred thousand people reside within Vivencia's walls. It's hard to wrap my head around that number when Accasy's largest city contains less than a third of that number.

Plenty of the citizens are going about their business on the stone-paved streets. They stroll past tenement buildings, duck in and out of shops, and lean on their window ledges to bask in the mid-day sun.

Everyone I see looks contented enough. I suppose as long

as their actions don't clash with the emperor's plans, he treats the people of his own country benevolently.

Why order them into back-breaking labor or let his soldiers run wild among them when he can exploit those he's conquered instead?

As we weave between the tall buildings, the breeze dwindles. The spring warmth turns to mugginess within the confines of the carriage.

I swipe at the long brown waves of my hair in an attempt to cool the perspiration beading on my neck. Cici tuts at me and leans over to tidy a few particularly errant strands.

Back home, I'd have had my hair pulled back in clips or braids to keep them out of my way. Why does a country with a significantly hotter climate make a fashion of unmarried women keeping their hair loose?

When I left Accasy, the air still held the crisp freshness that arrives with the spring leaves. I could have walked into the dense woods beyond the castle if I was seeking a deeper cool relief.

The homesickness wells up inside me so abruptly I nearly choke on it.

It's a long trek north. I can't imagine my future husband will be all that enthusiastic about regular visits.

A lump rises in my throat, but I swallow it down.

It doesn't matter. I'm entering this marriage to free my people from the worst of the tyranny, even if I'm not there to see them thrive.

I still have my memories to hold on to, whatever else happens.

Cici peers outside with wide eyes. "The city's so *big*. I wonder how far it is to the palace?"

The maps I studied swim up through my memories. "The

imperial compound is at the south end, by the river. We'll have to pass through a lot of Vivencia to get there."

"I guess that gives us some time to take a look at the place." She offers me another smile, this one softer around the edges.

I return it with a pang of gratitude. We're both venturing into unknown territory. The uncertainty is easier to bear with a companion on the journey.

Cici came on as my maid just four years ago. She's always kept a certain respectful distance, but she's gamely aided when I'm working on a concoction and never grumbled about how many hours I spend outside like my childhood maid used to.

Maybe once we're caught up in the imperial court together, we can become something more like friends.

The buildings on either side of the broad road grow taller and more sprawling. We pass an expansive park of grassy fields, flower beds, and fountains amid only a few stately trees. Men and women in flowing jackets and dresses meander along the paths or ride on horseback.

After passing a few more grand estates, we stop at another gate.

It takes our driver longer to make his case for entry into the imperial palace grounds. Finally, our horses draw us past elaborate hedges and a towering sculpture of Creaden, the godlen who presides over leadership and justice. He's been carved with the imperial crest clasped in his hands: a majestic hawk soaring over a grand oak, with the motto *CONQUER ALL* framing them.

That statue is followed by several life-size busts of imposing men and women I assume are past emperors and empresses. Then the carriage turns with an arc in the drive, and the palace comes into view.

I find myself staring at the three-story building of silvery marble that could encompass my family's castle ten times over.

My jaw goes slack before I can control my shock. In the first instant, I can only stare at the massive columns carved with leafy designs and the lofty windows reflecting the glare of the sun.

As the carriage rasps to a halt, several men in the purple-and-gray imperial livery stride down the stairs outside the yawning palace entrance. A few move to the back of the carriage to retrieve my two trunks. Another places a step beside the carriage while his colleague opens the door.

Girding myself, I paste a smile on my face, gather my silk skirts, and ease out into the tiled courtyard.

The stoutest of the staff, a jowly man who looks at least ten years older than his apparent underlings, is waiting for me. He dips his head in a motion of deference that's not quite a bow. "Princess Aurelia. It's a pleasure to welcome you to Dariu and His Imperial Majesty's home. I hope your journey went smoothly."

He speaks in Darium, of course, knowing I'll understand. Every royal throughout the empire learns the language of our conquerors alongside our native tongue.

At his question, the image of the corpses hanging by the road flits through my mind. I hold my smile in place. "Quite, but I'm certainly glad to be at the end of it."

"We'll first be—" He cuts himself off to frown at Cici, who's positioned herself beside me with her own bag by her feet. "Was there something you needed from your mistress before you return?"

Cici blinks. "Return? I'm Princess Aurelia's maid, sir." She dips into a brief curtsy.

"And I'm sure you've tended to her well during her

travels," the emperor's man says evenly. "But His Imperial Majesty prefers to select all the staff who work within these walls. The princess will be assigned a very capable maid of our own."

My stomach sinks. Cici darts a nervous look toward me.

If we argue rather than accepting the supposed generosity, will the emperor suspect some ulterior motive?

What are the chances he'll bend his usual policy for a woman he barely knows, soon-to-be-wife of his son or not… rather than string Cici up at the side of the road as punishment for our defiance?

I speak cautiously. "We weren't informed. My parents assumed—"

The stout man cuts in with a brusque tone. "She and your driver can inform them of the arrangements when they return. You should find our hospitality warrants no complaints."

The note of warning in his words sends a sliver of ice down my spine. I'd *better* not complain.

I don't want to start off my time here on the wrong foot. Or see an innocent woman harmed simply because it wrenches at me to lose the comfort of her presence.

I touch Cici's arm in reassurance. "It's fine. Tell my parents that Emperor Tarquin is taking care of everything for me."

Her expression stays worried. I dip my head in a slight nod, holding her gaze firmly. "Safe travels."

I'll be all right. I was born for this.

She gives my hand a quick squeeze, her eyes shimmering with sudden tears, and then one of the footmen is ushering her back into the carriage. I watch it pull away with a tearing sensation in my chest.

Now I'm utterly alone.

The man who greeted me clears his throat. "His Imperial Majesty is eager to welcome you personally and introduce you to his court."

Including his son, my future husband. We had better get that over with.

My smile might be a little stiffer than it was before, but I follow my escort through the immense doorway obligingly.

I will not tremble. I will not falter.

I'm a joyful bride thrilled to have made such an incredible match.

And if a whiff of hysterical laughter bubbles inside me at that thought, I certainly won't let it out.

Inside, the imperial palace is just as overwhelming. The central hallway sprawls as wide as my bedroom at home. The ceilings loom far above my head, painted with vines and flowers framing open sky as if to give the impression they aren't ceilings at all.

I suppose the spaciousness makes sense given the difference in climate. Accasians prefer narrow halls and cozy rooms that are easy to keep warm during the frigid winters. These airy open spaces must be much cooler during the southern summer.

More marble gleams everywhere I look, alongside panes of etched gold, delicate mosaics, and oil paintings of majestic landscapes. Flute music carries faintly from up ahead, mingling with distant laughter. Potted plants with crimson and fuchsia blooms give off a heady floral scent.

Our footsteps tap across the tiled floor until we reach a set of double doors framed with gold. My escort marches a few paces ahead of me and declares my arrival to the room at large: "Princess Aurelia of Accasy!"

Clearly my impending arrival was noted well in advance.

The vast audience hall I step into holds dozens of people, all turning to watch my approach.

Most of my audience is gathered on either side of the violet rug that runs the length of the room. The men and women wear similar clothes to those I saw in the nearby park: gauzy dresses and silky shirts.

I wore my lightest gown in recognition of the warmer weather, but it seems to drag against my limbs as I make my way past their curious stares.

On the dais I'm heading toward, two gilded wooden thrones gleam, their backs pointed in elegant spires as if to mimic the crowns on their occupants' heads.

In the larger throne in the middle of the dais sits a tall man with a sharp-edged face and a pale scalp nearly as shiny as his seat. I've heard Emperor Tarquin took to shaving off all his hair as soon as it started to thin.

His eyebrows, just below the rim of his ornate golden crown, are such a light blond they blend into his skin, giving the eerie impression that he has none at all. A suit of black, gray, and indigo covers his sinewy frame.

As I force my legs to keep moving toward him, his steady gaze pierces straight through me.

I drag my attention away from the emperor's ominous presence to the younger man in the throne at his right.

This has to be Marclinus. A matching if simpler crown adorns his hair, which is nearly the same shade of gold as the metal. His angular features echo his father's, though much more appealing with some lingering softness of youth.

Unlike his father, he sprawls in his throne as if he's lounging at a tavern rather than conducting an official audience. His golden-blond curls drift carelessly across the tops of his ears and down to the nape of his neck.

When our eyes meet, he licks his lips.

That's how he greets his future wife?

The emperor is flanked by a few pensive-looking middle-aged figures I'd guess are advisors of some sort, one of them in a cleric's robes. Beyond the imperial heir's throne stand four men too young to have likely risen to such prominence. Three of them can't be much older than me, and the other looks to be in his teens.

Who are they? As far as I know Emperor Tarquin only has one son, and they don't look anything like him besides.

The tallest fills out his silk shirt with broad shoulders bulky with muscle. The cream-colored fabric sets off his tawny skin. His dark brown hair is pulled into a short ponytail at the nape of his neck.

His eyes, so light blue they're noticeable even from a distance, sear into me along with his scowl.

The leaner but still well-built guy next to him has a rich brown complexion in starker contrast with the imperial men. His thick black hair appears rumpled even cropped close to his handsome face. His dark eyes follow me, his hands balling at his sides.

Their somewhat shorter companion looks as if he's been denied a few meals. There's a hint of gauntness to both his pale face and his frame. But his features are still striking, his reddish-brown hair and deep green eyes giving his expression a kick of intensity. He's folded his slender arms tightly across his chest.

Even the teenager is glowering at me from beneath the fall of his white-blond hair. His gangly limbs make me think of an overgrown puppy, but his fierce expression is all guard dog.

What about me has provoked all this hostility?

I jerk my attention back to the emperor and stop a

couple of paces from the dais. There, I drop into my lowest curtsy.

I need to stay focused on the man with the real power here.

"It's an honor to be in your presence again, Your Imperial Majesty." I've only seen the emperor once before—a brief introduction when he toured his territories when I was six— but he'd expect me to remember that.

The emperor's smile is as sharp as his face. "Welcome to my court, Princess Aurelia. Let me formally introduce you to my son, His Imperial Highness Marclinus."

He sweeps his hand toward the lounging, golden-haired man, who sits up only a little straighter and gives me a jaunty wave. His eyes, the same gray as his father's, slide down my figure as if he's stripping off my gown with them.

The corner of his mouth quirks upward in what's closer to a smirk. "I think I'll enjoy making *your* acquaintance."

Great God help me, this is the man I'm supposed to live out my days with?

Emperor Tarquin doesn't appear fazed by his heir's attitude. He motions to the figures at his left. "The key members of my cabinet and all of my court look forward to celebrating your arrival." He tips his head toward the crowd around the room and pauses before glancing beyond his son as if he'd almost forgotten who else was present.

"Ah, and my foster sons: Prince Bastien, Prince Raul, Prince Lorenzo, and Prince Neven."

Foster sons? All princes?

Before I can even start to puzzle out that statement and his dismissive tone, the emperor goes on. "Given that your family suggested this match, I assume you've come willingly, Princess Aurelia."

I bob my head again. "Of course, Your Imperial Majesty."

"Refresh my memory and confirm what I was told. How old are you?"

"Twenty-one."

"And you're where in line to the throne of Accasy?"

"I'm my parents' second child, Your Imperial Majesty." Does he really need to hear me rehash all this?

Emperor Tarquin lets out a low chuckle. "The full title can become a mouthful. I give you permission to simply call me 'Emperor' for the duration of this conversation."

"Thank you, Emperor."

He lifts his chin toward me. "Which godlen have you dedicated to, and did you make a dedication sacrifice?"

I'm not sure how much detail he's heard from the imperial representative who conducted the betrothal negotiations, but I have no reason to obscure my answer. Nearly everyone in the realms dedicates themselves to one of our gods at twelve years old in the typical ceremony. It would be a shock if I hadn't.

At least half of the people I've met, nobles and commoners alike, took the greater opportunity presented by the dedication ceremony. It's the one chance we have to be blessed with a gift of magical talent. But of course we must offer something of ourselves in return.

"I dedicated to Elox," I say. "I sacrificed my spleen for a gift for making healing potions and other cures."

The emperor's eyebrows rise. I can't tell if he's genuinely startled or putting on an act to try to loosen my tongue. "A medic princess. That might be a first."

I give him the simplest honest explanation I can. "I wanted to be able to help people. I can't heal anyone directly, though, only concoct things that can."

"And have you faced any adverse consequences from the loss of your organ?"

I think of the tiny scar on my stomach. "Nothing significant. Illnesses tend to hit me harder and take longer to recover from, so I'm careful to look after my own health as well."

"Very wise."

The back of my neck prickles with the sense that he's subtly mocking me, but Emperor Tarquin leans back in his throne as if he's satisfied. "You appear to be exactly who we were promised."

I summon my brightest smile to cover my next lie. "I'm glad to have pleased you and look forward to my marriage with great joy."

The emperor rubs his thumb along the point of his chin. Something in his expression sets the hairs on the back of my neck on end before he even opens his mouth.

"*If* you marry. Let's not be hasty."

CHAPTER TWO

Aurelia

As the emperor's words reverberate in my ears, the bottom of my stomach drops out. *If* I marry?

My mind scrambles for an appropriate response. My face has gone rigid around my smile.

Is he putting me off-balance for his sadistic enjoyment, not really meaning what he implies? Or maybe he's only referring to some additional step before the final confirmation, like having one of the imperial medics check me over to confirm my good health?

My parents hashed out all the details with his representative before I even left Accasy. That man inspected me as if I was a brood mare he was considering adding to the palace stables. Emperor Tarquin just said I'm who he was promised.

What could cause any hesitation?

The emperor is studying me as if evaluating my reaction.

I reach for my deepest well of inner calm and keep my voice steady. "I would never overstep and rush Your Majesty."

If there's something more he wants from me, let him say so.

Emperor Tarquin pushes to his feet. His limbs might be as sharply angled as his face within the folds of his embroidered suit, but there's still plenty of heft to his aging body, a sense of strength it'd be hazardous to challenge.

Marclinus watches in his casual pose. My future husband's lips remain curved in a smirk as if he finds the proceedings amusing.

The emperor sweeps his penetrating gaze over the crowd of assembled nobles. I catch the briefest hint of a smirk, not unlike his heir's, before his expression returns to impenetrable cool.

He spreads his sinewy hands toward our audience. "When I announced my son's engagement, many members of my court expressed... concerns that I had selected a suitable match from abroad. Some felt that their daughters were not given an equal chance."

A chill seeps through my skin down to my bones. This doesn't sound like a lead-up to a medical exam.

The nobles stay as silent as I am. They know better than to interrupt a proclamation.

Emperor Tarquin peers down at them. "I would not wish to deny any of my loyal subjects your due. Marclinus must have the most suitable wife we can arrange. I believe all those who expressed their objections are with us today, so let us see your daughters. Leonette Cento, come forward."

A curvy woman with chestnut-brown hair and deeper brown skin steps from the crowd and walks up to stand where the emperor indicates, just a few paces away from me on the thick violet rug. Her pretty face shows nothing but determination.

"Rochelle Salacia."

A tall, broad-shouldered woman emerges with her fingers curled into the layers of her airy skirt. Her cloud of wheat-blond curls sways as she approaches the dais, her cheeks flushed beneath a sprinkling of freckles.

"Cadenza Leppum."

This woman looks like barely more than a girl, her blue eyes innocently wide and her smile giddy as she hustles over to join us.

I hold my own posture still and straight despite the thudding of my heart. What exactly is Emperor Tarquin playing at?

He calls out several more names, bringing lady after lady to stand by me. It's hard to keep track through the pounding of my pulse and my whirling thoughts.

The twelfth name comes with a note of finality. "Fausta Amata."

The last noblewoman to join our array strides forward with an air of total assurance despite her petite frame. Her flame-red hair spills in loose waves down her back, artfully untamed. Her bright green gaze burns into mine for an instant before she focuses all her attention on the emperor.

He nods to the gathered women with a benevolent air, but I catch a bit of an edge in his next words. "In the interests of fairness, these ladies will be given an equal opportunity alongside Princess Aurelia to prove how loyal and dedicated they are. Marclinus and I have devised a series of trials to evaluate their devotion. Whoever impresses us most will win her place at my son's side."

I have to grit my teeth to stop my jaw from dropping.

The lurch of my gut threatens to send my breakfast up my throat.

Murmurs break out among the nobles behind me, but most of them sound *pleased.* And why shouldn't they? Now their daughters are being considered, when my marriage was meant to be settled with all certainty.

Emperor Tarquin can't be serious. This is some kind of joke—or a brief test, to confirm my commitment and mettle—

The emperor returns to his throne, motioning toward his heir. "The first trial begins now. Listen well. Whoever performs worst will be removed from the competition."

Marclinus slides forward in his gilded seat, appearing energized by the turn of events. His gray eyes sparkle as he aims a cocky grin at the ladies gathered before him.

Merriment rings through his voice. "You will each tell me what you admire about me so much that you wish to take me as a husband. Please spare no detail."

Gods help me, this is really happening.

Before I can fully wrap my mind around that fact, the petite, redheaded noblewoman—Lady Fausta—struts forward without a second's hesitation. She kneels at the base of the dais in front of the imperial heir's throne and bows her head deferentially.

"Your Imperial Highness, you are the standard all men should aspire to meet. You stand up valiantly to threats abroad and keep us ever entertained while you're in court. No one could look upon you without appreciating the perfection of every aspect of your being."

Her honeyed but confident voice cuts through my bewildered daze. She's been clever, jumping in to make her case first. Praise won't sound as sincere if it's simply repeating what others have said.

She's both demonstrated her eagerness and ensured she's the act the rest of us have to follow.

Lady Fausta goes on in the same fawning tone. "You always have the right answer at the ready as well as a quip to delight us. Every party is brightened tenfold by your presence; every decision you make guides our empire toward further grandeur. I have lived in awe of you since the moment I met you."

As she rises to her feet, applause breaks out from the rest of the court. Marclinus gives a little bow as if to welcome her assessment, followed by a suggestive wink. A glint of triumph lights in Fausta's eyes.

She's the act we have to follow—and the more we follow, the more trite our veneration will appear.

If I don't want to see the brighter future I meant to bring my country crumble to dust, I need to stake my own claim, *now*.

Lady Fausta steps back from the dais. I propel myself forward before any of the other women can take her spot.

My mind is spinning. I rummage through the little I know about the imperial heir—he hasn't accomplished much while his father still rules, but he was apparently instrumental in quashing a minor rebellion in Rione—and what I've observed in the short time since my arrival.

I don't just need to speak quickly; I need to speak well.

And I need to lie through my teeth.

I bend down in front of Marclinus's throne as Fausta did. He stretches out his legs as if preparing to bask in my adoration.

Gods smite me, how I'm going to have to lie.

Let's start with the biggest one, then.

I pitch my voice to carry but keep my tone soft, as if I'm as awed as Lady Fausta claimed to be. "Your Imperial

Highness, I've only just met you, but I'm already struck by your incredible wisdom. I could never ask you to bind yourself to me before you've confirmed that I'm your ideal match. I came to find the best of husbands, and such an astute man would only want the best of wives."

I'm assuring him that there are no ruffled feathers, making myself look generous and understanding in a way none of the other ladies can. Where can I go from there?

"I heard tales of your military successes all the way in Accasy and can see you're every bit the champion I hoped to marry. You have a commanding air that will hold the whole empire in your sway. I was struck by it and your obvious charm from the moment I entered this room. Your generosity toward your court shows you have a commendable heart as well."

We won't speak about his lack of generosity toward his supposed betrothed.

I grope for an ideal ending note and bow a little lower as I choose my phrasing. "Looking at the women I stand among, it's clear you're also a discerning judge of character and beauty. Any of us would be lucky to win your hand. I'll strive with every fiber of my being to show that I'm worthy of your greatness."

When I lift my head, the smattering of applause isn't quite as enthusiastic as it was for Fausta. I hope that's only because the nobles are balancing their approval of my compliments with loyalty to the ladies of their court.

The imperial heir looks gratified enough, his grin stretching broader as he watches me get to my feet. A small scar cuts through his full upper lip on the lefthand side—the only imperfection on his stunning face. "Well spoken, princess of the wild north. I look forward to your striving."

He makes the statement sound like an invitation into his bed. I don't know how to answer it other than with a modest smile and another dip of a curtsy.

With my heart still racing, I pull back in the wake of another lady who's already rushing over. As I place myself off to the side of the cluster of court noblewomen, narrowed eyes and sharp frowns flick in my direction.

I don't think I've earned any good will among my companions with my performance.

Better that they hate me than that I fail in the purpose that brought me here.

I cling to that knowledge, tensing my body against a tremor that ripples down my spine. Now that I've said my piece and thrown my hat into the ring, every nerve has gone wobbly with the enormity of what's happened.

Twelve other ladies. Twelve rivals who know the imperial heir far better than I do, who are familiar with his whims in order to cater to them, who might have caught his eye long before I arrived.

Why would Emperor Tarquin pit me against them? Why summon me at all if he decided a local match would suit his and his son's political agenda better?

The way the emperor spoke about his court's concerns… I don't think he appreciated their criticism. Maybe this is all a sham of sorts—put the nobles in their places by dragging their daughters into a public spectacle and then declaring me the winner all the same.

He doesn't care if I'm humiliated along the way. That shouldn't surprise me at all.

While I concentrate on appearing cool and collected, I give each woman's deluge of praise a cursory listen in case there's some useful insight into Marclinus's tastes and opinions. They all blur together, none particularly notable. Most mention his leadership and bravery and how captivating he is at court.

Lady Cadenza, the girlish noblewoman who hasn't lost an ounce of her giddiness, blathers on for a few minutes about every facet of his stunning looks, from his "hair a richer hue than gold itself" to his "strapping form" that according to her is particularly magnificent when astride a horse. She finishes with a breathless overture about how much she'd like to wake up to his dazzling face every morning.

Lady Rochelle with the boundless curls seems a bit rushed about her petition, but she refers to Marclinus's kindness to her family in a time of need. Possibly he's occasionally less of a jerk than he's appeared so far.

I'm not yet ready to take comfort from that idea.

When the last of our number has spoken, the imperial heir contemplates the line of women before him with a satisfied expression. He clearly enjoys having his ego stroked.

His voice comes out jaunty. "You all are quite eager to join me in matrimony, and I wish I could honor every one of you with the title. But I'm afraid thirteen wives would be a bit much even for a man of my talents."

As a titter of laughter passes through the crowd, Marclinus glances toward his father, adjusting his hands against the arms of the throne.

Emperor Tarquin turns his head in what might be a subtle shake before speaking in a dry tone. "I was glad to hear so many of our candidates recognize your importance as a ruler in addition to as a husband."

His son's expression shifts slightly. I'm not sure exactly what message the emperor conveyed, but I'm abruptly certain that he's had the final say in their choice.

"Just so." Marclinus leans forward on his throne. "Even Princess Aurelia from far-off Accasy praised my leaderly prowess. And yet Lady Cadenza, you didn't say a word about anything other than my appeal on the eyes. Should I assume you see me as nothing but a handsome face?"

The giddy noblewoman blanches. She takes a step forward, wringing her hands. "No, not at all, Your Imperial Highness. I—I only meant— I was overwhelmed being so close to your magnificence— I have every faith—"

Marclinus interrupts her with a dismissive flick of his hand. "You were the only one who mentioned nothing beyond the superficial. It shows a lack of ingenuity as well. I must narrow down my options, and you gave the weakest effort."

While Lady Cadenza stands there stunned, he makes another brief gesture that I don't understand until one of the imperial guards marches forward from his post at the edge of the room.

Even though this woman—this *girl*—would have usurped my place with my promised husband, a pang of sympathy forms in my chest. I brace myself for protests and wails as the guard reaches for her arm to escort her out.

Except that's not what he's doing at all.

In a motion so swift I barely understand what's happening before it's already over, he unsheathes the dagger at his hip and slashes the blade across Lady Cadenza's throat.

A startled noise I can't quite stifle bursts from my lips. A couple of the other noblewomen shriek, those closest to Cadenza stumbling backward to avoid her crumpling body and the blood splattering across the tiled floor.

Her head hits the tiles with a fleshy smack. Her eyes have already glazed, unblinking as the blood pools beneath her.

An urgent muttering rises up among the nobles. All of the other ladies pull closer together, away from the murdered woman.

A few of them, including Lady Fausta, aim accusing glares at me, as if I carried out this slaughter by being the better example Marclinus pointed to.

Emperor Tarquin stands. The entire audience room falls into tense silence.

I clamp my jaw in place against the scream I'd like to let out, willing my expression to stay blank. Any horrified response beyond my brief display of shock could be taken as treason.

I can't stop myself from tracking the crimson puddle creeping farther at the edge of my vision.

The emperor glowers at his courtly subjects. "These are trials of devotion, and those who fail to convince us of their dedication must be eliminated from my court and our country. All these ladies will have their chance—as well as the consequences of the gamble they wished to make. I sincerely hope that none of you have so little faith in your own or your daughters' loyalties that you would attempt to withdraw them now?"

Not a single voice speaks up.

Nausea wraps around my innards like clammy fingers.

He's saying every trial will end in death. Every trial… until only one of us remains?

The emperor offers us all a smile that can only be described as smug. "I'll see you at dinner, then."

I ease backward, wanting to put myself farther from his gaze while I struggle to hold on to my placid mask.

A servant approaches and dips into a quick bow. "Princess Aurelia, I'm to show you to your room. Your luggage has already been conveyed there."

I nod mutely and trail behind her as she leads me toward a side door. My gaze drifts of its own accord over to the four princes, Emperor Tarquin's self-proclaimed foster sons.

They're staring back at me with a venom I can almost feel searing into my skin. As if today's horrors are all my fault.

CHAPTER THREE

Raul

I t's no surprise that Bastien and Lorenzo took off for the library the moment our blasted "foster father" dismissed us. As if burying themselves in a heap of books is ever going to make our shitty lives any less appalling.

I hung back in the audience room long enough to check whether I still had Baronissa Dalbina on the hook—under the peevish glare of her husband, whose impotent seething is my real reward. So when I stalk into the sprawling room with its maze of bookshelves, my two princely foster brothers are already pawing through some old tomes they pulled off the shelves.

As I head over to them, I wrinkle my nose. The imperial staff keeps every inch of the palace polished clean, but this room always smells sour to me. All those aged papers are ever-so-slowly decaying around us.

It's a mass graveyard of fanciful ideas and histories no one ever bothers to learn from.

But it's also my safest bet for finding Bastien and Lorenzo, especially if I want them together.

At my approach, Lorenzo looks up from his book immediately, his deep brown face and gaze turned even darker by his mood. Bastien takes his time even though he can obviously hear my footsteps.

He wants me to know he has other things he'd rather do than talk to me. Too fucking bad.

When he does raise his head, his messy auburn hair drifts forward to shadow his pine-green eyes. At the moment, they're as sharp as pine needles too, his frustration echoed in the slant of his mouth.

Good. These two had better be just as pissed off as I am. Great God knows we'll get farther if we work together for once.

The thought sends a sudden twinge of loss through me. A memory flickers through my head from when there were four of us gathering together in quiet corners of the palace, tossing out ideas like logs we were heaping into a pyre for the empire.

But it wasn't enough. We weren't enough. I—

I shake off the gloom I don't need and swipe my hand through the air to beckon the two men toward the workshop.

In the far corner of the library lies a much smaller room no one bothers with unless a noble stumbles on a crumbling book. Jars of glue, spools of flax cord, and slabs of pasteboard and leather for rebinding line the shelves against one wall. A long desk stands against the other.

It smells even stuffier in this cramped space, but I'll take old leather over dying paper.

As the door swings shut to cast the room in darkness,

Bastien flicks on the lantern—a magic-blessed one, of course, since flames and books don't mix well. A wavering amber glow washes over us, yellowing his sallow skin.

"What?" he demands, as if he doesn't know.

I glower at him. "What do you mean, 'what'? She's even worse than we thought. You heard that Accasian bitch gushing over Marclinus like she'd want him and the damned empire to take her from both ends."

Lorenzo makes a brief gesture that basically amounts to, *Fuck her and her whole accursed country.* At least he agrees with me.

Bastien simply shrugs, though his jaw has clenched tighter. "She's hoping to marry into the power. What did you expect?"

"She's a spoiled brat who wants to sit on a high horse shitting on the rest of us!" A growl creeps up my throat. "She got to loll around in the wild north while the empire shoved us around, and now she's going to sweep in and stomp on us side by side with the imperial prick?"

Lorenzo's mouth twists. He twitches his hand past his throat. *Or maybe she'll die.*

I don't know if some additional communication passes between the two of them that I can't hear, but Bastien nods. "Lore's right. His Imperial Majesty decided to orchestrate a bloodbath." He says the emperor's title with a sneering tone. "Eleven-to-one odds now, and she's the odd one out. Not much chance she'll survive to see her wedding day."

I grimace. "There is still a chance. And you know if she hitches herself to Marclinus, anything good she arranges for Accasy will be taken from *our* countries, not his precious Dariu. The empire already has our kingdoms on a leash tight enough to choke, and she'll cater to hers at our expense."

Bastien narrows his eyes at me. "What exactly do you think we should do about that?"

I can tell from his rigid stance and the tautness of his voice that he's as angry as I am. He just thinks I'll be stupid about it. As if he's the only one capable of keeping a clear head just because he's a year my and Lorenzo's elder.

As if he's been accomplishing anything more than I have in the past decade, burying himself in books and pretending "research" will somehow fix the crap we're mired in.

I jab a finger at the desktop. "She had it easy her whole life, off in the outer reaches where Emperor Tarquin barely paid attention. I say we make it as hard as fucking possible for her now. Make her regret whoring herself to the empire every way we possibly can. Throw her off her game. If she trips and falls in Marclinus's estimation, it's her own damn fault for asking to come here. At least with one of the local nobles playing wifey, nothing will get *worse*."

The door bursts open, and my mouth snaps shut. At the sight of the towheaded teenaged boy pushing inside, I feel only a faint whiff of relief.

Neven shoves the door shut behind him, his brown eyes blazing beneath the tufts of his pale hair. "You're planning something, aren't you? You have to be. That cunt of a princess thinks she can march in here and end up ruling over—"

My stomach twists. I swivel to grasp Neven's shoulders as if I can steady his temper with my hands.

He scowls at me, but he stops. I'm the only one of us still slightly taller than him after his last growth spurt a couple of years back. The only one who'll snarl right back at him.

I've got just five years on him, but sometimes that feels like a century. He wasn't here when everything went wrong.

I can't look at him and not see the gawky seven-year-old

kid the imperial guards escorted into our shellshocked midst a few months later.

Although in a lot of ways the consequences were the worst for him. Which is why I can't criticize his anger even though it scares me.

"We're not making plans," I say, which is technically true. Bastien hasn't deigned to admit that maybe we should, and Lorenzo is probably waiting to follow his lead. "Just venting some steam. It's a good place to do that—in here where no one else is going to hear us and stab *us* through the throat for it."

Neven scoffs as if the suggestion is somehow absurd rather than a fact of our lives. That right there is what really scares me—what scares all three of us, I know.

He's been teetering on the edge of control for an awfully long time. The drive for vengeance vibrates off every move he makes, every word he speaks.

And if that control ever snaps and he goes for it, it'll be his broken corpse in a coffin.

His hands ball into fists. "How could she fawn over that pompous asshole as if he's some kind of hero? How could she have wanted to marry him in the first place? Unless she's just as bad as him... She walked out of the room cool as anything, like it didn't matter that he'd had a girl murdered right in front of her."

I shake my head. "When has the royal family of Accasy ever given a fuck about the rest of us? They barely bother to speak to anyone beyond their border. Tarquin admitted the marriage was *their* idea—she's obviously looking to get whatever she can out of it."

"Why would he agree to that? Why doesn't he just keep Accasy crushed under his heel?"

We didn't include Neven in most of our earlier, bitter

conversations when we first heard of Marclinus's engagement to Princess Aurelia. Maybe that was a mistake. If he was going to rage about the injustice, it'd have been easier to cool him off when he had some time before she was right in his view.

Bastien speaks up in the pedantic tone he takes on when he's being a know-it-all. "Out of the countries the empire still controls, Accasy is the farthest flung. It takes more effort for the emperor to extend his 'heel' that far, and it's the least populated too, so less need to fear rebellion. He simply doesn't bother with them as much—didn't even ask them for a foster. I suppose bringing their princess into court was just a convenient way to stop the local nobles from getting overly comfortable."

"But she has to know—they must *hear* things from the other realms up there—" Neven sucks a breath through his teeth in a hiss. "Which doesn't make a difference if she doesn't care. She'll try to arrange it so her kingdom is even more favored above all of ours, won't she?"

It's the same argument I've made, but I like it a lot less hearing it from him in that livid tone.

I squeeze his shoulders. "She's not arranging anything yet. Chances are she'll get a blade through the throat. There's nothing for us to do about it."

Lorenzo lifts his hand and swivels it in a brisk motion. *It'll be okay. We're together.*

Except if we're going to make any actual plans, we need to get Neven out of here first. He won't know where to draw the line.

If we let him career into motion, we may not ever rein him in.

Bastien aims a slightly wry smile at the prince of Goric. "You know what else is good for letting out steam? A little archery. You haven't practiced in a while. Go set the targets up, and I'll meet you down there. I need to bring a couple of books back to my room."

Neven frowns, but he's always eager to improve his combat skills, and Bastien doesn't offer to show off in his area of expertise often. "All right. The rutting princess better not walk in front of my bow, though."

He storms out of the room, leaving the three of us alone again.

I glance at the two men I consider closer than my brothers by birth. We might not get along the way we once did, but I see the same conviction that's pealing out inside me mirrored on their faces.

We can't watch another casket sent back to Goric. Anything that sets Neven off is a threat to the makeshift family of outcasts we've struggled to hold together.

And as long as the princess of Accasy is joyfully prostituting herself to our enemies in front of him, she's a flint that could spark the explosion.

Bastien's voice comes out even but quiet. "Fine. We'll all feel better if she's as miserable as possible. That shouldn't be hard to accomplish. Shake her nerve, unsettle her, distract her—how much it throws her off in the coming trials isn't our concern."

Lorenzo dips his head in agreement, his jaw flexing.

My lips pull back in a feral grin. "Wouldn't it be a shame if she can't enjoy the luxuries of her new home one bit? Let Princess Aurelia's every moment here be torture and regret."

CHAPTER FOUR

Aurelia

There's a kind of meditation to making tea. Breathing in the herbal scents as I pick out the leaves I want to mix. Sprinkling them into the bottom of the cup. Pouring the steaming water with a faint hiss.

As I sink into the padded armchair next to the table, I cling to the temporary calm brought by the ritual. It's masking a well of turmoil I don't dare show.

The maid Emperor Tarquin appointed me with, an eversmiling woman named Melisse who can't be any older than me, hovers at the other side of the table with obvious uncertainty. She eagerly brought me the teapot of hot water I requested, but I may have put her in fear of her job by insisting on doing the pouring myself.

She starts to twist a lock of her fawn-brown bob around

her finger and then jerks her hand back to her side to stop herself from fidgeting. "Is there anything else I can get you, Your Highness?"

A fast horse and the key to the palace gate, I want to say, but I bury that longing deep.

The image of Lady Cadenza crumpling with a gush of blood runs through my mind for the hundredth time. A chill races from my throat to my gut.

What is the emperor playing at? Not just any game, but a fatal one.

This is how he operates, isn't it? How every Darium emperor in the long line has enforced their brutal control over this half of the continent—how up until a century ago they tyrannized the countries in the western half too.

No doubt the imperial family only ramped up their ruthlessness after losing so much territory to rebellion, determined to ensure that no one ever slipped free of their rule again.

It wouldn't have been enough for Emperor Tarquin to humiliate the noblewomen whose families claimed unfairness. No, he had to show he could cut their daughters down in front of them without them being able to lift a finger.

Question his authority, and he'll make you regret ever asking for more.

A different yearning wraps around my heart—to have my family and friends next to me. To be able to talk my horror through with someone who'd be on my side as I certainly can't trust the woman in front of me to be.

How furious would my sister have become if she'd witnessed the scene in the audience room? What absurd remarks would Lady Nica have said to raise my spirits?

Would Lady Cataline's unconditional encouragement have erased the uneasiness that grips me?

The tightening of the knot in my stomach reminds me that I couldn't have really poured out my worries to any of them either. Even back home, I couldn't tell them everything.

We always knew I'd have to leave my family's side eventually, even if none of us would have guessed how far I'd end up going. The distance loomed between us well before I ever set foot across the border. And a princess can't indulge in weakness.

I've always been at least a little alone.

Melisse is waiting for my response. I push my lips into a careful smile of my own. "I'm sorry. I'm still sorting out my thoughts about everything that happened this afternoon. Perhaps the court was more prepared for these 'trials' than I was."

I keep my tone mild with the slightest nudge of inquisitiveness. I'd be surprised if Emperor Tarquin *doesn't* have my personal servant reporting on our conversations— and everything else she observes about me.

Will he be satisfied now, after this one shock? Surely he isn't going to cull *twelve* young women from his court in a matter of days?

Today's bloodshed could have been a simple message to them and a test for me, one I hope I've passed. If he keeps going…

It must be mostly Emperor Tarquin's will. I don't think the imperial heir was going to order Lady Cadenza's murder before his father prompted him.

Marclinus will have grown up with these ladies. I can't imagine he'd prefer to see them all slaughtered.

I won't make any assumptions about how much he or the

emperor care about my own survival, but between the two of them, I have a better chance of swaying him.

Melisse is shaking her head with a nervous giggle. A flicker of a starker emotion passes through her eyes before she regains her upbeat façade. "Oh, no. That was His Imperial Majesty's first announcement about the trials. I don't think anyone knew."

I had the same impression, but it's good to have my judgment confirmed.

I let out a soft laugh of my own. "I suppose I'll have to wait and see what else this competition entails."

My maid offers nothing further, but why would she know what the emperor is planning? Why would she spill his secrets even if she does?

I search for another question I could ask that won't sound too pointed or paint me in a concerning light. "I hope His Imperial Highness doesn't already have a favorite among the local ladies—that I do still have a chance."

"I don't think he's at all settled on anyone, Your Highness," Melisse says hastily. "He hasn't seemed like the settling down type—I mean, of course he wants to be married—we were all very much looking forward to your arrival."

She stops with a blush staining her peachy cheeks. I'm not quite sure what to make of her stumbling response other than I'm guessing my ogling husband-to-be may have been getting cozy with quite a few of the ladies of the court.

With his good looks and the power he represents, I doubt he's lacked for offers to warm his bed.

The memory of him lounging in his throne reminds me of the four men who flanked him, who he paid no mind at all to and the emperor introduced like an afterthought.

I knit my brow. "Who are the four princes—the ones His

Imperial Majesty called his foster sons? I hadn't heard that he'd expanded his family."

Melisse brightens as if relieved to be able to weigh in on a less precarious topic. "Oh, it's not like that at all. They're princes from the other countries of the empire—Rione and Cotea and all those. He fostered a second-born child from each of the royal families to establish better relationships between their kingdoms and Dariu."

Better relationships? I restrain a shudder.

I've heard of past emperors doing this. My great-grandfather's younger brother was summoned to the imperial palace when they were only kids.

What they really are is hostages. The emperor leaves the other kingdoms' rulers with the knowledge that any uncooperative move they make could be taken out on their child.

I'm second-born—but my great-grand-uncle is the last Accasian royal I've heard of in that situation. Maybe after that, Emperor Tarquin and his predecessors felt we were so beaten down there was no need to fear rebellion.

How long have those four princes been stuck here under his watch, subject to his whims? I can understand those circumstances having put them in a perpetual sour mood.

It's probably not *me* they resent but their entire situation.

"Do they participate much in the court?" I can't help asking.

"Well, it's not the same since they aren't Darium—and I don't know how much they—ah, that is—" Melisse flushes again, foot partway in mouth as she must recall that I'm not from Dariu either, but she manages to recover with a sly glimmer in her eyes. "Prince Raul—he's the one who's especially... filled out"—she motions with her hands to indicate height and muscular breadth—"seems to get along very well with the ladies."

Her voice drops to a whisper. "Mostly the married ones, they say."

My mouth twitches with amusement at her conspiratorial tone. "Is that so?"

"Yes. I mean, that's only what I've heard. And Prince Lorenzo—he's something to look at too, all dark and mysterious—plays music for the court sometimes. That's his gift. He sacrificed his whole tongue to Inganne for it, so you can imagine how lovely it is to hear."

I'd just been raising my teacup to my lips. At her last sentence, my head jerks up. "He gave his *tongue*?"

I don't know anyone personally who offered a dedication sacrifice that large. The man mustn't be able to speak.

Did he really think appealing to the godlen of the arts for improved musicianship was worth it?

Although for all I know, it wasn't entirely his choice. At his dedication ceremony, he'd have been a boy just turned twelve and likely already living under the emperor's roof. Even a decision meant to be so personal could be manipulated.

Melisse nods emphatically, looking pleased to have earned so much of my interest. "They all gave a lot, I think. Prince Bastien sacrificed a lung—for control over rain, for when Cotea has its droughts, I heard he said. His Imperial Majesty has him send off rain clouds if they threaten a festive day."

I think of the auburn-haired prince who was slim to the point of gauntness. I wondered if he'd lacked food—perhaps it was a lack of breath.

"I'm not sure about the young one," Melisse goes on with a thoughtful frown. "I mean, he gave a bunch of his back teeth, replaced them with steel. But he mostly keeps out of the way. There hasn't been much gossip about him."

"And I assume Prince Raul has some talent that appeals to the ladies?"

My maid gives a snort. "It sounds like he has lots of talents that don't come from magic. His gods-blessed gift has to do with knowing what people are carrying on them. I've seen the court men get mad at him after he announced some questionable thing they meant to keep secret that they were concealing in their pocket or a belt pouch."

Seeking out hidden objects could come in handy for one's protection. I wonder how far his talent extends.

My fingers curl a little tighter around the cup handle. I sip the brew I intended to steady my nerves, letting the familiar warmth flow down my throat with its sharp herbal tang.

Really I should be more concerned about my rivals in marriage.

I peer at Melisse over the top of my cup. "Are there any other interesting gifts within the court?"

She rubs her chin. "Nothing like that. Most of the gentlemen and ladies don't want to give up much of themselves in a trade—and I guess they don't really need to, in their position—not that I have any idea what it's like—" She clamps her mouth shut for a moment. "I probably shouldn't be talking so much about any of them."

She'll freely share gossip about the fostered princes, but not the Darium members of court. Her loyalties are clear.

I won't badger her when I'm not sure I'd get much of anything useful out of her regardless. The more comfortable she feels with me, the better.

Clutching my cup, I get up and move across the guest bedroom I've been assigned. I can't complain about the hospitality here. I've been given an opulent space with delicately carved wooden furniture, a canopy bed draped in moss-green silk, and matching curtains embroidered with tiny flowers drifting in the breeze from the broad window overlooking the eastern gardens.

My trunks were waiting for me when I arrived with all my belongings as I packed them. Which I was particularly grateful for when I lifted out my box of assorted tea leaves.

The other contents might pose a bit of a problem. I peer down at the heap of dresses that may as well stay in my luggage. I'm already wearing my lightest gown, and it's clinging to my skin with a dampening of sweat that I can't entirely blame on stress.

I turn back to Melisse. "Is there a dressmaker who works with the court ladies? I think I'm going to need to commission at least a few gowns to match the Darium style and climate."

She inclines her head. "You'll want Madam Clea. I can arrange an appointment for you, maybe tomorrow?"

"Tomorrow would be wonderful. Thank you."

I reach into the other trunk and retrieve the glazed clay offering bowl I brought with me. I doubt any luck the daimon might give me will overcome the emperor's will, but it can't hurt to leave an offering for the roving spirit creatures that flit through our world. I always had a few tidbits set out near my bedroom doorway at home.

"And if I could also get a few bits of fruit or scraps of bread for the daimon—"

I cut myself off at Melisse's sudden pinched expression.

She ducks her head as if afraid of reprisal. "That's not really… done here. Anywhere in Dariu, really, but especially at the palace. Their Imperial Eminences always say we make our own luck."

Ah. Of course they'd rather not appeal to any power other than their own.

I manage to smile again and return the bowl to my trunk. "That makes perfect sense. Thank you again for attending to me."

Melisse dips into a brief curtsy, canny enough to sense her dismissal. "I'll go straight to Madam Clea, Your Highness. Dinner should be in a couple of hours—I'll come back to show you to the dining room."

I wait a few minutes after she's left, drinking the rest of my tea. Seeing whether she'll make a sudden return.

When she doesn't reappear, I retrieve my journal, pen, and inkwell. Pausing to sort through my memories, I jot down every observation I've made about the emperor, my supposed betrothed, and the other people of their court that might help me in the future.

I don't write it blatantly, of course. In precarious circumstances, I'd rather have notes that anyone could look at than try to keep illicit accounts hidden. One of the earliest lessons my sister and I learned from our tutors was to come up with a form of code to make our most private thoughts appear innocuous.

Anyone perusing my journal will think I've simply prattled on about the palace décor and the terrain I saw on my journey here.

Despite the tea and the unloading of my thoughts, tension remains twisted through my chest. Setting the empty cup aside, I sink to my knees on the soft forest-green rug.

I sketch the gesture of the divinities down my front and rest my hands on the floor beside my legs. When I tilt my head, the sunlight filtering through the window dances across my closed eyelids.

Elox, I need your guidance. I prepared for my duty so

thoroughly, but I wasn't ready for this. *How can I best move onward toward my goals?*

I let my mind unspool, my focus detach. Blurred shapes pass across my eyelids with the movements of the curtains.

Then the image comes to me of a bandage wrapped around a wound. Binding the injury. Setting it to heal.

I blink and lean back against the chair, tamping down on a sudden bittersweet pang.

The message is undeniable. I must make my peace with the emperor's demands and set things right however I'm able to.

What else is there to do, really? I doubt Emperor Tarquin would let me leave the palace alive unless it's as his son's bride, even if Elox nudged me in that direction.

With a few measured breaths, I dismiss my uncertainties. I still have my purpose here, even if a few more obstacles have been thrown in my way.

I return to my trunks and paw through the folded dresses for a suitable gown for dinner—something not at all soiled by travel.

Something that'll illustrate the attitude I want to convey.

I settle on a dress of layered white silk with a draping of lace like snowflakes tumbling across its gauzy surface. White is my godlen's color. The color of healing and peace.

It also sets off my lightly tanned skin and the bronze luster in my hair. I might not be aiming to hop straight into the imperial heir's bed, but stirring up a little desire certainly can't hurt my chances of seeing our marriage through.

I tug the sleeves to make sure they completely cover the splatter of scars on my forearms, purple as bruises that have never quite faded. As I consider myself in the gold-framed mirror, my hand rises so I can run my thumb over my ring.

I look down at it, tracing the shallow grooves that weave

through the gold like currents in a stream. They frame a glinting sapphire that's cool to my touch. It's almost the same deep hue as my father's eyes, which I inherited.

I've carried my family here with me—the hopes and needs of our kingdom. They're watching over me even from all the way up in Accasy.

This is what I was raised for. I can do this, no matter what Emperor Tarquin throws at me.

CHAPTER FIVE

Aurelia

As temple bells peal the seventh hour of the evening, Melisse arrives to lead the way to dinner as promised. We travel along a couple of sprawling hallways and down a sweeping staircase to a room nearly as large and grand as the one where I met the emperor earlier this afternoon.

A line of gold-and-crystal chandeliers glisten overhead amid a ceiling painted with animals in elegant outfits frolicking across clouds. And they literally do frolic. My breath catches when I realize they've been enchanted to twirl and dip in their fanciful dance.

Tapestries and paintings of hunting scenes adorn the walls between gilded panels, blessed with more illusionary magic. Animals poke their heads from around trees; hounds run in place amid horses' clopping hooves.

Several sturdy but gleaming wooden tables stand in a

couple of rows at the nearer end of the room, each capable of holding a dozen diners. A massive banquet table twice the size dominates the farther end, with a throne-like chair at both the head and the foot.

Those two seats are currently empty, but it's easy to guess who'll be sitting in them. I recognize several other faces around the table: women who were called to compete for Marclinus's hand, nobles from the crowd who are perhaps relatives of theirs… and the four foster princes.

Keeping Melisse's comments in mind as I approach, I attach names to their faces.

Prince Raul, the tall, brawny one with his cocoa-brown hair pulled back in a ponytail, sits a couple of seats over from one of the throne-like chairs, flashing a smile at the noblewoman seated next to him.

Leaning back in his seat at the opposite end of the table is Prince Lorenzo, the well-built but not quite as massive man with the rich brown skin, intense dark eyes, and apparently no tongue. He has Prince Bastien—hair the reddish brown of cinnamon, pale and slender and missing a lung—as a neighbor.

I can only see the back of Prince Neven's white-blond head and wide shoulders, but his teenage gangliness sets him a little apart from the figures around him.

Prince Bastien's gaze flicks my way briefly. His dark green eyes seem to harden before he tugs his attention away.

Each of the place settings with their gold-rimmed plates and polished silverware appears to have been assigned. Melisse directs me to one specific chair, with a woman whose name I think was Lady Iseppa at my left and Lady Rochelle with her cloud of pale curls at my right.

I'm a little relieved not to directly face any of the princes' glowers, understandable or not. Across from me sits a woman

I haven't met yet, perhaps in her late twenties, with her black hair arranged in sleek, coiled braids. The upswept style tells me she's married.

She's an odd pairing with the flame-haired Lady Fausta next to her—as voluptuous as Fausta is slim, her smooth brown skin contrasting with Fausta's porcelain pallor.

When I looked at myself in the mirror a couple of hours ago, I was decently satisfied with what I saw. Across from these contrasting beauties, it's hard to imagine I'll catch the imperial heir's eye. In comparison with their striking coloring, I'm a much drabber alternative. My figure is neither as gracefully delicate as Fausta's nor as impressively curvaceous as her neighbor's.

But both Marclinus and his father made it clear that looks are hardly the only factor that matters.

The unfamiliar woman cocks her head at a coy angle, studying me through her eyelashes. "And here's the wild princess in our midst."

There's nothing outright insulting about her words. Accasy is often referred to as the "wild north" even among those of us who live there, if more tongue-in-cheek when speaking of our home. But her arch tone suggests she means it as a subtle jab.

Lady Fausta gives her neighbor a teasing nudge with her elbow, a familiar enough gesture for me to gather that they're friends. "Let's not nag at the poor thing, Bianca. She'll have little enough time to appreciate the splendor of the palace before she's gone."

My competitor's smirk leaves no doubt about how exactly she imagines I'll depart: with my throat slit in a pool of blood.

I keep my returning smile demure. "It is a lovely palace. I'm actually thinking I'll stay quite a while."

One of the ladies a little farther down the table makes a sound like a muffled guffaw. At the edge of my vision, I think I see Prince Raul's head twitch our way.

Bianca trails her graceful fingers along the edge of her knife. "Such high aspirations."

Fausta has narrowed her eyes. "You're going to find—" she starts.

A chime rings through the room, and everyone falls silent, their gazes dropping to the table. When I tense in confusion, Lady Rochelle leans a little closer with a rustle of her unruly curls. "Their Imperial Eminences," she murmurs from the corner of her mouth.

We're not supposed to look at the emperor and his heir as they arrive at the table? Restraining my eyebrows from shooting up at this absurdity, I flash her a grateful smile and fix my gaze on my plate.

It's then that I recognize the distinctive whorled grain of the ruddy wood beneath it. This table was built from bream cedar.

A vise closes around my chest. I knew the Darium shipbuilders favored breamwood above all else, but I didn't realize it was being imported for other uses as well.

Bream cedars, those towering evergreens so vast it'd take three of me to wrap my arms around the trunk, only grow in Accasy. How many men and women did the emperor drag from their homes and force into the arduous trek across the continent to deliver the trees that made this piece of furniture, with his "gratitude" as sole payment?

My family compensates the conscripted workers once they return. But they don't all make it back. And the ones the emperor's representatives like, who they call back to the job with barely a break, are lucky to see their families more than a few days a year.

All so His Imperial Majesty and his nobles can dine at this damned table.

My teeth have set on edge. I inhale and exhale slowly, expelling the prickle of anger. It won't serve me right now.

This is simply a reminder of why I have to beat the emperor's game. Of all the people who need me to be in a position to advocate for them.

With a rasp of chair legs, Emperor Tarquin and Marclinus take their seats.

"Your respect is noted," the emperor says in a wry tone, as if the nobles are offering deference of their own accord and not because they fear for their heads if they disappoint him.

Postures straighten around the table. Servants circulate the room, carrying carafes of amber-colored wine.

That looks familiar too.

I don't react as it's poured into my goblet, glancing around the table instead. The emperor sits confidently erect at his end, his lips curving slightly as the man next to him says something with an ingratiating expression. Marclinus lazes in his seat like he did in his throne in the audience room, carelessly flicking his hand at a server to add more to his glass.

Between them, a number of the ladies have stiffened. Bracing themselves in case another trial is announced.

The voices I can hear sound studied, performative. With every statement, eyes dart across their neighbors to gauge the response. Even the laughter of the lady at my left sounds more artful than spontaneous.

The homesickness that hit me earlier swells between my ribs. Suddenly, all I can picture are the dinners back home with my family's closest allies, the jovial ribbing and spirited debates. The warmth that filled the space from far more than just the hearth.

Rochelle's gaze slides toward me. She wiggles the handle of her fork. "So… how long does a carriage ride from Accasy take, anyway?"

The genuine if quiet curiosity in her voice relieves the strain just a little.

I keep my voice light but low so only she will hear. "The better part of three weeks. It would have been faster riding horseback, but harder on my ass."

I wait to see if she'll blanch with revulsion or sputter indignantly at my undignified language. Instead, Rochelle presses her knuckles to her lips against a chortle.

All right, at least one person in this place isn't completely awful.

My new acquaintance opens her mouth as if to say something else, but at the same moment, Emperor Tarquin raises his goblet. Another silence sweeps over the table in an instant.

"We have such wonderful company for dinner tonight," he says in a regal tone pitched to carry throughout the room. "So many fine ladies for my son to consider. In honor of the most recent arrival among those ladies, we're drinking creekvine wine tonight, transported all the way from distant Accasy. I hope Princess Aurelia will enjoy the taste of home. But drink cautiously—I hear this is a potent vintage."

Who did he hear that from? The soldiers and overseers who tramp into our taverns to demand the stuff, who call it "wild wine" and let themselves *run* wild in the most savage possible way while they're drunk on it?

I force a grin and lift my goblet to match his informal toast. My first sip burns down my throat, tart and heady.

Every Accasian knows half a glass of creekvine wine is enough, meant to be savored slowly.

The servants pass around slivers of fresh-baked bread

dipped in pungent oil, then collect our plates before bringing the first full course. Each plate arrives covered in a silver dome.

Rochelle receives her food first: a roll of crisp pastry stuffed with herb-speckled cheese and drizzled with crimson sauce. As the server deposits mine, my eyes drop to the plate —and my heart skips a beat.

There at the base of the roll, small enough that no one would notice it except at the angle of my seat, the sauce appears to have congealed into the blurred but readable shapes of seven letters. They burn into my vision like a message written in blood.

TRAITOR.

CHAPTER SIX

Aurelia

I walk down the hall with brisk but careful steps, my hands gripping the edges of the small silver tray. My gaze darts from side to side toward the doorways I pass.

The strange accusation on my plate lingers in the back of my mind. How can I not be unnerved?

No one made any overtly hostile comments to me during dinner. Lady Fausta and her friend Bianca aimed a few elegant sneers my way, but it's obvious they simply see me as Fausta's rival. And I don't know how they could have gotten access to my plate before it was served anyway.

Who in the palace would feel I've *betrayed* someone?

Who would they think I've betrayed? Have I let a comment slip that hinted at my true feelings about my betrothal—and the trials I'm now facing to see it through?

Was my gasp at Lady Cadenza's death enough for one of the emperor's people to consider me a traitor?

I have no way of answering any of those questions. My only comfort lies in the fact that no guards have brought their blades to my throat.

Emperor Tarquin indicated that many members of his court resented his bringing a bride for his heir from elsewhere in the empire. The simplest explanation is that it wasn't a literal accusation at all, only an attempt to shake my nerve however they could.

I can't let that happen. So I'm going forward as I best know how, as if that blood-red word never appeared before me.

The footman I probed said that His Imperial Highness Marclinus retired to his private office after dinner. This could be my first chance to speak to my supposed fiancé alone, away from his father's hawkish gaze.

I can make an appeal with both my words and the gift I'm carrying.

The footman told me I couldn't miss the office door. Half again as tall as my five foot six in height, it gleams with gold panels depicting a mass of armored stallions charging around a depiction of Sabrelle, the godlen of war. Apparently most of what the imperial heir works on is how to conquer even more.

I suppose that fits the family motto.

A guard stands outside the door, looking vaguely bored. I offer him a humble smile. "I'd like to see His Imperial Highness. I hoped we could take tea together."

The flick of the guard's eyes tells me I don't need to introduce myself. "A moment," he says impassively, and slips into the room to announce my request.

It is only a moment before he returns and waves me inside.

As I step past the door, the guard pulls it shut behind me,

staying in the hall. I pause just past the threshold, taking stock.

The office is unexpectedly modest in size as imperial grandeur goes, only half as large as my sprawling guest bedroom. No inch of the space is used frivolously. Built-in shelves cover two of the walls from floor to high ceiling, packed with books and record boxes. Two ornate armchairs and a small reading table stand next to the hearth, which is framed by glossy marble and currently unlit.

A massive desk of fine marlwood stands in the middle of the space, gleaming in the lantern light as if it's just been polished. One end rises up in an arch of dark wood containing a plethora of compartments and drawers.

At the other end sits the imperial heir.

Marclinus glances up from the paper he was considering —a letter, I think, from the format of the handwriting I'm too far away to read. He swipes his golden hair back from his forehead and leans his elbow on the desk.

His smile feels more calculating than the cocky smirks he offered me in the audience room. My skin prickles with sudden apprehension about the fact that I've put myself in this enclosed space with him alone.

There's nothing so improper about this visit when if all had gone according to plan, we might already be married. But I'm not sure I'd like whatever ideas might be passing through his head.

His tone sounds more measured than before, though still with a hint of a teasing lilt. "Have you not had your fill of me yet today, Princess Aurelia?"

I sink into a curtsy, balancing the tray deftly as I do. "I hope to spend the rest of my days with you, Your Imperial Highness. I don't think there can be such a thing as too much."

Even if the lie makes me queasy.

"And what have you brought me?" He contemplates the tray with an arch of one eyebrow.

I step closer to bring it to the desk. "My gift with medicine has also given me an appreciation for the more subtle benefits a cup of tea can offer. I prepared a blend tailored to your role, for clear thinking and expression of might. It should be just finished steeping." I tip my head toward the porcelain teapot.

Marclinus stares at the tray with an expression I can only describe as incredulous. "You made me tea." He lets out a short bark of a laugh. "There are three cups."

"I thought we could enjoy the drink together, and I know you have certain standards of caution." One of the servants sipped from his wine glass and sampled his plate before the imperial heir partook at dinner, just as one did for the emperor.

"How very attentive of you." His gaze lifts from the tray to my face, skimming over my chest in the process. "Was there anything else you were hoping I'd partake of?"

I have to bite my tongue, unable to suppress the flush that pricks at my cheeks—although maybe it's better he sees it and thinks I'm embarrassed by the insinuation.

He can't know my reaction is actually anger.

I lower my eyes as if in modesty. "I have no wish to circumvent the proper process of our engagement. I would like to get to know you better, but speaking will do perfectly well as a start."

Marclinus hums. "So you came to seduce me with tea. Well, I'm quite certain it isn't going to sway my judgment of the coming trials, and I'm not particularly parched, so I'll pass. But thank you for the gesture."

He doesn't sound remotely thankful. I grasp for

something I can say that might keep the conversation going without criticizing his methods. "If there's anything you want to know about me that the engagement negotiations didn't cover—"

The imperial heir waves his hand dismissively. "I can find you if I'm struck by any overpowering curiosity. I do look forward to seeing how a princess of Accasy conducts herself in the days to come."

There's no sign of doubt or concern about his choices. I hate to retreat, but I can tell from his tone and the straightening of his stance that he's becoming impatient.

If I push too hard too quickly, I'll destroy any hope I had of persuading him off his present course.

I drop into another curtsy. "I'll do my best to impress you."

"I expect you will."

When I reach for the tray, he makes a shooing gesture. "One of the servants will collect it. No need for *you* to go trotting around like a part of the staff."

My anger does come with a flare of humiliation this time. "It was my pleasure to serve you the best I know how."

I spin on my heel and walk out of the room before anything more truthful spills from my mouth.

I make my way back to my bedroom with my expression mild, my hands loose at my sides, and frustration curdling in my stomach. How impressed would he have been if I'd upended the contents of that teapot over his head?

He'd deserve it for dragging me all the way across the continent just to turn our betrothal into a contest.

With every breath, I will down the simmer of ire. Patience is my greatest tool.

I never assumed winning over the heir to the empire

would be *easy*, even if our marriage had proceeded as planned.

I come around the corner of the hall that leads to my room, and a looming figure pushes off the wall he was leaning against.

Prince Raul places his massive form directly in my path. With his hands loosely resting on his hips, his shoulders look even broader.

He glowers down at me, nearly a foot taller than my hardly deficient height, clearly intending to intimidate. His mouth forms a shape somewhere between a smirk and a grimace. "Where were you running off to this late in the evening, Princess? Already looking to skew the odds in your favor?"

His voice comes out dark as his cocoa-brown hair, but his gaze is pale as ice, with an equally biting chill. I don't know what he's after, but he obviously isn't here to make friends.

I keep my tone even. "I'm sorry if I've inadvertently kept you waiting. Was there something you wanted?"

If the fact that I've ignored his questions bothers him, he doesn't show it. He lets his lips curve into a smile as cool as his stare with a flash of white teeth against his tawny skin.

My heart skips a beat, and not only because of his imposing stance. It's not hard to see why plenty of the court women find him appealing—presuming he normally approaches them with an attitude less like he's about to bite their heads off.

"I simply thought you should know that you don't stand a chance," he says. "Soft little lamb of Elox coming down from the north without a day of struggle behind her. No one's going to pamper you here. The nobles will eat you alive while you dance to Tarquin's tune to entertain them."

Even as I keep my chin high, my skin turns cold. He sounds as if he's speaking from experience.

What does he know about the struggles I've faced or haven't?

I step to the side, intending to dodge him. "Thank you ever so much for the warning."

He matches my stride, cutting off my escape with his muscular body. "You can't ignore the shit you've thrown yourself into that easily. We're all wolves here. If they don't tear you apart quickly enough, we'll give you a good shove in the direction you deserve."

The impression I got in the audience room that he—and the other princes—were specifically furious with *me* strikes me again with a jitter of my nerves. I don't understand it.

Before I can settle on a response, another voice, equally low but flatter, speaks up from beyond Prince Raul's shoulder. "Speak for yourself, Raul. We're going to enjoy the show while it lasts."

Prince Bastien comes up beside his larger foster brother, the edges of his verging-on-gaunt face hardened by tension. His green eyes are far darker than Raul's but even more penetrating for it. He's followed by Prince Lorenzo, whose deep brown features are set at a hostile smolder beneath his close-cropped black hair.

Gods above, they do make a striking trio, even more so up close. It's a wonder the ladies aren't falling over the lot of them.

Bastien cocks his head to one side, his shaggy auburn hair shadowing his gaze. "Not that I think she'll last very long either," he goes on. "She clearly has no idea what she's actually walked into."

They've formed a whole intimidation squad now. What game are *they* playing?

My pulse thuds faster, but I refuse to let these men see they've gained any ground. Predators pounce harder when they sense a weakness.

I lift my eyebrows slightly. "Are you planning on enlightening me?"

Bastien clicks his tongue. "Do you really believe you have a chance here? If the emperor *actually* wanted you to marry into the family, he'd hardly have set up an extended, bloody charade to whittle away your chances. It's an excuse to lead you to the slaughter while blaming you for your failure."

Could he be right? I assumed Emperor Tarquin was aiming to teach the nobles a lesson—but he could very well have decided he'd rather have a known quantity as a daughter-in-law after all.

If I die here, that's one less bargaining chip my parents have to secure other allegiances.

Prince Lorenzo turns his hand and bends his long fingers in a gesture so furtive I almost miss it, and Raul snorts as if in response.

Interesting. The tongue-less prince has found ways of conveying his thoughts without his voice.

I wonder if even the emperor could follow that silent communication. How useful it would be for the four unwilling fosters to have a private means of chatter right under his nose.

Where is the youngest of them, Prince Neven, anyway? This afternoon, he looked just as irate as the rest of them, if not more. He didn't feel like joining their un-welcoming party?

When I glance down the hall, Raul scoffs. "There's no way out. You're stuck here now."

I fold my arms over my chest, evaluating the three princes in front of me. The animosity wafting off them still doesn't make sense to me, but I can't help thinking of all the things they must have seen and heard in their years at the palace while they've been chained at Emperor Tarquin's heels.

Things it might be useful for a newcomer to be aware of, if they were at all inclined to share.

They haven't lost their fire in all that time. The emperor hasn't beaten the mettle out of them. That says something in their favor.

Even though I've become the current target of their hostility, it stirs the flames I've been keeping a damper on deep inside me.

"Like you've been stuck here too," I say quietly. "I suppose that means we're in the same position now, doesn't it?"

Lorenzo's hand jerks in an obvious motion of defiance at the same moment as Raul snarls, "We're nothing like you."

Bastian's voice stiffens. "At least we know where we actually stand. You've got a long tumble ahead of you from your cushioned life."

It appears finding a common ground offends them more than it endears me to them. So be it.

I hold Bastien's gaze steadily. "You've had plenty of wisdom to share. I'll simply remind *you* that you don't know me at all."

Tucking my hands into my skirts, I step around Raul again.

He huffs a breath, starting to turn, but Bastien touches his arm. "She isn't worth more bother."

All the same, Prince Raul's voice carries after me as I hurry toward my bedroom door. "Go ahead and run, Lamb. You won't get far."

CHAPTER SEVEN

Aurelia

B eyond the broad windows that stretch from floor to ceiling all along one side of the expansive room, a private forest sprawls within the walls of the imperial compound. I rest my hand on a glass pane, peering down at the treetops.

Other than the fact that they're green, they don't bear many similarities to the forest that surrounded my family's castle back home—rounded and bushy rather than towering and majestic. The morning sun glares off their still, pale leaves.

It's hard to imagine a stroll through those woods being much of an escape.

I force myself to turn back to the rest of the room. I'm not sure what's more absurd: the fact that the so-called parlor is immense enough to make me feel small as a sparrow or that it's somehow claustrophobic at the same time.

With dozens of members of the imperial court meandering around the sofas and low tables, I can't walk more than a few paces without bumping into someone. The cloying warmth that's risen in the room might not bother them in their airy clothes, but my skin has turned sticky beneath my fern-green dress. My appointment with Madam Clea to commission new gowns isn't until this afternoon.

Nearly all of the courtly figures are wafting some version of lush perfume. The scents of innumerable flowers, herbs, and musks collide in a thick stew. I have the urge to find one of the few windows that will open and shove my head out into the fresh air.

What I really want is to be able to curl up in one of the chairs in Father's office and hash out the political factors I need to keep in mind. To flop onto my sister's bed and vent about the catty looks every lady in this place has been sending my way. To walk through the familiar gardens with my friends and share the awe and the horror of the past day.

I can't quite imagine it, though. The only person I never had to hold myself back with was gone long before I ever knew I'd end up here.

Melancholy wells up inside me for a moment before I shake it off and square my shoulders. Wallowing in what-could-have-beens won't get me anywhere.

My gaze lands on Lady Rochelle, standing by herself between two clusters of chattering ladies. Her head droops beneath its cloud of blond curls, her posture making her large-boned frame look more awkward than statuesque.

Not *every* lady has been staring venom at me.

I amble over to join her. My spirits can't help lifting at the way her expression brightens when she notices my approach.

Maybe we both need each other a little.

"Take a turn around the room with me?" I suggest.

Rochelle chuckles. "There is a lot of it to see."

As we stroll along the row of windows, she brushes her fingers over her lips. "The palace chefs really outdid themselves with that breakfast. I thought I wasn't that hungry, but then I couldn't stop until I'd cleaned my whole plate."

"It was pretty fantastic." To tell the truth, my first breakfast in the imperial dining room might have been the most mouthwatering meal I've ever eaten. I don't know if I should take that as a consolation prize or a sign that everything about this situation is mad.

Rochelle glances at me. "Is the typical food in Accasy much different?"

I consider the question. "There's quite a bit of variety. Darium recipes have made their way even that far north." Mostly to meet the demands of soldiers and overseers stationed in our territory. "Our native fare tends to be a little heavier and more directly spiced rather than relying on sauces."

She hums to herself. "I wish more cuisine from the outer territories came to us in exchange. It'd be interesting to try."

Has she given much thought to why that isn't the case? To why her country imposes its customs on the rest of us and never the other way around?

Why would anyone in the palace care when the treatment of our people doesn't affect them at all?

At the far end of the room, several paintings hang on the wall. Various austere figures in imperial purple gaze back at us.

One face sends a shock of recognition through me that jolts the words from my throat. "That's Emperor Tarquin, isn't it?"

He's a much younger man in the portrait, with golden hair much like his son's and a little more flesh around his high cheekbones, but the same sharp-edged features. It's his eyes that first caught my attention, though—the gray irises piercing even on canvas.

He's posed next to an elegant woman whose dark brown hair is sculpted in whorls over her head with several tendrils cascading over her shoulders. Her doe-like eyes give an unexpected impression of gentleness, but there's a firmness to her smile that suggests some fortitude.

"And his late wife." Rochelle's mouth slants at a discomforted angle. "Can you imagine having the birth of your first child go so wrong? Even with the gifted medics the imperial palace employs… I wonder if she ever got to hold her son before she passed."

I don't know what to say about the woman who might not have had much more choice in her marriage than I have —but who produced the arrogant, shameless jerk I might have to marry.

"Birth is a dangerous time," I settle on.

Less so for nobles than commonfolk, but there's no eliminating the risks completely.

A shaky laugh escapes Rochelle. "I suppose she at least survived long enough to actually marry." Then she presses her knuckles to her mouth, her cheeks flushing beneath her freckles. "I shouldn't have said that. I don't mean—I'm grateful for the chance—"

A flick of my gaze shows no one is close enough to have overheard. I offer Rochelle a sympathetic smile, one that's more genuine after the hint of uncertainty she's revealed. "It's all right. It's an… unnerving situation, as great as the reward might be."

"I didn't even know my father had complained." Rochelle

sighs and draws her posture up straighter, turning away from the wall of paintings. "Well, we'll all just do our best."

She sounds as if she's reassuring herself more than me.

As we drift along the inner side of the room, Bianca and Fausta sashay by. Even though she's nearly half a foot shorter than me, Fausta manages to peer down her pert porcelain nose when she looks my way. "Can't even dress herself properly for the imperial court. They really don't teach their princesses much of anything in the wild north, do they?"

Bianca lets out a snort that somehow sounds graceful. "Apparently not."

I did learn some politeness, because I manage not to roll my eyes at the two ladies as they swan off. If the worst thing they can find to criticize me about is unfashionable clothes, I'm not doing all that badly.

"They seem to be close," I remark to Rochelle. She might be more comfortable talking about the other ladies than my maid was.

She dips her head in agreement, the corner of her lips crooking up wryly. "There's a family connection—cousins twice removed or something like that. But they obviously get along beyond that. I remember seeing Vicerine Bianca had taken Lady Fausta under her wing during my early visits to court."

Vicerine—more prominent than a baronissa but not quite as respected as a marchionissa. She clearly feels secure in her position.

I arch my eyebrows. "It seems they don't think very highly of visitors from beyond Dariu."

"It might be just that they know you're only here because you were meant to marry Marclinus." Rochelle hesitates, her stance tensing as if she's realized she's ventured into precarious territory.

I match her previous wry smile. "It's fine to acknowledge that. We all know it's true, no matter how the situation evolved."

She shakes her head with a rustle of her curls. "I'm sorry. Anyway, I don't know much about how they've reacted to other guests from farther abroad. I'm usually only at court for a short time each month. There's a lot to oversee at home, and it's a day's carriage ride away. I suppose Bianca wants to see Fausta elevated with such an impressive match, but it is a little strange because… Oh. Well. That."

Something in her tone puts me on the alert. My gaze darts over the crowded room, seeking out Fausta's flame-red hair.

I spot Bianca's sleek braids first where her head is tipped close to one of familiar golden-blond.

Marclinus has been sauntering amid his subjects since we gathered here after breakfast. Now, the imperial heir leans against the back of one of the armchairs while Bianca appears to murmur something in his ear.

Her lithe brown hand trails down his chest over his silk shirt with the confidence of a woman who's touched him many times—and in much more intimate ways—in the past.

Ah. The sight makes me a little queasy, even though I have no desire to be touching Marclinus myself. Even though it's no surprise.

If one of the foster princes who has no real standing in Dariu can seduce plenty of the married ladies of the court, why in the realms would anyone assume His Imperial Highness hasn't partaken as well? I can't imagine any husbands would be bold enough to object.

Marclinus grins at whatever Bianca has said and grasps her hand, but his attention appears to be mainly elsewhere. I follow the direction of his wandering gaze and notice Prince

Raul working his own charms not far away, presenting a glass of wine to one lady before aiming a sly wink at another by his side. His crimson shirt with its loosened collar emphasizes his brawny form to even greater effect than yesterday's clothes.

The imperial heir must have noticed his foster brother too. Marclinus raises his voice loud enough to carry through the room, though his tone is jaunty. "Look sharp now, Prince Raul. Is there anyone in this bunch I should be worried about today?"

Raul's smile stiffens. He lowers his head obligingly, easing a little away from his two female companions.

I'm confused for a second before I recall what Melisse told me about the prince's power. Is Marclinus asking whether any of his nobles is carrying hidden weapons or other potential threats?

The imperial heir didn't sound at all concerned. He might simply be tugging on the prince's chain, reminding Raul that he can order him around.

Raul scans the nearby nobles, many of whom have tensed at his attention. He calls back to the imperial heir, matching the other man's careless attitude. "No signs of sedition, Your Imperial Highness. But Viceroy Antun must not appreciate your hospitality enough, considering the size of that flask in his vest pocket, and I think Baron Otho should give his wife a break until he clears up whatever that nixel leaf is for."

Several chortles ring out through the room. Nixel is mainly used to treat certain contagious sores of the nether regions.

Whatever Marclinus was looking for, Raul's performance appears to have satisfied him. "Duly noted," he says with amusement, and turns to one of the nearby lords.

How many times have they carried out that little charade

to embarrass the lesser nobles? It looked like the imperial heir enjoyed it more than the prince did.

A quiet but firm voice speaks right by my ear. "And if you have any tricks up your sleeve, we'll catch on to those too."

My head twitches around to find Prince Bastien standing by my side. His dark green gaze roves over the milling nobles in front of us, but it's obvious he was talking to me.

He's caught me alone—while I watched Marclinus and Raul's gambit, Rochelle has meandered over to a side table to procure herself a glass of wine.

Even though he only stands a few inches taller than me with his slender frame, the intensity Bastien gives off makes his presence loom larger. I study his chiseled face at the edge of my vision, copying his indifferent stance. "I'm not here to play tricks."

"Or it could be said you came to attempt the greatest ruse of all."

His odd animosity pricks at me. Why exactly is he so offended by my arrival at the palace? I didn't ask for my betrothal to be turned into a sick contest.

"I think I'm here for many of the same reasons you are," I say calmly, even though he didn't seem to appreciate having our situations compared last night.

Bastien lets out a light scoff. "You had your whole life to make the choice to place yourself in this room. I was all of seven when they came for me. So don't even try to claim we're alike."

He—and the other princes—were dragged to the palace when they were that young? My throat constricts.

Before I can decide what to say next, Bastien's posture goes rigid. He's staring across the room even more intently than before.

Several paces away, a few of the noblemen have closed in around Prince Lorenzo. I can't make out what they're saying, but their grins have a mocking edge.

One of them prods the silent prince in his well-built chest and lifts his voice just a little louder. "And you've nothing to say to that, do you?"

His companions burst into taunting laughter.

Lorenzo shakes his head, his mouth pulled into a resigned grimace. He pulls away from his hecklers.

As he starts across the room, Bastien strides away from me to join him. Lorenzo catches sight of him when he's halfway there and makes a quick motion with his hand that stops the other man.

He must have told Bastien he didn't want any kind of intervention. From the set of Bastien's shoulders, I don't think he's happy standing back.

Watching them, I have to wonder if an awful lot of the animosity I've seen is simple protectiveness. Bastien can't have that many years on the others, but there's no mistaking the older-brother vibe.

It reminds me of my sister's first pained gasp when my parents received the missive from the emperor confirming his interest in the betrothal. The fierceness of Soreena's voice while I bit my tongue. *You can't possibly marry her to that monster!*

I rub my finger over the rippled surface of my ring. It'll all be for the best in the end.

As long as I win.

That thought has barely crossed my mind when Marclinus raises his wine glass and his voice. "My court, my eager ladies—it's time for our next trial!"

Chapter Eight

Aurelia

The din of parlor chatter has faded to a faint buzz. We've crowded into one end of the sprawling room, with me and my eleven competitors gathered at the fore of the crowd.

My pulse drums behind my ears as servants carry a procession of equipment into the room. First, a wooden panel some ten-by-ten feet that they lean against the wall. Next, a large, lacquered box of uncertain contents. Then comes a huge longbow and a leather quiver stuffed with arrows.

Other servants have pushed the nearby chairs and tables off to the sides of the room. Marclinus stands in the middle of the open space, swiping his hands together as he peers at his assembled court with apparent satisfaction.

His father has positioned himself off to the side with a clear view of the goings-on. Emperor Tarquin's mild expression and glinting eyes give away nothing about the test he and his son are about to inflict on us.

Is the imperial heir planning on evaluating our archery skills? Is having a wife who'll join him competently on a hunt of particular importance to him?

It very well might be. Who knows how varied his priorities are?

I flex my fingers subtly at my side, remembering the feel of the bows I've practiced with. As one devoted to the godlen of peace, I don't have much taste for killing animals for sport, but we held annual hunts by the capital where every creature the nobles brought down was donated to families with little to put on their tables.

I'd hardly call myself an expert markswoman, but I can hit a target well enough.

Lady Rochelle eases up beside me and shoots me a nervous smile. I tip my head to her in return, hoping she finds the gesture reassuring.

If she spends most of her time managing her family's affairs on an estate farther abroad, surely hunting has come up in her education?

Once we hear exactly what the imperial heir has in mind, I'll pass on any strategies that occur to me. Rochelle is the only person here who's shown me any kindness. If I can see her through this trial alongside me, I will.

Marclinus takes his time preparing, pulling on a pair of supple leather gloves and opening the wooden case. A hint of a smirk plays with his full lips, lifting the small scar near the corner. I think he's enjoying drawing out the tension, making us wonder and worry.

What will it take for him to recognize the horror of this ridiculous competition? Or at least to get bored of it, which might be easier to accomplish?

He draws something slim and shiny from the case. As he flips it in his hand, the metallic surface flashes in the sunlight.

My gut tightens in recognition. It's a throwing knife.

Is he testing our abilities with blades as well? They're hardly typical courtly weapons. I've certainly never seen one used in a hunt.

The imperial heir turns toward us, holding the knife at a seemingly careless angle. He cocks his head, his cool gray gaze sliding over us clustered ladies.

His voice comes out in its typical laconic drawl, if a touch curter than usual. "Yesterday many of you spoke of trusting me to lead our empire to greatness. Today you'll get to prove just how far your trust extends. Each of you will present yourself in front of this wooden panel. I will demonstrate the accuracy of my throws and later my bowmanship. I expect you will not flinch or cower, since naturally you have complete faith that I can avoid wounding you."

Marclinus gives a brief grin like a baring of teeth. I stare at him, his words sinking in slowly.

He can't possibly mean—

He waves his knife toward us. "We'll go in the opposite order from yesterday, for *fairness's* sake. Lady Rochelle, that means you get to do the first honors."

Rochelle's face goes sallow, but to her credit, she doesn't hesitate. I'd imagine she's no surer than I am whether the imperial heir would take any delay as a sign of doubt and penalize her for it.

She strides over to the panel by the wall.

"Right in the middle," Marclinus calls over, positioning himself about twenty feet away, directly across from her. "Arms at your sides. Looking straight at me. Stay perfectly still, and you'll be fine."

And if she doesn't?

As he readies himself with the knife, my fingers curl. The nails dig into my palms with tiny nips of pain.

Great God help us, let his aim be as good as he's boasting. Let my new almost-friend keep her cool.

The room has gone completely silent. I hear the rustle of Marclinus's sleeve as he jerks his hand forward, the thin hiss of the blade whipping through the air.

The point thuds into the wooden boards just an inch shy of Rochelle's right elbow. Her expression tics at the impact, and then her jaw clenches.

Marclinus's grin widens. "Very good." He selects another knife from the case.

How many of those things is he going to hurl at her?

Three, it turns out, as I watch with a clammy sweat beading on my back. One by her left arm, nearly level with the first. And one so close overtop her head that her curls ripple around it.

Rochelle's lips purse tight in the same moment, as if she's clamped them against a shriek.

The imperial heir beckons her back to our side of the room. "Well done. Since Lady Cadenza has been eliminated, it'll be Lady Giralda's turn next."

As the buxom brunette hustles over and a servant collects the knifes for His Imperial Highness, Rochelle returns to my side. A slight tremor runs through her tall frame.

I give her forearm a gentle squeeze to steady her. But the trial isn't over yet even for her.

There's still that damned bow resting against the table next to the quiver of arrows.

"Slow, even breaths," I murmur to her. "Unfocus your

eyes if you can, so you don't even really see him, and picture something calming in front of you."

She nods and flicks her hand down her body in a hasty three-fingered tap.

If the gods notice her gesture of the divinities, they don't seem inclined to intervene.

I follow my own advice even now, knowing there are several more ladies to go before it's my turn. If I can sink into a meditative state before I even step in front of Marclinus's blades, it'll be all the easier to maintain the detachment.

Unfortunately, Lady Fausta decides to take the opposite tactic, now that it's clear what the trial entails.

With a flick of her scarlet hair, she eyes the noblewoman who's positioned herself in front of the panel and tsks her tongue. "I don't think she really does trust you, Your Imperial Highness. Look how her hand trembles."

Giralda tucks her fingers closer to the gauzy drift of her skirts. Her chin, which had been set firmly, quivers instead.

Marclinus twirls his first knife between his fingers, apparently unbothered by Fausta's attempt at sabotage. "I suppose we'll see."

He flings the knife without warning. Giralda flinches as the blade slams into the wood by her shoulder. Then she stiffens her posture even more.

"Let's have a little more faith than that," the imperial heir chides teasingly.

Fausta shakes her head, her bright green eyes flashing with triumph. "Such a shame she faltered right from the start."

My own hands clench against the desire to march over and smack her across her cruel mouth. As if this test isn't horrible enough without one of us adding to the anguish.

It goes on like that through the procession of potential

wives: each displaying herself in front of the increasingly
notched panel, Fausta heckling them to rattle their nerves,
Marclinus tossing his knives. I descend as deep as I can into
my well of inner calm.

*Elox watch over me. Help me remain at peace and show no
fear.*

When it's my turn to stand before the imperial heir,
Fausta lets out a disdainful laugh. "The wild princess looks
like she's marching into battle. I don't see any loyalty at
all."

Ignoring her, I will my stance to loosen, my expression to
stay placid. I gaze straight toward Marclinus, his tall form
blurry before my unfocused eyes, and picture the statue of
Elox in our main temple back home. The way the godlen's
kindly face tips toward the lamb nestled at his feet. The
willow bough draped across his shoulder.

Loyalty. Faith. I have plenty of them, just not for the
man with the knives.

The first two blades hit the wood on either side of my
upper arms. My breath barely catches. Distantly, I hear
Fausta's voice take on a sharper tone, as if she's peeved that
her previous remarks have had no effect.

"Frigid as those northern cities. Who would want to
marry a woman that cold?"

I simply breathe.

The last knife soars over my head. As I step away from
the panel, Marclinus smiles. "The princess isn't easily
shaken."

Fausta can't say much about that, because it's her turn
now. She approaches the panel with her chin high and
endures the onslaught of knives without the slightest wince,
although of course it's easier when no one's picking at you at
the same time.

Then Marclinus reaches for his bow. "Lady Rochelle, we return to you."

I give her a quick squeeze of her hand and a murmured reminder. "Focus on your breath."

The imperial heir waves us back with him several more paces so he has more room to shoot. He aims his arrows much as he did his knives—one on either side and one over the head. But the twang of the bowstring and the warble of the fletching through the air make the process all the more unsettling.

Fausta resumes her heckling, but thankfully my coaching appears to have helped Rochelle stay centered. She shivers briefly when the arrows smack into the wood around her, but nothing you could even call a flinch.

And so it goes through the same order, until a willowy lady named Timille approaches the panel.

Her steps are already shaky, her knuckles white where her hands are balled at her sides. Fausta pounces on the visible weakness with malicious glee.

"Look how she's quaking. How can you stand there and make any claim on our great Imperial Highness when you're practically falling apart in front of him? He should have you put down right now."

I've held my tongue during her previous jabs, not wanting to provoke her further and fluster the other ladies even more. Now, seeing the gleam of tears welling in Timille's eyes, I can't keep silent.

I pitch my voice as soothing and serene as I can while letting it carry across the room. "You can do this. You've seen what excellent aim he has. Those arrows won't touch you."

Fausta's head snaps around with a searing glower, but I don't care. Timille draws in a ragged breath and appears to gird herself at my words.

As the first arrow flies, Fausta lifts her voice again. "You barely belong here in this court, let alone at an emperor's side. What a pathetic display."

A tear trickles down Timille's cheek, and Marclinus makes a scoffing sound. My throat constricts.

"You're making it through," I tell her in the same calming tone. "You know you can. Focus on that and not her."

Emperor Tarquin has shifted his gaze toward me. I don't glance over at him, but his attention burns into my skin.

Is my intervention a mark in my favor or against me?

Even if it's the latter, I can't regret speaking up.

After the third arrow has landed above Timille's head, she hustles back to our cluster of ladies, swiping at her eyes but uninjured.

My opposition has clearly soured Fausta to me even more. When it's my turn, she starts up her sneering commentary before I even have a chance to move forward.

"Here comes the ever-so-generous princess. I don't think she really wants you if she's so eager to help the rest of us, Your Imperial Highness. She's probably hoping you'll send her back to her backwater country since there's no way she'll survive here."

Her jabs bounce right off. I don't give a shit what that viper thinks of me.

One arrow whines through the air to pierce the wood by my right arm. Marclinus gives a low laugh, but I can't tell whether he's mocking me or Fausta for her failure to rattle me. He pulls back the string again—

Just as he's releasing it, a sudden crash shatters the quiet of the room.

I'm lucky the imperial heir is as skilled a marksman as he is. The din makes his stance twitch, but the arrow veers only an inch to the side of where he would have been aiming.

The pointed head carves a line through my sleeve and the side of my arm before digging into the wood behind me. Pain flares through my bicep.

I stifle a gasp with a hiss of breath, clamping my jaw tight. The pain flares hotter as blood seeps into my sleeve, dampening the fabric against my skin.

Every particle of my body wants to yank away from the arrow, from the panel, from this whole wretched game. I lock my legs in place, waiting for the imperial heir's—and his father's—response.

Marclinus has swiveled to peer toward the source of the noise. My gaze finds Prince Raul standing farther back in our audience, lifting his hands in a gesture of apology, the feral glint in his eyes turning it into a lie. "Forgive my clumsiness, Your Imperial Highness. I knocked over one of the wine trays."

His threatening words from last night come back to me. *If they don't tear you apart quickly enough, we'll give you a good shove.*

I don't for one second believe that was an accident. The prince is making good on his ominous promise.

Uneasiness curdles in my stomach, but when Marclinus turns back to me, there's a gleam in his eyes that might be appreciative. I'm not sure Raul's gambit harmed my chances the way he was hoping.

"The court certainly can't complain that you haven't endured this trial with more fortitude than the other ladies required," the imperial heir says in a wry tone. "One more shot, without any further disruptions please, and a medic will see to your arm."

No apology from him. Not the slightest sign of regret that his absurd test could have ended with that arrow through my heart.

I push my mouth into an accommodating smile and wait out the last arrow above my head with only a brief skip of my heart.

There is a medic already waiting when I step away, a devout of Elox in the typical white robe. As she seals my arm with her gift for healing, I watch Fausta pose regally amid her three arrows.

Marclinus sets down his bow. His gaze slides along us assembled ladies, his mouth fixed in a smirk but his gray eyes hard as stone. It's difficult to tell whether he's taking pleasure in this announcement.

His voice is equally cool. "The lady with the weakest faith must be eliminated." He glances toward Emperor Tarquin, who gives a tiny nod of confirmation, before going on. "Lady Timille, I'm afraid your lack of trust was quite dispiriting. We can't let that stand."

My gut lurches. The willowy woman claps her hand against her mouth to muffle a sob.

"No, please," she babbles, stepping toward the imperial heir. "I can do better, I swear—"

There's nothing I can do. An imperial guard has already marched forward. I hold my face in a mask of perfect indifference.

Marclinus's expression shows nothing but disdain as the man gouges open Timille's throat.

CHAPTER NINE

Lorenzo

The melody flows from the strings of the vielle with every slide of my bow across them. With my eyes closed, everything but the music has disappeared.

There is no crowd of nobles chattering through my performance. There is no ruthless emperor watching, confirming that I'm paying my keep in accordance with his expectations.

The warmed wood of the instrument fits against my shoulder as if it's a part of my body. My arm glides through the movements of the song as if guided by the godlen of creativity and dreams herself.

The music courses over me like warm sunlight beaming down from on high. For those fleeting moments, it's nothing but joy.

I can only maintain the illusion for so long, though. As I

play on, the effort of using my gift starts to prickle through my nerves.

A faint ache spreads through my limbs. The first jab of an emerging headache pierces my artistic reverie.

I have to keep going longer. I have to keep compelling my magical talent through my music. Everyone in my audience has expectations of how skillfully I'm supposed to work this instrument.

I've always had a knack for song. My unenhanced performance would still be enjoyable to the ears. Just not quite as impressive as they require.

Not for the first time, regret nibbles at my gut with an edge of resentment.

Why in the realms did I ruin one of my favorite pastimes for myself? There are few enough pleasures we're allowed under the emperor's roof, and I might as well have asked Inganne to destroy this one for me.

Nonetheless, the gift my chosen godlen blessed me with in exchange for my great sacrifice holds true. I carry on through a few more compositions before the pain expands far enough that I know it's best to call it a night.

No one wants to see the entertainment vomiting his over-exertion all over the polished floors.

When I lower the vielle, scattered applause breaks out through much of the crowded gallery room. Emperor Tarquin sweeps his arm toward me. "Another lively performance from our Prince Lorenzo."

He speaks as if I'm a dog he trained for his court's amusement. I force a smile and imagine ramming my bow right down his wizened throat.

A pageboy appears at my side to take the instrument back to my chambers. My foster father avoids treating his royal hostages as common servants as well as circus animals, most of the time.

I remain on the low platform that served as my stage for a few moments longer, my gaze traveling over the nobles who've fallen back into their conversations. The dull headache continues to pulse at the back of my skull.

I can't do much about my status here in the imperial court, but I sow more than musical appreciation when I'm able to. Who most deserves to be unnerved tonight? The prick who led his friends in badgering me this morning?

A new arrival at the nearest doorway catches my attention. Neven prowls into the room, his face set in its usual discontented scowl. He must be finished with his tutoring for the afternoon.

I'm never sure whether to be glad the emperor decided my older foster brothers and I had completed our necessary education or to miss the years past when I didn't have to spend quite so much time in the company of his fawners.

Raul has positioned himself not far from the platform like he often does when I play, ready to stroll over in full intimidation mode if any of the nobles decide they'd rather hassle me than appreciate the music. I twist my hand in his direction with a few flicks of my fingers and a point toward the pale-haired teenager. *Kid's here. Better keep an eye on him.*

The prince of Lavira gives a slight tip of his head in acknowledgment and saunters through the crowd to join Neven. I hop down from the platform with a roll of my shoulders.

It's a couple of hours before dinner yet, but performing both my music and my gift always leaves me hungry. My stomach gurgles. I spot a server weaving through the crowd and pluck a morsel off her tray.

Eating anything more solid than pudding is always a

careful process. I break off small pieces and nudge them between my teeth, chewing carefully.

The tart flavor of the berry-laced pastry absorbs into my cheeks and the stump left where my tongue used to be. With a twitch of my jaw, I swallow.

Such a great sacrifice for such a great gift, and so little I can accomplish with it.

By the time I've polished off the pastry, my headache has retreated, my legs feel perfectly steady again, and I'm sick of the thoughtless blathering around me. It's not as if I can contribute to the nobles' conversations anyway.

Now that I've done my part, the emperor won't mind if I duck out for a bit. I haven't seen Bastien in a while. Maybe he's gone to the library.

I weave through the bodies clad in billowy silk and escape into the relative silence of the hall.

It's only a short trek along that hall and down another to our usual meeting spot. Easing past the heavy wooden door into the vast space with its labyrinth of bookshelves, I suck in a deep breath of the still, utterly silent air.

No rustle of turned pages or padding of careful footsteps reaches my ears. Bastien must be occupying himself elsewhere.

He could always turn up before long, and I can occupy myself perfectly fine in this room on my own. The stories in the volumes lining those shelves provide no shortage of inspiration.

I've just picked out a couple of promising titles and carried them over to one of the padded reading chairs when the door sighs open.

I lean forward in time to see Princess Aurelia slipping inside.

My body goes still, mostly tucked out of view behind one

of the jutting bookcases. As she gazes around the cavernous room, I study the intruder in our midst.

She's traded the more fitted, stiffer dresses she's worn since her arrival for a flowing, airy gown in the Darium style. A paler blue than her sapphire-dark eyes, the thin silk courses around her elegant hourglass figure like water streaming over a fountain.

The billowy sleeves reach all the way to her hands. A lot of the ladies prefer to keep their arms covered to avoid the sharpest rays of the sun on their skin, but the princess's tan suggests that's not a significant concern of hers.

She might simply have wanted to cover the lingering scar of this morning's arrow wound.

Raul was probably pleased with the result of his supposed clumsiness, but the memory of the flare of crimson blood against her sleeve makes my stomach knot.

I don't like that she's here either. I don't like what her ambitions would mean for the four of us and the kingdoms we were torn from. But I can't help connecting that burst of blood to the stuff splattered on the floor when the imperial guard slit one of the other ladies' throats.

We're better than the emperor and his heir. Better than all of the toadying nobles of his court.

I have to keep believing that, even if I've lost most of my faith in anything else that might comfort me.

As Aurelia wanders farther into the room, she nudges her hair back over her shoulder. The rich walnut-brown waves that frame her soft features remind me of the polished frame of my favorite lyre.

Her looks definitely won't be what could turn Marclinus away. If I didn't know what she stands for, I'd enjoy gazing at that pretty face.

But I do know, and any moment now she'll glance my

way and notice me. I'd rather she didn't realize I've been sitting here gawking at her.

Setting my books on the chair arm, I get up and step forward as if I'm just emerging from one of the aisles between the shelves.

Aurelia startles at the rap of my shoes and then lets out a brief laugh. "Oh. I'm sorry—I didn't know anyone else was in here."

She smiles at me, the friendly light in her deep blue eyes like the last rays of evening sun warming the sea outside the palace where I was born. As if we could be friends.

As if we aren't both aware that everything she's striving for threatens the home I'll someday return to.

What has she sacrificed? Up until now, she's lived her life freely while empire shoves the rest of us around. And she thinks she should be able to barge into our midst and rule over us?

She seemed to show a little kindness to one of the other ladies during the trial, but I saw no emotion whatsoever on her face when that lady was murdered. I can't even say whether Aurelia was trying to help or simply to make Fausta look worse in comparison.

I offer a noncommittal shrug, refusing to return her smile. Uncertainty about how to proceed prickles over my skin.

I might have turned and left, but Aurelia moves toward me.

She stops with one of the narrow tables between us, resting her fingers on its smooth edge. "You were wonderful on the vielle. I've never heard anyone play like that before."

I dip into the slightest of bows. Ever so pleased to have entertained her.

"Of course, I've never met anyone who's created an entire

language before either." Aurelia looks down at her own hand and then at mine. "I'd like to understand you better, if you're willing to show me."

A chill shivers under my skin. She's been here less than two days, and she already noticed some of my silent communication with my foster brothers?

Feigning ignorance, I pull out one of the small papers I keep in a sheaf in the pouch on my belt, along with a small pencil. I have to lean over my side of the table to write. *I can talk this way if you need a longer answer.*

When I turn the paper toward Aurelia, she shakes her head. "That's not what I mean. You say things to the other princes using your hands." She pauses. "If you don't want to share that with me, I won't push. I only wondered. After hearing the music you create, I have to think there's a lot you could say."

What does it matter to her? Why would she even care?

She sounds like she honestly does. The thoughtful curiosity in her expression tugs at something deep in my chest.

No one's ever bothered to ask before—not a single one of the nobles who could have witnessed my vocabulary of gestures in the decade I've been developing them.

Even my family back in Rione, on the brief occasions I see them, has never known quite what to make of my muteness. On my first visit after my sacrifice, my older sister turned so despondent that I was afraid sharing the truncated secret language I was developing would make the situation worse. After five years trapped in the imperial court, my foster brothers felt far more like my siblings than she did anyway.

Bastien said we should unsettle Aurelia, trip her up. That'll be easier to do if we find out more about her. If I accommodate her request in some small way, who knows what she might reveal to me?

I spread my hands in the fairly universal motion that says, *I'm at your disposal.*

What does she want to know?

She tilts her head as she considers. "How would you show that you agree with what someone's said?"

I bring my thumb to my palm and curl my fingers around it.

"And if you disagree?"

I flick my thumb across my forefinger from tip to base.

Aurelia watches the motions and then imitates them. Not only observing but feeling the signal from the inside out.

My foster brothers sometimes use the gestures if they want to convey something between us when we're around uncertain company, but only them, and not often. It's far stranger watching her slender hand form the shapes like a secret message meant only for me.

She tilts her head toward the nearest bookcase. "And if you wanted to refer to books or reading?"

I aim two fingers out straight and brush my thumb over them a few times.

As the princess copies that gesture, some impulse drives me onward. I flick a finger toward her, make the reading gesture, and then expand the space between my thumb and forefinger wide.

Aurelia tracks the series of movements. "Do I read a lot?" she confirms.

She does pick things up fast. I nod to indicate that was the question I meant to ask.

"Some," she says in answer. "The more I learn about practices of potion-making and healing herbs, the more I can use my gift without it becoming a strain. And I've always been curious to read the histories of both Accasy and the continent's other realms."

Those studies didn't give her any sympathy for the rest of the empire's conquered countries? Make her realize how privileged she's been?

She seems interested enough in someone beyond herself now. She nods toward me. "How about you?"

I pinch my finger and thumb to almost touching. *Just a little.* My hand ripples with the sign I use for music, and then I lift my arms to mimic the pose of playing the vielle so she'll grasp my meaning.

Her expression brightens with understanding. "You like to read about music."

And stories of the macabre, but I don't see how it'll help anything to let her in on that distinctive hobby.

My pulse has quickened at her enthusiasm. I come around the table so we're standing only a few feet apart, giving her a clearer view. Then I twitch a finger toward her again, graze my fingers past my temple with a discreet tap, and swivel my forefinger around the head of my thumb.

Aurelia's brow knits. "What do I think about…?"

I angle my thumb so it stands upright and circle the tip more slowly. Then I raise my hands to form a crown of fingers on my head.

The princess's mouth twitches. "The emperor? Or the imperial heir?"

I have ways of distinguishing, but I don't see the point in getting into them here. I shrug again with a swift tap of two fingers together. *How about both?*

The light fades from her eyes, sending an unexpected pang of loss through me.

"I think they're the most powerful men in this half of the

continent, if not the whole thing," she says in a careful tone. "And they require all due praise."

She doesn't indicate that she believes they *deserve* that praise. I can't help thinking she hardly seems excited about the prospect of her marriage, although maybe that's been diminished by the bloody trials leading up to it.

I motion toward her again and then wave my fingers away from us—once, twice, three times, as if to indicate the palace, the lands beyond, the entire damned country.

Aurelia's canny gaze absorbs it all, and her expression firms. "Am I going to leave? No. Just because one's goal has become harder, that doesn't mean it isn't still worth obtaining."

The sympathy that was twining through me snuffs out in an instant.

That's all this scenario is about for her, isn't it? Obtaining her goal. Setting herself on a throne, no matter who lies bleeding along the path there.

And here I was admiring her lovely smile. Regretting the dulling of her shine.

She wanted me to.

A burst of anger laced with guilt propels me straight toward her. Aurelia scrambles backward in my wake. Her shoulders hit the bookshelves behind her.

I glare straight into her deep blue eyes and drag my finger across her throat just shy of touching the skin. A gesture every human being can recognize.

Aurelia swallows audibly. When I ease back a step, she peels herself off the bookcase and lowers her head. "I can see my company is no longer welcome. I apologize for interrupting your reading."

She strides out of the library with a swish of her pale

skirt, and I tell myself the burn at the base of my own throat is all fury, no regret.

CHAPTER TEN

Aurelia

I gaze up at the tapestries decorating the hallway, my ears pricked for any sound of footsteps. Marclinus didn't grace us with his presence in the dining room for breakfast, and the page I spoke to said he'd taken his meal in his private chambers.

The apartments of the imperial family lie beyond this hallway. If I meander it for long enough, I may get another chance to speak to him apart from his court.

There has to be something I could say that will lessen his interest in continuing these trials. It couldn't be clearer that his father is the driving force behind them.

Can I work a wedge between them? It'll need to be subtly done, but if there's a way to stop the madness before another lady lies slaughtered in front of me, I'll take my chances.

A faint tapping does reach my ears, but the pace and

weight of the steps don't fit the imperial heir. When I glance over, it's Vicerine Bianca approaching.

At the sight of me, her lips curl into a predatory smile. She saunters closer with a pat of her upswept braids.

What was she doing over by the imperial apartments? Or *in* the imperial apartments?

The image flickers through my mind of her voluptuous form pressing close to Marclinus's side yesterday in the parlor. He didn't appear all that engaged by her charms then, but that doesn't mean he never is. Rochelle indicated they have enough of a history that she'd be displeased to see him marry.

"Why, Princess Aurelia," Bianca says in a saccharine tone she doesn't even try to make sound genuine, "have you gotten lost all alone? How sad."

I keep my own smile mild. "Not lost. Simply admiring the imperial art collection."

"Ah. Yes. Certainly the most compelling feature of this part of the palace is the *art*."

She pauses a few paces away from me and lifts her slim black eyebrows. "If you were thinking of paying a private call on His Imperial Highness, I'm afraid he's quite satisfied already."

After an interlude with her? Given her animosity toward me, I suspect there's at least as much chance that she's spinning fables to intimidate me as telling the truth.

"I'm glad to hear he's well, since I had no such intention," I say evenly. "I'm quite content to wait for my wedding night."

Bianca presses her hand to her lips against an elegant snort. "How confident you are with so many trials still ahead of you. As if you can offer him anything that would suit him better than the ladies of his own country and court."

"He had those ladies before, and yet he asked me to come

all the way from Accasy. I'm sure he can make up his own mind about who would make him happiest."

A full laugh spills out of her. She shakes her head. "You naïve little girl. If you think his choice will have anything to do with what makes him *happy* and not what serves his purposes best, there's nothing I can do for you."

She saunters off down the hall, and I don't bother to call a retort after her. It's not as if she has any interest in helping me.

That entire conversation was about serving *her* purpose—to needle me in every way possible.

I draw my gaze back to the tapestries before me. One depicts a view over Dariu's capital city, the beige and tan buildings rising in stately rows beneath the stark blue of the sky. An ache fills my throat at the thought of the much more colorful streets of the capital I left behind—the oranges and yellows and pinks that brighten Accasy's homes.

No doubt the Darium court would consider them gauche. I haven't felt a trace of that sort of friendly warmth within these walls.

Back home, some of those bright buildings have lain empty since before I was born, cobwebs clogging the windows, roofs sagging. Haunting memorials to families displaced or "eliminated" as utterly as the two ladies whose throats I've seen slit.

We could see their windows filled with light and merriment again. See every town and village thriving as they haven't in centuries.

It all depends on me.

I drift farther down the hallway, taking in sweeping landscapes and fanciful scenes from tales of the godlen. None of Elox, I'm not surprised to see—most feature Creaden in his lordly acts or Sabrelle spurring on a battle.

When footsteps next approach, they're the heavier tread of a man, though a little errant in their rhythm. Marclinus emerges from around the corner with his fine purple shirt carelessly askew and a goblet clasped in one hand.

I paste on a sunnier smile than I offered Bianca and turn to meet him. "Your Imperial Highness. How wonderful to see you."

The imperial heir's gaze rakes over my body in one of my new, filmier dresses. The fabric is hardly transparent, but the openness of his leer makes me feel uncomfortably naked.

So much for what Bianca claimed about all his needs being "satisfied."

Her other comments stick with me, though. I'm aware he must want a wife as a political tool as much as anything else, but maybe I haven't focused on that aspect enough. On showing how my differing experiences from the ladies of his court are an asset rather than a flaw.

Marclinus grins widely at me, swirling his goblet in his hand. A tang of wine wafts from it, but he looks sober enough, if a little looser than he seemed yesterday.

"Did you come up here looking for me?" he asks. "But no tea this time?"

He sounds amused rather than disdainful. I suppose he's in a better mood than during my previous overture.

Does that mean he'd be more open to hearing an appeal?

I glance down at my hands as if wishing I could make a tray appear. "You didn't seem very enthusiastic about it. I wouldn't want you to think I have no concern for your tastes."

"Hmm. I won't deny I can be rather changeable at times." He laughs as if this is a great joke and then crosses the last distance between us. Slipping his hand around my elbow, he nudges me to walk with him down the hall.

I keep my stance relaxed through sheer force of will, fighting the urge to recoil from his nearness. He might be stunning to look at, but everything else I've seen from this man so far inclines me to maintain as much distance as I can get.

I have to bring out another side of him. A better side of that changeable nature he admitted.

It seems wisest to start by addressing the trials in the same jaunty attitude he's displaying. "Should I be looking forward to more excitement today?"

Marclinus clicks his tongue at me. "I can't be spilling my secrets. It's more fun if you're kept on your toes."

Fun. Yes, that's exactly how I'd describe watching a woman slump into a pool of her own blood.

I make my smile soften. "It must be a little difficult for you seeing ladies you grew up with fail. I'd imagine you've considered some of them friends." And perhaps more, if Bianca is anything to go by.

The imperial heir strokes his thumb over my arm. "If they consider themselves my friends, they should make a better show of it! There's no need for you to worry yourself about them."

He pauses and glances at me sideways with a gleam of curiosity in his eyes. "But you did worry. You tried to reassure poor Timille yesterday."

Despite his words, his tone remains amused. I can't detect an ounce of sympathy for the "poor" woman who was reduced to tears and then a corpse at his command.

Is he testing to see if I'll criticize his approach?

I phrase my answer carefully. "I am dedicated to Elox, after all. I feel I owe it to my godlen to help those in distress when I'm able to."

"Even if that makes the competition harder for you?"

I lift my shoulders in a slight shrug, wishing I could detach his hand. "I would rather earn your approval through my own merits than someone else's lack of them."

Marclinus lets out a bark of a guffaw. "Well, that is a way of looking at things, isn't it? I can tell you're a woman of many... merits."

And there's that suggestive tone he's brought out with me before. I ignore the crawling of my skin and latch on to the small opening he's offered. "I have gotten the impression that some members of your court feel rather resentful of my presence. They believe the entire competition was spurred by my arrival."

"In a way it was, but they're bigger asses than they seem if they didn't catch on that their own demands sparked the idea." The imperial heir gives another chuckle. "So sour about what they asked my father for. I hope you're not the type to be shaken by a few jabs here and there."

I echo his laugh. "Oh, not at all. I did wonder if it might teach them even more of a lesson if they had the opportunity snatched away now that they've gotten a taste of it. Declare that the trials have already proven all that was needed and proceed with our wedding."

Marclinus shoots me a sly look. "Aren't you the crafty one. What happened to showing off your merits?"

I beam at him as winningly as I'm capable of. "I thought I'd given an excellent demonstration of them already."

I don't really have much hope in that particular gambit, and what's there snuffs out with his laugh. "But we have so much more planned. It'd be a shame to miss out."

Tipping my head closer to his shoulder, I shift tactics. "I've no doubt. And I can see that your father's approach has its place, even if the loss of life seems a shame. Would you conduct the same tests if you were emperor yourself? It's thrilling to imagine what brilliant strategies you'd have for taming your court."

Let him think about the legacy he could be creating. Remind him that he can make decisions apart from his father.

But Marclinus simply smirks. "I think what we have is pretty brilliant as it is. There hasn't been this much excitement in the palace in years. A good time for all."

Except for the women dying in the process.

My stomach sinks. I don't think I've gotten through to the imperial heir at all, from any of the angles I've attempted.

As we reach the next bend in the hall, Marclinus lets go of my elbow, but only to sling his arm right around my shoulders. He leans in so close his breath tickles over my cheek. "Keep impressing me, Princess, and imagine how much more fun we can have together."

At the same moment, the youngest of the princes steps out of a room up ahead. Neven glances our way and stiffens with a fierce flash of his eyes beneath his white-blond hair.

Marclinus nips my earlobe and saunters away. The young prince glares at me for a few seconds, his jaw working, and storms off like he's trailing a thundercloud with him.

No doubt his older foster brothers will hear about my apparent dallying with the imperial heir before the next hour's bell rings. But every nerve in my body is wound too tight for me to care.

Marclinus's suggestive whisper echoes through my mind. *How much more fun we can have together.* With the exact same enjoyment as he spoke of the trials as "good times."

Gods help me, even if I'm the last bride standing, what will I be able to say I've actually won?

Chapter Eleven

Aurelia

The bathwater rippling around my body has cooled, but I'm not ready to budge from the tub yet. I stretch my legs out through the lukewarm liquid and exhale more tension from my lungs.

At home, I bathed at night so the cozy warmth could relax me into sleep. Here, in the hotter Darium climate, I've found it's most pleasant to take to the tub in the starkest heat of the middle of the afternoon, keeping the water milder from the start.

The sweet floral scent of the soap lingers in my nose. I scrubbed my arm and the side of my neck up to my earlobe extra thoroughly as if I could wash away the memory of Marclinus's intrusive touch.

Will it be easier to accept his attentions when the trials are over, once we're officially bound together? *If* I win—I can't let myself get over-confident.

I'm not sure if an end to the bloodshed will make up for all the corpses left on the sidelines of our journey to the altar.

It will have to. I will make it work, whatever it takes.

Elox give me the peace to guide me through.

I tap my fingers down my front in the gesture of the divinities, displacing the water to reach my belly and then the sigil branded between my breasts. The motion brings a deeper whisper of calm.

The brush of my hand against my skin and the direction my thoughts had headed in stir up other sensations. I trace my fingertips down my side, indulging in a fleeting memory of the only touch I once welcomed.

But that desire has too much grief and guilt tangled up in it now to provoke more than a flicker of enjoyment. I swallow thickly and finally clamber out of the bath.

After Melisse insisted on setting out the soaps and oils and a whole heap of towels, I told her she could take her leisure until dinner. She looked a tad shocked, but she'll have to get used to my peculiarities if she's going to stay on as my maid. I'd rather bathe with full privacy. Most of the Darium-style dresses are loose enough that I can get myself into them without assistance, and all my hair requires is a comb I can run through it myself.

If Cici were still with me, maybe I'd feel differently and appreciate the time to ourselves. But no matter how cheerful and obliging Melisse acts, I can't forget who's paying for her service.

I dry myself and pull on the silk dressing gown my maid also left behind for me. Sweeping my damp hair back over my shoulders, I head to the main bedroom to pick from the few premade gowns Madam Clea was able to supply me with that fit my shape and coloring. She promised a set of custom dresses within the week.

I thanked her as much for believing I'll survive here that long as for her work. Although I suppose she'll be paid from the royal treasury of Accasy even if I'm dead.

The opening of the bathing room door lets a waft of drier air dispel the humidity from the bath. I've just stepped out onto the rug when an unexpected figure rises from the armchair near my bed.

I freeze, staring at Prince Raul. His massive, muscular form feels even more intimidating in the seclusion of my personal chambers.

His pale blue eyes sear into me from his tawny face, like they did on our first meeting. His mouth is curled in an expression that's part sneer, part scowl.

My arms rise instinctively to fold over my chest, hiding the way the thin fabric clings to my breasts. A shiver runs over my skin at the realization of how little barrier there is between my skin and his penetrating gaze. I can't help remembering how Prince Lorenzo closed in on me out of the blue yesterday, the fierceness of his finger slashing across my throat.

I don't trust that this man won't go even farther.

"What in the realms are you doing in here?" I snap. "*How* did you get in?"

Melisse locked my bedroom door when she left—I heard the bolt slide over.

Raul prowls closer, probably to take full advantage of his imposing height. He speaks in the same low, ominous tone he used to threaten me before. "I wouldn't want you to think you're safe anywhere in this palace, Lamb. No matter where you hide, we can get to you."

My composure has returned underneath my burst of alarm. My voice comes out tart rather than shrill this time. "I wasn't 'hiding.' I was taking a bath, as one sometimes does when they believe they're in the privacy of their own chambers. I'll ask again—what are you doing here? Devising new ways to murder me?"

His eyebrows arch. "Murder you? Your beloved fiancé is taking care of all the slaughter at the moment."

"You seemed happy to hurry him along yesterday in the parlor."

Raul hums. "You asked to be part of these bloody trials, Princess. I didn't put you in front of his arrows. I just thought we should make sure you were thoroughly tested."

His gaze drops, the first time he's looked at any part of me other than my face, but his assessment feels less like Marclinus's ogling and more of a strategic scan, as if he's checking me for weapons. As if I could possibly be hiding any under this flimsy robe.

Not that I wouldn't be tempted to stab him if I happened to have a blade nearby right now.

"Were you preparing yourself for another interlude with the heir?" he asks. "You have moved quickly, haven't you, for all your pretenses at playing fair?"

I narrow my eyes at him. "Not that it's any of your business how I spend my time with my future husband, but seducing my way into his favor isn't part of my plans."

Raul gives a dark guffaw. "That's not what I'm hearing. It seems the two of you were very friendly this morning."

Prince Neven reported his observations as I figured he would. "Whatever you heard is the full extent of our 'intimacy' so far."

"Which I'm sure you eagerly encouraged."

"A strange assumption from someone I'd imagine is quite familiar with His Imperial Highness's inclination to take whatever he wants without asking."

That last remark appears to draw Raul up short. He

studies me even more intently, with a glint of interest that unnerves me. "Are you saying you don't welcome your betrothed's interest?"

It takes all my willpower not to grit my teeth. "I'll welcome the joys of marriage once the marriage has taken place. I didn't welcome *you* in here at all. You can leave of your own accord, or I can yell for the nearest guard to escort you."

A deeper smolder comes into the prince's eyes. He takes another step toward me, bringing him close enough that he could touch me if he reached out. Close enough that a musky amber scent that must be his seeps into my lungs with my next breath.

"Ah, but what would the guards think if they found the visiting princess consorting with one of Marclinus's foster brothers in her dressing gown?"

I glare at him. "That you're an asshole who doesn't respect people's personal space, presumably."

"The visual could change so easily, though." With another step, the heat of his brawny body grazes my skin through the silk. His voice drops lower with a husky note that sends a shiver straight to my core. "All I'd have to do is steal a kiss, and they'd be wondering why you look so ravished with a man other than the one you're meant to marry."

Something about the claim sets off a pulse of attraction that condenses between my thighs. Maybe it's the confidence in his voice and the fact that he's waiting for my response rather than simply manhandling me like Marclinus did. Maybe I'm simply pissed off about the imperial heir and that's addling my good sense.

Either way, I still have enough sense to ignore the twinge of desire and ease backward. As much as I hate to retreat, staying where I was feels too much like an invitation.

"You think very highly of your skills," I say.

"With good reason." A grin crosses Raul's face, turning his handsome features so stunningly gorgeous that for a second I can't breathe. "Which I think you already suspect. I haven't set a finger on you, and you're already wet."

Heat flares in my cheeks. I will it down as well as I can and reply evenly. "I just came out of the bath, in case you forgot."

"Oh, I know the difference. In case *you* forgot what you saw last night, I have a gift for knowing exactly what people are hiding within their clothes."

I don't know if I'm more pissed off at him for intruding and provoking this reaction or myself for responding to his innuendo. "I've already told you what I want—for you to get out of my room."

"I don't think you've given my offer full consideration." Raul lifts his hand. "Why don't we both find out how much you mean that?"

I brace myself to strike out at him if he's going for a grope, flimsy robe be damned. But the gesture he makes is so tender, almost innocent, that it startles me.

He simply strokes the backs of his fingers ever so gently across my cheek.

My pulse stutters. A shock of warmth blooms in my face and washes straight through the rest of me.

Including my sex, with a pooling of arousal.

I can tell Raul has picked up on that fact from the triumphant edge to his grin. With a flare of frustration, I pull farther back, out of his reach—and my gaze snags on the paler marks crisscrossing the knuckles on his raised hand.

My medical understanding—and the concern that comes

with it—kicks in instinctively. "What happened to your hand? Where did all those scars come from?"

The question comes out soft with a compassion the man in front of me hasn't earned, but he jerks his arm to his side as if I've insulted him.

"What do you care?" he retorts with an edge of a snarl.

I gaze back at him, confused by the shift in his attitude but recognizing that I've hit on a vulnerability.

As much as this man is trying to hurt me right now, he's been hurt himself, for years longer than I've had to endure in this prison of a palace. He's aiming his rage at the wrong person, but I can't say it isn't justified.

I wish a few *more* people in this place were angry.

The words I wish I could have said to Marclinus this morning rise up. "I don't like to see anyone suffering."

Raul sputters a laugh. "You came to the wrong place, then, didn't you, Lamb?"

He strides forward so swiftly I don't manage to stumble backward before he's tucked his arm behind my back. "Since you want me to leave so badly, why don't I stroll right out your door and see what that does for your reputation?"

I'm not sure what kind of reaction he's trying to provoke this time, but my sympathy crackles right back into a surge of my own anger. My hand whips out before I can think better of it.

I slap him across the side of his face hard enough to leave a reddish blotch in its wake. As Raul jerks away, my fingers curl toward my palm. "That should settle any question of my willingness. Grab me again, and we'll see how your nose likes my fist."

The prince stares at me for a moment as if he's been shocked into silence. His jaw has tightened with what I'd take for wrath, but he mostly looks incredulous, as if he can't believe what just happened.

Then his eyes blaze with a different sort of heat.

A chuckle tumbles out of him. "Lambs who try to spar with the wolves end up getting eaten that much faster."

He strides out of the room as quietly as he arrived, leaving me clutching my robe and wondering what deeper mess I've mired myself in now.

CHAPTER TWELVE

Aurelia

By the time Melisse arrives to see if I need any assistance before dinner, I've discarded my bathrobe for a proper gown. Regardless, the ghost of Prince Raul's touch lingers on my skin.

He's rattled me, which would have been his intention. But I can't set aside the curiosity his intense presence provoked.

"Melisse," I say as my maid insists on giving my hair one last brushing before we head to dinner, "you told me about Prince Raul's gift the other day, and I saw him use it, but you didn't mention what he sacrificed for it." I haven't noticed any visible indication.

"Oh." Melisse's cheeks flush where her reflection hovers behind mine in the mirror. "I mean, I wouldn't know from experience, but they say he… he's been gelded."

My head jerks around of its own accord. "He had the clerics *castrate* him?"

My maid's blush deepens. "They say. It doesn't seem to have held him back any in the area you might think, does it? From the gossip among the ladies, it seems... it might actually be a benefit. No need to worry about protection from certain sorts of consequences."

He couldn't get them pregnant. I suppose that would be a boon for a lady who disliked taking mirewort to prevent it —or who didn't want the herb to interfere with her chances of having a child with her husband.

He decided having just turned twelve that he'd never have children of his own. What could he have said to the cleric at his dedication ceremony to convince them he understood what he was giving up?

Or maybe Emperor Tarquin told them to accept whatever his foster sons offered. I'm sure he's amused to know one of his charges won't supply their royal line with additional heirs.

If it's true, Raul's imposing physique is even more impressive. From my medical knowledge, castration usually slows growth in any male not already fully matured.

Perhaps he was an early bloomer, or perhaps the cleric left him with enough to retain a few benefits.

As Melisse sets the brush aside, I graze my fingers over my cheek where the prince touched it a couple of hours ago. A heated shiver passes through me that's at least as unnerving as it is enjoyable.

The loss certainly hasn't diminished his confidence in his masculine appeal.

I gather myself, pressing my hand against the sigil of Elox on my chest. Releasing every shred of emotion the prince stirred in me, good and bad, into the well of serenity I've cultivated with my godlen's guidance.

When I set off for dinner, I'm impenetrable again.

A few steps into the dining room, I pause, taking in the revised layout. The longest table now stands in the very middle of the room. Only eleven chairs are placed around it: five on each side and one at the foot.

The two regal chairs where the emperor and his heir will sit have been placed a few feet back from the head of the table, as if they don't mean to eat, only to watch. Indeed, the other, smaller tables encircle the main one from all sides, making it the center of attention as well as the room.

Eleven chairs. Eleven potential brides left.

My gut knots with trepidation, but I push myself onward. One of the pages directs me to my assigned chair.

Only silverware and a goblet wait for me at my spot. Well, those and a silver bucket next to my chair.

A few of the other ladies arrived before me. Their faces echo the same apprehension that's prickling through me.

Lady Rochelle ends up across from me, one seat over. We exchange tight smiles. She curls her fingers around the handle of her fork, rocking it against the table restlessly.

Lady Leonette, the pretty but solemn woman who was called first in the announcement of the trials, ends up at the foot of the table. When Fausta arrives, she casts her gaze that way and lets out a disdainful sniff, as if she sees it as an honor she deserved more. She settles into her chair a couple over from me.

It's a good thing for her one of her fellow noblewomen is sitting between us. A buffer in case she starts harassing the other ladies again and I'm tempted to stab her with my steak knife.

I believe in peace, but if it's a question of her peace or that of the ten other women at the table, there's such a thing as prioritizing the greater good.

As the last of us settles into her chair, the chime rings through the chatter from the surrounding tables. I now dip my head automatically, though I watch our judges make their appearance from the corner of my eye.

Emperor Tarquin reaches his gilded seat with his usual steady stride. Marclinus saunters over right behind his father, his mouth already curved into a wide smirk.

He doesn't sit at first, simply propping his elbows on the back of his chair in a casual pose. His merry voice rings through the room. "Good people of the court and ladies of our competition, we have something special for you tonight."

At a clap of his hands, we look up. Servers slip between the tables, carrying covered plates. They stop just behind us to wait for their next cue.

Marclinus sweeps his hand toward us with a flourish. "You lovely ladies will get to feast on every one of my favorite foods tonight. I want to see that our tastes align in cuisine as in all else. You should appreciate every morsel. But I do favor rather a lot of dishes, so downing them all may try your appetite."

A manic gleam lights in his gray eyes. "The first one to fail to *keep* it all down is clearly the least qualified to be my wife."

Fail to keep it— Oh.

The significance of the silver buckets hits me with a lurch of my stomach. They're for us to vomit into if we're stuffed beyond our tolerance.

Even as the queasy chill trickles through my veins, my gaze flicks toward Fausta's scarlet hair with a jolt of recollection.

At lunch, she was being oddly friendly with the ladies near her, encouraging them to try more of one dish and another. While her plate remained barely touched.

Had she guessed what our next test might be, or did she manage to ferret out a forewarning?

Marclinus snaps his fingers at the servers. "First course: stuffed quail eggs."

As my server steps forward, I glance around and catch a glimpse of the four foster princes seated in a row at the table just behind me. For once, their hostile gazes aren't aimed at me but at the imperial heir instead.

I think Bastien's face looks a tad more sallow than usual. Lorenzo's mouth has tightened with a trace of revulsion.

I yank my attention back to the plate being lowered in front of me before I can focus on Raul's or Neven's expression. At least I don't have to watch them glowering at me while I endure this meal.

Four small half-eggs nestle in the middle of the plate, their yolks whipped to a froth and mixed with bits of some reddish vegetable. Hardly an intimidating appetizer.

But from what I've seen of Marclinus's sense of "fun," that's no cause for relief.

Lifting the first egg to my mouth, I catch Rochelle's nervous eyes from across the table. "Take small bites and chew thoroughly," I murmur. We'll want the food to settle as well as possible into our stomachs and to digest quickly.

A server comes around to pour wine, and I add, "Careful how much you drink." It won't do us any good to fill up on anything not part of the trial.

The other ladies closest to me have heard my advice as well, but I'm not going to resent them that, even if they've spent more time glaring daggers at me than offering friendliness. The moment any of these trials begin, we're equal victims.

As I chew my first morsel, Marclinus sprawls out in a typical languid pose and waves his hand to one of the other tables. "I could use an appetizer of my own. Vicerine Bianca, you'll keep me company, won't you?"

I can't imagine any of his court would refuse him, but Bianca sashays over beaming eagerness through her coy smile.

The imperial heir pats his lap. She sinks onto him, leaning against his well-built chest as if they're a pair of ardent newlyweds.

The viceroy I've gathered is her husband watches from the table she left with his expression set in stiff indifference.

Beneath that mask, is he angry with his soon-to-be ruler for the liberties taken? Or simply resigned that his wife is no more truly his own than anything else in this palace?

Bianca gives a slight tip of her head to Fausta, who flashes a smile in return. My chest tightens with the abrupt certainty that my suspicion was correct.

Through her associations of whatever sort with the imperial heir, Bianca found out something about the coming trial and passed the knowledge on to her friend.

Heedless of his potential brides arrayed in front of him, Marclinus tucks the lowest loops of Bianca's sleek braids aside so he can nibble at her neck unimpeded. Her eyelids flutter, and a breathy sigh slips from her lips.

My face flushes. I drag my gaze back to my meal.

The public intimacy in the middle of a formal dinner would fluster me even if the man involved *wasn't* my supposed future husband. Does he often show off his proclivities so blatantly, or is this just another part of our test?

None of the nobles I can see look surprised by his

display. Even Emperor Tarquin looks more bemused than offended by his son's antics.

Surely Marclinus will rein in his appetites once he's married? Once he's officially dedicated to another woman?

I want to believe that, but a niggling voice in the back of my head points out that he doesn't seem to respect anyone else's vows all that much.

We finish the quail eggs with no trouble. The imperial heir cups Bianca's breast through her dress and announces the next course. "Seared, butter-glazed scallops!"

So it proceeds through plate after plate. I'm not sure what the rest of the room is eating—they've been brought one course for every two of ours. Each of ours proves larger than the one before.

By the eighth plate, a slab of roast pork drenched in a creamy wine sauce, my belly is aching despite my best precautions. Across from me, Rochelle's shoulders have tensed as she chews, a fine sweat shining on her forehead. Her neighbor's milky skin has taken on a greenish tint.

At the foot of the table, Lady Leonette remains stoic, but she's gripping her knife tight enough for the dark brown skin of her knuckles to lighten. Only Fausta looks reasonably relaxed, spearing her next bite with a triumphant air as if she's already won.

The tender meat tastes like ash in my mouth. I force myself to grind it between my teeth rather than gulping it straight down the way I'm tempted to, as if getting it over with would spare me additional misery.

Nearly as nauseating is the sight by the head of the table. Marclinus has called over one of the married baronissas to perch on the arm of his chair. He's teasing his fingers back and forth along her thigh, although Bianca keeps drawing his attention back to her with strokes of his jaw and chest.

Fausta doesn't appear at all concerned about the imperial heir's straying eyes. She probably has the same views on happiness in marriage as Bianca does. No wonder the vicerine doesn't feel threatened by her friend's interest in the man.

By the time the ninth plate arrives, my stomach feels as though I've swallowed a boulder. I stare at the heap of sauteed fish with queasiness bubbling at the base of my throat.

"Dig in!" Marclinus calls cheerfully. He's giving every indication of reveling in this trial.

He did say he was enjoying them. I just hadn't wanted to believe he did quite this much. He didn't seem so zealous in his delight during yesterday's test.

My main rival must decide it's time to speed the process along. Fausta brandishes her fork. "So much lovely food. Isn't it just wonderful to feel it filling your bellies, ladies? Mouthful after mouthful stuffed down there? It's almost *sickeningly* good."

The woman at my left shudders. My gaze darts to her with a pang of compassion.

"Keep going, slow and steady," I whisper. "Don't listen to her."

Someone farther off in our audience makes a gagging noise that sets my stomach churning harder. I'd think it could be accidental if another noble didn't imitate the sound a moment later, and then another.

Some of them are having a good time, just as Marclinus suggested. They're trying to speed along the impending humiliation.

None of the attempts have come from behind me. Is this where the princes draw the line in their sabotage?

More likely they know that any efforts they make would

affect all of us, not just me. I'm the only competitor they're looking to unbalance.

I force down the fish through sheer force of will. Sweat trickles down my neck.

The lady next to me shifts in her chair. Her hand shakes where she's clutching her fork.

A set of shallow bowls appears before us, filled to the brim with a cloying stew. One whiff makes my gut wobble. I grasp my spoon.

Fausta raises hers with a light chuckle. "Oh, I can't wait to gulp down even more. Can't you just *feel* the hunger burning in your throat—"

My neighbor buckles over with what must be anything but hunger. I gasp a breath, groping for the words to calm her.

It's too late. She retches into her bucket, vomit splattering the metal sides.

Even as the horror of her fate hits me, I snatch up my napkin and press it tight to my nose. Just the sound of her retching has acid searing the back of my mouth. If I smell it too…

The lady at her other side succumbs with a heave of her own vomit. Across the table from them, another doubles over with a horrible sound that's part sobbing, part gagging.

Marclinus straightens up in his chair, his eyes unnervingly bright. He points to my neighbor without so much as a glance toward his father. "She broke first. Put her down."

The last word has barely left his mouth before a guard is yanking the woman out of her chair and slashing her throat.

I squeeze my eyes shut against the grisly sight. But I can't stop myself from hearing the fresh splatter, now of blood, or the peal of Marclinus's laughter.

When I dare look at the table again, Rochelle has just bent over her own bucket. My hands ball as I watch my friend heave and shudder.

There are still six of us who've kept our meal down. I hold myself rigidly still, waiting for the emperor or his heir to call an end to this horrific meal.

Instead, Marclinus lounges back in his chair, one arm around Bianca's waist, his other hand caressing the side of the baronissa's breast. He grins at us. "You can all keep going. We'll see who outlasts the rest."

Through my nausea, the last tiny spark of hope I've been holding on to sputters out.

He's celebrating our suffering.

He likes the torment so much he's asking for it to continue even after the main outcome of the trial—the culling of our ranks—has been decided.

I'm never going to convince him to give up this sadistic competition. I'm stuck here until I die or I take his hand in marriage.

Despair sweeps through me, but it dredges up a deeper resolve than has ever gripped me before.

I won't die. I'll see my purpose through, marry this hateful man, and bring my people the relief they've so long deserved. No matter what I need to do.

The image of Raul's looming form rises up through my mind. Of Bastien's accusing remarks. Of Lorenzo slashing his finger past my throat.

The disgust on their faces when Marclinus announced this trial.

The princes might have it out for me, but they're the only people in the entire palace who've been remotely honest about how awful the emperor and his son are. As much as they seem to despise me, they hate the tyrants who might as well be their jailers even more.

They may be the only ones I can count on… if I can find enough common ground for them to let me in.

I've been cautious in my approach so far. I have to make the most of every opportunity going forward.

If I want to be sure of surviving the next week, I need to turn the enemies of my enemy into my greatest allies.

Chapter Thirteen

Bastien

Clutching the metal bar, I haul my body off the ground. The strain ripples through my shoulders and biceps with a familiar burn.

I bring my chin to the level of the bar, hold there through a carefully even breath that prickles through my single lung, and lower myself again.

I still have three more repetitions in my standard sequence, but the squeak of the opening door diverts me. I let go of the bar and turn around, swiping my stinging hands together.

My stance has tensed in case it's one of the court nobles or a member of the imperial guard. I generally restrict my exercise sessions to the privacy of my bedroom, where there's no chance of anyone mocking my thin body or my lack of endurance. Every now and then, though, I sneak down to the chambers dedicated to physical training to make use of the equipment I otherwise don't have access to.

It's nearly midnight—both nobles and guards off duty tend to be asleep or deep in their cups by now.

No doubt they are tonight as well, because it's Raul crossing the room toward me. My foster brother's expression is typically intense, but there's an unusual spring to his step as if this once he's more energized than pissed off.

What does the prince of Lavira have to be elated about? Princess Aurelia passed another trial with unsettling composure, even when she was expelling the contents of her stomach. And we all had to watch the entire repulsive show Marclinus giddily put on.

I'd have liked to empty a few of those buckets of vomit over his head and see how he enjoyed it then, but his next act would have been ordering me drowned in one.

Lorenzo trails along behind Raul with enough distance to suggest that while he agreed to be part of this conversation, he doesn't share Raul's enthusiasm. The prince of Rione twists his fingers in a swift gesture only I see. *His idea. Don't know what.*

I roll the lingering ache out of my shoulders and wait for Raul to reach me. "What's going on? Shouldn't you be tumbling whichever ladies Marclinus hasn't dragged off for the night?"

My foster brother rolls his eyes at me. He seems to think that bedding as many of the married women of court as he can serves as some kind of revenge against them and their husbands. I once tried to suggest that they might be using *him* at least as much as he's using them, and then he did nothing but glare at me for the better part of a week.

Nothing we can do here has ever made all that much difference, at least not in the ways we'd have wanted. A bear with its paw caught in a trap would have more room to maneuver.

A sly smile has curved Raul's lips. "I had a different thought about tumbling."

I restrain a sigh. "And what about this thought was so important that it has you arranging midnight meetings?"

He folds his arms loosely over his chest. "I paid the princess a visit in her chambers this afternoon. Mostly to judge whether Neven was right that she's been whoring herself to His Imperial Highness already—and it appears not —but I learned something else even more worthwhile."

"Which is…?"

His grin is getting cockier by the second. "She's not as unaffected as she likes to pretend. I caught her just coming out of the bath. She didn't like me interrupting, but she was turned on too. No denying the tells of the body."

Especially to a man with Raul's gift.

"How does that help us?" I ask. Will he get to the point already?

"Unnerving her hasn't stopped her from coasting through the trials so far. But there are other ways to mess with her—and Marclinus. It'd be some kind of victory if one of us—fuck, all of us—could claim her before he can. Cuckold him and then if she makes it to the end, reveal it right when he's got no other contenders left? He and his damned father will look like idiots."

Lorenzo's mouth has twisted uneasily, but a glimmer of some hotter emotion shines in his dark eyes. I'd be lying if I said Raul's suggestion hasn't kindled something in me.

His plan isn't completely absurd. It'd be another way of undermining the traitor in our midst, if nothing else. If we can win her over, gain her trust, and then turn on her, we'll leave her completely off-balance.

I imagine a blush staining Princess Aurelia's pretty face, her lips parting with a sigh of passion, and a flush of my own creeps over my skin.

The possibility of seducing her is more appealing than I like. How much is Raul being guided by strategy and how much by his own base desires?

Entangling ourselves with her could upend our own plans as much as hers.

"I doubt she'll be all that interested after the reception we've given her, no matter how her body might react in the moment," I point out. "If there's anything she's shown in her performance before the court, it's self-control."

Raul shrugs. "There are always cracks. She's alone without anyone here she knows. She's still human—she has needs." He flashes another grin at me. "I think you're just afraid I'll beat you to the punch if you give it a shot."

I grimace at him. "I don't see why that would matter if your idea is that we'd all have her. I'm simply not convinced this would be the best use of our energy. She must have other weaknesses."

"This will be the most fun to prey on."

I lift an eyebrow at Lorenzo, who makes a noncommittal gesture. He isn't fully on board, but he's not outright against the idea either.

If I encourage Raul, there'll be no stopping him. As always, it's my job to be the voice of reason among us.

I turn away as if I'm done with the conversation. "I'm sure you'll do whatever you want regardless. Just make sure you're listening to your head at least as much as your cock, will you?"

Raul's tone becomes slightly mocking. "Thank you so much for your not-quite-blessing, King Bastien."

That's what he always calls me when he thinks I'm being a hard-ass.

He spins on his heel and strides off. Lorenzo meets my eyes with a look that seems to say, *That's Raul for you*, and lifts his hand to his mouth to stifle a yawn.

I wave him off. "Go get some sleep. Who knows what tomorrow's going to bring."

For us or for the princess of Accasy and her fellow hopeful brides.

Despite the workout, I don't sleep much, shifting restlessly beneath my sheets. A couple of hours before the leisurely court breakfast time, I crawl out of bed and head to the library to settle my mind.

As I stalk through the halls to that vast room stuffed with books, I chart the aisles in my head. Over the past sixteen years, I've scoured every volume on military and political tactics, along with a plethora of historical accounts that only provided the occasional tidbit of strategic philosophy.

What's left that might offer some new information? If there was any scrap that could topple Tarquin, Marclinus, or their entire damned empire, I'd have found it by now.

A little more insight into the culture of Accasy could be helpful, but the imperial library is sparse on materials relating to any of its conquered countries beyond the tales of the initial conquering. Would it be worth slipping into the theoretically locked records room and giving the accounts of imports and disciplinary actions another perusal?

From what I recall, those are sparse too. Accasy sends the empire some wood and wine, and occasionally soldiers to wage war on the border with the half of the continent the empire would like to regain. No significant uprisings have occurred since the first few decades after the invasion centuries ago.

They've turned complacent. The empire's wild northern lapdog.

I haven't quite decided on my best course of action when I push past the heavy door and find myself faced with the opportunity to get a much more direct accounting.

Princess Aurelia is standing by one of the nearer sets of shelves, contemplating its contents with the serene assurance that seems to be her natural state—or else her most practiced façade. When she catches sight of me, she... smiles.

With Raul's insinuations wriggling around in my brain, it's hard for me not to notice how that smile brightens her tanned face and adds a sparkle to her deep blue eyes. How her burnished brown hair gleams in the early morning sunlight streaking through the tall windows at the other end of the room.

How her delicate lavender gown flows over her limbs while clinging to curves an interested man might call tempting.

No, I don't think Raul is only looking to indulge his sense of vengeance with his new proposal.

As I walk over to the princess of Accasy, I study her openly. Let her feel the weight of my scrutiny.

It isn't as if I've made any secret of what I think of her presence.

If my gaze unsettles her, she doesn't show it. When I halt a few paces away, she dips her head to me in a gesture of respect. "Prince Bastien. I hope you're well."

I have to choke back a guffaw. "Do you?"

Aurelia considers me for a moment. "We got off on the wrong foot, didn't we? I'd rather it didn't stay that way."

I prop myself against the table I've stopped beside. "What does it matter to you?" She's barely reacted to the court's ladies being slaughtered right in front of her, so it's hard to imagine she's all that concerned about my feelings. Other than how provoking friendlier ones might be useful to her.

Her smile returns, soft around the edges. "I know you care a lot about your people. It must be hard having been separated from your family and your country for so long."

How would she know what I care about or how much? An easy stab in the dark, an attempt to show sympathy.

"I'm managing as I am," I reply.

"Then I hope you'll understand that I am too. Simply... managing. There's nothing that matters to me more than the people I left behind. If it was up to me, if I could choose freely—"

Her voice catches—just for an instant, but it's enough of a lapse that I mark it. And the fact that she never quite finishes that thought.

"I have a duty to my kingdom and the people in it," she goes on. "What I want isn't relevant beyond that I want to serve them as well as I can. I'm lucky that I had so long before my duty took me from my home, and I won't insult you by saying our situations are the same. But I take no joy in any of the bloodshed that began when I arrived."

She sounds genuine enough that a tendril of sympathy unfurls inside *me* before I stamp it out.

Easy words to say. And whether they're true or not makes no difference.

I already knew she hadn't come here for love but to serve her family's purposes. Whatever she gains for her kingdom will be stolen from mine and my foster brothers', and I don't see a trace of guilt in her over that consequence.

She might not be rejoicing in the brutality of the trials, but she hasn't shrunk from it either.

Annoyance at my spurt of compassion pushes me forward so I move incrementally into her personal space. I draw my spine up straight to make full use of the few inches I have on her in height. I can't tower over her like Raul might, but let's see how she reacts to a different sort of imposition.

"None of that means anything to me, Princess."

Her hands close at her sides, her thumb rubbing over the ring on her left forefinger. There's something almost defensive about the motion—as if she feels she needs to protect the ornament from me—that I file away for future consideration.

She doesn't back down, though. Her brow knits. "What is it that bothers you so much about me? If I've caused you harm, I honestly didn't realize, but I'd want to know so I can set it right."

Is she really so ignorant about how her schemes will affect the rest of us or simply playing at it? I've gotten the impression she's reasonably clever, but even the most brilliant thinker has their blind spots, and I doubt Princess Aurelia qualifies as brilliant.

It could be her awareness shouldn't matter either. I knew it might be useful to get her to let down her guard and reveal more of herself, and she's all but laying herself on a platter—however much she's willing to share now.

I can't let my frustrations prevent me from exploiting every potential advantage I'm offered.

I dip my head, smoothing out my voice with the benefit of much practice. "Perhaps I'm merely bothered by the additional chaos that's come with your arrival. That may have been unfair of me. It's clear you were totally unaware of what Marclinus had planned."

There. A little of the tension in her stance relaxes.

"I was." Aurelia lets out a soft laugh that quivers through my nerves. "I had no idea what to expect from him at all. You must know him well after growing up together, but I gather the trials were a surprise to the court too."

"Their Imperial Eminences sprung them on all of us."

She tilts her head to one side as if mulling over the situation. "Well, I've discovered he's fond of praise, knives, archery, and rather a lot of food. How else has he liked to spend his time?"

She asks the question casually enough, but I sense her goal at once. She's prying for information, hoping I might shed some light on the upcoming tests.

The princess is at least canny enough to realize what an excellent source of information I could be for her. I can use her trust to my advantage.

What could I tell her that would trip her up rather than boost her chances?

I hum as if in thought. "As much as he enjoys praise, he does admire the boldness of a blunt statement as well. And he's always tickled when he finds an opponent with combat skills to rival his own, if you have any skill for sparring. He plays a lot of games—cards, board, those of sport—to pass the time, and I can tell it bores him that his companions always lose."

Bores him so much he cackles gleefully with every win. I can't imagine what he'd make of a prospective wife who could best him or dresses him down to his face, but it wouldn't be a pretty picture when he's through.

One of Aurelia's eyebrows rises. "Hmm. I'm a believer in politeness over bluntness, and I can't say combat or sports are my forte. I may have a struggle ahead of me."

The subtle wry note in her voice leaves me uncertain

about whether she's poking fun at herself or skeptical of my advice.

I might as well say one true thing that's obvious enough, in case it'll make her more likely to act on the rest. "He does also love a good ball, of course. Music, drinking, dancing."

"Maybe I'll survive here long enough to participate in one of those." She pauses and then rests her hand on my forearm. A feather-light touch, but the warmth of it tingles over my skin. "He hasn't ever been kind to you, for all you're supposedly a brother, has he?"

Interesting. I step even closer and set my hand over hers, holding her gaze. Does her breath quaver just slightly at my nearness?

Raul might have been on to something—something that applies to more than just him. Could it be that all the princess needed was a little kindness to break down her walls?

I summon a brief smile. "We make do as best we can with what we're given. As you clearly recognize."

Aurelia offers me one last smile of her own, quiet but radiant as dawn on the horizon. I've never seen her look at Marclinus quite like that. "Thank you for talking with me. And for listening."

She steps back and walks out of the library. I stare after her for a few seconds, my heart thumping a little too loud, before I notice another sensation down below.

Great God smite me, I'm half hard.

The recognition comes with a flood of shame like a deluge of cold water, which solves the immediate problem.

What the fuck is wrong with me? It hasn't been *that* long since a woman last offered me an affectionate touch.

Of course, the affection a few women of the court have shown was only about a momentary getting off. In the case of the few members of staff I've entertained, it was the thrill of a dalliance with a foreign prince. Never anything really to do with *me*.

Not that I'm dim enough to think Aurelia's overtures come from anything other than a selfish place either.

Jaw clenching, I find myself striding over to the narrow windows. I look through the glass toward the tufts of cloud floating across the lightening blue of the sky.

My hand taps down forehead, heart, and gut before balling over my sternum. Gods only know what the godlen whose brand I bear—the master of travel, communication, and weather—would make of this scenario.

I extend my thoughts toward the sky. *Jurnus, the road I'm on has become twisted. How should I weather this storm?*

The clouds drift on before my eyes. Then one draws my attention with a twitch of my pulse.

It stretches across the sky toward me in a thin but straight line, like something steady and true.

I can only think he means that I should stay the course. Remain loyal to my principles.

Raul is an idiot. He's going to let his dick lead him away from the path we were already walking. Giving in to those urges can only muddle the situation.

I'll stick to the track we first agreed on, wear the princess down in every other way I can, and we'll see who topples her first.

CHAPTER FOURTEEN

Aurelia

T t isn't difficult to get lost in the sprawling hallways of the imperial palace. I set out to do so, curious to see what I might discover if I ventured off my typical routes, and I can honestly say I'm now not entirely sure how to get back to where I started.

As I wander down yet another vast hall, a door opens at the other end. A lady I vaguely recognize—I think she's a marchionissa—slips out.

Even from a distance, I can see the flush in her cheeks, the mussing of her pinned-up hair. She pats it down hastily as she hustles away in the opposite direction.

I must have made my way into one of the sections of the palace containing the court's private quarters.

I don't think much of it, continuing on my way, until I'm just a few paces shy of the doorway the marchionissa emerged from, and the door opens again.

This time, it's Prince Raul who steps into the hallway, tucking his elegant shirt into the waist of his trousers in a way that immediately tells me what he and his married lady companion were getting up to.

Our gazes lock. Raul's icy blue eyes spark in a discomforting way that makes me want to flee, but I force myself to stop.

If I'm going to obtain the princes' help to get me through the coming trials, I need to ingratiate myself with all of them. I didn't make much progress with Bastien this morning. He played friendly enough after my appeal, but his remarks sounded far too calculating.

He's still suspicious of me. Prodding him for more information when he was already skewing his answers would only have given him more justification to feel that way.

I smile at Raul with a wryness to acknowledge the tension of our past interactions. "I've finally stumbled on someone I know. I seem to have lost my way. I don't suppose you'd summon the kindness to direct me to the parlor?"

A slanted grin crosses Raul's breathtaking face. "It seems to be an afternoon of servicing ladies. I could do even better than giving directions."

From the look of the marchionissa, it's not a hollow promise. If flirting is the closest I can get to friendliness from this man, perhaps I should entertain it a little rather than shutting it down.

I lower my eyes modestly. "I think the directions will do for now. Do you think you can manage to get me to the gardens with my honor intact?"

Raul chuckles at the coy remark—and the implication that I might be more open to his advances later. He swipes his hands together in front of him, and my gaze catches on the blotches of scars marking the knuckles.

I only noticed the one hand yesterday. The other's scars look fresher, like skin that's only recently shed its scabs.

I can't stop my medical inclinations from kicking in—and maybe I shouldn't want to. The more ways I can establish good will between us, the better.

I nod toward him. "You've injured both of your hands recently. If there's any lingering pain or you want to ease the scarring, I have a salve that speeds along the healing process."

Raul follows my gaze and snorts. "Scars add character. I'm perfectly fine."

For a second, I think his tone has stiffened, but then he touches the small of my back and nudges me down the hall. "Let's get this lost lamb back to the flock."

He guides me along with an air of total assurance. I glance up at him, ignoring the tingling of my skin at the nearness of his impressive form. "You must know the palace awfully well by now. Prince Bastien says he arrived when he was seven years old. Was it the same for you?"

"The emperor's chosen age for fosters," Raul says in a nonchalant tone. "I turned up a year after Bastien did. Hard to believe it's been fifteen now. But I've found whatever ways I can to make good use of the time."

His thumb strokes across my back in a subtle caress. As little as I intend to succumb to his advances, I can't help thinking his approach is an awful lot more pleasant than Marclinus's forceful grab of my arm and unprompted nip.

The imperial heir requires only his station to seduce any lady in court. Raul will have needed to actually charm them. And he must prove good to his word, or disparaging gossip would quickly spread between the ladies and he'd find his options dried up.

I probably shouldn't be thinking about his seductive

prowess when I need to focus on gaining his friendship, not access to his bed.

"Does His Imperial Highness ever resent the competition for his court's attention?" I ask, partly because it might reveal more about Marclinus's attitudes and partly out of honest curiosity.

Raul sounds as if he's choked back a guffaw at my baldness, but it's not as if I could be unaware of my betrothed's lustful pursuits after yesterday's dinner. His smirk grows. "The court is large enough that our interests don't need to overlap. I do believe in keeping my liaisons more private. Easier for all involved to relax."

He leans a little closer, lowering his voice. "I could make you just as satisfied as Marchionissa Poinette. Set that lovely body alight with all the pleasures it's craved."

I peer at him through my eyelashes. "I don't doubt your skills. But *I* believe in a certain amount of loyalty to one's partner... even if the match hasn't been settled."

Raul lets out a hum that resonates over my skin. "You're not married yet. Marclinus has never bothered to care how his partners feel. Shouldn't a woman deserving enough to become empress get to experience true gratification at least once before she consigns herself to a life where she's expected to do all the worshiping?"

His words quiver through me, stimulating both my heart and my sex. Gods smite me, he can probably tell my drawers are dampening.

I can still play along. "Is that what you'd do? Worship me? It's seemed as if you'd rather savage me like the wolf you claim you are."

"Perhaps we could split the difference and make it a ravaging instead." Raul's thumb skims over my back again. "I'd be willing to set aside our differences momentarily for the sake of mutual enjoyment. I have more of a bone to pick with your husband-to-be than you, after all."

And no doubt he enjoys the idea of bedding me before that husband-to-be has a chance to. For all his provocative words, a hint of the hostility he's shown me in the past has emerged in the brief sharpening of his tone.

I know he can put on a performance when he feels the need to. His overtures don't mean he likes me any more than I imagine he's truly fond of the various other ladies he tumbles.

His larger animosity allows me a change of subject. "His Imperial Highness has given you a difficult time in other ways, then?" Maybe if I learn more about how Marclinus has hassled his foster brothers, it'll reveal something about how he might challenge his potential future brides.

"Marclinus never wants anyone to forget how much power he holds," Raul says lightly. "So why not take back a little of our own when he never needs to know? You can't deny you're tempted." His voice drops to a murmur. "Just imagine how I could make your body sing while I devour every inch of it in the best possible way."

A deeper shiver ripples through me, this one all heat. My cheeks flare of their own accord.

I offer another modest smile. "I think that's a proposal best left to the imagination. As thrilling as the idea might be."

My tone must be firm enough to tell him he isn't getting any farther with me at this particular moment. Raul teases his fingertips over my back once more and then prods me forward. "We'll see if you change your mind once it sinks in just how skilled these hands are. You'll find stairs to the garden entrance just around the next bend, Lamb."

He leaves me to continue on alone, mulling over exactly

what he meant about his skills "sinking in." But I do recognize the bright hall around the corner, lined with paintings that flicker with bits of illusionary magic.

As I head down the staircase to the broad doors that have been propped open, laughter carries from gardens beyond. I hurry out into the warm sunlight and floral-scented air.

It appears that most of the court has already assembled amid the flowerbeds and hedges since our luncheon, including Their Imperial Eminences and my remaining competitors for Marclinus's hand. Fausta glances over at me from a cluster of other ladies and immediately narrows her eyes.

I amble along a path past her only to hear her sharp laugh peel out. "It looks like the wild princess is wild with her clothes as well."

As several nearby heads swivel my way, I'm abruptly aware of the loosening of my bodice. I hastily reach behind me.

This Darium-style gown is meant to emphasize the bosom and waist amid the airy sleeves and skirt. The sparse ribbon lacing at the back maintains that form.

But my grasping hands find that the tight bow Melisse tied for me has slipped completely apart, the lacing spreading wide.

My temper prickles with the realization. This is what Raul meant. As we strolled through the halls, he must have surreptitiously worked the bow loose without my even noticing.

He wanted me thinking about him after he'd walked away—wanted the memory of his seductive mischief burned into my memory with embarrassment.

That's how he still sees me: as prey. An innocent maiden who'll be flustered by his rakish behavior.

His assumptions might not be a bad thing. But I do need to fix my dress.

"You really should guide your maid more effectively, Princess Aurelia," Fausta adds in her snide tone.

As I turn my back to a hedge and tug at the ribbons, Rochelle comes up beside me. "Here, I can fix it quickly."

"Thank you." I hold still with much gratitude as my friend secures the lacing again with a firmly knotted bow.

She speaks under her breath as if embarrassed by the admission. "My sisters and I often help each other at home—there's more of us than maids."

Not the richest of noble families, then. I'm not surprised by the admission after what I've seen and heard from her so far. She's never seemed truly comfortable putting on courtly airs.

How in the realms did *she* end up in the middle of this miserable game?

I wish I could ask her that without giving away my own reservations too blatantly.

When she's finished her efforts, I find the bodice melds to my torso even more neatly than it did before. My belly looks almost as sleek as Fausta's.

I smooth my hands over it. "You've done an impressive job. I think I've come out of this mishap looking better than I might have if it hadn't occurred at all, thanks to you."

Rochelle gives a soft laugh. "Your figure isn't difficult to enhance. None of us in my family are great beauties. When you don't have much to work with, you learn certain tricks for making the most of what you have."

Her self-deprecation sends a twinge through my gut. "You have plenty of appealing features," I tell her firmly. Her pale blond curls may be unruly, but they're certainly eye-catching with that striking color. Her face is reasonably comely. And she does have a figure, even if it's a little awkward.

More confidence might be enough to solve that problem.

Rochelle shrugs. "It's all right. I never think about it much except when I'm here. Back home, we're out roaming the fields and pastures as much as we can get away with, and the birds and bunnies don't care how pretty a picture we make."

I smile at the wistfulness in her voice, feeling it echo inside me. "There's a huge, old forest behind the main royal castle in Accasy. I'd sneak out for a walk there every day that I could. Sometimes you need a little time away from all the trappings, just you and the untouched world."

A glimmer lights in Rochelle's eyes, her smile widening. "Yes. I don't think many of the other ladies here appreciate that. These tamed gardens don't quite compare."

As if on cue, two of our fellow competitors wander over to join us with rather timid expressions. One is holding two wine goblets, the second of which she offers to me. "I appreciated your advice during last night's dinner. It's—It's good to know we can still look out for each other."

I take the goblet and turn it between my fingers, resolving to swap it for a fresh one off one of the servants' trays when I have the chance. Even if her gratitude is genuine, I'm still standing between her and the marriage she's vying for.

Between her and her very survival, quite possibly.

I'm not sure I'd accept a drink even from Rochelle, as much common ground as we've found.

"I'm glad I could help," I say. "We all deserve the best possible chance."

In these wretched, ridiculous tests, I can't add with Emperor Tarquin and Marclinus standing nearby.

A ruddy-faced man with a similar large-boned but slightly awkward build to Rochelle's ambles over and sets his hand on her shoulder. His gray-blond moustache flutters as he speaks. "You've been more than kind to my daughter, Your Highness. I hope your poise can rub off on her."

Rochelle's face pinks beneath her freckles. "We were all a little taken aback by the announcement at first—" she starts in a meek tone.

Her father barrels right over her explanation. "You've never wanted to reach for enough. We have a good name! You can do it proud. Just keep that head high."

My friend's smile looks resigned. "Of course, Father."

Ah. I no longer need to wonder why she was thrown into the competition.

Perhaps I can offer a diversion from the uncomfortable turn the conversation has taken. My thumb rubs the side of my ring absently as I look around.

My gaze skims the flowerbeds and pauses on the emperor and his heir. They're standing in profile to me by a hedge sculpture like the imperial hawk spreading its wings over a column. Emperor Tarquin is holding a wine glass of his own.

I furrow my brow and drop my voice to a hush. "Did His Imperial Majesty's hand just wobble? It almost looked as if he's having trouble carrying his goblet."

My four companions all cast hasty glances that way. Rochelle's father frowns. "I hadn't noticed."

I glance away with a brief laugh. "It was probably nothing. I was only startled because he normally seems so strong and steady."

I'd direct the conversation to another new topic, but Fausta saunters over to our little cluster just then, trailing several of her noblewomen friends behind her. She tosses back her flame-red hair and wrinkles her pert nose at me.

"Lady Giralda, Lady Iseppa, let's not fawn over our princess from the north. We can't let her think she's as superior as she likes to act."

I act superior? The kettle would like to have word with the pot.

I keep my smile in place. "We were only having a friendly conversation."

Fausta's scoff is as delicate as the rest of her petite frame. "*Friendly*. As if we haven't all seen how you look at us, heard how you talk about us. Oh, yes, please bestow more of your patronizing wisdom on me."

She's framing my attempts at help as condescension. My teeth grit against a barbed retort.

If I snap at her, I'll only appear to be proving her right.

I smooth the anger from my voice. "And what do you call it when a lady purposefully demoralizes her peers, Lady Fausta?"

My rival sniffs as if she couldn't possibly dignify such a question with a response and turns away from me. "Let those of us who understand the greatness of Dariu stick together and avoid those who'd look down their noses."

The two ladies have gone rigid. When Fausta starts to drift away, they scurry after her with nervous backward glances as if they think I might retaliate.

"You were wonderful during the knives," one of them simpers to Fausta before they step out of hearing behind a fountain.

I can't blame them for caring more about what one of their own thinks of them than my opinion. But it's hard to take comfort from that thought when Vicerine Bianca sweeps by in Fausta's wake.

She motions to the other nobles who've paused to watch the altercation, directing them away from me and Rochelle.

"Who has time for such pathetic figures. What do you make of the latest shoes on offer in Vivencia, my ladies? Far more refined than anything you'd find in the wild north, no?"

None of those nobles were ever my friends, but my stomach sinks to see the gap widening around my friend and me. Fausta and Bianca have discovered a means of warfare that extends beyond the trials.

Even Rochelle's father seems affected. "My girl, there is something I wished to discuss with you alone..."

As he drags her away, my gaze slides back to the emperor and Marclinus of its own accord, only to find the two of them watching me with an evaluating air.

I lower my gaze and stride off to find myself a fresh glass of wine. And try not to speculate on how it might hurt my chances if the man I'm meant to marry thinks his whole court already hates me.

Chapter Fifteen

Aurelia

Cheerful voices warble through the drawing room. The warmth of the hearth wraps around me. When I look up, my mother's smile reaches me from across the room.

My heart leaps with the most painful sort of joy. I'm home. Somehow, I'm *home*.

Fiddle music lilts through the air. A few of my friends spring up to dance. My sister catches my hand, tugging me into the whirl of bodies—

And I find myself spinning past the doorway, all the way through the castle gates. The capital city of Costel sprawls before me, the brightly colored faces of the buildings beaming under the sun.

The music keeps playing, as if it's a festival day. The city folk are emerging from their homes and businesses to romp together on the streets.

I weave between them, tasting the tang of ale and sweetness of fresh-baked pastries lacing the air. I grin wider at every bob of a head, every merry greeting.

"So happy you could join us, Your Highness."

"Thank you for the castle's generosity, Princess Aurelia!"

The celebratory atmosphere pulls me in—but a flicker of shadow snags my attention with a lurch of my heart.

A dark shape lurks at the mouth of an alley. Black uniform painted with white bones as if it's a living skeleton—a Darium soldier.

I've barely noticed him before he's yanking a little girl off the street into the alley. A yelp breaks from my throat.

I run down the street toward him, and the people around me stumble. More skeletal figures appear everywhere I sweep my gaze. They snarl and snatch at the civilians, wrenching them out of view.

Whipping around, I grasp after their victims, but I can never reach fast enough. They're always just a little too far away.

A sob builds in the back of my mouth.

Strong arms embrace me with a waft of a cedar-sweet scent. A steady but gentle voice that hits me right in the heart speaks by my ear. "It'll be all right, Lia. We'll see this through."

I choke up so abruptly I can't breathe.

We won't see it through. Our story has already ended. Any second now the blades will flash and the blood will spray—

I jolt out of sleep with my heart pounding and my skin clammy with sweat, my fingers clutching the sheet. The darkness weighs heavy on me with the thick rosy scent of the potpourri the cleaning staff replenishes every day.

I'm not home. I'm still in the imperial palace, trying to see the future I want through all on my own.

The ache of that knowledge barely has time to sink in before a sharp chuckle rings through the air from just beside my bed.

I'm not alone after all.

I jerk upright on the mattress, one hand groping beneath the heap of extra pillows next to me. My fingers close around the handle of the small dagger I decided to keep there after Prince Raul proved he could enter my chambers regardless of locks.

Light flares at the other side of the room. The lit lantern casts an eerie yellowish glow over the three figures arrayed next to my bed.

Raul brought two of his fellow princes this time.

It's actually Bastien standing closest, as if he's leading this invasion. He holds the lantern to the side so I can see his striking face.

The wavering light turns his narrow features harsher but blazes off his auburn hair and in his deep green eyes. Which are fixed, with stark intensity, on me.

"Welcome back to the world of the waking, Your Highness," he says flatly.

My gaze darts from him to Raul standing by his shoulder with a smirk and Lorenzo poised near the end of the bed, his deep brown skin and black hair nearly blending into the shadows beyond. They're watching me too, Raul looking amused and Lorenzo more pensive but neither of them at all friendly.

I keep my grasp on the hilt of the dagger but don't draw it out. The moment they see the weapon, I'd lose all benefit of surprise if I need to use it. And they haven't done anything worthy of outright murder just yet.

Or maybe they have. Bastien adjusts his free hand, and a gleam of gold brings my attention snapping back to him.

He's holding a thick gold ring. A thick gold ring with a sapphire nestled amid its rippled band—

My pulse stutters. My gaze plummets to my hand still resting on top of the sheet—to my now ringless forefinger.

In my shock, I hadn't registered the missing pressure. How in the realms did they manage to pull it off my finger without the movement waking me?

My heart settles into an even but quickened beat, more rapid than when I woke up from the nightmare. A chill winds through my veins.

I keep my voice steady through sheer force of will. "Have you decided to become common thieves now? Breaking and entering wasn't enough of a crime?"

Raul sinks down on the edge of the mattress and lets his gaze travel over my form beneath the sheet. The nights in the palace are warm enough that I can't bear to keep on a blanket, and the thin fabric shows every slope of my torso and legs.

"Maybe we simply wanted to keep you company," he purrs. "The lamb must get lonely in this big bed all by herself."

Bastien flicks an irritated glance toward his foster brother before focusing back on me. He turns the ring between his fingers. "You wear it even to bed. It must be very important to you. Why does it bother you so much to lose it?"

The chill descends straight to my gut. How closely has he been watching me that he realized the ring was more significant than a random piece of jewelry?

Or maybe he's simply more perceptive than most of the nobles I've been surrounded by. I doubt even Marclinus for all his evaluations of his potential brides has given my jewelry a thought.

I swallow thickly. "It's special to my family. My mother gave it to me just before I left as a parting gift, a connection to home. It's the *only* thing I can easily keep with me that I brought from the place where I spent my entire life until now. So yes, it's rather important."

Bastien studies me as if searching for a lie. What other significance could he imagine the ring has?

Everything I've said to him is true, but he seems set on distrusting me. Despite his brief apology in the library, he's gone straight back to looking at me like I'm a villain.

I hold out my hand. "So I'd appreciate having it returned to me."

The prince closes his fingers around the ring. "I don't know. I think it might be good for you to experience what it's like having something that matters to you taken away."

My jaw clenches against a surge of emotion, rawer after the dream I just came out of. "What makes you think I've never experienced that before?"

Bastien scoffs as if it's a ridiculous question, and Lorenzo's face hardens. Even Raul's eyes turn flinty despite his seductive airs.

Maybe it does sound absurd when they've lost a decade and a half of their lives to the empire. But I've had far worse than a ring wrenched from my grasp.

I'm not sure how to play this situation. What can I do that will sway them toward sympathy rather than hostility?

The thought of letting them walk away with the ring makes my chest clench up. Even with the dagger, I've got no hope of overpowering all three men. And I doubt I'll ever turn them into allies after tonight if I attack them that blatantly.

Or if I turn to the imperial justice system. Gods help me, I don't know if I even believe that Emperor Tarquin would side in my favor rather than declaring it better for me to set behind all traces of my kingdom.

The fatigue of my broken sleep rolls over me alongside a suffocating swell of anguish. Why does every second of every day here have to be some kind of battle? Why can't I keep one small thing that I care about safe?

Tears prickle behind my eyes, and I instinctively stiffen my resolve against them. Every bone in my body balks at the idea of weeping in front of the princes, letting them see their cruelty has affected me.

But it has. They already think I'm weak. Maybe they'll find some kind of a conscience if they see how much I'm struggling.

I swipe at my eyes, and the burn intensifies. Moisture gathers with every blink. "Please. I've never been this far from home before. I've never been separated from my family for so long. I realize it's nothing like you've been through, but I don't know—if I don't have even that one thing to hold on to—gods, I miss them so much—"

My words break off with a hitch of a sob. The tears trickle out, streaking down my cheeks. And I find I can't stop.

I thought I'd just make a show of a little misery, but the moment I open a crack in the dam holding back the emotions inside me, all the grief and horror and homesickness crash over me in a wave. My tears turn into a torrent.

I clap my hand to my mouth against a wail, not quite muffling it. Shame sears through my despair—that I have so much weakness in me still, that these men are seeing it—but it isn't potent enough to push back the deluge.

Somewhere inside the maelstrom, I find the wherewithal to at least drive my point home. To prod them for answers of their own.

My voice breaks around the words. "I don't... know what... you want from me. I'd try. If I knew."

But maybe all they want is to keep barging into my room, stealing my things, tossing their cutting words in my face.

Another sob tumbles out of me, and Lorenzo makes a rough noise. He stalks around the foot of the bed so stiffly I'd think he's furious with me.

But if he's annoyed by my outburst, I must have tugged at some compassion in him as well. He sits on the bed an arm's length away and rests his hand on my shoulder.

His touch is nothing but gentle. When I glance at him through my tears, he squeezes my shoulder and looks past me to the other two princes.

His expression still looks gloomy. He motions to his foster brothers with sharp twists of his free hand.

I can't follow the entirety of his message through my blurred vision and with my limited knowledge of his self-made vocabulary, but it's clear he's saying something about me. One hasty gesture he repeats a couple of times makes me think of an exchange, an item passed between two sides.

Bastien exhales with a disgruntled sigh and appears to answer with a few skeptical twitches of his own hand around my ring. Whatever Lorenzo answers, the other prince's mouth sets in a flat line.

Raul watches the silent conversation, his smirk returning. I don't trust the gleam in his eyes when he returns his attention to me.

"He has a point," he says to Bastien.

The unexpected support from Lorenzo has taken the edge

off my despair, even if I'm not sure exactly what they're discussing now. I brush aside the last lingering tears, gathering my self-control.

Bastien turns to me. "Perhaps we could make a trade of it."

The exchange I thought Lorenzo was indicating. I offer him a grim smile. "You want me to barter for what's already mine?"

My voice comes out a little too watery to be convincingly incredulous.

The corner of Bastien's mouth ticks upward just slightly. He rotates the ring between his fingers so the sapphire flashes with lantern light. "It appears to be mine at the moment. Do you want it back or not?"

A very small part of me is tempted to yank my dagger out from beneath the pillow and see how he likes having the blade shoved right through his thieving hand. A much larger part of me recognizes that the offer of a deal is some kind of victory. And that a moment's revenge isn't going to benefit me in the long run.

I leave the dagger where it is. "What payment are you looking for?"

Raul's smirk grows, and for a second I'm afraid he's going to leverage the situation into a much more violating proposition than he's suggested before. "I have a thought."

Bastien grimaces at him. "Of course you do."

For all they've coordinated their animosity toward me, the two of them don't actually get along that well, do they? A fact I'm filing away for future reference.

Lorenzo makes a circling gesture I can tell means, *Get on with it.*

Raul leans back on his hands as if he's perfectly at ease lounging on my bed. "Let the princess spend a whole day constantly reminded of how exposed she is, no matter what locked doors she hides behind. You wear no undergarments under your gown from first dressing in the morning through turning in for the night, and you get back your ring the next day."

Bastien's jaw works, but it doesn't appear he has a proposal he likes better. "That will do."

Walk around the palace with whatever trials tomorrow might bring—perhaps quite literally—with nothing on beneath my dress? My skin crawls at the thought.

But it isn't as if anyone would *know*. My skirts barely lift above my ankles even when I'm seated.

Well, Raul would know, with his penetrating gift. No doubt he's looking forward to confirming my compliance.

It's not as if he hasn't invaded my privacy before. I survived.

I fix Bastien with a firm look. "I'll accept the deal—*if* you swear to your godlen that you'll fulfill your end and not make any new demands. And that you won't give the ring back only to steal it again later."

It's a bit of a gamble. Some people don't worry all that much about what the god they dedicated themselves to thinks of them. But for Bastien to have offered such an immense sacrifice to his, it seems likely he'd rather not risk divine wrath.

I don't think he'll accept my condition unless he actually means to follow through.

He glowers at me, but he sets the lantern on the bedside table so he can press that hand to his chest over his godlen mark. "I swear to Jurnus that if Princess Aurelia carries out her side of the deal in full, I'll return her ring for her to keep, as soon as I'm safely able to."

Conviction resonates through his words, sending a tingle over my skin. I believe him.

"Then it's settled," I say. "Perhaps you'll let me finish my sleep now?"

Lorenzo pulls away from me. Raul gets up with a jaunty tip of his head. "Sweet dreams, Princess."

I don't release the hilt of the dagger until my bedroom door has closed behind them.

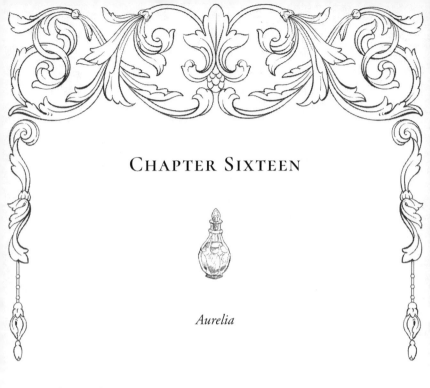

Chapter Sixteen

Aurelia

Melisse enters my bedroom with her usual courtesy —knocking on the door with a soft call of, "Your Highness?" and waiting for my acknowledgment before entering. Much more respectful than certain princes I could mention.

She halts a few steps into the room. "You've already dressed."

I offer her a reassuring smile from where I'm sitting at my vanity. "I was up early and it seemed silly to wait. You know I'm not much for being fussed over."

The press of my bare bottom against the silk skirt of the gown reminds me of the true reason. I couldn't explain to her why I'm forgoing a chemise and drawers.

I can be grateful that Madam Clea delivered a new series of dresses yesterday evening, ensuring I have a selection fit for a princess. I picked the one with the most fabric around the bodice, an extra layer of pale green that flutters over my chest, to help conceal my lack of undergarments.

The skirt, flowing in the typical Darium style, should reveal nothing. As long as the imperial heir doesn't require any table dancing from us, my indecency will remain a secret.

I wish I could fully trust that table dancing is, well, off the table. It's difficult to imagine what Marclinus might ask of us next.

The next trial can't be too far off. He gave us all of yesterday as a reprieve, though it was hardly relaxing when we spent every minute around him braced for the next announcement.

To mollify my maid, I haven't done more than comb my fingers through my hair. She picks up the brush and runs it over the dark brown waves until they shine like polished bronze.

"There's been a lot of chatter around the dining room," she mentions in a hushed voice. "I heard Their Imperial Eminences have already taken their seats."

My stomach knots. "I suppose I should head over early and see what the fuss is about, then."

It's more distracting than I expected to navigate the world without a single scrap of cloth covering my sex. As I walk, the fabric of my skirt ripples against my mound and the air tickles over my folds in an unnervingly provocative way.

I have to think Prince Raul was perfectly aware of the effect his bargain would have on me. Is the idea simply to put me in a more impious mood?

That can't be why Prince Bastien agreed. *He* must be hoping the embarrassment of my secret immodesty will affect my performance in the next trial.

Or maybe he simply wants me to be miserable. It's certainly seemed that way most of the times I've spoken to him.

As I walk down the hall toward the dining room, my thumb rises instinctively to rub the now vacant base of my forefinger. Anxiety quivers through my chest.

I'll have my ring back by tomorrow. Bastien swore to his godlen. I simply have to endure a single day of new discomforts.

I turn onto the main hallway that holds the dining room and spot Fausta and Bianca huddled together at the far end. It looks as if Fausta has just pushed a morsel of something into her mouth, chewing hastily while Bianca hands her a goblet.

There's something oddly furtive about the exchange. Fausta takes a few swift gulps from the goblet and presses it back into Bianca's hands.

An uneasy chill wraps around my gut. What are they up to now?

What do they know that I don't?

As Bianca saunters away with the goblet, Fausta swipes her hand past her mouth and turns to notice me. With her usual sharp smile, she sashays into the dining room ahead of me.

I follow, swallowing down my trepidation.

The room beyond the doorway looks the same as last night, back to its standard layout with the table of honor at one end of the room and the others in neat rows alongside it. Emperor Tarquin and his son have indeed already taken their seats, the servants acting as their tasters hovering behind them.

Marclinus has procured himself a full goblet of something or other. The table itself is empty other than a few centerpieces, porcelain vases with sprigs of vibrant flowers. He tips his glass languidly to his mouth, watching us over the top of it.

A couple of my fellow competitors have arrived ahead of Fausta and me. As servants direct us to our seats, more enter behind us.

It appears the ten of us remaining are all being arranged on the far side of the table today, where we have a view over the entire dining room. Rochelle ends up at the chair two down from mine and acknowledges me with a nervous smile.

Bianca has opted not to join us as she often does. I spot her with her husband at one of the smaller tables. Maybe she feels she needs to give the viceroy a little attention here and there to ensure some kind of harmony in their home.

All four of the princes take seats at the other side of our table—first Lorenzo, catching my gaze and then looking away. Next Bastien and Neven together, in murmured conversation my tormentor doesn't bother to glance up from.

And finally Raul, ambling over to the chair directly across from me, his cocky grin widening with every step.

Wonderful.

As he drops into his seat, he tips his head to me in acknowledgment. "Good to see you looking so unhampered today, Your Highness."

Oh, he can tell I've followed through on my end of the deal, all right.

I smile back at him. "It's amazing what a good, uninterrupted night of sleep can do for you."

Not that I would know about that today.

The rest of the chairs around the room are filling up before me. Just moments after the last spot at our table has been taken, Marclinus rises to his feet. At the flourish of his arms, the chatter around the room falls away.

He beams at his audience, so much glee shining in my betrothed's eyes that my stomach starts to roil before he's even spoken.

A matching feral delight rings through his voice. "Good morning to you all, good people of my court. With this new day, we are beginning a new trial."

He makes a dramatic gesture toward the line of us along the one side of the table. "Not long ago, the ladies eager for my hand enjoyed a night of indulgence. Now we will evaluate their self-restraint. From now through sunset tomorrow, they will refrain from ingesting so much as a drop of water or a crumb of food."

Someone farther down the row stifles a sound of dismay. An ache forms in my throat as his words sink in.

Nothing to eat or drink for nearly two days.

The lack of food will be uncomfortable but not unendurable. I've heard of devouts and clerics fasting for longer in an attempt to leave behind the concerns of the body to commune with the gods.

Going that long without anything to wet our throats? By tomorrow evening, our bodies will be dangerously close to dehydration.

I've never felt more grateful for the water with its light steeping of tea leaves that I mixed this morning. I intended the herbs I picked to fortify me for the day ahead, but the liquid they soaked in could be my actual saving grace.

The memory of sipping from that glass draws my gaze down the line toward Fausta's petite form. My jaw tightens.

She knew. Or, more likely, Bianca caught wind of the next trial and quickly saw to it that her friend would go into the day with some initial refreshments to give her an edge over the rest of us.

Will she keep sneaking relief to Fausta over the next two days?

As if hearing my thoughts, Emperor Tarquin lifts his voice from his end of the table. "Naturally, the guards will closely monitor all of the competitors to ensure they follow the rules of the trial. You will be accompanied anywhere you go, including your bed chambers. Cheating will not be tolerated."

Marclinus rocks on his heels. "But for those who prove their forbearance, you can look forward to a fabulous feast tomorrow night!"

He claps his hands. "Now the rest of us will dine."

As he sprawls back in his chair, servers move around the room. Plates wafting the savory scents of fried eggs and spiced meat clink against the tabletop in front of the breakfast-goers across from us.

My mouth starts to water. My stomach gurgles, empty of anything other than tea after the long night.

Raul catches my eye and digs into his meal with flamboyant gusto. He sniffs the food with a happy sigh, hums ecstatically as he chews, and makes a show of smacking his lips before he spears the next morsel.

A couple of seats over, Prince Neven notices his foster brother's display. He shoots a glare my way and takes an extravagant bite of his own breakfast, all but groaning to emphasize how delicious it is.

The lady at my right has turned wan, watching their goading alongside me. She wets her lips, and her stomach rumbles loud enough that her cheeks flare pink.

Raul tips his goblet to his lips with exaggerated swallows, and my mouth feels even drier. But my gaze settles on the band of cloth he's wrapped around his knuckles.

Focusing on his hands rather than his food helps me

ignore my hunger. His other hand bears the same narrow bandage.

I don't remember seeing those during his middle of the night visit, although Bastien drew most of my attention then. And I wasn't exactly at my most alert. Has he injured himself again?

What is Raul doing that's scarred his knuckles that way? Or is it something someone else is doing to him?

As he waves a tidbit of meat in the air with his fork as if to waft the tempting smell toward us, I find myself studying the set of his broad shoulders, the working of his jaw as he chews. For all he acts like the most confident of the four princes, impervious and imposing, there's so much tension simmering behind that front.

Lorenzo has swayed between warm and cold, and Bastien's been nearly frigid, but Prince Raul is all fire. I know what's driving him better than the others.

There's so much emotion in him that might be shifted in my favor if I could only convince him that I'm not his opponent.

Those thoughts percolate in my head for the rest of the torturous meal. When Emperor Tarquin gets to his feet and dismisses us, I head straight to the nearest imperial guard I see patrolling the room.

"I know we're not to go to our rooms alone," I say, "but I forgot something I promised to give a friend. Would you escort me?"

CHAPTER SEVENTEEN

Raul

I've made my mid-afternoon naps a known habit so no one so much as blinks when I leave behind the blathering of the court. They all think I'm catching up on lost sleep after entertaining ladies at all hours of the night.

None of them need to know that I simply want to escape their inane conversation and pompous airs for an hour or two. I rarely actually sleep.

The bed my esteemed foster father has provided me with is an ideal place to lounge about, though. I'm looking forward to doing just that when I push past the door and spot a small jar nestled on the bedcovers.

I sweep my gaze across the room as I approach, but there's no sign of anyone lurking in here now. Closer, I make out the tiny note balanced on top of the jar.

For your hands, says the compact but elegant writing on the scrap of paper.

A sudden certainty balls in my chest. I flick the paper aside and pick up the jar.

The gel inside is translucent greenish-yellow. The sniff I take after unscrewing the lid has a pungent herbal quality.

The medic princess decided to gift me her healing salve even though I told her not to bother.

My hand tightens around the jar, setting off a sting through my bandaged knuckles that only fuels my annoyance. I toss the container back onto the bed.

Marclinus has her starving for the day, and she's going to pretend to care about my hands? How the fuck did she even get in here?

I find myself inhaling deeply as if I might catch a lingering hint of her coolly sweet scent. But the answer is probably much simpler. All she'd need to do is pass the offering along to the manservant assigned to me, who could have dropped it off.

That doesn't mean she had any right to. I want her trembling with unfulfilled need, not consumed with *pity* for me.

Discarding all pretense of napping, I stalk out of the room. Her Highness has to be reminded that I'm the last person who needs any coddling.

She thinks she's so stoic, sitting there with her stiff upper lip through breakfast and luncheon, flicking her gaze away from the carafes of wine and fresh-pressed juices the servants have carried through the halls for those allowed to partake. I noticed Tarquin has instructed that filled glasses be left out on some of the tables as a temptation.

Several of the other ladies have eyed them with obvious distress. I haven't caught Aurelia so much as glancing at one.

She's hardly unshakable. I've seen how she's responded to

me. She broke down in tears over her precious *ring*, of all idiotic things.

It's a shame our little deal won't have interfered with her performance in this trial. If anything, her hidden brazenness might give her a welcome distraction from focusing on thirst and hunger.

I couldn't have known that when I suggested it. Bastien is probably fuming in his quiet, scowling way. But how much could he have expected to get in exchange for a mere bit of jewelry, no matter what meaning it holds for her?

At the very least, she'll have been thinking about me and what's missing between her thighs for the entire day. If that hasn't ripened her for the picking, I don't know what would.

Most of the court is where I left them in the hall of entertainments. Some of the nobles are gathered around tables for games of cards or dice—with more temptations in the form of bowls of nuts and dried fruits in easy reach. A few fling darts at one of the boards mounted on the wall. Others simply sway vaguely to the tune a couple of the imperial musicians are playing on flute and piano.

Tarquin had Lorenzo give another demonstration of his talent right after lunch. The emperor pushes for longer performances than ever these days. My foster brother looked more gray than brown by the time he was finished.

I don't see him around at the moment. Gods willing, he's gone off for a nap of his own to ease the pain of straining his gift.

Where's the princess of Accasy gotten to?

I scan the edges of the room. The sheen of her brown hair draws my eye from the opposite end. She's standing next to that tall, clumsy daughter-of-a-baron who seems to be the only lady Fausta and Bianca haven't scared off from her.

I saunter toward them, evaluating my approach. I need to

be reasonably subtle—if Marclinus thinks I'm moving in on his pet princess of the north before he's had a go at her, I'll need bandages on a lot more than my hands.

As I check to confirm he's still at one of the cards tables, my gaze snags on another familiar figure.

Neven is easing across the room in Aurelia's direction, his gaze trained on her with a fierceness that sets off a peal of alarm in my head. He's clutching a flower vase of all things, though the flowers have been discarded.

What in the realms is he up to? If he's focused on her, it can't be anything good.

Which would be fine, except I'm not convinced it'll be particularly smart either. The kid does have a habit of following his temper rather than his brain.

He pauses near the wall with its display of illusion-enhanced paintings. They're intended to reflect the purpose of the room: a bear cavorting with a tambourine here, a fox hurling darts there.

Aurelia drifts away from her friend toward the same wall. Neven's stance tenses.

Several paces away, one of the imperial guards turns his head toward them.

With a hitch of my pulse, I hurry forward. The damned kid is going to get himself into a heap of shit if someone doesn't catch him first.

I reach him just as he takes his first urgent step toward Aurelia, his hands clutching the vase. Snagging him by the elbow, I jerk him around.

"What do you think you're doing?" I demand, low enough that only he can hear.

Neven's face flushes beneath his pale hair, but it's at least as much anger as embarrassment. His voice comes out in a harsh whisper. "I'm getting rid of her. I can say I saw her about to sneak water from the vase—splash it on her and drop it so it looks like I smacked it out of her hands."

I grimace at him. "Brilliant plan, with at least one of the guards watching you every step of the way."

Neven glances past me, and the color drains from his face. "Oh. I thought— They didn't seem to be paying attention… It was the perfect chance!"

"Obviously not." I prod him toward the door. "And we're not lowering ourselves to outright murder, for fuck's sake."

His gaze jerks back to me with a fresh blaze of anger. "How many deaths are we going to let *her* get away with?"

A lump clogs my throat. Does he really hold Aurelia responsible for the ladies killed in the trials prompted by her betrothal? Or is he simply latching on to an opening to avenge any death at all?

The one he'd most want to avenge, she had nothing to do with. But the man who orchestrated it is out of his reach, unlike the princess of Accasy.

I squeeze his shoulder a little more gently than I might have otherwise. "I just know you don't need any on *your* conscience. Put that thing back wherever you lifted it from, and let the princess dig her own grave like we said."

"She hasn't gotten very deep so far," Neven mutters, but he trudges off.

When I turn back toward his target, she's paused by the freestanding cabinet that sometimes serves as a buffet table. Naturally, her gaze doesn't even veer toward the few platters of appetizers placed on its polished top.

Her attention is fixed on me.

I stroll over as if nothing's amiss, but she glances from the doorway Neven vanished through and back at me. "Did you just spare me from some kind of assault?"

I glower at her. "The kid's a little hot-headed. I was setting him straight."

She folds her arms in front of her, which only emphasizes the appealing curves of her breasts. An appeal that's made twice as enticing by the knowledge that there's no further barrier beneath her fluttery dress. "I suppose I owe you for that favor now?"

I hadn't thought quite that far yet, but the idea is enticing in its own way. I lean against the buffet to consider and shoot her a sideways glance. "Maybe I'd like you to continue with your trials wondering what I'll collect and when."

Aurelia turns her back to the cabinet as well and gazes up at the assorted paintings. "You do seem fond of teasing."

I give a short guffaw. "It isn't teasing when I'm more than ready to deliver. Although speaking of delivering, if you're going to leave little presents on my bed, you can skip what I've already said I don't need."

She shrugs, the silky fabric shifting over her tempting chest. "There are plenty of things we don't *need* that can still make our lives more pleasant. I'd have thought you'd be a major advocate of that philosophy."

Is she trying to compare her salve to my seduction? And not doing a half bad job of it either.

I'd be more irritated if she hadn't given me a perfect opening to pursue my own gambit.

I shift closer to her along the buffet, putting me where I can extend my arm just a little to the side and disturb the edge of her skirt. The cabinet stands high enough to block my overture from the rest of the room. "I'd rather indulge in what could be pleasing for both of us. A little distraction to help you get through the rest of this trial of endurance?"

Aurelia tsks her tongue. "Wouldn't you call that cheating?"

I might if it involved any suitor other than me.

A glance over my shoulder shows that the nearest guard has diverted his attention elsewhere—and the furniture shields most of us from his view regardless. I trail my pinky finger back and forth over her skirt, not pressing close enough to graze her skin but making the motion of the fabric do the stimulation for me.

I lower my voice to its most provocative tone. "A few minutes in my bed, and I'd have you shaking with bliss. There's already so little between you and me. Imagine how quickly I could raise your skirts and spread your thighs, stir every delight between those legs until you were crying out for more."

"I hardly think this is appropriate conversation for the hall of entertainments."

And yet her breath has quickened. I extend my gift toward her with a tingle through my senses and grin. "It's the highest sort of entertainment. And you're already imagining it, judging by how wet you are from my words. I assure you, I'm even more talented with my fingers, and my tongue, and my—"

Aurelia turns her head toward me abruptly enough that I hesitate. Her dark blue eyes capture me, and for one uneasy moment I have the impression she's looking right into my soul.

I'm not wrong that I've turned her on. The evidence is there between her thighs and in the faint flush that's come into her cheeks. But something about her gaze looks inescapably sad.

Her voice has gone even quieter. "I'm not the emperor or

his heir or even a lady of this court. You don't need to perform for me. I wouldn't ask you to—I don't *want* you to."

She makes me sound like I'm that damned dancing bear in the painting. My jaw clenches automatically. "What are you trying to say?"

Aurelia's gaze doesn't waver. "If anything were ever to happen between us, it would only be if you're indulging your wants as much as I am any of mine. Not playing a role to gain some bit of power. Not getting off on merely the challenge of it. Not adding some new layer to this ridiculous game. Just straightforward, honest desire."

Hearing her lay it out so baldly feels like the slap she gave me in her bedroom the other day. It brings the same flare of conflicted emotions—fury that she's struck back at me and a kick of lust that she dared, the latter shooting straight to my groin.

This time, a pang of something else pierces through my chest as well. Tarquin *does* treat us like his dancing bears, doesn't he?

I wouldn't have thought she'd notice. I wouldn't have thought she'd realize it rankles me.

I wouldn't have thought she'd care.

She probably doesn't. This is just one more dimension to a game that's more complicated than I anticipated.

If I'm no longer sure what the rules are, I'll just have to wing it.

She wants honesty? I can measure it out as it suits me.

I recover my grin, letting it turn wry. "What if I told you I already crave you more than I've ever wanted any woman in this place?"

Aurelia arches her eyebrows. "Even though you hate me?"

She's not pulling her punches today, is she? I summon an appropriate answer. "I wouldn't say I hate you. Not *everything* about you. Besides, a little hate can be excellent spicing."

Even as I say the words, I know that's not quite right. I don't hate who she is right now, not exactly. It's who she's aiming to become—who she will be, if she claims the spot next to Marclinus, if she has all that power within her grasp.

I don't want to fuck the selfish, brutal empress she will be. But the blunt, naïve and yet knowing princess she is right now?

The thought sends a throb of desire through my veins.

Aurelia returns her gaze to the paintings, but she doesn't move away from me. "I don't hate *you*."

"Maybe you should. Because I'm not going to stop reminding you how much you want me too, even if you won't say it out loud."

I lift my fingers toward her dress, this time extending them until they come to rest against the pliant flesh of her thigh. The spot right where her legs meet her hips, which any other day would present multiple layers of fabric to dull my touch.

Today it's only a single swath of silk.

I stroke my fingertips slowly up and down. Aurelia wets her lips, but she speaks steadily enough. "Is that all you want out of life? An occasional craving satisfied, a sprinkling of spice here and there?"

"I take what I can get while my life isn't really my own." What it'll be when I'm finally released from the emperor's clutches… it's easier not to think about that future while it's still so indefinite.

She frowns, which is definitely not the reaction I wanted to provoke, but more color is rising in her graceful neck at the same time. "Was it Emperor Tarquin who damaged your hands? Or Marclinus?"

I let out a raw laugh. "It wasn't. And I don't want you thinking about either of them when I'm touching you like this. I don't want you thinking about anyone but me."

I sweep my fingers around to the front of her thigh, just inches from where she's nearly drenched for me. The faintest sound escapes her throat.

"Raul," she begins.

I don't give her a chance to make excuses, to pull away. I jerk forward as if I've dropped something and bend down to retrieve it.

The moment I'm at the floor, I cup Aurelia's ankle. As I rise, I skim my hand over her smooth skin, lifting her skirt with it.

It takes less than a second—the beat of a heart. The swiftest of kisses against the skin just above her knee, and then I've released her, straightening the rest of the way up.

Aurelia steps to the side, increasing the distance between us, with a quiver that tells me exactly why she felt she needed that space. The heat of her body lingers on my hand.

She's so close to melting.

I open my mouth to draw her in even more—and the sudden thunder of footsteps brings me spinning around.

The guard isn't marching toward us. He's storming toward one of Aurelia's competitors, a pale slip of a thing who's crouched next to one of the side tables.

Right by a goblet someone left behind.

"Trial breaker," the guard bellows, towering over her.

The lady only manages to stammer. "I—No, it was only —I wouldn't have—"

The guard lifts his head with no acknowledgment of her protests. He looks across the room toward the emperor and his heir. "She had her hand around the goblet and was tilting it to her mouth."

Tarquin sighs as if disappointed. "She knew the rules. If she can't stay true to them, she won't be true to us. Deal with it."

The lady raises her hands beseechingly. "Please, I was so thirsty I lost my—"

Her last words are cut off with the hiss of a blade and the gurgle of blood from her severed throat.

I tamp down my disgust and turn away as if I'm bored by the display, only to find my gaze on Princess Aurelia again.

Aurelia, who's staring at the slaughtered lady with her lips pressed tight and all trace of a flush vanished.

When I blink, the hint of uneasiness vanishes. Her face settles into its usual serene expression.

A thread of uneasiness winds through my gut.

That's one fewer obstacle on her way to the throne. Shouldn't she be glad to see the competition eliminated?

Was her subtle show of distress a trick to shake my resolve, or is this the lie now? Could she actually have cared about that simpering fool?

I can't ask her even if I wanted to, because the next thing I know, she's striding off beyond my reach.

CHAPTER EIGHTEEN

Aurelia

S imply walking into the dining room intensifies the burn of hunger in my belly. Over the past day and a half as my body has adapted to the emptiness, my appetite has mostly dwindled from a sharp throbbing to a dull ache, but even the faint scent of the doughy rolls already laid out on some of the tables sets off a fresh jab.

As I walk toward the head table, I avert my gaze from the carafes of various beverages. The gravelly sensation in my mouth and the pinching of dryness in my throat has only deepened the longer I endure this trial.

Perhaps I should just be glad for the minor relief of wearing undergarments again. One of the female guards played chaperone in my bedroom overnight, but she didn't interfere with my dressing any.

Normally when I reach the head table, one of the palace

staff directs me to my assigned seat for the meal. Today, the woman who approaches motions me off to the side near Marclinus's throne-like chair. "You won't be sitting for this meal. All of the seats are taken."

The emperor and his heir are going to make us stand through the entire luncheon we're not allowed to partake of? A prickling of dizziness ripples through me even imagining it.

Rochelle has come up behind me in time to hear the instructions. We exchange an uncertain glance, but we don't speak about it.

At this point, we need to preserve all the moisture in our bodies that we can—and all the energy. Talking will only expel both.

I fight the urge to lean against one of the unoccupied chairs, also in the name of conserving energy. I suspect that would be considered cheating too.

Our tyrants are determined to make this latest test as taxing as possible.

No one else has slipped and tried to sneak nourishment since the lady who was slain yesterday afternoon. I suppose she served as warning enough. But just as with the trial of over-indulgence, the imperial heir has shown no inclination to end this one early simply because he's eliminated a contender.

More of the competing ladies join our unsteady cluster while the other nobles file in and take their seats. A nearby marchion pops a grape into his mouth with a juicy crunch that sets my parched throat on fire.

Marclinus saunters in alongside his father and takes his seat with barely a look at the ladies waiting for his approval.

Emperor Tarquin scans his assembling court, frowning.

"Where has Prince Lorenzo wandered off to? I think we'd enjoy some music with our meal—he can have his after."

As several of the nearby nobles shake their heads in ignorance, my stomach twists for a different reason.

This would be the first time I've seen the emperor demand that Lorenzo play twice in one day. The prince already performed for nearly two hours in the parlor this morning and looked rather ill by the end of it. He's had less time than that to rest.

Straining one's gift can have severe adverse effects on the body. Not that I'd expect Emperor Tarquin to care about how his demands might harm anyone else.

My gaze flits over the growing crowd too. I don't spot Lorenzo's darkly handsome face, but the other three princes are standing nearby.

Neven is saying something to the other two with obvious anger. Raul puts a hand on his shoulder, and Bastien tips his head closer while he replies with a solemn expression. Neven scowls, but he follows them the rest of the way to their seats without further argument.

The older princes protect their younger counterpart as well as they can, don't they? I only fully recognized it yesterday when Raul intervened in Neven's planned assault.

Raul didn't care that much what the teenager might do to me. He didn't want Neven to have to face the consequences if he was caught overtly harassing me.

Looking after his younger "brother" mattered more to him than whatever animosity he still holds toward me.

Emperor Tarquin sighs. "I'll speak to him when he arrives." He continues on to his seat—and treads on a spoon that must have fallen while the table was being set.

His balance wobbles before he grasps the edge of the table to steady himself. With a grunt, he kicks the spoon out of the way. It's a totally understandable lapse—even a man half his age would have lost his footing momentarily.

From the neighboring table, I catch a murmured comment. "You see—he really isn't quite himself."

Ah. My remark the other day about his tremor must have entered into the palace gossip.

When I glance toward the nearby doorway to see if everyone has finally arrived so we can get this meal over with, the last of the princes is just stepping over the threshold. Lorenzo still looks a bit weary, some of the richness dulled in his deep brown skin.

A twinge of sympathy runs through me despite my own discomforts. Before I can think better of it, I catch his attention with a twitch of my hand.

Remembering the signs he showed me in the library, I swivel my thumb like a crown over a forefinger to indicate the emperor, flick my finger toward Lorenzo, and then jerk my fingers tight like claws in an effort to indicate discomfort to come.

Lorenzo blinks at me. I can't tell whether he's drained enough to have trouble concentrating or simply startled that I've adopted his surreptitious means of communication.

Then the message appears to sink in. He stiffens, takes a backward step toward the hall—

Too late. Emperor Tarquin's voice carries over the court chatter. "Prince of Rione! Come delight us with more of your musical talent."

Lorenzo's jaw tightens as if he's suppressed a grimace. With a resigned air, he stalks past me to the corner of the room the emperor indicated, where a page is waiting with what seems to be his other preferred instrument: a gleaming lyre.

Marclinus straightens in his chair. He waves to the nine

of us ladies gathered nearby and calls out his announcement. "My hopeful brides will be demonstrating other kinds of self-control and devotion at our last meal of their trial. They'll each help serve me my food."

A few giggles and guffaws pass through our audience. Now he wants his noblewomen to play servants?

I don't really care about being humbled. From the looks of my companions, they're too wrung out to be embarrassed by this new development. Even Fausta's posture has started to droop, though she's keeping her chin rigidly high, her eyes darting over the rest of us.

Various staff circulate the room, bringing meals that are already portioned. One carts a wooden stand holding a platter with a large serving dish and sets it up next to Marclinus's spot at the table. She moves around him and poses at the opposite side of his chair, ladle hovering over his bowl.

The imperial heir beckons the closest of us ladies over to the serving dish. "Hold it up so I can receive my soup. Prepare yourself—the dish is hot."

His words set off a peal of warning in my head. I bite back my own plea for caution as the noblewoman reaches for the porcelain sides.

The moment she grasps the dish, her features twitch with a flinch she can't suppress. A tiny gasp escapes her lips.

Marclinus raises his eyebrows at her. "Get on with it, then."

With her lips pressed so tightly the skin around them pales, she hefts the serving dish off the platter and holds it within reach of the woman with the ladle. Her arms tremble, and the whites of her eyes look starker with every passing second.

The other woman calmly spoons three dollops of the

soup into Marclinus's bowl, and the lady yanks the serving dish back to the platter. When she wrenches her hands away, dark pink blotches of burns show against her palms and fingers.

My gut lurches with a sensation very different from hunger. The first victim retreats to the back of our cluster, her shoulders trembling and her hands tucked close to her skirt.

We wait in tense silence as Marclinus eats his soup while exchanging dry remarks with the nobles closest to him. I can't decide whether his cool cruelty is more disturbing when he's in a calmer mood like now or when he's more animated in his antics.

The next course to arrive is roasted vegetables in a similarly sized serving dish. Lady Leonette moves to hold it up to the serving woman's tongs, her curvy frame going rigid, a breath passing through her teeth with a soft hiss.

Rochelle stirs restlessly at my side and stiffens when she starts to sway. Her face has already turned wan beneath her freckles.

I touch her arm, deciding it's worth straining my throat to see her make it through. My voice comes out in a thin whisper. "Distance your mind like we did with the knives. Like you're not in your body."

I'm not sure I conveyed my meaning as clearly as I'd have liked to, but she makes it through her turn with only a few shakes and shudders. Then comes a dish filled with risotto, and I'm the next in line.

Following my own advice, I detach into a meditative state as I step forward.

I'm not really here. I'm floating somewhere above my body, unaffected by its pains.

My hands lift to the sides of the dish. The heat sears

through my skin, yanking at my consciousness. Tears would well behind my eyes if I had the moisture to spare.

The rich savory smell fills my nose, and a tiny bit of saliva manages to form around my tongue. I separate myself from that sensation too, holding the dish firmly and lifting it to the server.

I will survive this agony. I will not be broken.

What is this discomfort compared to the weeks of brutal labor endured by the common folk the empire forces to convey the bream cedar logs across the continent? To the slashes of swords and pelting of arrows faced by those compelled to fight along the empire's border?

Some part of me can't help wondering if the pain that's being inflicted on me is some kind of punishment for ever daring to wish I'd never end up in a position like this at all. For imagining I deserved any kind of freedom while the people of my kingdom suffer.

The server lowers her spoon. I set the dish back on the platter and peel away my stinging hands.

Marclinus looks up at me with a crooked grin. "The steadiest of them all so far. You do know how to carry yourself as more than a lady, Princess Aurelia."

His compliment leaves me cold. There's a faint snort behind me that I'd imagine comes from Fausta.

Who edges a little out from our cluster just as I'm passing by. She whips out her foot and snags my ankle.

My weakened body stumbles, my capacity for balance dwindled with my thirst. It's only thanks to Rochelle's hasty grasp that I don't fall face-first to the floor.

When I glance back at my rival, she smirks at me for the two seconds it takes before Marclinus lifts his voice.

"Lady Fausta, are you hoping to win my hand by your own merits or not?"

I hadn't realized he was paying attention—and clearly, neither did she. She whirls around with a flush splashing across her delicate features. "I'm so sorry, Your Imperial Highness. It was an accident. I wasn't thinking about where I set my feet."

From the imperial heir's narrowed eyes, I don't think he believes her any more than I do. As he beckons to the next lady, Fausta shoots a glare over her shoulder at me, as if it's my fault that he chided her.

She handles her own turn steadily enough, with just a brief quiver of her arms and a stifled whimper. I'm just starting to think that we'll all make it through without significant incident when the seventh lady hefts up her serving dish—and yelps.

Her hands spasm against the porcelain sides. The dish slips from her grasp and crashes onto the floor. The chunks of curried meat it contained splatter the rug in the midst of the chunks of broken pottery.

Marclinus glowers at her. "I was looking forward to enjoying that course. It seems you value your own comfort over mine."

The lady cringes. "No, Your Imperial Highness. I wasn't totally prepared. I got dizzy. I'll try again."

"There's nothing else for you to try with. Pray your showing isn't the worst."

The staff are already scrambling to collect the mess. The noblewoman ducks away to the back of our cluster, her whole body trembling. She looks as hopeless as I feel.

What can I say to her? What can I do that will make any difference?

There's nothing. The last two ladies manage to hold their serving dishes. Marclinus polishes off his dessert and flicks his hand toward one of his guards. "You know who failed. Bring the others to the medic to see about their burns."

The blisters on my fingers are still throbbing, but I clench my hands all the same when the guard draws his knife. When he slashes it across the woman's throat like so many before.

The pain means I'm still here. The pain means I'm alive, no matter how little any of our lives matter to my husband-to-be.

Chapter Nineteen

Aurelia

As the cleric's baritone reverberates through the imperial temple, Rochelle and I lean against each other as discreetly as we can, since we're not meant to sit beneath the expansive marble dome overhead.

I can't help feeling that Emperor Tarquin is rubbing salt into the wound. He called us to the temple that adjoins the palace while the sun was sinking toward the horizon, forcing us to stay on our feet through the last half hour. And he appears to have instructed his cleric to lecture us.

The silver-haired man pivots beneath the peak of the dome, his multi-colored robes that represent all of the godlen and the All-Giver who made them swishing around his plump form. "Let us remember that greatness can come from both submission and struggle. When the plague of scourge sorcerers challenged the gods with their twisted magic centuries ago, our Great God rained down fire for our arrogance and then abandoned these realms. But from those ashes rose our empire, faster and stronger than the rest. We must humble ourselves before the gods who still watch over us but also honor authority when our fellow mortals earn it."

Worship the gods and the emperor… just make sure not to worship the emperor *quite* as much. So very helpful.

I find it difficult to focus on his words—to think about much of anything other than getting to wet my throat and fill my belly again.

When he stops with an air of finality, Rochelle and I manage to stir ourselves to join the rest of the assembled audience in tapping our hands through the gesture of the divinities and then respectful applause. The last strains of daylight beyond the stained-glass windows fade away.

A servant's voice calls out. "Proceed to the dining room!"

My heart skips a beat, but I turn toward the doorway carefully. As we tramp down the hall and up the stairs toward the dining room, a burning sensation fills my throat from the back of my mouth all the way down to my collarbone.

Melisse finds me before I even reach the room, clutching a glass of water. "They said we could bring this right away—I thought you'd want it—"

I manage to rasp a thank you and yank the cup to my lips. The water is lukewarm, but no beverage has ever tasted as refreshing as this one does right now.

After the first gulp, I force myself to slow. My deprived stomach might rebel if I fill it too quickly.

With each swallow, relief spreads through my limbs. I still feel weak, but already steadier.

As Rochelle's maid hustles over bearing similar cargo, I gather my voice. "Moderate yourself as much as you can. Taking in too much all at once after a fast can end up making you sick."

Rochelle nods and all but wrenches the glass from her maid. Her throat works with a few large swigs before she gets her frantic thirst under control.

We've continued walking as we drink. The smells of creamy sauces and roasted meat drift from the doorway before we reach it, and my stomach shudders eagerly. Now that I've got the moisture to allow it again, my mouth floods with saliva.

Rochelle wets her lips. "This is going to be the most incredible meal in existence, no matter what they feed us."

I let out a rough laugh. "Agreed."

The dining room's layout has changed again, with a few tables pushed together in the center of the room holding a buffet of platters and bowls. Servers poised around the spread hand out plates and set various delicacies on them.

Before I've made it to the table, Prince Bastien appears in front of me, holding a plate that balances a small bowl of stew with a slab of buttered bread on the side. When he offers it to me, my lips part to express my confusion. Then a glint of gold catches my eye.

He's nestled my ring between the bowl and the bread. A simple but surreptitious way to return my stolen jewelry as quickly as possible. He couldn't exactly sneak into my bedroom while I had the imperial guard watching over me last night.

I snatch the plate from him and dip my head in thanks before hurrying to the head table where Marclinus's ladies have always sat. The second I drop into my chair, I slide my ring back onto my finger. Then I grab my spoon in one hand, the slab of bread in the other, and throw myself into my meal.

I intend to moderate my pace, but my hunger rears up like a savage creature, and for the first several seconds I can't seem to do anything but shovel stew and bites of bread into my mouth. My bowl is already half empty when a mocking laugh carries from farther down the table.

"The wild princess has become outright feral tonight," Bianca says in an arch tone.

I glance up to see her sitting next to Fausta, who's popping morsels of roasted chicken off her fork into her mouth much more daintily than I was. She slants her gaze toward me with a sniff of disdain.

The reminder that I *am* supposed to be acting like a princess, that my betrothed will be watching me, reins me in. I finish the bowl of stew and every crumb of bread at a more measured pace, draining another cup of water in frequent sips between bites.

By the time I'm finished, my stomach feels oddly bloated, even though this is my first meal in two days and only a fraction of what past dinners included. It seems wisest to listen to my body's signals.

I can catch up more tomorrow. And if I find myself starving later in the evening, I'd imagine Melisse can slip down to the kitchen to scrounge up some sort of snack.

With the gnawing hunger sated, a restlessness creeps over me despite my fatigue. I've spent the past two days cooped up in the palace, constantly monitored, never allowed a moment alone.

What I'm most craving now is fresh air and space to move around unimpeded.

The nobles around me are immersed in their feasting. I get to my feet and amble toward one of the doorways, and no one speaks to stop me.

After several bends in hallways and a couple of wrong turns, I emerge from the palace into the back gardens. The lanterns along the back wall of the immense building cast a glow through the darkness over the grounds.

The flowers in their rectangular beds drift in the breeze, which is still warm from the day but not unpleasantly so. A fountain burbles to my right, where a statue of Prospira, godlen of fertility and agriculture, appears to summon water from her hands to course down over the mass of vines she's standing on.

I let the cool spray fleck my skin and then meander onward. Gradually, despite my still slightly wobbly steps, my shoulders ease down.

There are no judgmental stares here, no guards, no games. The knot of held-in tension in my chest gradually unwinds.

A few flowering trees stand amid the gravel paths, and an orchard in spring blossom sprawls to my left. But my gaze is drawn to the taller trees that form a semi-circle farther ahead and to my right: the palace woods.

The oaks and ash trees stretch nowhere near as tall as the evergreens back home, but they're the closest thing I've got here. I drift toward them, called by the pang of homesickness I can never quite shed.

The woods are hardly wild. It's clear the paths between the trees are carefully maintained, the shrubs kept trimmed and brush culled back to make for easy riding—or even walking. The shadows thicken, but enough moonlight filters through the leaves overhead that I continue onward, not yet ready to return to the stuffiness of the palace. The earthy scents in the air invigorate me out of the lingering weakness from the trial.

I've barely moved all day. My limbs are aching as much from disuse as fatigue.

As I meander on, a faint strumming reaches my ears. It lilts in a scrap of melody, halts, and then starts up again.

Who else would be out here in the dusk?

I hesitate and then ease along more cautiously than before, peering in the direction of the music. Several paces farther, a gleam of lanternlight comes into view.

I pad on until I make out the tall, well-built figure leaning against a tree trunk, lute tucked under one arm, long fingers dancing nimbly across the strings.

Prince Lorenzo might have played himself ragged on the emperor's orders earlier today, but it looks as if he's still able to take some pleasure from his talent. Although the tunes spilling from the lute's strings don't sound as vibrant and assured as his past performances that I've heard.

From the way he's pausing and restarting, I think he's getting used to the instrument. Learning how to work with it rather than already sure of his skill.

That doesn't make the music he's producing any less enjoyable to listen to, though. His rambling practice has a rawness to it, a sense of discovery that sends a little thrill over my skin.

Does he feel the same way I do when I'm assembling a new potion or ointment for the first time?

Maybe it's that sense of connection that brings me forward. Maybe it's the memory of how he moved to comfort me two days ago when the princes stole into my bedroom in the middle of the night—the only one who showed any concern about my grief.

Or maybe I simply know I have to take every chance I can get to win over my most likely allies.

At the rustle of my feet through the scattered leaves, Lorenzo's head jerks up. His hand stills over the lute's strings.

I come to a stop a few paces away. "I think I might like hearing you play like this even more."

He raises his eyebrows at a skeptical angle. After a moment, he wiggles his hand over the strings as if to say he was shaky.

I shrug. "You still brought a better melody out of it than I could have managed. Why are you practicing all the way out here?"

He jabs his thumb in the direction of the palace, touches the instrument, and pulls a grimace.

"They wouldn't appreciate it?" I can believe that easily enough. Emperor Tarquin wants his pet princes performing to the best of their ability.

Lorenzo nods in confirmation. He pauses, taps the lute, and then points to himself.

I can't quite follow what he's getting at. "You like to play it?"

With a shake of his head, he casts around. Setting the lute against a tree, he picks up a stick long enough that he can drag it across the ground without bending over. He sweeps the debris away from a flat stretch of dirt and draws a series of letters. *It IS me.*

Before I have to ask what that's supposed to mean, he motions toward the palace again and mimics the swaying of a vielle's bow. Then he rotates a finger against his shirt, over the spot where his godlen sigil will be branded into his deep brown skin.

Understanding clicks in my head. "What you play in there feels like it's your gift more than your own abilities. You come out here so you can get back to how it was when it was just you?"

A hesitant smile crosses Lorenzo's lips. He gazes at me for a moment, his expression turning graver.

He mouths a couple of words alongside a curl of his hand, but I can't decipher the shape of them. At my look of confusion, he picks up the stick, wipes away his previous statement, and replaces it with a simpler one.

Sorry.

My gaze snaps back to his face—to his solemn, dark eyes. "What for?"

He sputters a choked sort of laugh. I guess the question is kind of absurd.

I spread my hands. "I'm just trying to narrow down the possibilities."

My wry tone brings back a trace of his smile. He draws a finger past his throat, an echo of what he did to mine in the library.

"Oh," I say. "I can overlook that. I realize none of you were very happy about me showing up."

Or should I say none of them *are* very happy? Lorenzo isn't giving me a hard time right now, but he didn't at first in the library either.

His attention has shifted to my hands as I've spoken. Abruptly, he beckons me closer.

At the same time, he sets down the stick and strides to meet me. He grasps one wrist and turns my palm toward the lantern light.

The medics worked their healing magic on this afternoon's burns, but their magic isn't powerful enough to erase an injury in an instant. Pink marks remain on my skin —from past experience, I'd expect them to take a few days to vanish completely.

Lorenzo scowls and jerks his fingers in his gesture that indicates the imperial figures. He halts as if catching himself, his hand closing into a fist.

"It's over now," I find myself saying, as if he needs the reassurance. "The burns don't even hurt anymore."

He lowers my wrist and lets go. His chest rises with a strained breath. Then he seems to gather himself.

He makes a questioning gesture, points to me, and then indicates the woods around us.

"Why am I out here?" My own smile falters. I look up at the trees looming overhead. "I needed a break. And this is the only part of the estate that feels just a little bit like back home."

Lorenzo grasps the stick again. *You miss it a lot.*

Not a question. He saw how I reacted to losing the small piece I still have left of Accasy.

I drag the cooling night air into my lungs and feel as if I might burst with how much I miss my kingdom. "Yes. I try not to think about it, but if I let myself, it's always there. I guess the homesickness must get better with time."

My companion should know something about that, but his gaze has gone distant. He starts another series of motions that I interpret to the best of my ability.

"You… when you were small… when you first came to the palace?"

He forms an anguished expression and streaks his fingers down his cheek like tears.

My gut twists. "You were awfully homesick too, were you?"

I can interpret his next gestures clearly enough. *More than the others. A long time.*

"Eventually you'll get to go back to your kingdom, won't you?"

Lorenzo makes a face as if to say, *Who knows?* With another swipe of his foot, he scrawls his stick across the cleared earth. *What do you miss?*

"Gods. Everything?" My laugh snags in my throat.

Images of home swim up through my mind. "People aren't totally wrong in the way they talk about Accasy. There's so much that feels free and wild—vast forests with ancient trees, fierce rivers, perilous cliffs. It's not the easiest place to survive, but that means we celebrate the surviving together instead of fighting about who's doing a little better than anyone else. I haven't gone this long without talking with my parents or my sister in my whole life. And silly things, like the fresh sap syrup we'd have on our pancakes…"

Just talking about it makes the lump of loss expand. I will my grief down and focus on Lorenzo. I've only overheard a little talk about where he came from. "What do you miss most about Rione?"

He considers, a current of emotions rippling across his face, and sketches out a list.

Ocean close by
Family
Other music
Exploring cities and hills
Coconut jam

I have to smile at the last one. "I've never tried any kind of coconut. Not something we have in large supply up north."

Lorenzo lets out a sound of disbelieving horror and makes a gesture I can understand well enough. *Not okay.*

My amusement at his hyperbolic response is bittersweet. "Maybe I'll have the chance to fix that oversight before much longer."

The prince lowers his head, the shadows shifting across it with the flickering lantern light. I think of the pain knotted deep inside me after just a few weeks away from home. Of him arriving here at age seven, just a kid who hadn't had time to come to terms with the role he needed to play to ensure his family's safety.

My next words come out quiet but vehement. "I know I'm lucky that I got to have a life of my own for as long as I did. I promise you, if I can make it through these trials and marry Marclinus, any way I can help you—or Raul or Bastien or Neven—I'll do whatever I can."

Lorenzo jerks his gaze up to stare at me. There's nothing playful about his shock now. His stick wobbles for a second before he draws one word. *Why?*

Is it really that hard to understand?

I swallow thickly. "We came from the same place, in a way. We're not the heirs, just the extras who had to accept whatever bargain was offered, let ourselves be traded away for our country's security. You all deserve more of your own lives than you've gotten. And I came here… I came here because I wanted to help everyone who deserves it."

I can't tell if he believes me. An odd sadness comes over his face even though I was trying to offer hope.

Abruptly, he picks up his lute with one hand and catches my elbow with the other. At his tug, I follow him through the woods toward the gardens. "What…?"

He lets go of me long enough to make a simple message clear. *Wait and see.*

We skirt the edge of the gardens and approach the orchard. Toward the back of the rows of hunched trees, one stands in a secluded plot, its silvery leaves quivering in the breeze.

The moonlight glints off not just the leaves but the pure white fruit nestled between them, like the palest of apples. My lips part in awe.

"Twilight pumellos. I didn't realize—"

But of course the emperor would have the rarest of all edible fruits growing on his grounds.

Lorenzo brings his finger to his lips for silence and reaches up to pluck one of the fruits. The give of its skin looks more like a plum than an apple, despite its size.

My eyes widen. "Are we supposed to…?"

The prince shrugs with a hint of a grin and motions as if to say, *It's just one.*

He takes a small bite from one side, closes his eyes with a dreamy expression, and then hands the pumello to me.

I sink my teeth into the pliant flesh on the opposite side. A buttery sweet and yet delightfully tart flavor washes over my tongue.

I have to press my hand to my mouth to hold back a moan of satisfaction. Lorenzo watches me, looking utterly pleased to have given me this little gift, even if it's a stolen one.

As I offer the fruit back to him, our fingers brush with a brief tingle. "I suppose now that we've started, we'd better finish it."

He gives a soft chuckle, his eyes never leaving mine. Something in his gaze makes my heart flutter.

He steps forward and lifts his hand to my cheek. The gentleness of his touch sets off another flutter. I can't look away from his stunning face.

When I don't jerk back, Lorenzo leans in and kisses me.

It's been a long time since I've been kissed. The prince's lips are tender but fervent against mine, the incredible flavor of the twilight pumello lingering on them. A surge of giddiness sweeps through every inch of my body.

I might as well be an instrument left to gather dust, and he's strumming me to life with the deepening of the kiss, with the stroke of his fingers down my neck.

I don't know if I've *ever* been kissed like this.

That last thought sends a jab of guilt through my gut.

This is good. He's warmed up to me in one way or another. But I ease back a step, ignoring the frenetic beat of my pulse and the longing coursing through my veins.

"Thank you," I say softly. "But I—we really shouldn't—"

Lorenzo makes an accommodating gesture as if to indicate he understands. No sign of dejection shows in his expression.

He might have thought less of me if I *hadn't* drawn a boundary.

Another pain lances through my belly. This one I can't blame on my stirred-up emotions.

I frown, my attention drawing inward. My stomach has gone unusually tight. As I notice that, the sickly chill of nausea seeps through my limbs.

It can't be the fruit I just ate—twilight pumellos aren't remotely toxic, and Lorenzo looks fine. Perhaps my stretch of starvation is catching up with me in an unexpected way.

Not a way I want him seeing me, not after the progress I seem to have made.

I gather myself and smile, pretending sweat hasn't started beading on the back of my neck. "Thank you again. For talking with me. For sharing this. It's been a long two days. I think I'd better finally get to bed."

Lorenzo frowns and swivels his hand. *Are you okay?*

"Yes. Just very worn out." I reach out and squeeze his forearm for emphasis. "All I need is some rest."

As I set off for the palace building, I hope to all the gods who might be listening that's true.

CHAPTER TWENTY

Aurelia

By the time I reach my bedroom, the queasiness has given way to wracking shivers. My hand shakes as I bring the key to the lock. It takes me three tries to fit it into the keyhole.

I stagger into the room and shove the door shut behind me. A sudden rush of feverish heat leaves me sagging against it.

A lantern is glowing on the vanity, my nightgown laid out on the bed, a fresh carafe of water on the side table. Melisse arranged everything for my arrival but must have assumed I'd have returned earlier if I wanted her direct help.

I can't blame her for thinking that way. I've dismissed her early most other nights, preferring to prepare for bed in privacy.

More chills and searing heat sweep through me in waves.

My legs wobble, but I push myself off the door toward the bathroom.

A dip in the tub might help settle the strange sensations surging through my body. Bring me back into proper equilibrium.

I'm halfway across the room when my stomach lurches even more emphatically than before. I race the last several steps and throw myself over the toilet just in time for it to catch the mushy remnants of my dinner coming back up.

My stomach heaves again and again until I'm sputtering nothing but saliva. My throat burns with acid and the rest of me with the prickling hot fever that seems to have won over the chills.

This is more than just a struggle to recover from my trial. I'm outright ill.

Even though my limbs feel as though they're on fire, shivers keep coursing through them. I slump over on the floor, fighting for focus, for clarity of thought, for steadiness.

My hand presses against my sternum over my godlen sigil. *Elox, help me through this, give me the strength to recover. The focus to use my gift…*

First, I need to drink something. Hydrate myself after all the fluids I just lost. I need—

My mind flips over on itself and sends me crashing into darkness.

In my faint, I must knock my head against the floor. When I surface back into consciousness an uncertain amount of time later, a sharp ache is pulsing through my skull—and the side of my forehead that's pressed against the tiles feels particularly tender.

Fever still crackles beneath my skin. My stomach has settled into a slow boil of nausea, nothing left in it to expel.

I inhale and exhale in ragged breaths, holding on to the locus of calm at the center of me.

I haven't come this far just to die on a bathroom floor. I can heal myself.

Gritting my teeth, I reach out to my gift and train it on the symptoms raging through my body. How can I fix whatever's wrong with me?

Images waver through the haze of my thoughts, but they drift away just as quickly. Swallowing makes my throat sting. I grimace at the sour flavor.

Water first. Then medicine. I won't accomplish much if I faint again in the middle of the concocting.

Cool resolve gathers in my chest. It takes enough of the edge off the fever for me to ease myself onto my hands and knees.

With every step I crawl across my bedroom, my head throbs in tandem. I let my awareness sink down into the center of me, into that one small still place like a tiny temple within.

Find your peace, and anything is possible, the devouts of Elox like to say.

I don't register that I've reached the side table until my head bumps into one of the legs. After a minute or two gathering myself, I sit back on my heels.

I spill more water than makes it into the cup, but the liquid feels gloriously cold against my scorching flesh. I swipe a damp arm across my forehead and sip.

Three shallow swallows, and my stomach starts to cramp. I clench my jaw and my fingers around the glass.

Should I yell and hope a guard will hear me who can bring one of the palace medics?

That thought provokes a series of more unnerving

questions: What will Marclinus think if I turn into an invalid after his trial? How will the emperor evaluate me?

Will Tarquin decide I mustn't be hardy enough to stand beside his heir after all? They executed one of the other ladies for simply dropping a dish.

I manage to tamp down my nausea and take another sip of water. The fever blazes on, but in this moment I feel as if it's burned away everything but my path forward.

I can take care of this setback on my own. I don't have to appear weak in front of anyone other than myself.

If Their Imperial Eminences never find out, so much the better.

Through some combination of inner fortitude, feverish delusion, and sheer force of will, I scoot along the side of the bed and across the rug to reach my trunks. My tea box sits right at the top of the one containing everything that's not clothes. I pause to recover my strength and lift it out.

The wooden container isn't *only* a tea box. With trembling fingers, I pry free the upper layer that holds the tins of various dried leaves and flowers and set it aside.

The larger compartment beneath that offers more of a mishmash: a couple dozen small linen bags of herbs, nearly as many vials of ingredients best preserved in liquid or gel form, a few jars holding premixed concoctions I thought it might be useful to have ready, no longer including the salve I gave Prince Raul.

As I stare down at them, my gift surges to the forefront of my mind. The components I need swim up before my eyes.

Fuck. That's quite the combination.

Whatever's gotten into me, it's serious. The ingredients tell me it's going to take a real kick to propel this illness out of my body.

I pluck out a few of the bags, a vial, and a pot of a thick gel that'll emulsify the mixture together. But two of the items whirling through my aching head aren't in the array before me. They're ingredients I assumed would be on hand at my destination, without considering that I might end up in a position where both leaving my room and asking for help were precarious propositions.

There'll be plenty of garlic in the kitchen. And the palace cooks gather most other herbs fresh each day—I've seen thyme growing in the herb garden.

I just have to get to it.

My gaze slides to the mortar, pestle, and tiny oil stove among my brewing equipment. With all the throbbing and searing that's taken over my body, I'd like nothing more than to sit and do what work I can right here.

But the longer I wait, the more the infection will take hold. I don't know if I can count on being able to move around the palace even in ten minutes' time.

Gods help me, I don't know if I can count on it *now*.

I have a couple of aids that should dim the worst of the agony for a short while. Rummaging through the box, I fish out a sliver of ruddy root that I hastily chew. An astringent taste fills my mouth. Within seconds of swallowing, my nausea starts to ease.

I grasp a chunk of papery bark and suck it against my cheek. Its flavor is more bitter, but it should gradually ease at least some of the pain radiating through my body.

These are only temporary solutions, though. I have to take advantage of them quickly.

I set my feet flat on the floor and gradually unfurl myself upright. Heat continues sizzling beneath my skin and my headache pounds, but after a few breaths, my legs stop wobbling.

The chill of resolve I felt before thickens, spreading through my limbs. It doesn't remove the discomfort, but it sets me apart as if my mind is sealed off in that serene chamber within.

Elox is watching over me. He's lending me the strength I asked for.

He doesn't want me faltering from my purpose either. The peace I'm hoping to bring my people honors him more than it does any other godlen.

I take a few tentative steps forward. It's easiest when I hold my head high and my posture stiffly erect, as if my body is a machine I'm directing with a whirring of clockwork rather than my own physical essence.

I'll have to navigate two hallways, a staircase, another hallway, and then I'll come to the kitchen. I think there's a door straight from that room into the garden I need. Not far at all, on the measure of it.

Ha.

As I propel myself forward, I sink my teeth into the bark in my mouth, gnawing more bitterness out of it. The throbbing in my skull fades a little more.

One foot after the other. I cling tightly to the threads of calm I've found.

The hallway outside my chambers seems quiet. I suspect my fellow competitors will have taken right to their beds, as I probably should have rather than roaming the woods. If the rest of the court is indulging in some frivolity, it's far enough away that I only catch one bellowing laugh diminished by the distance.

It'd be nice if my luck held. But I reach the end of the first hall just as the three princes who've plagued me come striding around the bend.

"...get complacent," Prince Bastien is saying to his

companions in a flat but insistent tone. At the sight of me, his voice dies and his feet jar to a halt. Lorenzo and Raul stall in their tracks where they're flanking Bastien.

The slender prince flicks his gaze over my body. A harsh edge creeps into his voice. "Well, look at this. The princess of Accasy appears to be perfectly alert and off on late-night adventures."

It seems my efforts at looking as if I'm perfectly fine and not about to keel over are working.

I don't have the time or energy to wonder why Bastien sounds annoyed by the fact that I'm wandering the halls.

"Good night," I manage in a stiff voice, because it'd be odd if I didn't acknowledge the men right in front of me at all, and step around the trio as gracefully as my mechanical grip on my body allows.

The princes are startled enough that I've made it a few steps past them before their footsteps scuff against the carpet, spinning and hurrying after me. Bastien mutters something about how "she was making excuses to get away from you," which doesn't make much sense either, because I haven't attempted any justifications.

He calls after me in a low but disdainful tone. "Where are you going, Princess?"

I keep my response efficiently short. "Kitchen."

He snorts, as if there's something ridiculous about my answer. "Still so hungry after that feast? Off to raid the palace cupboards? And it seems you don't even trust your maid to fetch a snack for you."

I don't know why he has a problem with any of that. What's it to him? Shouldn't he want me to eat the emperor out of house and home if I take a mind to?

It's easiest to say nothing. I keep my mouth clamped

shut, bark braced between my teeth, and my feet moving onward, step after step.

The stairwell is just up ahead. I'll be able to hold on to the railing going down. It won't look strange at all as long as I don't clutch it like a drowning woman.

Bastien picks up his pace, his boots thudding against the thick carpet behind me in time with the fever blaring beneath my skin. "You're not answering because you're up to something. I think you need a little company on this expedition."

The thought of the princes tagging along through my entire awful trek sends a renewed shudder through my gut that I almost can't rise above. My frustration slips my control instead. I spit the words through my clenched teeth. "Fuck *off.*"

There's a moment of stunned silence and then a rough noise of consternation melding with an amused tsk of the tongue I can tell is Raul.

"Watch out, Bas. You're bringing out that wild fire. I knew it had to be in her somewhere."

I ignore him too, veering toward the staircase.

Unfortunately, all three princes march after me down the broad steps. My palm skids against the gilded railing, sweat beading there in the brief moments I grasp on for balance.

Bastien comes up with a retort about a minute too late. "Cursing at me isn't going to stop me from keeping an eye on you."

No, I hadn't really expected it would. I go back to ignoring him, drawing relief from the knowledge that the kitchen doorway is just around the next turn.

No clatter of pans or clinking of dishes reaches my ears—the staff will have cleared out for the night. No one needs to know I slunk in there… except for my increasingly irritating pursuers.

Lorenzo must convey some comment with gestures, because Bastien speaks again in a more hushed cadence as if replying. "She obviously lied. She didn't flee because she was ever so tired. Half the palace is already in bed, and here she is roaming."

Through my sickly daze, it sinks in that he's talking about my excuse for leaving Lorenzo in the orchard. He's claiming that I made up a story.

I can't tell him off without revealing how close to incapacitated I actually am. After Emperor Tarquin and his heir—and I suppose Fausta and Bianca—Bastien is the last person I want aware of my weakened state. Especially when he's acting like such an ass.

I'm not sure I *could* defend myself without the calm center I've held on to cracking and everything else falling apart.

"Why so rigid tonight, Lamb?" Raul says in a cajoling tone. "I know you enjoyed my company yesterday."

I swerve through the kitchen doorway in silence. I might have to repair every smidgeon of progress I've made with these men after tonight's performance, but at least I'll be alive and well to do it.

My years of potion-making in the kitchens of my family's royal residences have left me familiar with the typical layouts. The Darium approach to organization isn't much different. It only takes a swift scan of the vast counter space to spot a basket in one corner with several bulbs of garlic poking their white faces from the top.

As I stride stiffly over to pluck one up, my gaze catches on a kettle tucked away on one of the storage shelves. The images brought by my gift shift and flow through my thoughts.

I'm going to require some boiled water.

I slosh a little from the kitchen taps into the spouted metal pot and set it on the main stove. The fire within must be intended to burn all night, perhaps with magical enhancement to ensure it never dwindles too much. The heat that wafts over me barely feels warm compared to the blaze of my fever.

The princes have followed me into the room. Bastien scowls at me. "If you're hoping to confuse us by grabbing random objects—"

I don't bother to wait to hear what new accusing remark he's going to make. The flavor has leeched from my bit of bark—its numbing effect on my pains will be dwindling.

My headache pounds harder on my way to the small door at the far end of the kitchen. My fingers stumble over the deadbolt but manage to shove it over.

I step out at the edge of the herb garden I've encountered during my occasional strolls outside. My eyes are going bleary, but with several hasty steps amid the tight rows, I spot the tufts of thyme in a dense patch.

I don't need that much. As I bend down to snap off a few sprigs of leaves, I quietly spit the scrap of bark into the dirt.

When I straighten up, a wave of dizziness rocks me. I stiffen my limbs against it and skirt the watching princes on my way back into the kitchen.

Their stares follow me. Lorenzo makes a rough sound in his throat that I can't decipher.

Raul follows me to the cupboard where I pull out a mug. "What in the realms are you playing at, Princess?"

He's kept his tone jaunty on the surface, but it's hardened

underneath. Is he getting annoyed with my lack of explanation?

Perfect. The frustration can be spread all around.

The kettle is already steaming. I drop the thyme into the mug and pour in just enough boiling water to fill the vessel by a quarter. Then I start my journey back to my room, clutching the mug in one hand and the bulb of garlic in the other.

I'd thought I felt terrible before. I hadn't known how much more capacity for awfulness my body contained. My initial measures must have held off the worst of the symptoms more than I realized.

With every step, the feverish heat turns starker, raking claws through my flesh and fogging my vision. My stomach starts up its roiling again. The throbbing in my head expands down my back and through my very bones.

I've probably made the illness even worse by pushing myself to keep moving. But if I'd just lain there in my bedroom, I might have been dead by morning.

My awareness of my princely followers dwindles as I retreat even farther into the shrinking calm inside me. Bastien is demanding an explanation and Raul cajoling me, and I just keep striding forward, step after step, as quickly as I can.

I didn't bother to lock my bedroom when I left it. With a waft of gratitude for that oversight, I push the door open with my shoulder and walk inside.

Just a little farther. My tools and the other ingredients wait a mere ten paces away.

But as I wobble toward them, the princes barge after me into the room. Because of course they still have no concept of privacy.

"Whether you speak to us or not, we are going to get answers," Bastien insists.

The fever has eaten away at the cool place inside me so it's little more than a scrap of stillness. The battle raging inside my body rises to a roar.

My control is slipping from my fingers.

"Get out!" I shout, or maybe it's only a mumble, my tongue tripping over itself.

Either way, it makes no difference. Bastien marches even closer.

With my last bit of strength, I set the mug on top of the closed trunk.

And my legs give beneath me.

I crumple to the floor, my limbs gone so limp I can't even grope out with my arms to soften my fall. My skin smolders, and my stomach lurches. I'm vaguely aware of retching a sputter of acid-laced water onto the carpet.

I think I hear my name. My mind wavers in and out of darkness, the impressions of shapes and sounds around me fragmenting.

Fingers brush against my forehead and jerk away. Bastien: "She's burning up with a fever."

"What the fuck? But she seemed—"

"She was so quiet—the effort it would have taken her to talk… If I'd realized—"

"She couldn't really have been hiding *that* bad an illness."

My thoughts spiral away. I gag and retch again. Pain batters me from all sides, as if beating me up for daring to fight.

I almost had my cure. I know what I need to do. But I can't—I can't—

Through my haze, I catch fractured sentences from an unfamiliar voice. "You knew— What did you do to—?"

Has Prince Neven joined them—or has a guard overheard and rushed in?

No, no, no, I don't want—

Bastien's voice has gone raw. "I didn't think— Gods smite me, it was only a bit of spoiled meat and juices in her stew. I meant to upset her stomach a little, slow her recovery. I wouldn't have wanted it to hit her like *this*."

Raul sputters a humorless laugh. "Who knows what that crap had in it?"

And the voice I'm not sure of, as if from farther away— someone at the door? "Her sacrifice—her spleen—she said—"

Then Bastien's remarks about my stew sink in.

That fucking prick. Anger flares alongside my fever.

He did this to me on purpose. He might not have expected me to get so sick, but the result is the same.

The princes keep talking.

"Should we call a medic?"

Bastien sounds even more agonized than before. "How are we going to explain how we found her? We couldn't have seen her collapse through the closed door. And they might be able to piece together what happened to her—that I did it."

"If we leave her, who knows what'll happen to her?"

"Weren't you the one who insisted we're all better off if she dies?"

"Not like this. We're not the butchers in this place... I wasn't finished with her."

"Then give me a chance to think."

"How about you think faster!"

I'm losing track of which voices are which. Maybe I only hallucinated that there was a third. But the thought that the princes might alert the rest of the palace to my condition sends a spike of panic through me alongside my anger.

Deep inside, I gather every particle of will I can.

Elox, stay with me. Let me make this cure.

"Wait! There is that one medic we—"

"She's waking up!"

Straining my muscles, I manage to push myself off the ground. I stare foggily at the equipment spread out next to me.

My gift tickles at the back of my head, flashing images of how the parts combine, how I need to bring them together.

A voice I know is Raul's comes from behind me with a sputter of disbelief. "Look at her, picking up the pieces even now."

The floor creaks as he must step closer, but I ignore him. My shaking hand grasps one of the linen bags and shakes some of the contents into the mortar. Then the second and the third.

Clutching the pestle, I start to grind the crystals and dried leaves into a finer powder. My body sways with the movements of my arm.

With another heave of my gut, I have to pause to retch more spittle.

Bastien crouches down beside me. His voice has evened out again, devoid of emotion. "Aurelia, you're using your gift to make something that'll set you right, aren't you? Is there anything we can do?"

I lift my gaze to him, taking in his face, even paler than usual beneath the rumpled fall of his auburn hair.

Wasn't he considering leaving me for dead? I'd laugh if I remembered how.

My incredulity must show all the same. Bastien's mouth tightens. "If you die, it'll be because you failed one of these stupid trials or pissed off Marclinus, not because of me. I'm not standing by when you're this ill. What else do you need?"

I wonder if he even notices he said "if" I die. He seemed awfully certain of that outcome the first time we spoke.

Regardless, I only seem capable of producing one answer, effective even with my voice little more than a creak. "Fuck off."

Raul lets out a strangled sort of guffaw.

As I go back to my grinding, a hand rests gingerly against my back.

I can tell it's Lorenzo without needing to look. That's the only reason I don't shrug off the steadying touch.

He hasn't said anything horrible to me in the past half an hour. Of course, he can't say anything at all, but some mildly coherent part of me would like to believe he wouldn't have after our conversation in the woods.

My work is almost done anyway. I light the pot of oil under the tiny stove and set my miniature cauldron over the flame. In goes the hot water steeped with thyme, then the crushed mixture from the pestle, then a few drips of silvery oil from the vial.

Unpeeling the garlic nearly proves my undoing. My trembling fingers jitter across the papery skin.

Lorenzo's hand firms against my back.

If he's thinking of intervening, Raul beats him to the punch. The massive prince leans in to snatch the garlic from my hands.

Both Lorenzo and I make noises of protest, his more forceful than my weak grunt.

Raul glowers at both of us. "You're not dying over a fucking piece of garlic."

He tears the skin off both the bulb and one of the cloves. I stretch out a wobbly arm. "Enough."

He hands the clove over. Ideally I'd cut it up, but I don't

have the coordination for that right now. Instead, I dig my fingernails into the smooth surface to pierce it and toss it into the bubbling concoction.

The mixture has turned into a thick gray sludge. Hardly the most appetizing substance I've seen in my life, but my gift tickles through me like a balm, confirming I've done everything needed.

I let the potion simmer as long as I dare, closing my eyes against the impression of spikes driving through my skull and joints. Then I spoon a few dollops of the stuff into a little bowl.

I blow a ragged breath over the concoction to cool it. As I bring it to my lips, the princes remain braced around me, though what they think they're going to contribute at this point, I can't fathom.

The sludgy substance coats my tongue with a sour and slightly metallic flavor. Wincing, I swallow once, wait to make sure my stomach doesn't immediately expel the stuff, and gulp the rest.

The furious determination that gripped me dissipates. I lean over on my side and let myself sag onto the floor.

The carpet is comfortably soft when I'm embracing it purposefully rather than collapsing onto it.

Lorenzo reaches over to squeeze my hand. I find myself squeezing back, even though I have no idea what he's thinking right now.

"Aurelia?" Bastien says tentatively.

I hold myself still and quiet. Gradually, the ache jabbing through every part of my body starts to fade. The fire searing through my veins dwindles.

Raul touches my cheek. "She's less hot already." There's a hint of a question in his voice.

Bastien answers it firmly. "We stay until we're sure she's fully well."

Fine. It's not as if they'd leave just because I told them to anyway.

My eyelids slide shut, and my mind drifts into a healing sleep.

CHAPTER TWENTY-ONE

Aurelia

I've never been inside a building so enormous before. The smoothed stone tiers sprawl out on either side of our cushioned benches, rising dozens of rows above us and encircling a span of packed bare earth that could contain the entire imperial palace.

Our cluster of nobles sit in leisurely fashion along the cushions: all eight of Marclinus's remaining prospective brides and some thirty of the court nobles, with Their Imperial Eminences on a pair of matching thrones in our midst. On the narrower, unpadded benches that fill the rest of the vast arena, the spectators squeeze much closer together.

There must be thousands of figures crammed into this venue to watch the spectacle their emperor has arranged.

I rest my hands against the velvet fabric on either side of

me to aid my balance. My gift-brought cure had completely alleviated my fever and aches by the time I woke this morning, but between the earlier starvation and the illness, I expect it'll take another day or two before my body truly feels well.

My fellow ladies don't appear to be as daunted by our surroundings as I am. I suppose they've attended these arena shows many times before.

At my left, Lady Giralda peers down at her gown's sky-blue sleeves against the peachy skin of her arms and lets out a disgruntled huff. "I swear this color looked good in my chamber's mirror. This much sun makes it look wretched on me."

Rochelle leans forward at my other side to study our companion. "With your complexion, I think you'd do best in pinks or oranges. If you want something really vibrant, maybe a bright yellow?"

Giralda shoots her a cautious glance and then hums to herself. "My mother always discouraged yellow. 'Too sunny,' whatever that means. I'll have to try it sometime."

None of us mentions that we have no idea whether we'll actually get the chance to add to our wardrobes again—or if Marclinus will cull us first.

One of the palace staff comes by with a carafe of wine and a platter of goblets. Rochelle hesitates before reaching to take one. As she cups it between her hands, she lets out a shaky laugh. "After the past two days, I keep thinking I'll still be punished if I take any food or drink."

I offer a crooked smile. "That kind of lesson sinks in fast."

"Yes."

Her expression when she peers down at the wine turns so desolate it wrenches at me. I didn't check on my friend after dinner last night to make sure she was recovering well. Maybe she's not feeling at her best either.

If so, it doesn't seem wise to draw attention to that fact in public. Instead, I opt for potential distraction, lifting my chin toward the immense yard below us. "Does Emperor Tarquin hold these exhibitions often?"

Rochelle blinks out of her momentary daze and nods. "Once every month or so, I think. I only happen to be at court when they're held a couple of times a year. It's quite a spectacle."

Something about the way she says those words makes me tense up inside. I've gotten a sample of the sorts of spectacles the emperor and his heir enjoy, and I can't say I share their tastes so far.

Marclinus is in his most energetic form today. He ushered us all off on this trip into the city with jovial comments that showed no trace of concern for the women he deprived. As soon as he sat in his throne, he grabbed the nearest lady to toss her in his lap.

Possibly by design, that lady was Bianca. She looks nothing but pleased to be sprawled across him, trailing her fingers over his jaw and chest, giggling when he leans in to kiss her neck or nibble her ear.

I notice her husband is keeping his gaze fixed very rigidly on the arena grounds.

Lady Giralda sips her own wine and shifts impatiently on the cushion. "When are they going to begin? The stands are full."

I look toward the thrones and frown as if in thought before lowering my voice. "The emperor looks a little wearier than usual, doesn't he? Perhaps he's not quite ready to give the exhibition his full attention."

Both Giralda and Rochelle follow my gaze, Giralda letting out a pensive hum.

Before we can talk any further, a man in a bright red jacket and trousers walks into the yard in front of us. He glances toward our part of the stands, and it's Marclinus who waves his hand in a *Go on* motion.

The announcer must have an amplification charm, because his resonant voice booms through the entire arena. "Welcome, fine citizens of Vivencia and beyond! Today, our great emperor has ensured that you'll be awed and thrilled by feats of might and courage. Let us ask for Sabrelle's blessing for all today's fighters. May they do our godlen of war proud."

Even the emperor and his heir dip their heads in respect to the gods, Tarquin flicking his hand through the gesture of the divinities. The announcer does the same before lifting his voice again. "First, some of our most skilled warriors will battle each other. Let them and our Imperial Eminences hear your approval!"

Applause reverberates through the arena, bouncing off the tiered walls. In the bright sunlight streaming through the uncovered roof, several armed figures in leather and chain-link armor stride out from doorways set on the ground level.

My pulse hitches as I realize I recognize one of the fighters. Prince Raul is unmistakable with his brawny frame and cocoa-brown hair, which is drawn back in its usual short ponytail.

Swinging his sword casually, he strolls over to face off against another warrior who's nearly the same size.

I can't suppress my startled curiosity. "Is it normal for the princes to compete in these exhibitions?"

Giralda giggles. "Only Prince Raul. He almost always

does. He's very good—obviously, or he'd have been cut down by now."

A chill seeps under my skin. Is that a real possibility? Surely Emperor Tarquin wouldn't risk losing his hostage in a bit of entertainment?

Or maybe he'd find it amusing to see one of his conquered royals die in the dirt.

A horn sounds, and the five pairs of warriors around the arena rush at each other.

Blades clang and spiked clubs thump together. Yells break out throughout the crowd in a cacophony that's impossible to pick apart, but they're obviously egging one or another fighter on.

The pairs shove apart, circle each other, slash and dodge and stab.

It's hard for me to drag my attention away from Raul to consider the other battles. Both because he's the only one I know, the only one whose fate I can't help feeling some personal stake in—and because he *is* very good.

Great, even.

Despite his massive body, he sidesteps and lunges with incredible speed. Even at a distance, I can see the muscles rippling through his arms with unleashed power.

He only has an inch or two over his opponent, who can't weigh much less than him either, but he drives the other man back pace by pace with a growing sense of inevitability. When a swipe of the other sword draws a bloody line on his forearm, Raul simply bares his teeth in a grin and pushes harder.

The emperor watches with a serene expression. Does he realize how much of that normally bottled aggression must be actually aimed at him?

Raul isn't the first to end his fight, though. At the other

end of the arena, one in the pair of female warriors heaves her rival to the ground. She plants her boot on the other woman's chest and aims her sword at her opponent's throat.

More cheers blare from the stands. Through the furor, the announcer declares the fight in her favor.

For a second, I think the winner might simply walk away, leaving the other woman bruised, bleeding, and beaten but alive. Then Marclinus leans around Bianca toward a metal fixture on the arm of his throne, which has an amplification charm of its own.

His voice peals through the arena. "Let's see this fight properly ended. Don't hold back on the losers. We came to see the strong conquer the weak: blood, guts, and all!"

His eager tone makes my lungs constrict, but apparently plenty of his citizens agree. A louder roar sweeps through the building.

The woman adjusts her grip on her sword with a flourish and plunges it through her opponent's neck.

Raul doesn't wait for a similar admonishment. If he's been participating in these shows regularly, I suppose he already knew what to expect.

The second he's knocked his rival's legs out from under him, he's springing at him. He kicks aside a jab of the other man's blade and slams his own sword deep into his opponent's chest.

As the other man's body goes limp, I restrain a wince. At least it was a quick death.

Which apparently isn't enough for the voracious imperial heir. When one member of another pair starts to falter, staggering between bashes of his attacker's club, Marclinus speaks into his amplification charm again. "Make him dance! Let's see a real show."

With one smack of the spiked club and another, blood

sprays over the dusty ground. My wobbly gut lurches. I avert my gaze to one of the pairs not yet at the outright-slaughter stage.

Rochelle's hand slips around mine where it's braced on the bench. She speaks in a murmur so low no one could overhear. "With your dedication, this must be especially hard for you to watch. Pretend we're having a lively conversation about it."

I focus my attention on her with a grateful smile. "It *is* quite the spectacle. Do they always follow the same pattern?"

My friend nods with more energy than the question really deserves. "From what I've seen, pretty much. The people know what they like."

And so do their rulers.

At another thud of a body that I've thankfully missed witnessing, Marclinus whoops in approval. I flick my gaze toward the thrones and catch Emperor Tarquin's lips curved in a thin smile.

When there are only the five winners of the warrior-to-warrior fights left standing, the announcer declares that it's time for the animals. Several wild beasts I'm familiar with and a few others I've never seen before hurtle into the arena with snarls and snorts.

Most of them charge straight at one or another of the fighters. I can only imagine how their keepers have been mistreating them that their first instinct is to attack.

As cries and squeals mingle with the thunder of applause, I turn to Rochelle again. She gamely chatters with me about the sorts of animals we'd consider the greatest threat and which are most impressive to look upon, the strain in her expression suggesting she doesn't find the spectacle much more appealing than I do.

By the time the exhibition is over, more than a dozen

animal carcasses lie slumped on the arena's grounds along with seven human corpses. Raul has taken a gouge to his lower leg, limping as he heads to one of the doorways. I suppose the imperial medics will heal up the victors.

Those of us who are the emperor's special guests rise and take our leave through a private exit before the main mass of spectators departs. In the broad street outside the arena, the carriages that brought us have pulled around to collect us.

I move to beckon Rochelle to join me in one, but she's no longer standing next to me. My steps slowing, I scan the mass of nobles around me.

Her cloud of blond curls is nowhere in view.

Where could she have gone? I veer a little to the side where I last remember her being, searching for her familiar form.

As the other nobles start piling into the carriages, an urgent shout catches my attention from farther down the street. I hurry over and spot one of the imperial guards ushering Rochelle out of a neighboring street.

Her face is flushed, her hands fluttering aimlessly in the air. "I saw a kitten run off that way, and I thought maybe I could bring it back to the palace. I didn't mean to wander off so far."

The guard answers in a gruff undertone, but he lets Rochelle continue on alone as soon as we're close to the carriages. She notices me watching and offers an embarrassed grimace, but there's a frantic cast to her eyes that makes me hesitate.

"Here," I say gently, and motion her into one of the carriages that still has room.

We're tucked in with a few other court ladies, who rave about the excitement of the battles while the carriage rattles through the streets toward the palace. I hold my silence, studying Rochelle from the corner of my eye. The way her hands fidget with her skirts, twisting the fabric. The way she worries at her lip as she stares out the window.

When we disembark within the palace gates, I touch her arm. "I feel like I need a walk after all that sitting. Join me for a stroll in the gardens?"

Rochelle summons a smile. "That sounds lovely."

I wait until we're well out of hearing range of any imperial staff, meandering close to one of the warbling fountains. "Are you all right? What happened back there by the arena?"

A flash of panic crosses Rochelle's face. Her hands ball at her sides.

"I'm not going to judge," I add quickly in a hushed voice. "Whatever's going on—I'll help you if I can."

She stares at me for a long moment as if weighing my honesty. Then her shoulders sag. "I suppose it doesn't matter if I tell you. I'm stuck either way. If you go tattling to the emperor, it'll just speed along the inevitable."

The hopelessness in her voice makes my throat tighten. "What do you mean, Rochelle?"

She ducks her head to gaze at her hands instead. "I thought maybe I could slip away. Run off, pay someone for a ride back home, hide out there until Marclinus has his wife and maybe wouldn't care anymore about the rest of us who were supposed to vie for the spot…"

But the guard spotted her and dragged her back.

My spirits sink, but I make myself ask the obvious question. "Have you asked about being released from the competition?"

Rochelle lets out a shaky sigh. "Not directly. I talked to my father a bit, and when he was done berating me for not appreciating the opportunity he created for me, he told me he's heard the emperor saying a refusal to participate will be taken as treason. I just thought—if I wasn't even *here* for them to think about me... I don't know. It was probably stupid."

What can I say that would provide any comfort? My gift doesn't show me how to conjure cures for impossible terms set by tyrant emperors.

The best I can tell her is the truth. "I don't blame you for trying. The trials, everything he's putting us through... You never asked for this."

"Neither did you. None of us did. Although some seem happier about it than others."

Her eyes narrow briefly, maybe thinking of Fausta. Then she shakes her head. "The ridiculous thing is, even if I won, I wouldn't be happy about it. He isn't who I want to marry."

Her phrasing tips me off without her saying more. A pang fills my chest. "There's someone else you do want."

Rochelle's voice drops to nearly a whisper. "There's a man in the town by our estate... Not noble, but his family have been the main medics in the area for generations, and he's trained into the same calling. It's an honorable profession. Father wouldn't accept it, not yet, but I thought—maybe in a few years, if I haven't found a better match. If one of my sisters makes a particularly good one. Then he might ease up."

And there's no chance of that now. Now her only options are failure and death or success and marriage to a different man.

A rush of emotion wells up inside me—echoes of love, frustration, grief, and anger I can no longer separate apart.

It isn't fair. But it was never meant to be "fair" for me. Fair for a princess is an utterly different thing.

Rochelle is only a minor noble. She shouldn't have to put

her entire happiness aside over her father's selfish power play, over the sadistic inclinations of the emperor and his heir.

If anyone should get to break the rules, it's her.

"Maybe there's still a chance," I find myself saying. "Maybe we can uncover a way out."

I just have no idea what that could possibly be.

Chapter Twenty-Two

Bastien

I probably should have avoided the records room for the entire duration of Marclinus's "trials." Even though today passed without incident, the palace guards are twice as alert, not wanting to be blamed for any oversights.

But the events of the past few days have left an uncomfortably restless energy coursing beneath my skin. I need to do *something*—or to at least feel as if I've done something—to temper it.

I don't want to find out what might happen if I let my agitation continue to build.

So I'm here in the library just shy of midnight, navigating the aisles between the shelves in the dark with the benefit of years of practice. The emperor and his staff trust their locks; they don't bother to guard the records room otherwise.

It never occurred to them that I might have ways of

getting around their basic protections. And I'm always careful to ensure there's no evidence of my interference.

I ease open the door and am just stepping inside when a voice reaches me from several paces away. "What's in there?"

With a lurch of my heart, I whirl around.

Princess Aurelia is just pushing herself out of one of the nearby armchairs with a swift swipe of her eyes. Had she… fallen asleep there?

What would she have been doing in the library in the middle of the night without even a lantern?

Curse it all. Now I have to answer her.

I'm not sure which is worse—that or the fact that I can't stop my gaze from traveling over her, checking to confirm that all signs of her sickness are gone. Not that I could count on being able to tell anyway. The way she was striding around the palace last night, I had no idea she was remotely ill until she crumpled like a puppet with its strings cut.

The memory makes my stomach twist all over again. Up until that point, I was berating myself for not sabotaging her better, annoyed that my gambit hadn't affected her at all. Meanwhile I almost killed her.

Gods help me, I never would have outright *poisoned* her. Not purposefully.

There are only two people in this world I've ever wanted to murder, and both of them are untouchable. I did let my frustration get the better of me yesterday, let it cloud my mind so I forgot about the consequences of her sacrifice…

Does she even fully know that? I'm not sure how much of what I said she absorbed in her feverish state.

Why is she even talking to me if she does?

The knot of guilt in my gut doesn't change that for all she impressed me with her fortitude, she's still a potential enemy.

I set aside my many questions and keep my tone as even as possible with my answer. "Nothing of much importance."

If Aurelia was dozing, she's snapped back to alertness quickly enough. She glances at the sign mounted over the door and then back at me. "I heard that's where the imperial records are kept. Finances and trade and all that. You don't consider them important?"

I clench my jaw to stop it from twitching with annoyance. If she already knew, why did she ask?

To find out what I'd say. Whether I'd lie.

We are still at odds, no matter how much Lorenzo insists that we should go easier on her—that she isn't out to undermine the rest of us and our kingdoms. That she actually wants to *help* us.

The man's closer to me than my own brother, but he gets so swept up in his fanciful notions sometimes.

She didn't trust him enough to admit she was feeling unwell yesterday. Instead she lied and said she was merely tired.

And then she didn't look even fatiged when we first encountered her afterward.

I thought the constant assured calm she's shown throughout the trials meant that no part of Tarquin and Marclinus's tests bothered her all that much. But if she can pass for nothing worse than irritable while she's burning up with fever and ready to vomit her guts out, maybe I don't really know anything about her at all.

Why in the realms would she trust *me* not to lie, after everything I've said and done before?

In the midst of my inner conflict, one particular detail from my mental inventory of the records room jumps out. I might be able to discern more of her motives without resorting to anything harmful.

Although I suspect I should kowtow a little first. She has earned some kind of apology.

I motion for her to follow me into the smaller room. "If you're curious, I can show you around. It's all rather dry and boring, but I like to take a look at the data every now and then."

Aurelia walks closer but stops a few steps from the doorway. Her expression turns puzzled. "Emperor Tarquin gives you free access to his records?"

I shrug in a nonchalant way that I hope looks convincing. "He wants us to make use of our skills however we can."

It isn't even a lie. I just didn't directly answer her question.

Aurelia peers past me toward the shelves of record books and scrolls before returning her pensive gaze to me. In the faint moonlight cast through the far windows, her deep blue eyes look even more striking than usual.

"And should I be concerned that you've changed your mind about murdering me and are simply looking for an out of the way spot to give it another try?"

So, she did catch that part of our conversation. My face flushes with shame I can't suppress. "That was—I misjudged, badly. I swear to you that I never intended more than a mild discomfort, and I'm sorry I put you through all that unpleasantness. And it seems I may have misjudged *you* altogether, and I should never have interfered in the first place."

Her eyebrows arch. "Does that mean you'll stop with the threats and the sabotage completely?"

I don't want to answer that, since I'm not sure myself. It feels wrong to lie to her face.

I dip my head, a motion of deference that could be taken

for a nod. "I'd like the chance to make up for my mistakes. If you'll let me."

And in doing so, I can determine exactly how much of my previous conduct has actually been a mistake.

Aurelia doesn't look completely convinced, but I must sound genuine enough that she's assured I won't turn around and stab her. She brushes her fingers against the bodice of her gown where her godlen mark must lie beneath. "I suppose you're lucky I believe in peace."

"If you change your mind, you can always tell me to fuck off again," I say before I can think better of the remark.

It gets me the first upward tick of her lips into a wry smile. "I'm not going to apologize for my impoliteness, given the circumstances."

"Utterly fair." I hold up my hands in surrender. "I deserved much worse. Your forbearance and your fortitude are both shockingly admirable."

Aurelia lets out a light guffaw, but she finally follows me into the records room. "You should be familiar with the art of pushing through discomfort. I don't get the impression the emperor has made your life here all that comfortable."

She isn't wrong about that. But I don't know that I could have summoned the strength to carry on so purposefully through a raging illness. Lorenzo has two lungs, and I doubt he could have either. Raul, maybe, through sheer stubbornness, but he'd have done a lot more swearing along the way.

While smaller than the main library, the records room is hardly tiny. Between the shelves built into the walls, it has its own short aisles amid a few freestanding bookcases. A couple of desks stand in the more open area, each with a magic-blessed lantern.

I check that the door has firmly shut behind us and tap

one of the lanterns to light. Aurelia's soft features come into clearer focus.

She peers around the room, taking the contents in with a thoughtful air I have to appreciate. "Where would you start?"

Normally I'd start with the latest accounting ledgers of the court nobles, but I don't have an innocent explanation for that habit. I turn to the larger, leatherbound volumes on the nearby shelves. "We can see exactly what's been coming into the palace in the past few weeks and how much Their Imperial Eminences paid for the privilege."

"If anything," Aurelia murmurs under her breath, but she joins me at the table as I heft the heavy book onto it.

I flip through the pages to the latest entries. "There's always a lot of food—other than the herbs you've already seen and fruit from the orchard, not much is cultivated on the palace grounds. Materials for clothing—you'll have been responsible for some of that. New furnishings. Possibly an artistic commission or two. But to look at it, it's mostly rows of numbers."

"But you think it's worth knowing about."

"I think everything you *can* know is worth knowing about. Every gap filled means you go forward on firmer ground."

Aurelia aims a softer smile at me, one that makes my pulse skip despite myself. "I think your desire to learn is rather admirable too."

I can't let her pretty face distract me from my goal.

I wave vaguely toward one of the other shelves. "It can be a bit tedious, is all I'm saying. Sometimes it's easier with a little treat to smooth the way. The accountant keeps a bottle of ambervin liquor behind the box on the top shelf, if you want to make this investigation a little more enjoyable. Consider it part of my apology."

"Hmm." Aurelia walks over to have a look.

I let her retrieve the bottle herself and carry it back to the table. She can't imagine I've doctored it in any way when it'll have been obvious I wasn't expecting to run into her.

She uncaps it and takes a sniff. "I've never had ambervin liquor before."

"It's popular in Lavira. Quite a nice flavor, meant for sipping. Which makes it easier not to give away that any's been taken without permission."

I shoot her a sly grin. She doesn't need to know it's also quite potent. I'd never have more than a single capful when I'm in here on my own.

Aurelia hasn't abandoned all sense of caution. She pushes the bottle toward me so I can take the first drink. Also fair.

I drizzle a little into the cap, feigning that I've poured a more generous portion and tossing it back before she can get a good look. The sharp fruity tang burns down my throat.

When I nudge the bottle back to Aurelia, she pours closer to a full cap. Her gulp makes her cough and then grin. "That *is* nice."

If I can get one or two more shots into her, her tongue should get looser—and perhaps more honest.

As I check the tallies of the past couple of weeks, Aurelia considers them and then studies the other shelves. "Are there records for the entire empire in here? For goods brought in from countries outside Dariu and that sort of thing?"

"Some, but the imperial accountants aren't quite as detailed in their reporting of those." The emperor's people are always happy to leave off what was outright taken rather than bargained for.

I point her to the shelves that hold the most recent reports from Dariu's conquered countries. She pulls out the one labeled *Accasy* and brings it to her side of the table.

Naturally. Focused completely on her home territory when that's the one she must already be most familiar with.

I go through the motions of pouring another drink but only drop the slightest splash into the cap. Then I offer the bottle to Aurelia again. She tosses back another capful without so much as wincing this time.

I've never seen her show that much enthusiasm for the wines the imperial staff supply us with, but this woman does know how to drink.

The record book she's taken gives me a direct opening. "Lorenzo told me you have plans not just for Accasy but all of us if you make it to the throne."

Aurelia's gaze darts to me. Is she surprised that he'd have mentioned her comments?

She pauses for a moment before answering. "I think there are a lot of wrongs being done in many places and to many people other than in my own kingdom. My main goal has always been to heal as much as I can. I'm not going to refuse what help I can offer when it's needed, regardless of where that is."

A very measured answer. I swallow another tiny sip of the liquor and slide the bottle over in the hopes she'll take more. "I suppose you must have problems in Accasy in mind already, that you're hoping to start with."

Aurelia simply toys with the bottle, her gaze going distant. "As you must have your own concerns for Cotea. I suspect some of the simplest solutions might benefit all of us."

She pours perhaps half a capful. A short laugh hitches out of her in its wake, her cheeks starting to flush.

Another pinch of guilt has me reaching for the cap. I'm not risking overdoing another gambit. "I think I'd better put this away now."

Aurelia relinquishes the bottle without complaint. I return it to its hiding place while contemplating my next remarks. "And you think Tarquin and Marclinus will go along with your suggested solutions?"

Her expression tightens slightly, a little slip of her placid mask. But it doesn't reveal the haughtiness or guile I was braced for.

If anything, she looks pained.

"I'm going to do my best, as my godlen guides me," she says quietly. "This is what I was born for. I hope I'm up to the task."

It hits me then as it never really has before just how mired she is in this shitty situation.

She got to grow up free as I didn't, true. But I know that once my older brother's second child is old enough for Tarquin to foster, my nephew will become a new hostage from Cotea and I'll go relatively free.

If Aurelia doesn't die in the trials, she's going to be chained to Dariu and its tyrants for the rest of her days.

Compassion nibbles at the edges of my skepticism, but Aurelia's comments could still all be for show. She knows I've put her life on the line before. She'd want to earn my support to ensure that doesn't happen again.

There's talking vaguely about healing and then there's outright treason. Let's see just how honest she's willing to be.

I rest my hands on the table, watching her. "You hate them, don't you? Emperor Tarquin and Marclinus?"

Aurelia lifts her gaze from the book. She looks at me searchingly enough that my skin starts to prickle under her regard.

Her voice stays quiet, but it's even steadier than before. "Maybe not as personally as you must, but yes. It hardly matters."

Gods smite me, she actually admitted it.

I choke on my laugh. "Hardly matters? You're trying to marry into the family."

"And I must take the best match I'm in a position to, just as you had to accept your fostering. Would you ever have fled your duty, knowing how he'd retaliate on your people?"

The answer tumbles out without any thought required. "No."

There's something bittersweet about her next smile. "Neither would I. This is the most amazing chance I could have gotten to do something good for my country, maybe for the entire empire. The only kind of chance I *could* get, since I wasn't first-born and meant to guide my kingdom directly. I can't be selfish about it—I'm not going to let everyone who's counting on me down."

Enough vehemence runs through her words to convince me, with a shiver down my spine that's partly regret.

I don't know if she'll be able to accomplish even a fraction of what she imagines, but I believe that she's imagining it. Not just paltry benefits for a chosen few. An actual better world.

Aurelia's head tilts to the side with a hint of tipsiness. "You must know the palace and its procedures better than just about anyone. Are there ways to get out of the grounds without the guards noticing?"

I stare at her. "I thought you just said you weren't going to flee?"

She raises her hand to her mouth, stifling what sounds like a giggle. "That wasn't a very good change in subject, was it? I'm not asking for myself. For a friend. Seeing if I can get started on making a difference sooner rather than later."

I'm not sure what to make of that statement. What friend could she have who wants to escape the palace?

Even if she's lying now, it doesn't make a difference. I don't have any solutions for her.

"We roam pretty freely in and around the palace," I say. "But the gates are tightly monitored. If your 'friend' wanted to leave without being noticed, I don't think that would be possible alone. They'd need a collaborator willing to smuggle them out, hidden."

Aurelia's brow knits in consternation. "I don't think she has that. At least not at the moment. And by the time…"

She shakes herself out of her reverie. "Never mind. I'll continue to think on the problem myself. Thank you for sharing your thoughts."

So determined even though she knows I've had time to study every inch of the palace and its workings. How much would she risk to assist this unknown person?

"If the emperor finds out *you* arranged something like that," I start.

Aurelia waves off my warning before I can finish it. "I realize. It's just a matter of finding a risk worth taking."

Perhaps I've drunk more of the ambervin liquor than I meant to, because I feel abruptly off-balance. That's the only explanation I can come up with for what I say next.

"Do you want to see what I actually come in here to do?"

Curiosity sparks in Aurelia's compelling eyes. "Absolutely."

I move to the smaller ledgers on the lower shelves. "These are the accounts of all the nobles who reside with the imperial court at least some of the year. Let's see. Why don't we start with Viceroy Ennius and his lovely wife, Bianca?"

The corners of Aurelia's mouth tick upward. As I open the ledger, she comes around the table to stand next to me. Not close enough to touch, but my body tingles into sharper alertness at her presence.

I retrieve a pen and a small pot of ink from the desk drawer and consider the most recent items on the list. "These requisitions haven't yet been fulfilled. Why shouldn't they pay a little more for that new mirror? This three can easily become an eight."

I fill in the lines with swift strokes and consider my other options. "And it'd certainly be a shame if they ended up needing to decide what to do with several reams of lace rather than linen." I adjust the shorthanded *li* into *lace*.

Aurelia's laugh makes my pulse sing in return. "Do you alter the accounts a lot?"

"Only a little here and there. So the adjustments can still appear to be mistakes rather than malice."

She turns to peer at the other ledgers. "Who do you think we should tackle next?"

Her use of "we" gives me more of a thrill than it probably should. I select a couple more volumes, nobles whose purchases I haven't messed with recently.

It's hard to look away from Aurelia's eager face as she points out another cost we could increase. Her arm brushes against mine, and warmth blooms over my skin even with our sleeves between us.

I wouldn't have expected the stoic, impassive woman I've seen in front of Marclinus to delight in this minor sabotage, but here we are.

After we've tweaked an entry in the third book, Aurelia's enthusiasm dims. She looks up at me, so close I feel as if I might fall into her gaze. "Don't you ever want to do *more* than this?"

The question prods a sore spot buried deep inside me. I snap before I can catch my tongue. "What makes you think I haven't?"

Aurelia flinches and steps back, her retreat tugging at my

gut. I scramble for the right thing to say, my thoughts abruptly muddled.

I'm not angry at her. I'm angry at myself, for all the ways I've failed.

"I have wanted to," I say. "So much more. But the most important things... I couldn't."

Aurelia's bittersweet smile comes back. "I'm sorry," she says, even though I should be the one apologizing to her. "But even if you couldn't before—there will always be more chances. We might even do something important together."

I don't know if it's the liquor or the resolve in her gaze or everything about this unexpected encounter, but a spark of hope like I haven't felt in longer than I can remember flashes to life inside me. I find myself reaching for her hand as if I need to touch her to convince her of my words. "I don't want you to die at all. Not in the trials, not by Marclinus's orders —not any way."

Her smile widens. "I'm glad to hear that."

She looks down at our joined hands and turns hers over to wrap her fingers around mine. Even as the jolt of that contact shoots straight to my groin, she eases in and brushes the gentlest of kisses to my mouth.

It's over before I can even kiss her back, though heat has flared across my lips.

Aurelia's cheeks flush pinker than before. "I'm sorry. I wasn't thinking. I'd better—it's late."

Before I have a chance to decide what I'd even want to say to her, she's ducked out of the records room and vanished behind the swing of the door.

CHAPTER TWENTY-THREE

Aurelia

When I walk into the dining room for breakfast, I'm probably not as alert as I should be. It took me too long to get to sleep last night, replaying my conversation with Prince Bastien in my head.

I'm increasingly convinced that he was honest about not having meant to nearly murder me. Whatever resentments led him to his mistake with the stew, I can't afford to hold unnecessary grudges against my only potential allies when I have so few.

He does feel like something close to an ally now. By the end of our talk, he trusted me enough to reveal his more illicit activities. I believed him when he said he wants me to survive the trials.

He looked so earnest in that moment, with his hand tucked around mine…

Perhaps it's not surprising that a little affection sparked in me before we parted ways. But was that goodbye kiss a clever strategy for deepening whatever connection I've finally forged with him or an ill-advised impulse I should have known better than to follow?

Could it possibly have been both?

Whatever the case, I'm too distracted to give Fausta's cluster of friends a wide enough berth. I've barely noted her flame-red hair at the edge of my vision when a murmur and a couple of giggles rise up from their midst.

They surge toward the head table, even though nothing edible has been brought out yet. One lady contrives to step straight into my path at the last second, forcing me to stumble backward to avoid plowing into her.

In the same moment, an unnerving ripping sound hits my ears alongside a tug of my skirt.

I glance down just as Fausta flits deeper into her friends' midst. I have no doubt she's responsible for the ragged tear that now splits the mauve silk of my gown from mid-thigh to calf.

My teeth set on edge. I spin toward her, half a dozen cutting remarks leaping to my tongue to tell her off once and for all—and my gaze catches on Marclinus lounging in his throne-like chair by the end of the table.

He's come early today. He's watching the bunch of us while he twirls his butter knife in his hand as if it's flying between his fingers.

I've never been very concerned what Fausta thinks of me, but I still need to keep the imperial heir's favor. He's seen me unshakably serene and composed. I'd like to maintain that image.

Another flurry of giggles breaks out from the ladies. Bianca swans by at the back of the pack, adding a tsk of her tongue. "You really should be more careful with those fine gowns, wild princess."

I swallow my frustration, the comments I'd like to make searing in my throat.

Well, now I need to put on a new dress. The walk will give me time to simmer down.

The moment I step out of the dining room, I can't stop my hands from balling. Why does Fausta have to be such a wretch to all of us? Does she really hate the ladies she grew up with so much that she's happily ushering them to their deaths alongside me?

By every appearance so far, yes, she does.

And she also hates me so much simply for existing that she sees every petty inconvenience she can create as some kind of victory.

It's of no consequence. I have other gowns. But the events of the past few days and the knowledge that we should expect the next trial sometime soon have worn away at my temper.

I'm breathing slowly, willing the anger down, when I catch voices up ahead. Male voices, a mix of jovial and sneering, with mocking guffaws mixed in.

"Why do you even bother coming to breakfast, silent man? Shouldn't you be asking the cooks to grind all your meals into mash like a swaddled babe?"

"My theory is you had them carve out your tongue because your singing was so horrifying."

"Right—he had to make sure no one ever asked it of him!"

My jaw clenches harder. I round the bend just in time to see one of the younger noblemen elbowing Prince Lorenzo in the ribs while his companions snicker.

Lorenzo is striding straight ahead, his gaze fixed on his

destination, his well-built form rigid. There's obviously no point in him even trying to communicate with these jackasses.

They're not looking for a conversation, only a punching bag.

All at once, I'm twice as furious as before. And right now, there's no emperor or heir around to judge me for my remarks.

I pick up my pace to meet them with a muffled rapping of my shoes against the carpeted floor.

"Come on, open wide and let's see the horror for ourselves," one of the men is cajoling Lorenzo.

I plant myself directly in front of their gaggle, my feet wide and hands on my hips. "It's not often I hear such blatant disrespect for the gods. You all must not care to receive any good favor from them."

Both Lorenzo and his hecklers draw to a halt. The prince twitches his head in what might be a shake of refusal, but I need to put *someone* who deserves it in their place today or I might explode.

The nobleman who was elbowing Lorenzo furrows his brow at me. "What are you talking about? We're just having a bit of fun, a little jest."

I scoff. "A bit of jest calling a sacrifice made to the godlen a 'horror'? Insulting the purpose of that sacrifice? Inganne might appreciate playing around, but somehow I think she'd draw the line there."

The men shuffle uncomfortably, most of them looking suitably chided. One fool, I think the fellow who was speculating about the prince's eating habits, doesn't know when to shut up.

"What's it to you either way?" he says. "You don't make any laws around here."

I give him the most disdainful look I can summon. "Forgive me if I'd prefer to walk these spectacular halls without hearing them sullied by blasphemous idiocy."

That provokes a couple more snickers, these ones are aimed at my target. His friends jostle him teasingly. With a huff, he marches around me, continuing on to breakfast with the others hustling after him.

Lorenzo pauses for just a few seconds, scowling at me with the force of a thunderstorm. His hand jerks at his side. *I was okay. Don't need protecting.*

Then he sweeps past me too, without so much as a sideways glance.

As I whirl after him, my stomach sinks. I didn't mean to make *him* angry by telling off those spoiled bullies.

The memories wash over me of the vulnerabilities he revealed the other night, the beauty he showed me, the tenderness of his kiss and his supportive touch after I collapsed in my illness.

I thought we'd founded something more real than I might ever get from his foster brothers. Have I just ruined it?

"Lorenzo." I hurry after him, my quest for a replacement gown abandoned. "Lorenzo!"

He doesn't slow down, and I don't want to outright run —especially as we pass the area of the dining room and other nobles heading that way. But Lorenzo keeps going past the common rooms, down one side hall and then another, studiously ignoring me.

"Lorenzo, can we just talk—"

Without looking back, he makes a gesture that clearly says, *Go away.*

I frown. I've dealt him an injury accidentally. Leaving it to fester doesn't seem wise, especially when I don't know when I'll get another chance to speak to him without witnesses.

How many times have he and his closest companions barged into *my* space when they had no right to, even when I've told them directly to leave? Turnabout should be fair play. At least my reason is more honorable.

He swerves through a doorway, and I speed to a jog just in time to catch the door before it shuts.

As I push into the room after him, Lorenzo spins on his heel to face me, his gaze accusing. Pinned by his dark stare, it takes the rest of my awareness a moment to catch up—to realize I've followed him right into what must be his bedroom, based on the furnishings.

Of course. Isn't this the same hall where I saw Raul emerging from his chambers the other day?

A four-poster bed stands off to one side of the room, a couple of armchairs arranged in a sitting area at the other. The shelves across from me hold an assortment of scattered books, papers, and at least a dozen instruments, all of their wooden surfaces polished to gleaming.

Lorenzo makes the same gesture as before, more emphatically. *Go away!*

I step to the side of the door, staying close to the wall so it's not too much of an invasion but making it clear I'm not leaving. "When did any of you ever listen to me when I asked for the same? You're angry at me. I'm sorry. I was only — They were being awful. They deserved to have someone knock them down a peg."

Lorenzo's hands flick through another series of movements, a little too hasty in his agitation for me to totally understand. At my puzzled expression, he makes a rough sound. He pulls a paper and pencil from his belt pouch and leans over his bedside table.

His handwriting slashes across the page in fierce strokes. *I can handle them. Don't need you rescuing me. I'm not feeble.*

His anger starts to make more sense. The realization of how my defense came across makes me wince.

I soften my tone. "I'm sorry. Really, I am. I've never thought you were weak. I never thought you *needed* me to step in. I just… could. They were right there in front of me, and I don't like seeing *anyone* treated cruelly. It was only about them being asses, not anything to do with my opinion of you."

Lorenzo gives me a skeptical look. He scribbles another note. *Would you have done the same for Raul?*

I can't help snorting at the picture that question paints. "I have trouble imagining any of those pricks daring to go at *him* quite that blatantly. But Bastien or Neven? Of course. I mean… isn't that what the three of you tried to do for me when you realized I was sick? You wanted to help because you could, because it'd have bothered you not to. Or do you think I'm feeble?"

The corner of the prince's mouth cants upward. The tension in his shoulders appears to be relaxing. His next few gestures sketch more smoothly through the air.

I think he says, *That night, you were a little.* His tentative smile suggests he doesn't mean it as a criticism.

I wrinkle my nose at the point made but can't deny it. "So maybe you can agree I have a slight advantage dealing with spiteful idiots because I can talk to them more directly?"

Lorenzo glowers at me for a second, but as his animosity fades, so does any lingering tension in the air. He sighs in a long rush and twists his hand in the shape I recognize from when he apologized that night in the woods.

Sorry. I'm bad at taking help. Sometimes it's worse.

Worse because his bullies hassle him more after the

chiding or worse because most people who might defend him end up turning around to inflict similar treatment?

Probably some of both.

I nod, my throat tight. "I can understand that. I shouldn't have barged into a situation that had nothing to do with me without checking with you first. In the future, I'll do whatever you'd like."

Lorenzo considers me. Now that his annoyance has dissipated, a glint sparks in his eyes nearly as sly as when he stole the fruit in the orchard for us to share.

He picks up his pencil again. _Anything I'd like?_

The emphasis and the heat in his gaze send a tingle over my skin. The kiss we shared after the twilight pumello tickles up from my memory again.

I wet my lips without meaning to. Lorenzo tracks the movement, and my whole body warms with the sharper awareness that we're alone in his bedroom.

Is it wise to become more entangled with any of the princes? Especially when I've now kissed two of them, regardless of how fleeting a peck I gave Bastien?

Especially when desire is already pulsing through my veins at the thought of experiencing Lorenzo's kiss again?

But I do want them utterly on my side. If I'm going to win over this man, wouldn't it help more than hurt to play to his interest in me a little more?

The more invested he is in me being alive, the more likely he'll do something to ensure I stay that way if the opportunity arises.

And damn it, it'd be nice to feel _good_ for a moment or two amid all the awfulness of the court.

I meet Lorenzo's eyes without shrinking. "What are you thinking?"

He steps closer, his gait languid now, his gaze burning

into me with its intensity. At the stroke of his fingers along my jaw, my chin rises automatically.

As he claims my mouth, he nudges me closer to the wall. My arms loop around his shoulders instinctively. I'm caught in his embrace, in the thrilling slide of his mouth and the heat of his body washing over mine.

So why does it feel like he's opened the door to my cage?

My fingers trail up into the short tufts of his thick hair, and a rumble emanates from his chest. He kisses me harder, his hand coming to rest on my waist.

Just a little fun, I tell myself. A little pleasure before I have nothing left ahead of me but duty.

I recite that excuse through another scorching kiss, through the experimental brush of Lorenzo's fingers up my torso. Through the jolt of bliss when he palms my breast through my gown.

A whimper slips from my throat. Lorenzo drinks in the sound. When I can't help arching into his touch, he swivels his hand against my chest with more assurance.

My nipple pebbles at the friction, more giddy quivers racing over my skin. Arousal pools between my thighs.

I should stop this soon. I should stop before I'm dragged under more than he is.

He eases a little lower, and the torn fabric of my dress shifts. A current of air wafts over my leg.

The sensation hits me like a bucket of cold water.

I'm supposed to be at breakfast right now. I've already taken far more time away than should be required to exchange gowns.

My body tenses. Lorenzo draws back immediately, his gaze searching mine.

I touch the side of his face to soften the partial rejection. Can he feel how hard he's set my heart thumping?

"I need to fix my dress and make it to breakfast before it's over."

That's all I have to say. He knows what's at stake. It doesn't stop Lorenzo from stealing one more swift but sweet kiss, but then he ushers me out the door without attempting to change my mind.

I can't help noting that I've already won enough loyalty from him that he'd prefer to see me survive the day rather than ruin me in more ways than one.

It's a victory. I have to hold on to it.

I rush to my own room as quickly as I can, trade the ripped dress for an intact one, and stride back to the dining room. The smells of buttered bread and fried cheese set my mouth watering as I approach the table.

Most of the nobles at the head table are still eating. But as I drop into my chair, Marclinus dabs his fingers on his napkin and rises to his feet.

"My ladies," he says with a dip of his head in acknowledgment, his lips curved in the cruel smirk I've come to know so well. "Take this as your notice that the next trial will begin in the hall of entertainments on the hour."

Chapter Twenty-Four

Aurelia

I approach the hall of entertainments braced for catastrophe.

Just moments after I step over the threshold, bells ringing in the tenth hour of the morning peal beyond the palace walls. The last of Marclinus's prospective brides hurry in behind me.

Most of the court nobles have already gathered in the vast room in anticipation of the new spectacle. They stand in clusters murmuring to each other and studying us rather than partaking in any of the offered entertainments.

Rochelle comes over to join me, her mouth pressed tight. I nod to her in acknowledgment.

I might not know how to send her back to the man she loves, but we'll face this next challenge together.

Perhaps if we're the last two remaining in the end, the emperor will accept some kind of victory that doesn't need to be fatal. I could step in with whatever minor authority I might earn as the champion and official betrothed to ask for a show of mercy against my final opponent.

Right now, the imperial heir stands near one of the windows, talking with his father. I think Emperor Tarquin looks vaguely exasperated, which I'm not sure bodes well for the rest of us.

Marclinus laughs and makes an animated gesture. The emperor responds with a motion as if to say, *Go on, then.*

As Tarquin settles into one of the high-backed wingchairs, Marclinus saunters into an open stretch of floor where he can address his entire audience. His wide grin does nothing to ease my nerves.

"My friends, my ladies," he says in a buoyant voice, "today we will all appreciate the greatest beauty the gods can create, so often hidden away. It will be a trial of surrender and welcome. The lovely women vying for my hand will demonstrate that they fully and freely accept my gaze and my attentions by remaining bared before me until nightfall."

I stare at him for several thuds of my heart, his words not quite sinking in. Remaining bared? He can't possibly mean—

At our obvious uncertainty, Marclinus chuckles and sweeps his hand through the air. "You may disrobe now. Leave not a scrap on. Your maids have been summoned to assist you as needed. No modesty between us today—no attempts to evade my view or my touch. It is only a small sampling of what you will enjoy if we are wed, after all." He flicks his gaze toward the rest of the nobles. "The rest of you will keep your hands to yourself, naturally."

Even the most boisterous members of the court appear to be stunned into silence. Melisse arrives at my side with downcast eyes and a faintly apologetic expression. "If Your Highness would like some help…?"

I can hardly refuse, can I? Defiance would earn me a trip straight to my grave.

My lungs have constricted, but I reach for the folds of my skirt. Melisse hefts the fabric higher so I can peel off the gown with a minimum of disturbance to my hair.

Before I've even grasped my chemise, a renewed ripple of murmurs passes through our audience. A couple of my fellow competitors pause in their own undressing to peer at me—even Rochelle hesitates, blinking at my uncovered arms.

I knew I wasn't going to be able to hide the marks there from everyone forever. I just hadn't expected their exposure to be quite so abrupt and beyond my control.

Marclinus is eyeing me too, his eyebrows rising. His representative saw my scars and I would assume noted them in his report, but Mother had me powder them even more than my face to diminish the purple hue. The imperial heir might not have expected them to be so obvious… or, knowing him, he might not have bothered to read the report to begin with.

It's his father who speaks first, though I'm sure *he* would have insisted on being thoroughly informed. Emperor Tarquin has pushed to his feet, frowning. "What is the matter with your arms, Princess Aurelia?"

His tone is dry but ominous. He's asking me to give the explanation he's already aware of to his court—and no doubt evaluating how I handle the awkwardness.

I skim my fingers over both forearms to show there's no discomfort, not even a change in texture to the smooth purple blotches that stand out against my tan skin from just above my wrists to my elbows. "It's only a discoloration, nothing more. Lingering scars from a minor accident years ago."

Marclinus cocks his head. "What sort of accident produces scars like that?"

I smile disarmingly. "I've told you about my gift. When I was still learning how to use it, I made a mistake with a healing potion I was brewing. It erupted from the cauldron and splattered my arms above my gloves. The properties of the potion meant our medics couldn't completely erase the marks. But they haven't caused me any pain since the first day, and I got a lesson in always wearing *long* gloves when attempting a new concoction."

I speak calmly and warmly, as if it's a harmless story only worthy of amusement now, but my gut stays balled tight. There's no telling how Tarquin or his son might react, whether I'll be deemed soiled goods and cast aside for the superficial flaw, no matter how forewarned they were.

It has no bearing on my ability to support my husband's rule or bear him healthy children, but I know better than to expect a purely logical reaction from these men by now.

To my relief, Marclinus laughs. "You nearly have gloves painted right on you. I do like a woman who isn't afraid to get her hands dirty."

The leering slant of his next grin suggests a more provocative meaning to his words, but I'll take his acceptance either way.

While we continue undressing, the imperial heir ambles from one of us to the next as if inspecting his goods. Fausta strips down with a determined expression, revealing all of her petite but perfectly proportioned frame. As Rochelle proceeds with obvious discomfort, I realize just how clever she is at dressing even though she tends toward plainer styles.

The gowns she's always chosen have played down her broad shoulders and added more curve to her smaller chest and square hips. Without the benefit of their enhancing effects, her sturdy physique looks outright gawky.

Naturally, Fausta rubs in the fact by shooting a pointed look Rochelle's way and pretending to stifle a giggle.

Other than the scars on my arms, which are hardly a selling point, I don't think there's anything all that remarkable about my own body. My regular walks have kept my limbs toned but hardly as dainty as Fausta's. I have two breasts in the right place and reasonably sized, which my childhood maid once said is all a man cares about. Who can fathom an emperor-to-be's tastes, though?

My thumb lingers against the side of my gold-and-sapphire ring. Are we expected to remove all jewelry too?

Before I can fret over losing that bit of comfort, one of the other ladies asks for me. She holds up her wrist, where a thin gold chain dotted with tiny pearls glitters. "Should I take off my bracelet as well?"

Marclinus appears to consider. "Ah, leave your minor adornments on. They cover nothing and enhance the rest of the landscape."

I tuck my ringed hand close to my side. The warm air moving over my bare skin feels unsettling with so many gazes traveling with it. Keeping my breaths even, I hold tight to my inner calm.

For the first time, I'm discovering which of the lesser gods each of my fellow ladies dedicated themselves to. Fausta's sternum is branded with Inganne's sigil, though I've never seen her show any artistic interest. Maybe she considers her cruel antics a kind of play and assumes the childlike godlen would approve?

Not at all to my surprise, Rochelle is a dedicat of Prospira, the godlen of agriculture and abundance. That fits her generous attitude.

Do any of the others have gifts like mine? I resist the impulse to trace my fingers over the small scar near my stomach where my spleen was removed nine years ago.

I don't see any missing digits or skin on the women around me, but nobles are often cautious in what they sacrifice. Especially ladies hoping to catch the eyes of discerning bachelors. Teeth can be replaced with ceramic counterparts that pass for the real thing. Bits of flesh can be offered from spots normally hidden by hair or the shape of one's body. A lesser internal sacrifice might not leave a scar years later.

Of course, smaller sacrifices mean smaller magic. I haven't seen any sign that my competitors are wielding gifts I need to worry about.

I hate to think what Fausta might have asked for if she'd *known* she'd one day find herself in a fight to the death for the imperial heir's hand.

Now that all eight of us are nude, Marclinus meanders past us again, testing how we respond to his touch. When he trails his fingers up Fausta's arm, she tilts her head coyly. Rochelle visibly tenses at his stroke of her belly but doesn't pull away.

When he reaches me, I tap into my inner reserves of serenity even more deeply. Every particle of my body wants to cringe at his caress of my cheek and neck, but I hold still with a mild smile.

If I can detach from a raging fever, I can endure this indignity.

"I'd say your markings make you all the more exotic, Princess of Accasy," he says in a teasing tone. "They certainly don't detract from your fine figure. Curves in all the right places."

His fingers skim down the side of my breast, the slight concave of my waist, the slope of my hip.

I'm not here. It might as well be a sculpture he's touching, not any part of me.

Bianca's mocking voice breaks through my silent meditation. "Not all that much of them, though. Hardly impressive to simply fill a man's hand when you could be spilling over in bounty."

My gaze darts to her voluptuous form, but Marclinus simply chuckles. "Now, now, Vicerine. Jealousy doesn't become any lady."

Bianca's eyes flash with anger, but she snaps her mouth shut. She reserves her glare for me rather than the man who chided her, the moment he turns his back.

The imperial heir compliments Lady Leonette's athletic yet curvy figure, bringing a reserved smile to her lips. Then he returns his attention to our larger audience in their scandalized but avid hush. "We'll continue with a typical day. Let us revel in our entertainments—and the beauty of my ladies! How about a little music… Where's that foster 'brother' of mine?"

It takes me even more effort not to stiffen at the sight of Lorenzo walking past. He keeps his gaze studiously averted from our nakedness, but of course he'll have seen something.

The other princes are somewhere in the room too, taking the situation in. Taking *me* in.

Raul has talked about getting me naked. There've been times when the idea sounded a little bit tempting.

I'd never have wanted him to get his first glimpse like this.

As Lorenzo takes his vielle and launches into a sprightly tune, Marclinus motions us to the room's various activities. I stick close to Rochelle for moral support—mine as much as hers—and end up spending the better part of an hour playing cards with several other members of the court.

Marclinus calls me over to have a go at a game of darts. I manage not to cringe at the raking of his gaze over my body as each throw makes my breasts sway.

At lunch, we find ourselves arrayed all on one side of the head table again, with Marclinus sitting directly across from us. His leering eyes roam over all of us whenever he's not attending to his meal.

We're not even allowed napkins on our laps, not that he can see them through the table. We're instructed to keep those next to our plates.

When we've finished eating, the emperor directs us all out into the gardens. The bright sun prickles over my skin, highlighting every nook and cranny on our bodies in contrast.

I've never wished more for an overcast day.

As we walk over to the lawn for whatever games Marclinus has gotten it into his head to play, the wind picks up. It ruffles through our hair and nips at places wind is never meant to reach.

Rochelle shivers but keeps walking. "We just have to make it through dinner," I remind her under my breath.

Another hot gust sweeps over us—and one of the other nude ladies walking nearby wraps her arm around her chest against it.

It's obviously an instinctive gesture. She's shielding herself from the wind, not anyone's gaze.

But Marclinus's jaunty voice carries from a few steps behind us. "Lady Jovitte, you wound me by hiding from my view. So I'm afraid you must be wounded in turn."

Jovitte yanks her arm down, her face blanching. "I didn't mean—"

My own lips have parted to protest on her behalf, but it's already too late. One of the ever-present guards lurking on the fringes of our gathering leaps forward with his sword drawn.

The blade slices Jovitte's throat. Her body slumps onto the grass, blood dabbling the flesh the imperial heir was so determined to leave on display.

Rochelle sucks a tiny gasp through her teeth. I force myself to drag my attention away and nudge her to keep walking.

Gods save me, what else can we do?

CHAPTER TWENTY-FIVE

Aurelia

I t's hard to imagine what my parents or my sister would say if they found out I spent my eighth day in my betrothed's presence playing croquet on the lawn while utterly naked before him and his entire court.

I'd like to think they'd take one look at the scene and whisk me away, out of Dariu and Marclinus's sights forever. I know Father's voice would reverberate with rage, that Mother would look sick with horror, that Soreena would happily throw herself between me and all those prying eyes.

But in the end, they'd leave me here, wouldn't they? They'd mourn the better husband they hoped I'd have, they'd weep and rant to each other in the privacy of the family castle, but they wouldn't risk the destruction of our entire line by openly defying Emperor Tarquin.

I'm a piece in the game, and that's all I've ever been

meant to be. It's just not quite the game any of us were expecting.

As we sprawl on picnic blankets sipping wine and then stroll amongst the garden beds with Marclinus roving between "his" ladies like a bee from flower to flower, I hold on to one kernel of comfort. The guards have removed Jovitte's corpse and splashed water to rinse away the blood, but this trial has already claimed a life.

If the rest of us suppress our modesty for the rest of the day and let the imperial heir ogle us at his leisure, then we'll all survive. The last couple of trials, he's only culled those who made overt mistakes from the competition.

Rochelle and I can look forward to discovering what fresh torments he'll have in store for us tomorrow.

That doesn't mean today's torments are over. When we head into the dining room to await dinner, Marclinus sprawls in his gilded chair and motions me over. "I'd like to spend a little more time up close with each of my ladies."

As I approach, tamping down my trepidation, he grasps my hand with a tug. He expects me to cuddle up on his lap like I've watched Bianca and a few of the other court ladies do in the past.

My stomach churns, but I paste on a smile and sink onto his outstretched legs.

Elox, let me be as serene and steady as stone.

Marclinus teases one hand into my hair while the other traces across my pelvis from one hip to the other, just inches above my sex. If I were any less deep in my distant reverie, the muscles would have twitched as if trying to repel him.

Is this how it'll always be? Will he see his wife as nothing but a toy?

His attitude could change with marriage. With

familiarity and the chance for me to speak a little more freely once my position is somewhat secure.

But as he flicks his thumb over the peak of my breast with a chuckle of amusement, the flame of hope I've kept stoking nearly gutters out.

He only plays with me for a few minutes before calling Leonette over to replace me. I barely feel my legs as I return to my seat. I'm not just pulled back deep inside my body but hollowed out.

It's almost over. We're almost through.

The other members of court chatter away through Marclinus's lecherous display as if there's nothing horrifying about it. Emperor Tarquin's expression holds a trace of disdain, but so mild that might be wishful thinking on my part. He's certainly made no moves to interrupt his son's behavior.

Dinner tastes like ash on my tongue. When the dessert dishes are cleared, Marclinus stands and announces that we'll dance in the ballroom until the sky is completely dark.

Of course. It's not nightfall yet.

In the vast room across the hall, the regular court musicians strike up an energetic tune. The imperial heir takes each of us for a turn around the dance floor but seems content to see other partners lead us through the motions while he's occupied.

Each of the noblemen who approaches me keeps his hands very carefully only on mine, not straying too close to the rest of my body. But their gazes drop to my naked form at least as often as they're peering back into my eyes.

My feet follow the steps I know. I check the hue of the sky every time I swing past one of the windows.

Then the music dips into a brief lull between songs, and I find Prince Raul looming over me, claiming my hand.

All day, I've ignored the princes as well as I can. There's no avoiding the most imposing of them right now.

I set my jaw and lift my feet with the first swell of the new melody.

I'll give him this—Raul looks only into my eyes, not once gawking at my unclothed form farther down. The sear of his pale blue gaze somehow makes me feel twice as naked.

I fix my own attention in the vicinity of his chin.

We haven't spoken since the night I was sick—when he insisted on helping me with the garlic for my potion. When he seemed to be arguing in favor of getting help even when Bastien was hesitating.

Where do I stand with him now?

Apparently, that night's events didn't temper his seductive inclinations at all. After a minute of silence, he speaks in the low, husky tone that's shivered through my nerves before. "I'd tell you that you look lovely, but I don't think that's my place."

Tonight, my nerves are too raw for me to feel anything but irritation at his overtures. "Funny, that didn't seem to stop you from saying much more brazen things before."

"Before, we were on equal footing." We step apart with a bob of the dance, and he catches my opposite hand. His head dips closer to mine. "A woman like you deserves a man who wouldn't flaunt your body for everyone to see. Who'll treat it like the treasure it is."

Is he implying that he'd be that man?

I manage to swallow the burst of hysterical laughter that bubbles up my throat, but my eyes snap up to stare into his.

My voice comes out equally low but tart. "I'm well aware. How do you propose I fix that problem? Are you going to act out all the promises of pleasure you made to me right here in front of Marclinus?"

Raul's smoldering expression stutters. "Are you asking me to?" he says, but his provocative tone is edged with sudden uncertainty.

"I'm not an idiot. I simply thought I should remind you just how powerless *you* are here, since you thought I'd enjoy having you do the same for me. Or is it not all that fun to have salt rubbed in a wound after all?"

Raul opens his mouth and closes it again. I think this is the first time I've seen him lost for words, whether angry or seductive.

Anger comes first, with a roughening of his tone. "I never offered to rescue you, Lamb."

Maybe this is a mistake, rebuffing his advances. But I'm too wrung out right now to care.

I've gotten two of his foster brothers to warm up to me. Who says I need Raul's help too?

"No," I reply as the melody peters out. "You offered me an alternative that's not really an alternative at all, just a sham of passion. You'll have to forgive me if I decline."

I leave him staring at me, his face flushed and his jaw tight.

I drift through two more dances before the view beyond the window shows total blackness. Marclinus motions for the musicians to stop. A row of maids appears by the doorway, each of them clutching a dress for us.

With the remaining threads of my self-restraint, I stay where I am rather than dashing over to claim mine from Melisse. Marclinus rubs his hands together with a self-satisfied air, as if he's immensely pleased with how the latest trial has gone.

Well, why shouldn't he be? He got everything he wanted from us.

I ready myself to walk calmly over to the waiting maids

on his dismissal. Once I'm moving at all, it'll be harder not to dash.

The imperial heir sweeps his gaze over us once more, an arrogant grin playing with his lips. "Today has given me plenty of opportunity to consider all the assets my potential brides possess. Unfortunately, not all of them are quite as pleasing to my tastes as the others."

Emperor Tarquin speaks up from his chair. "A factor their elders surely should have considered before putting them forward as candidates."

My spirits start to sink. We aren't through with the trial after all. Is he really going to cut down our number again over something as out of our control as his physical preferences?

What if he's decided my scars repulse him after all?

"Yes," Marclinus says, so cheerful about it I'd like to strangle him. "A grave oversight that speaks to selfishness and lack of consideration for one's rulers. I must eliminate the least suitable of you now. I'm afraid you should have known there could never have been any passion between us, Lady Rochelle."

My heart plummets so swiftly it might crash through the floor. A sound like a whimper escapes my friend where she's standing beside me.

A guard strides toward us, drawing his sword just like the one who slaughtered Jovitte this afternoon.

In a matter of seconds, it'll be Rochelle crumpling in a spray of her own blood.

No. I can't let it happen. I can't make my peace with this act.

The guard moves to brush past me, and my voice bursts from my throat. "Wait!"

The guard's steps falter. He pauses with a flick of a glance toward me and then a questioning look at Marclinus.

The imperial heir studies me with a bemused expression. No one's outright protested any of the executions before, have they?

He speaks in his usual careless tone, but a silky note of warning runs through it. "What reason do you have for concern, Princess Aurelia?"

I thought I'd been overly ogled all day, but nothing compares to the pressure of the gazes burning into me now from all around the room. The whole court is waiting to see what I'll say, whether I'm going to call the blade to my neck as well.

What in the realms *can* I say?

I drag in a careful breath to delay my answer, my gaze flitting across the room as if I might find an answer there. It snags on Prince Bastien's sallow face where he's staring from the sidelines.

The answers he gave last night come back to me in a jumble. How a person could escape the palace. *They'd need a collaborator to smuggle them out.*

If there's a way that I can bring Rochelle *with* me, right under the emperor's nose…

The rustle of the dresses in the maids' arms sets off a collision of ideas in my head. My pulse skips with momentary exhilaration.

But I'm going to have to sell the proposal with a pitch perfectly tailored to the man hearing my appeal.

I don't feel right trying to curtsy nude, but I bow my head low with a similar positioning of my arms, figuring that can't hurt my case. "I apologize for interrupting, Your Imperial Highness. It's only, I think I might be able to suggest an even better punishment for Lady Rochelle's failure."

An eager gleam lights in Marclinus's eyes. That remark has caught his attention.

He crosses his arms in front of him. "And what would that be?"

I give a sheepish laugh as if I'm a bit embarrassed by my boldness. "It's selfish, I'll admit. But it could serve both our purposes. I'm used to having multiple maidservants to call on. I'm not sure I've been able to present myself to you at my best while relying on one. Lady Rochelle has shown a keen eye for apparel. I'd be grateful to exploit her skill more directly, without the effort of feigning friendship. What if *Lady* Rochelle died and became Rochelle the maid?"

He needs to believe I couldn't possibly be making this request out of compassion rather than cruelty, that any evidence that I cared about her was merely a ploy. Please, let my act work.

A brief noise of consternation is muffled somewhere in the crowd behind me. Maybe Rochelle's father, who might actually think that seeing his daughter stripped of her title and status is worse than watching her murdered.

I'm sure Marclinus can't conceive of a humiliation much worse than having to serve the people who were once your equals. *He'd* probably choose death first.

He taps his finger against his lips near his scar. "And you wouldn't be worried about keeping around a woman who also had her aims set on me?"

I force a haughty chuckle, keeping my gaze fixed on him. Not letting myself look at Rochelle even though she's right next to me, her arms wrapped tightly around her belly now.

I can't let him see how much I actually care about her. I

can't bear to witness how she's reacting to the way I'm talking about her.

"How could I see her as a threat?" I ask. "You've just said you feel no passion at all for her. And I can't imagine you wanting a passionless partnership."

"True. Very true."

My heart thuds as Marclinus ponders the proposition. He shifts his attention to Rochelle. "What do you have to say about this, Lady Rochelle? Would you accept Princess Aurelia's offer and live on as her maid?"

My breath catches in my throat, but Rochelle gives him exactly the answer he needs to hear.

She bends into a pleading posture, her voice hoarse. "Please, Your Imperial Highness, let me receive my rightful execution with honor. To face that degradation, and from a supposed friend who's proven herself so false…"

Her voice breaks with a wobble.

A triumphant expression crosses Marclinus's face. "No one here should be getting off easy, especially those who've disappointed the imperial line. How clever was my princess to come up with such a fitting punishment? Princess Aurelia, she is yours."

I bob my head again, restraining the majority of my relief. "Thank you, Your Imperial Highness. You are so generous to those who earn your favor."

He wipes his hands together. "I am, aren't I?"

When I lift my gaze, Rochelle is still cringing by my side. Fausta's glare would be stabbing straight through me if it got any sharper.

And Prince Lorenzo has moved within my view, his dark face taut with revulsion.

I smile at all of them as winningly as I can while an ache

wraps around my heart. How much more hatred have I earned with an act I meant out of kindness?

CHAPTER TWENTY-SIX

Aurelia

Melisse's chin trembles as she helps me into my gown. "I didn't realize you were so dissatisfied with my services, Your Highness."

It appears my gambit has upset even more people than I anticipated. I'm not entirely sure *anyone's* happy about the turn of events I just orchestrated except for the imperial heir.

"It's not that at all," I reassure her while keeping my voice appropriately cool for our difference in status. There are still too many keen eyes and ears around us. "I would simply be better served by staff with a variety of strengths. It wouldn't do to place an overlarge burden on you alone. Speaking of which…"

Committing as fully as I can to my act, I turn toward Rochelle and clap my hands in summons. "Rochelle, I'd like you to attend to me in my chambers now to decide on tomorrow's attire." I raise my voice. "Can someone bring her an outfit suitable for her new station?"

Within minutes, Rochelle has donned one of the black and gray dresses worn by the female attending staff and we're proceeding down the hall toward my bedroom. She trudges along a couple of steps behind me, as is also appropriate.

And possibly for the best, because I'm not sure how well I could keep up this front if I had to look her in the face.

I unlock the door and let her follow me inside. She turns the bolt in our wake, perhaps on instinct from when she's entered her own room in the past.

She'll never have chambers to herself again as long as she dwells in the palace.

I turn around, an explanation I'm not sure she'll accept choking me on the way up—and Rochelle throws her arms around me.

"Thank you," she whispers as if she's still afraid of being overheard, squeezing me tight. Her curls spill against my face. "You did it, Aurelia. Gods, you actually *saved* me."

All at once, I'm choked up for a completely different reason.

I hug her back, thanking all the gods there are that the person who mattered most in my gambit understood my purpose. "You did well with your part. *I* believed you saying you'd rather die."

Rochelle pulls back, grimacing. "I just knew that would make him even more eager to go along with your idea. That absolute *prick…*"

I can't restrain a rough laugh. "You don't have to worry about marrying him now. You can stay with me as long as you need to until it's safe, and then I'll see you get back home to your beloved medic. Your father can't pressure you about a match befitting your station anymore."

A teary sheen fills Rochelle's eyes. She wipes at them, letting out a breathless guffaw of her own. "I can't believe— it's amazing that you pulled it off. Gods, Tevio will be so worried when he hears. Do you think there's any way we could send him a letter that won't give away the truth?"

"I'm sure I can figure out a reasonable cover story. Let me know how to address it, and I'll get something sent off in the morning."

"That would be wonderful. Thank you so much, Aurelia. I'll be the best maid you've ever had once I figure out how."

I squeeze her shoulder, my own eyes prickling. "You don't have to worry about that. Let's focus on getting me through the rest of these trials alive so I can make good on my promise. But first, I think we could both use some sleep." I pause. "I'm not sure where you *will* be sleeping from now on."

"I know where the servants' quarters are. I'd imagine they always have a few extra beds." She shakes her head, the light in her eyes fading, but only for a second.

With a renewed smile, she hustles over to my wardrobe. "But first I should make sure you have the absolute best dress to keep Marclinus's eyes on you tomorrow. Hmm. This one looked wonderful on you, but I think if we cinch it just a little more right here…"

"I trust your judgment," I tell her honestly, and drag myself to the wash basin to prepare for my own much-needed sleep.

I wake with a hitch of my pulse, not sure what interrupted my rest. With the first blinks of my bleary eyes, I half expect to find the three princes standing around my bed again, sneering at me for humiliating my supposed friend.

All three of them might very well see me as a spoiled, selfish outsider again, but none of them have interrupted my sleep tonight. The room around me is empty.

Knitting my brow, I peer through the expansive space— and hear a faint patter from behind the nearest set of curtains.

I ease out of bed and peer behind the heavy fabric. My heart skips a beat.

A pure white dove is fluttering by the window. It glides down almost to the outer ledge, then flaps its wings to ascend higher in front of the glass pane.

The dove is one of Elox's sacred animals. I haven't seen one anywhere around the palace since I arrived.

Is this a sign from my godlen?

If so, it's an insistent one. The dove flies in a wobbly circle in front of the window and then veers out into the yard. It swoops back to me and away again, as if it wants me to follow it.

I hesitate for only a second. Then I'm grabbing yesterday's dress, not wanting to risk sullying the one Rochelle adjusted for tomorrow. Once I've yanked it over my head, I hurry out and through the halls to the nearest way out.

I slip around the side of the palace, peering up toward the second floor. A glimmer of white catches the moonlight above me and then dips lower. The dove sails past me and onward over the gardens.

There must be something Elox wants me to see. Something that will help me fulfill the rest of my goals here?

I hustle after the bird as quickly as I can while staying

quiet. It never circles back, only flying straight ahead until its pale form disappears amid the shadows of the woods.

When I follow the dove between the trees, it takes a moment before I make out the white feathers in a streak of moonlight. The creature flutters onward, and I weave between the trees on its trail.

For a few fleeting moments, I catch a melody in the distance—notes strummed on a lute. Is Lorenzo out here practicing his new instrument this late at night?

If so, the dove isn't leading me toward him. As I pad on through the woods, the music soon fades behind me. Then there's nothing but the soft rustling of the leaves in the warm night breeze and the rasp of my feet over the twigs and pebbles that scatter the ground.

It's perhaps several minutes later when the dove finally lands on a branch and stays there. I squint through the darkness, taking in the spot it's brought me to.

One of the woods' largest trees lies on its side, moss coating the crumbling bark. It must have fallen months if not years ago. A deeper shadow marks the ground where its roots pulled up from the earth, a steeply-sided hollow left behind. I can't see anything else at all noteworthy about this spot compared to any other area of the palace woods.

I ease forward to take a closer look at the fallen tree—and at the corner of my eye, the dove disappears.

Not flies away, not hops behind a patch of leaves. Simply blinks out of existence in an instant.

As my head jerks toward the branch where it landed, four women step out from behind the nearby trees to form a semi-circle between me and my path back to the palace.

Fausta's fiery hair gleams bright even in the thin moonlight. Her eyes shine equally fierce. "Look at that. The princess fell for the simplest trick of all. Some cleverness."

As haughty as her voice is, it's also a little ragged. I re-evaluate the porcelain pale of her skin—perhaps turned sickly not by the dim lighting but by efforts expended. The tufts of hair along her forehead droop with sweat.

My hands ball at my sides. "It was an illusion."

One she appears to have conjured at significant personal expense. Whatever gift Inganne gave her, she stretched it to her limits with that small deception.

Next to her friend, Bianca lets out a soft but mocking laugh. "Too bad you didn't figure that out sooner."

They're standing with two other ladies of the court—young but married by their pinned-up hair. Friends who're part of their venomous pack.

I focus on Fausta and Bianca, who are obviously the ringleaders. "Why did you drag me out here in the middle of the night?"

Fausta's eyes narrow, glinting hard as emeralds. "What have you ever done for him to call you *his* princess? You've never really fought for him this entire time, not as I have. So let's see you fight now."

With her last word, one of the other ladies twitches her hand, and the ground beneath me lurches. Only a little, but so abrupt and unexpected that I stumble.

In the same moment, all four of the noblewomen launch themselves at me.

Bianca snatches my hair and yanks my head back so sharply pain lances up my neck. Fausta drives her knee into my back, a vulnerable spot just above my hip. Another of the ladies twists my arm behind me while the fourth drives the hard heel of her shoe into my foot.

A bone crunches, and agony explodes up my leg. I cry out, staggering away from them, thrashing with fists and elbows to try to fend them off.

A few of my strikes land to grunts and pained gasps. Every lady in Accasy's court learns at least a little self-defense.

But it would take a stronger fighter than I am to fend off four opponents all on my own. Especially when they've already gotten the upper hand.

I can't take more than a hobbling step before I'm shoved back into their ring of blows. Fingernails rake across my cheek; a kick brings me to my knees.

Bianca wallops me across the side of my head, leaving my mind spinning and my skull throbbing. Fausta slams her foot down on the back of my other leg, and my shin bone cracks with a blaze of pain.

I rasp a breath and start to scream, as little chance as there might be of anyone hearing my cry all the way over in the palace. Before I can get out more than a brief shriek, Bianca punches me right in the throat.

I choke and sputter. Fausta aims another vicious knee at my ribs, setting off a splintering ache through my side.

Then she motions to her friends, and they all shove me over the lip of the hollow into the deep cavity left by the fallen tree's roots.

Fausta lets out a laugh that's more a cackle. "I hope you enjoy your last day or two knowing no one will even think to look for you here."

She and her friends grab a few handfuls of sticks and other debris and toss them down on me in a battering rain. Giggling amongst themselves, they dart off into the night.

I sprawl on my side, my breath coming in short hitches of anguish. My elbow on my dominant arm is at best sprained, any movement sending pain stabbing out from the joint.

With my other hand, I swipe the sticks away from my face and peer at the depression I'm stuck in. Just a slight squirm toward the steep earthen side of the hollow has me whimpering in pain through my bruised throat.

One leg broken, the other foot fractured. I don't think I can even crawl.

I try to lift my voice in a shout, but all that comes out is a faint rasp. The impact of Bianca's punch has dulled my capacity for speech.

My head sinks down to rest on the uneven earth. When I stop moving, the pain dwindles to the edge of my consciousness.

My thoughts swim into clearer focus with kindling resolve.

I'm not letting my journey end here. Not letting those vicious shrews have the last laugh.

Closing my eyes, I direct a silent prayer toward my godlen. *I came out here out of faith in you, Elox. Give me the strength to make my return.*

A faint quiver of energy ripples through my nerves, stirring my determination. I squint at my surroundings again.

First I need to get out of this cursed hole.

With my jaw clenched tight, I dig my good elbow into the earthen side of the hollow. As I wriggle my hips upward with my arm for leverage, my ribs scream, but I end up leaning partly against the slope rather than sprawled at the bottom of the cavity.

I stop and pant, splinters jabbing through my lungs.

I can make it to the top. Bit by bit. One heave at a time.

I brace my elbow and squirm, brace and squirm. The ache in my side sears hotter, and my head throbs harder.

The forest floor has just come into view when my broken foot smacks against a stone, and the roar of pain drowns out my thoughts completely.

CHAPTER TWENTY-SEVEN

Aurelia

I don't realize I fell unconscious until my eyes flutter open again.

In that first instant of waking, my mind hasn't quite caught up to everything I've been through in the past several hours. I recognize that I'm lying on dry earth with morning sunlight wavering through leaves overhead, and move to push myself upright.

The spike of agony that pierces through me from head to toe shocks me right back to the present.

I crumple back down against the side of the hollow and make an attempt at clearing my throat. My vocal cords still sear with pain.

When I part my lips and attempt to call out, I sound more like I'm gargling than yelling.

I can see over the lip of the hole, but even lifting my good arm toward the surface makes me flinch. All my injuries have set in, and my initial rush of adrenaline has faded.

It's hard to imagine being able to pull myself the rest of the way out of the hollow, let alone all the way to the palace gardens.

What now?

I'm scrambling for some kind of solution when the crunch of footsteps reaches my ears.

My heart leaps. The sound was distant, but it can't have come from too far off if I was able to hear it.

Another twig snaps. The underbrush rustles with someone's passage.

And a voice that's low but pitched to carry wavers through the woods. "Aurelia? Are you out here?"

That sounds strangely like… Prince Raul.

Why would he be wandering the woods? Why would he be looking for me?

Both questions are better answered after I'm found.

I try to lift my voice again. "I'm over here!"

The rasping words are barely louder than a whisper. I don't hear any sign that my call was noticed.

There has to be another way. I grope around with my uninjured arm and grasp one of the larger sticks Fausta and her friends hurled down on me.

Extending the stick as far as I can without fainting with agony, I rap it against the base of the fallen tree. The stick clatters against the log.

Not quite loud enough. Gritting my teeth, I smack the mossy wood with all the strength I have left.

The distant footsteps stop. "Did you hear that?"

Another voice—Prince Bastien's even cadence. "That way."

I keep flailing at the log even as tears form at the corners of my eyes. The bruised and possibly fractured ribs in my side send a pulsing burn through my torso.

The approaching figures pick up speed, crackling through the brush. I'm just lowering my arm with a gasp for breath when they hurtle into the small clearing around the fallen tree.

It's not just Raul and Bastien but Lorenzo as well. They jerk to a halt. Lorenzo's dark eyes widen while Bastien's jaw goes slack.

Raul speaks first, with a snarl resonating through his words. "That treacherous bitch."

In my dazed state, I almost think he's talking about *me*. Then he scrambles down into the depression next to me, his hand hovering over my shoulder while panic flashes across his face. "What did she do to you?"

I swallow against the pain in my throat and manage a few brief croaks. "Broken leg. Foot. Ribs."

Bastien's mouth has twisted into a grimace of fury. "And hit her hard in the throat, from the sound of it. Fucking harridans. It *was* Fausta and her pack of vipers, wasn't it?"

I manage a nod, and he sucks a hiss of a breath through clenched teeth. "The way they were smirking at breakfast when Marclinus commented about you not showing up— Fausta even made a comment about how you'd probably run off. Thank the gods Lorenzo remembered he'd seen them wandering around out here last night. Hold on, let me…"

He eases down the side of the hollow more cautiously than Raul did, but his expression is no less fraught. His dark green gaze skims my jumble of limbs, tracking the damage.

I don't really understand why they're so concerned about my well-being all of a sudden. Considering how we made our acquaintance and the performance I gave last night, I'd be less surprised if they'd come to celebrate my downfall.

Lorenzo makes an urgent sound, crouching at the edge of the hollow. I can't follow his hasty gesture, but Bastien must understand.

"I don't know if it's safe to move her," he says, his own voice strained. "If we don't stabilize her properly, we could make things worse."

He peers down at me, his grimace deepening. "I don't suppose you know any brews for healing broken bones, Medic Princess?"

Even with all the pain I'm in, I can't restrain a snort. "It'll take… a real medic."

He curses under his breath and looks over at Raul. Bastien's face has tensed with frustration, which makes even less sense to me when Raul bares his teeth in silent comprehension. "That fucking prick Tarquin."

Now I'm totally lost. What has the emperor got to do with any of this? If *he* decided he no longer approved of me, he'd have his guards slit my throat, not send the other ladies to discard me in the woods.

Bastien grazes his fingers over my hair in an unexpectedly gentle gesture. Maybe trying to soften the blow of what he says next. "Early in the trials, Emperor Tarquin gave orders to the imperial medics that they're not to interfere if any of the potential brides manage to sabotage each other without getting caught in the act. That they should let nature 'run its course' and the strong prevail."

The disgust in his voice makes it clear exactly what he thinks of that attitude.

I know without even prodding my gift that there's no concoction in the world that can meld together a body broken like mine is. I could dampen the pain, yes, but I'd still be unable to walk, incapable of even sitting up without help.

Raul growls. "I'll drag that cunt out here by her fucking throat and make her account for what she's done. Cutting down the one woman in this mess who has anything like a heart…"

I look up in time to see Bastien glaring at him. "Assaulting Fausta is only going to get you thrown in a jail cell—or in your own grave. Being an idiot won't help Aurelia."

Raul glowers back at him, every muscle in his massive body flexing with his seething energy. "She's going to pay one way or another."

Lorenzo reaches out to tap Bastien's shoulder for his attention. Whatever he communicates, the other prince's expression turns pensive. "Yes, even in this situation, that might work. With the right leverage…"

He turns back to Raul. "You still haven't told anyone the thing about Flacos, have you? We didn't think it was worth humbling him."

Raul's pale eyes light up so avidly it would probably terrify me if I didn't know his rage is on my behalf. "I still have that secret in my back pocket. Has he got a gift that'll work for knitting bone?"

"I don't know, but even if he doesn't, it might be enough to persuade him to bring one of his colleagues on board to help."

"Maybe… Let's see if we can put a little fear into him and get the job done." Raul's gaze drops to me again. His hand, still extended tentatively over my shoulder without quite touching it, clenches into a fist. "And quickly."

I have no idea what they're talking about—or whether I'd agree to this plan. "What are you going to do?" I rasp.

A savage smile curves Raul's lips. "My gift told me a little something about one of the medics on staff that he wouldn't want anyone else knowing. We'll get you healed, Princess—he can be paid with my continued silence."

He sounds utterly certain, but as he and Bastien get to their feet, my stomach knots. "Wait."

What if he's overestimated the sway he'll have over this man? What if his ploy only exposes Fausta's victory over me so that it can no longer be concealed?

The princes stare at me.

"What?" Raul demands. "Do you have a better idea?"

Bastien's penetrating gaze takes the measure of me. "Or she isn't sure she can trust us. Which might be fair enough, but I don't think you have many options, Aurelia."

Lorenzo's fingers shift at his side in a few emphatic motions. *We'll help you.*

My throat constricts around the sting. I don't want to put my life in their hands… They've toyed with it enough times themselves.

But they're here. They came looking for me; they've raged on my behalf.

Isn't this why I started cultivating their good will in the first place? What would have been the point if I throw away their aid when I need it most?

I dip my head. "All right. Try your plan."

Raul simply grins.

Bastien points to Lorenzo. "Persuading Flacos is mostly going to take talking. Stay with her in case Fausta's crew decides to come back to gloat."

Lorenzo gives a gesture of agreement followed by something else that makes the other prince nod.

"Good thinking." Bastien casts his gaze down on me once more. "We'll be back as quickly as we can. Stay strong."

As he and Raul lope off through the woods, Lorenzo sits down on the side of the hollow to join me. He takes my hand in his gingerly and then twines our fingers when I show no sign of discomfort.

A sudden burn forms behind my eyes, as comforting as the gesture is. Maybe *because* of how comforting it is.

I thought I'd destroyed all the progress I'd made with these men with yesterday's stunt. But somehow the three princes I've clashed and sparred with are on my side—and more passionately determined to help me than I'd ever have expected.

Even with the evidence right in front of me, I have trouble wrapping my head around that idea. I peer up at Lorenzo as if I can read the answers to my confusion in his handsome face.

With him so close, I can get away with simply murmuring. "After last night, I thought you'd all be back to hating me."

Lorenzo's forehead furrows as if he doesn't know what I'm talking about.

I make a face. "The way I treated Lady Rochelle?"

He blinks and then sputters a sort-of chuckle. The motion of his free hand toward me, then covering his face, then pressing to his heart convey a clear enough message.

You were hiding that you cared.

A lump fills my throat. They recognized that? They trusted what I've shown them enough to believe my cruelty was an act and not my kindnesses before?

That's what Raul must have meant about me being the one woman with a heart. The horrified look on Lorenzo's face last night—it was prompted by Marclinus's attitude rather than mine.

It's possible saving Rochelle won the princes to my side more instead of pushing them away.

How is it that these three men who started out

terrorizing me know me better than the man who claims to be considering me as his lifelong partner?

"I also told off Raul quite a bit," I feel the need to add.

Lorenzo's mouth twitches with a grin. I think the next flicks of his fingers are meant to convey, *He likes that.*

My guffaw prickles up my throat. "Sure he does."

Apparently I didn't offend Raul so much that he wrote me off, though.

The effort of speaking has set off the pain in my ribs again. I let my eyes drift shut.

Lorenzo keeps holding my hand, using his other to brush stray strands of hair away from my forehead. His touch lingers on my face.

All at once, my heart is aching more than any other part of me.

The bell of the hour peals beyond the palace walls. It's hard to tell how long it's been before footsteps tramp back toward us, punctuated by hushed but urgent voices.

I open my eyes just as Raul and Bastien come into view at the top of the hollow, flanking a middle-aged man with wispy salt-and-pepper hair atop his narrow face. I saw him overseeing the medics who healed our burned hands in that previous trial, though I never spoke to him directly.

As he studies my crumpled form, he frowns. "What did you say happened here?"

"She fell," Bastien says flatly. "What does it matter? She needs healing."

"She fell three feet and managed to break several bones all through her body, *and* end up with a bruised throat?"

At the medic's obvious skepticism, my chest tightens. He's not easily fooled.

Raul narrows his eyes. "You're going to fix her up as well

as you can, or the emperor's going to find out just how much you've exploited his generosity in supplies."

I've never heard the prince sound so ominous.

The man's tan face grays. "I have no idea what you're talking about."

"No? You really don't think that *I* could have noticed what you're carrying on you when you take your little trips out of the palace—what is it, every tenth evening?"

A shiver runs through the medic's frame, but he makes one final protest. "I have orders from Their Imperial Eminences not to interfere—"

"*Fuck* your orders. Work your magic, or we're marching you straight to Emperor Tarquin right now."

My body stays tensed, but the man only hesitates for a moment longer. Muttering something to himself, he slides into the hollow next to Lorenzo and examines my legs. "I'd better start here."

Bastien folds his arms over his chest. "Be quick about it. We need her back at the palace as soon as possible."

The medic rests his hand on my shin. Warmth courses through my flesh, followed by a piercing sensation that makes me wince.

But the tension in Bastien's voice niggles at me. He bends down to pass a small drinking skin to Lorenzo, who brings the spout to my lips. The cool water dribbles down my sore throat.

As Lorenzo draws back the skin, I catch Bastien's gaze. My voice comes out a little smoother. "Why the rush?"

His mouth tightens. "Marclinus is calling for all his remaining ladies to attend to him at the next bell. If you're not there... I don't think there's any excuse that will appease him."

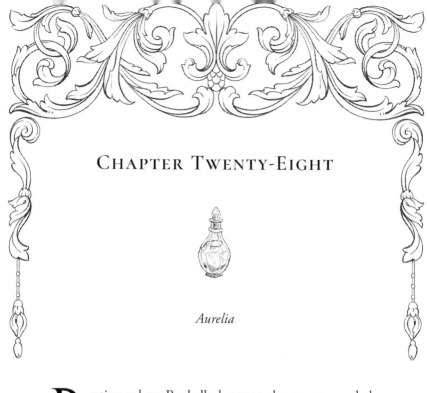

Chapter Twenty-Eight

Aurelia

Bastien ushers Rochelle between the trees toward the clearing. The moment she spots me, she dashes forward twice as fast. "Thank the gods! I brought the dress. You'd better hurry."

She hauls the gown she picked out for me last night from the large picnic basket where she had it heaped in beneath a blanket.

After spending all yesterday fully on display for the entire court, I don't even think about stripping to my underclothes to yank the new dress over my head, despite the three princes still on guard around me.

Rochelle babbles on as she helps me adjust the waist. "I had no idea what to tell anyone. I was so worried. And Fausta and Bianca wouldn't stop spewing out 'speculations' that you'd abandoned the trials. I said you were taking a little time to yourself to clear your head and prepare for the next trial, but I don't know how much the emperor believed me. Are you really all right?"

I can't do anything but smile at my friend and her frantic concern. "All right enough to keep going, and the rest of the healing will happen in its own time."

Flacos the medic set all my broken bones and sealed the cracks. He was able to smooth over some of the damage to my throat too. But there is no perfect healing magic.

I can feel the tiny tears that linger in my muscles with twinges every time I adjust my stance or turn at the waist. I don't think attempting a sprint would be wise for at least the next few days. And I'll be keeping speeches to a minimum until the stinging sensation has completely eased when I swallow.

While Rochelle runs the brush she brought through my mussed hair in a few swift strokes, Lorenzo shoves the old, soiled dress into the basket and covers it. The moment my friend is finished tending to me, Raul grabs the basket and shoves it into Rochelle's hands. "Get her where she needs to go, and keep your mouth shut."

I frown at him. "She's on my side. More than *you've* been in the time since I arrived here."

Raul clamps his lips together with a trace of a wince.

Rochelle peers at him and the other princes with obvious curiosity, but she takes his order to heart despite my defending her. Setting a steadying hand on my upper arm, she sets off for the palace alongside me.

"The princes found you?" she murmurs when we're out of hearing distance. "I didn't realize you'd talked much with them. They seem very... invested."

I mustn't be imagining their intensity if she noticed it too. I give the answer that makes the most sense while still being acceptable. "They know as well as I do what it's like to end up here from homes beyond Dariu's borders. It's hard not to bond a little over that kind of common experience."

"Oh! Yes, of course, I didn't even think of that." Rochelle flushes. "Honestly, most of the time it feels as if you fit in at the palace better than I do. I almost forget how new you are to court."

I reach to set my hand over hers against my arm. "I take that as a compliment. And thank you for doing your best to cover for my disappearance. If I'd had any way to get word to you—"

"I know. That's not *your* fault." Her expression turns fierce. "How are you going to deal with Fausta?"

My stomach twists at the thought of the petite redhead— at the memories of her caustic words and vicious blows last night. "Keep my distance and be twice as cautious. I can't accuse her without revealing that I was healed against Emperor Tarquin's orders, and gods only know what the emperor would do to me—or the medic who helped me —then."

Rochelle lets out her breath in a huff. "I always knew she could be conniving, but to go that far…" She cringes. "I think it's going to take a while before the other staff really see me as one of them, but if I overhear anything about her or Bianca that sounds ominous, I'll let you know right away."

I wish the loss of her title brought her more immediate benefits than just avoiding murder. Gods willing, it won't take too long after the trials are finished—assuming *I* can avoid being murdered during them—for me to send her where she truly wants to be.

We cross the gardens and clamber up the stairs to the audience room, where Marclinus demanded everyone's presence. Pain throbs from my recently healed foot and shin.

In the hall, Rochelle gives my arm one last squeeze and

heads toward my bedroom. She's no longer welcome as a participant in courtly affairs—and it's better for both of us if no one has a chance to pay attention to that picnic basket before she can stash the dirt-stained gown amongst my things.

Willing back the discomforts of my body, I march into the audience room.

In the first instant after I cross the threshold, I feel as if I've stepped back in time to my very first day here, when I entered this room before the entire court just like I appear to be doing now.

Back then, I hadn't the faintest clue what I was actually walking into.

I stride with measured grace to where the other five ladies still vying for my betrothed stand arrayed before the two imperial thrones. When Lady Fausta glances over and sees me, her face blanches almost as white as it looked after she'd exhausted herself conjuring the illusion of the dove.

Like she's seen a ghost.

I hold my satisfaction tight inside and aim a pleasant smile at my fellow competitors. When I reach the front of the room, I dip into a curtsy meant to encompass both of Their Imperial Eminences.

The ache in my weakened legs sears deeper, but I straighten up without a wobble.

Marclinus is watching me with one of his cooler expressions. He's toying with a dagger, running the point beneath one fingernail. "Princess Aurelia. You deprived me of your company for most of the morning."

As if on cue, the hourly bell rings out, marking just how close I came to missing his deadline.

"My apologies, Your Imperial Highness." I lower my head for additional deference. "It wasn't my intention to neglect you. I took a stroll through the woods to meditate on how I might best continue to please you and lost track of the time. It was a pleasure to see a little wildness celebrated here as it is back in Accasy. Perhaps we can take a similar walk together sometime."

Marclinus hums noncommittally. The brief tightening of his mouth emphasizes the scar notched through his upper lip.

An uneasy prickle runs over my skin. How much of his favor has Fausta's attack cost me, even if she didn't accomplish her greater purpose?

I keep my gaze trained on the imperial heir, but I can't help noting the moment each of the princes arrives in the room to join Neven on the platform in their usual places. Marclinus doesn't so much as glance their way.

He didn't care about them being on time. This was a test for *me* more than anyone else, even his other prospective brides.

And I don't think it's over yet.

Marclinus flips his dagger and slides it into the sheath at his hip. He speaks in a languid tone. "The six of you ladies have all proven yourselves admirably so far. The cream that's risen to the top. But we haven't finished our evaluations yet."

Emperor Tarquin lifts his dry voice from where he's been watching the proceedings from his own throne. "If anything, your continued dedication to my son is more important now than it ever was. We certainly wouldn't want to see complacency or faltering enthusiasm after making it this far."

Who the fuck does the emperor think could be *complacent* after what they've put us through?

I shouldn't have needed to worry about complacency in the first place. I should have been able to assume that my betrothal was set as agreed upon, not a promise dangled like bait.

I suppress all those thoughts behind my agreeable smile as Marclinus picks up the thread. He leans forward in his chair with a cool grin. "So we're giving you all the chance to confirm that you're still fully committed to seeing through the rest of the trials ahead, now that you've had a taste of them. Please present yourselves one by one and beg me for the opportunity to continue."

He wants us to *beg*?

Even as bile lurches up my throat, my legs are propelling me forward. I haven't forgotten the lesson Fausta schooled us in on the very first day of the trials.

Whoever gets to the imperial heir first has no acts to follow.

There's a slight scuffing of shoes against the floor behind me, as if Fausta started to throw herself forward but caught herself on seeing I'd leapt in first. Her trickery might have come back to bite her in one small way—she was so stunned by seeing me well it set her off-balance.

But I still have to figure out how to convincingly plead for the chance to go through all the additional torments Marclinus and his father have in store for us.

Prostration seems like an excellent place to start—and a way to buy my whirling mind a few more seconds to pull together a coherent plea. I drop to my knees at the edge of the dais in front of the imperial heir, bowing my head so low my hair drapes across the floor.

"Please, Your Imperial Eminences," I say in my humblest voice, deciding it can't hurt to speak to both of them even if I'm focusing on Marclinus. The heir might be making some of his own decisions, but it's Tarquin who holds most of the power. "I did not even know just how much earning your good favor mattered to me until these past several days. The challenges you've presented have impressed me to no end with how discerning you are. I have no thought left in my mind, no concern to occupy me other than what will serve you both, but especially Your Imperial Highness, best."

Someone, maybe Bianca, lets out a faint scoffing sound. I don't dare raise my head yet to take in Marclinus's expression.

"Thank you for honing my purpose and giving me the chance to prove my worth. There is nothing I want more than to keep doing so, in every way you can conceive of and to whatever lengths you desire, so that you know I will put in the same effort throughout any future I get to spend with you. Please, simply tell me what you would want of me next, and I will oblige with all I am."

The effusive lies leave my stomach churning. I remain prostrate in front of the imperial heir, awaiting his response.

A slow clap carries from the throne. "Very pretty, Princess Aurelia," Marclinus drawls. "You set a high standard to meet. It would be my pleasure to continue discovering how you might please me."

No doubt. I will down the shamed flush that flares in my cheeks and rise with one more dip of my head. "I'm immensely grateful for your generosity, Your Imperial Highness."

Naturally, the moment I step away from the dais, Fausta prances in to plead her case next. She practically sobs with her statement of how much the opportunity means to her and how she's appreciated getting to know Marclinus to new depths.

The imperial heir takes it all in with the same air of cool amusement. He's not in so much of a leering mood today, but his more subdued attitude leaves me on edge.

What else is he plotting?

Nothing quite yet, it appears. The other four of the remaining ladies beg with abandon, and Marclinus approves of us all without even looking toward his father. Perhaps they'd already decided in advance that my appeal was the only one they truly needed to evaluate.

After the last of the ladies has spoken, Emperor Tarquin gets to his feet with an authoritative air. "I'm gratified to see how much passion these ladies have for my son and heir. Before we have any further excitement, I believe it's time to eat."

CHAPTER TWENTY-NINE

Aurelia

My nerves stay jittery throughout the luncheon, but the worst threats I encounter are Fausta's and Bianca's glowers. They seem to have gotten over their shock and are now attempting to finish the job they started by glaring daggers at me at every opportunity.

They're only going to be more vicious now—more determined to remove me from the competition. And given Fausta's gift for illusion, however small, I'll need to stay twice as on guard.

I can't trust even my senses around them.

When I leave the table, I find Rochelle waiting near the doorway, her hands clasped awkwardly in front of her as she endures her former equals' stares.

"I thought I'd see if there's anything you might need," she murmurs once I reach her. "If you'd like me to fetch anything from your room or run you a bath…"

Her presence is one small bright spot in this awful day. I smile gratefully. "A bath would be lovely, but in a few hours. Right now, I think I'll retire on my own for a nap." I can't say my doze in the woods was exactly restful.

Rochelle bobs her head. "Shall I come at the fourth hour of the afternoon?"

"That sounds perfect. You can let Melisse know so she'll bring fresh towels." I don't want my original maid to feel I've cast her aside—or for Emperor Tarquin to think I asked for Rochelle's service to edge his regular staff out.

By the time I've navigated the halls to my bedroom, both of my legs are throbbing. Gritting my teeth, I unlock the door, step inside—and freeze just past the threshold.

The door thumps shut behind me. Prince Raul stands up from where he was sitting on the edge of my bed. His gaze rakes over me, as searing as always but not remotely cold this time.

"Why are you in here?" I demand.

He takes a step closer but stops before his height can become imposing. His eyes are completely fixed on mine now. "I couldn't eat. Not after watching you have to grovel in front of the imperial prick like that. I'd have spent the whole time holding myself back from launching myself across the table and bashing in his arrogant face. Or wringing that treacherous redhead's skinny neck for what *she* did to you."

The fury in his voice dwindles with a tightening of his tawny face. "And I can't do any of that. You were right. There's so fucking much I can't do for you."

A lump rises in my throat at those last words and the anguish running through them, but my tone stays tart. "And you thought startling me in my bedroom was a good alternative? How the fuck do you even keep getting in here?"

My profanity provokes a trace of a smile across Raul's lips. "We need to keep a few secrets."

In other words, no matter how much anger he showed on my behalf this morning, he doesn't fully trust me. There's a part of him that still wants to keep me on my toes.

Which means I can't trust him either.

I cross my arms over my chest. "You still haven't answered my first question. What are you doing here? I didn't expect you to beat up Marclinus or Fausta or anyone else for me, so you don't need to justify the lack of violence."

Raul spreads his hands. His voice takes on the husky note I find annoyingly compelling. "I can't get vengeance on those who deserve it yet, but that doesn't mean I can't do anything at all. I'd like to remind you of how a princess *should* be treated, in one of the few places where I can actually follow through. Whatever you want, you only have to ask for it."

The offer sends a heady pulse through me, but I arch one eyebrow in response. "I don't suppose you're angling for me to request any particular sort of 'treatment.'"

Raul's smile stretches into a grin, too crooked to be completely cocky. "Have I imagined having you gasping and moaning in that bed? Absolutely. I'd erase every memory of that asshole's touch. But I won't find it remotely satisfying if you're not just as eager for it. *I* don't put my hands where they're not wanted."

When I hesitate, he steps a little closer. His pale blue gaze holds mine. "You've been looking out for so many people other than yourself since you got here, haven't you? While everyone puts you through the wringer. No matter how strong you are, you must be getting exhausted. I mean it when I say you can ask for anything. What do you need most right now, Princess?"

Gods, what a question. I stare at him, doing my best to ignore the heat he's stirred beneath my skin.

I'm not tumbling into bed with this princely rake. I *would* like to get my weight off my aching legs.

My gaze slides across the room and lands on my vanity. The idea flutters up with a pang of longing that seems almost absurd.

It might be nice, just for once, to be taken care of in much simpler ways by someone who isn't obligated.

I walk over to the padded stool and seat myself in front of the vanity. My silver-handled brush is already lying out. I motion to it. "My hair has barely been brushed since yesterday, and my ribs still hurt when I lift my arms. You could see to that for me."

A snort escapes the prince. "Are you attempting to put together an entire collection of maids now?"

I glance at him over my shoulder. "Did you not mean 'whatever I want' after all, only what doesn't threaten your dignity?"

Raul narrows his eyes at me, but his smile stays in place. I don't think he's really offended.

Suddenly I can't help remembering the remark I thought Lorenzo made this morning when I mentioned telling Raul off. That he *liked* it.

Maybe he actually does enjoy being provoked, because he saunters over and picks up the brush. "I can't say I have much practice at this, but I'll give it my best shot."

"It's a remarkably simple process," I have to point out.

He chuckles and brings the brush to my hair. The moment the bristles graze my scalp, I realize I might have made a slight miscalculation.

He's standing so close the warmth of his body tingles

over my skin. The rhythmic stroke of the brush sets off even giddier quivers down my neck.

The act never felt quite so intimate when it was a maid handling it.

A flush starts to rise up my neck. I grope for a topic to distract us, and my eyes catch on the scarring across his no-longer bandaged knuckles in the mirror.

"Did the salve help at all? If you deigned to try it?"

Raul's fingers trail across the back of my neck as he eases some of my hair back over my shoulder for ease of access. "It does seem to move the healing process along faster. Too bad you can't use it on your bones."

I grimace at the reminder of my injuries, and the image floats up of a recent time when he took several wounds of his own. "Why do you fight in the exhibitions? Doesn't that just serve Emperor Tarquin's purposes?"

He shrugs with another stroke of the brush. "It serves my purposes just as much. I'm not sure I'd have been able to survive as long as I have without hurling myself at him and his heir if I didn't have other avenues to vent a little aggression."

"You couldn't find avenues that didn't require facing off against murderous warriors and savage beasts?"

The corner of his mouth kicks upward again. "I like a challenge. As I'd think should be obvious by now, Princess."

I suppose I walked into that one.

He moves to stand by my other shoulder, his fingertips gliding over my cheek as he gathers the hair there. More heat blooms in their wake.

"You've got a twig snagged in here. Maybe you do need more maids."

I glower at him in the mirror. "There wasn't really time

for a thorough job this morning. I'd appreciate you removing it now."

Somehow he manages to detangle the scrap of wood without any painful tugs. As he resumes his brushing, he studies me in the mirror. "You asked about my battles, but you're at least as much of a fighter as I am, even if you hide it. How did one of Elox's lambs end up tough enough to withstand a near-poisoning and a brutal beating in the course of a few days?"

How am I supposed to answer that? I tuck my hands together on my lap, my thumb running over my ring. "Elox doesn't reward *weakness*. There's a different sort of strength in being able to endure, to hold steady through chaos."

"Somehow I doubt most of even his clerics could have handled this situation with as much grace as you have. You'd put them to shame."

My mouth twists with a bittersweet smile. "I'm also the second princess of a conquered country. I've known from the start that my purpose will mean submitting to someone else's needs. And I had many years to prepare for that future, even if I didn't know exactly who or what it would entail until recently."

Unlike four seven-year-old boys who were thrown into this life before they'd had much chance to understand anything at all.

Raul's hand stills for a moment. "It shouldn't have to be like that. It's your life as much as your kingdom's."

"No, it's not."

I thought that once. For a short, glimmering stretch of time, I imagined a different kind of future.

I imagined, and the gods reminded me just how futile it was. Just how tragic those hopes could be.

It's better that I learned the costs of selfishness before I strayed down that path too far to recover.

Raul makes a rough sound. "You deserve better. In every way. You're so much more than a pawn."

"Sometimes a pawn is needed to make the winning move," I say softly. "It's not a role without any rewards."

He scowls and runs the brush through my hair once more. Despite his obvious frustration, the stroke is no less gentle than those before.

Even though he scoffed at my request, he's handled me so tenderly my entire body has lit up. He hasn't made a move beyond what I asked for.

This time, I can't tamp down on the swell of desire. As he sets the brush back on the table and straightens again, I look up at him.

His cool eyes meet mine, gleaming with a matching hunger. "What now, Princess?"

Would it be so horrible for me to claim one small reward right now?

I lift my hand toward him. "Lean closer."

He bends down, ducking farther at my beckoning gesture. When his chin is level with my temple, I ignore the twinge in my ribs and reach up to tease my fingers into his own hair.

The cocoa-brown strands are unexpectedly silky to my touch, pulling loose from his ponytail at my careful tug. As I unfurl my fingers against his scalp, Raul exhales over me in a heated rush.

His head dips even lower. His voice comes out strained. "Aurelia…"

Heat courses straight to the meeting of my thighs. All I can manage is a whisper.

"Do it."

He closes the last few inches between us to press his mouth against the side of my neck. Lightly at first and then, at my shaky sigh, parting his lips to swipe his hot tongue over the sensitive skin.

As I close my hand around the errant strands of his hair, he charts a scorching path from the corner of my jaw to the crook of my shoulder. Every flick of his tongue and scrape of his teeth floods me with more need.

He must be able to tell. I press my legs closer together beneath my dress to try to relieve the pressure, and the prince chuckles against my skin.

He eases the neckline of my dress over on my shoulder, branding the uncovered skin with kisses in its wake. The shifting of the fabric pebbles my nipples and sends even more arousal pooling between my thighs.

Raul's fingers skim across my other shoulder and down my side, and I'm abruptly aware that this encounter could spiral beyond my ability to corral it within a matter of seconds.

I grasp his hand as it reaches my hip, easing it away from me and scooting beyond his eager mouth in the same motion. "That's enough."

Raul grins down at me with a feral intensity that almost makes me regret my self-control. "No, it's not, Aurelia. It won't be enough until you're begging the only way you ever should—for me to bring all the pleasures you've imagined to reality. When you're ready for that, I swear you'll never feel as worshipped before or after. But I can wait."

I keep my tone mild. "You make a lot of promises."

"Only ones I know I can keep."

I hold myself still and calm until he's slipped out the

door. Then I set my elbows on the vanity and bow my head into my hands.

The heat Raul kindled in me burns on.

All three of these men are getting too far under my skin. I have to remember why I wanted them on my side—or the future I'm vying for might go up in flames.

CHAPTER THIRTY

Aurelia

In the hour before dinner, after a bath that's done much to soothe my unsteady nerves, I seek out the rest of the court and find most of them gathered in the parlor. I didn't think I could go any longer without my absence being remarked on again.

As I walk into the room, the first gaze that locks with mine is Prince Neven's from where he's standing just beyond the doorway. The young prince's bright brown eyes narrow into a glower with the tensing of his posture.

"Enjoying yourself, Your Highness?" he asks in a sharp tone. At the back of his mouth, I catch a flash of the steel teeth Melisse mentioned.

I can already tell this wouldn't be a productive conversation. I dip my head to him in acknowledgment while veering in a different direction. "As much as you are, I'd imagine."

I'm a little worried he'll follow me to let out whatever animosity he's apparently still harboring, but the next time I glance around, he's disappeared within the crowd.

Now that my only real friend in the palace has been relegated to staff, I'm more adrift than ever among the members of the court. Even my fellow competitors who I've talked to before in vaguely friendly ways turn the other way as I weave through the room. The other gentlemen and ladies eye me up and down and murmur to each other, but the best they offer me are thin smiles that hold no warmth at all.

When I cross paths with Bianca, she shoots a smirk my way before primping her sleek upswept hair and sashaying onward. She's done her work well, chilling the court against me.

I'm going to have an upward battle even if I win the marriage I came here for.

I end up near one of the doorways, watching for a server to enter and taking a glass of wine off his tray before anyone could have had a chance to meddle with it. When Fausta and Bianca are in the room, I'm not inclined to leave my safety to chance.

As I sip the tart liquid, a slender figure approaches at the edge of my vision. Prince Bastien inclines his auburn head as if examining the trinkets displayed on the shelves along the wall.

"How are you faring?" he asks. He doesn't glance my way, but there's no one else near enough for him to be talking to.

I adjust my weight, evaluating the ache lingering in my legs. "I've felt better, but I can get by. I'd imagine I'll be fully healed within a week."

He lets out a rough breath. "I wish we could have done more. If we'd found you sooner—"

"I'm lucky you did at all." I pause, measuring my words.

He's given me a perfect opening for the request I was already hoping to make. "There is something else that would help, though."

Bastien's head ticks slightly toward me before he catches himself. "What's that?"

With the prince who's always seemed the most practical of the bunch, I expect I'm best off taking a straightforward approach. "Lady Fausta has had an edge in the trials because Vicerine Bianca ferrets out information in advance. You spend a lot of time around Emperor Tarquin and Marclinus. If you pay extra attention to any comments they make or actions you observe that might relate to their plans, and let me know... It could even the playing field."

I wouldn't have dared to make such a request before this morning's rescue. Even now, my breath catches as I wait for his answer.

Whatever guilt he felt over nearly killing me, saving my life today has balanced the scales. He might laugh in my face at the idea of being my spy, or accuse me of attempting treason, or—

Bastien gives a short nod. "I can do that. Keep my eyes and ears open. They haven't discussed the specifics of the upcoming trials in front of me before, but I might pick up on something that'd be of use."

"Thank you." Relief sweeps through me, even though his agreement is hardly a guarantee of results. Simply knowing I have that kind of support within the palace eases the uncertainties that gnaw at me.

I know Rochelle will help me any way she can too, but in her new position she won't have many excuses to be around the emperor. I don't want to encourage her to stick her neck out more than is safe and risk Marclinus changing his mind about staying her execution.

At the edge of my vision, Bastien grimaces. "It's the least I can do."

While we've carried out our surreptitious conversation, my gaze has continued traveling around the room. It snags on a head of white-blond hair. Neven is standing near a few of the court musicians in the corner of the room. They'd just wrapped up playing when I arrived, and he looks as if he's asking the trim fellow who plays the harp about his instrument.

Maybe there's something more immediate I could seek Bastien's help with.

"I don't suppose any of you have bothered to let Prince Neven know that you've decided I'm not a villain after all," I say, keeping my tone light. "He still seemed rather peeved with me when he spoke to me this afternoon."

Bastien mutters a curse under his breath. "I'll talk to him tonight. With everything else that's happened, I didn't even think of it. You don't need to worry about it—he'll listen to us."

It's hard to see the puppy-dog-ish teenager as a huge threat, but I'd rather not take my chances there either. "Thank you for that too."

Neven definitely doesn't look hostile now. He gestures toward the harp and gazes avidly at the musician while the other man answers. When the harpist touches the prince's arm to emphasize some point, a blush spreads across Neven's cheeks.

My lips twitch with amusement. "It can wait a little while, of course. I won't ask you to interrupt his flirting."

"What?" Bastien jerks around to follow my gaze. "Gods help me, if that prick is encouraging him…"

I shoot him a sideways glance. "Why shouldn't he? Neven obviously likes him. If Raul's reputation is anything to go by, there aren't any rules against fostered princes pursuing whatever dalliances they want."

Bastien frowns. "He's only seventeen—practically still a kid. He has no idea what he actually wants yet. I don't think a court musician is the best person to figure it out with. They get around nearly as much as Raul does."

Somehow I don't imagine any of the older princes considered themselves "kids" at seventeen—or kept themselves chaste that long. But I suspect Bastien wouldn't appreciate me pointing that fact out.

"He won't figure out what he actually wants unless he gives a few things a shot." A pang of loss ripples through me, softening my voice. "And seventeen's plenty old enough to fall in love."

Bastien looks at me for the first time in our conversation, but at the same moment, there's a tap on my shoulder. Rochelle has slipped through the doorway and come up at my other side.

She offers a quick but warm smile. "We're supposed to escort our ladies to their seats for dinner."

My stomach gurgles in answer, reminding me that I missed breakfast and didn't have much appetite at lunch. I give Bastien a quick nod in farewell and turn to follow Rochelle. "Lead the way."

She's obviously doing her best to show total commitment to her new role. Only a few other maids and pages have arrived to start ushering the court to the dining room. I drift to the side of the hall so we can talk quietly without being overheard.

Rochelle speaks before I can, with a swift glance over her shoulder toward the room we left. "You were talking with Prince Bastien about Prince Neven?"

I laugh. "Briefly. He seemed rather concerned about his foster brother having any romantic pursuits."

Rochelle hums. "The other princes have always kept a close eye on Neven, from what I've seen. I suppose it makes sense they're so protective, given… everything."

I hadn't thought about the fact that Rochelle's been visiting court since the princes were much younger. Her comment rouses my interest. "What's 'everything'? I assumed it was only because he's a fair bit younger than the rest of them."

"Well, there is that, but also—have you not heard? I suppose no one really talks about it now since it's been ten years."

I tap my elbow against hers. "I haven't heard anything, so you'd better tell me before I expire of curiosity."

Rochelle's gaze darts around the hall. Her voice dips lower. "Neven wasn't the first prince Emperor Tarquin fostered from Goric. He's thirdborn. He had an older brother, Pavel, who was fostered before him… The first one who came to the palace, almost a year before Bastien. I wasn't here when it happened, but ten years ago, apparently he went mad and tried to murder the emperor. Of course he was executed. Neven was brought in to take his place."

My stomach hollows out. If Prince Pavel was less than a year older than Bastien, he and the other older princes would have grown up together—would probably have relied on each other for several years the way the three of them do now.

I can't even wrap my mind around how they must have felt to lose him. And to see another boy brought in as yet another hostage in their friend's place…

They have even more reasons for their anger than I

guessed. Gods, it must be torture for Neven to be living here with the man who executed his brother.

Rochelle's right—it's no surprise at all that the older princes would be committed to making sure he survives his time at the palace.

I've gained a small piece of the puzzle that I was missing, one that makes the picture so much more coherent.

I don't dare mention any of those thoughts here in the hall where I might be overheard. To even imply there was anything tragic about the execution of a boy who attacked the emperor would be treason in itself.

Before I can decide how to continue the conversation, Rochelle returns my conspiratorial nudge of the elbow. "The way you said what you did about falling in love at seventeen... It almost sounded as if you were speaking from experience."

She doesn't ask the question outright, but it's clearly implied. A pang resonates through my heart.

I don't see any reason to lie, though there's no need to spell out all the details. "I can't say no man ever caught my eye before I arrived here. What's growing up without at least one flirtation that was never to be? It's well in the past."

It's more than three years now since the news came that I'd never see his face again. The grief has long since dulled, and I set aside the echo of loss that's risen up.

It was my mistake, forgetting my place. My heart is full with the love of my family, my country, my people, and the peaceful godlen who watches over us all.

Rochelle looks as though she might pry for more of the story, but I'm saved by our arrival at the dining room. One of the gilded imperial chairs has been set in the middle of the head table tonight, and Rochelle directs me to the seat at its left.

"I'm not sure why they rearranged the chairs," she says with a furrow of her brow.

I gather my fortitude. "I suppose I'll find out soon enough. I'll see you later tonight."

As I settle myself in my seat, more of the court drifts into the room. I'm glad to see Fausta placed four chairs distant from me and Bianca at a completely different table, but my relief is short-lived.

Marclinus strolls over to the gilded chair that's next to mine and sprawls into it. He grins at me with an air much more relaxed than this morning. "It seems you'll be keeping me company through dinner, Princess Aurelia. We can get to know each other even better."

Beneath the table, he trails his fingers over my knee through my skirt.

I restrain a flinch, forcing my mouth into an ingratiating smile. "How wonderful."

My gaze trips down the table to where Emperor Tarquin has taken his own seat at his usual spot at the head of the table. The emperor's piercing gaze evaluates me.

I'm still being tested after this morning's lapse. Are they trying to provoke me into revealing that I don't really want to be here?

It isn't going to happen. I haven't come this far, endured this much, to slip up now.

But I can't forget that the greatest threat in this palace isn't Fausta or Bianca or any of the nobles who've sneered or glared at me. It's the emperor and his heir themselves.

CHAPTER THIRTY-ONE

Lorenzo

I didn't think I'd ever have anything in common with Lady Fausta or Vicerine Bianca. But glimpsing their pinched faces across the ballroom, I think they're just as displeased with Marclinus's current choices as I am, if for very different reasons.

He has six potential brides still in his macabre competition. All six of them are here in the ballroom. But this is his fifth dance with Aurelia while he's only drawn the others onto the dance floor once or twice.

It's got to be because of this morning's near-catastrophe. If we'd found Aurelia even minutes later, Fausta might have managed to completely sabotage her chances regardless of our efforts to see her healed.

Marclinus is suspicious of her disappearance, so he's pulling her closer, watching her, judging her. I've noticed Emperor Tarquin eyeing her more often than the others too.

But her rivals won't see that as a bad thing. They're simply peeved that he's giving her more attention than he's offering them.

What if they try to trip her up in some other way to get back at her?

Glancing around the edges of the dance floor, I spot Bastien halfway across the vast room, standing next to Neven. The shards of light that glint down from the dimmed chandeliers dapple both their forms.

I wait until Bastien looks my way and twist my hand at my side, indicating danger and the two women now outright glaring Aurelia's way. He's closer to them—and better equipped to intervene if we need to.

Bastien gives a slight nod. The flick of his fingers informs me that he's already monitoring them, as is Raul.

All right. The court's reigning snakes won't have a chance to strike tonight.

That doesn't help Aurelia out of the predicament she's already in, though.

At the dwindling of the melody, Marclinus releases Aurelia—but not without one last stroke of his hand down her side and an open leer at her retreating back. I tuck my hands into the pockets of my trousers so no one can see them clench into fists.

Every particle of my body is clamoring to stride over there and take her hand, to draw her into a dance I'd like to believe she'll welcome more. I tense my legs against the impulse.

We have to be careful. To engage her so blatantly in front of the whole court… I don't want to give Tarquin or Marclinus any reason to wonder just how interested I am in the princess of Accasy. Would I be able to hide my attraction when I'm holding her in my arms?

So I smother those feelings, as much as it feels like I'm suffocating with the effort. I watch as one of the marchions carefully invites her to a dance, darting wary glances toward the imperial heir in case Marclinus decides to intercept him.

It's obviously caught everyone's notice that he's become particularly fixated on Aurelia tonight.

Bianca starts to move toward the uneasy couple—and appears to trip over her own feet. She sprawls on her hands and knees and whirls around, but no one's near enough to have caught her ankle.

Raul stands nearby with his back to her and his hand loose at his side. A faint smile crosses my lips.

The darkened ballroom gives him plenty of space to work.

Another song ends, and the urge grips me again. But Marclinus goes straight back to Aurelia, snatching her hand and twirling her toward him.

She smiles at him and moves in time. She doesn't recoil when his hand drifts down to squeeze her ass or when he tugs her so close her breasts graze his chest, even as my teeth set on edge.

But there's no life in her expression. It's as blank as a doll's.

I'm not sure anyone who didn't really know her would pick up on the signs, but I've seen Aurelia laughing and awed and angry. I know how her eyes can spark and her cheeks flush with passion.

I also know the slightly glassy look that's come into her eyes now, as if she's drifted off behind her compliant façade. She's pulling away from him in the only way she can without him realizing.

How much more is he going to harass her this evening?

How much more can she take before something

crumbles? She was lying in the woods with multiple broken bones at the start of this day.

Resolve rushes up through me so sharp and certain I can't deny it too. Raul and Bastien will do their parts. I can look after her my own way.

The night is getting late. It won't be strange for her to take her leave now. I simply need to give her permission.

I ease along the edge of the dancing crowd. When Marclinus finally releases Aurelia again, I'm right within her line of sight as she turns around.

With a surreptitious gesture by my hip, I motion her toward the door, hoping she gets my intended meaning: *You should leave, now.*

The smallest twitch of her jaw is my only indication that she caught my message. She drifts toward one of the tables holding platters of appetizers and then meanders through the doorway as if on a whim, not with any particular purpose.

I wait through several thuds of my heart before ambling toward the room's other entrance, aiming for the same nonchalant air.

When I reach the hall, Aurelia has already vanished from sight, but I can guess that she's headed toward her chambers. I pick up my pace and catch sight of her around the bend.

At the thump of my footsteps, she glances back. A crease has formed in her brow.

I could wave her on toward her room and leave her be— but she must wonder why I signaled her in the first place. I don't want to leave her worried.

This isn't a good place to talk, and joining her in her bedroom probably isn't wise. I pause and flick my hand in the direction of the library alongside the reading gesture I've shown her before.

Aurelia nods and sets off again, staying a good twenty

paces ahead of me. I slow down now that I'm sure we'll end up at the same place so she can pull farther away.

We pass a couple of servants, but there's no reason for them to think the two of us are together. I lose sight of Aurelia completely for a minute, but when I duck past the library door, she's waiting by one of the tables in the broad central aisle.

A quick glance shows no one else in the room at the moment, but I'd rather not take the chance of someone stumbling on our conversation. I usher her over to the repair room where my foster brothers and I have many of our private discussions.

At the tap of the closing door, I flick on the magical lantern. Aurelia takes in the worktable and the shelves of supplies with a curious look before turning to face me.

Her wild, sweet scent, like flowers blooming in a winter forest, drifts through the faint tang of binding glue. All at once, I find it difficult to do anything but gaze at her in the wavering light, taking in the soft planes of her face and the luster of her hair.

Her voice, hushed but urgent, breaks me from my reverie. "What's wrong? Why did I need to leave?"

Of course she's worried. My fingers flex, searching for the right gestures to convey my answer.

You weren't happy with Marclinus. Here he can't touch you.

Her eyes widen, some of the color draining from her tan face. "Was it that obvious I wasn't enjoying myself? If he could tell—"

I cut her off with a hasty shake of my head and a hitch of my pulse that I've panicked her even more. My hands whip through a simple message. *I know you.*

"Are you sure?"

I nod emphatically and touch her arm in an attempt at reassurance, but she raises her hand to her face. "Maybe I should go back. He's already on edge with me since this morning." She hesitates. "But if it's obvious I wasn't simply turning in for the night, he'll wonder why I left to begin with. Curse it all."

I step closer so I can rest my hand on her shoulder, wishing the act didn't feel so inadequate.

Aurelia drags in a ragged breath. "I'm sorry. I just—*gods*, I hate this whole spectacle he and his father have created. They've made marriage into a total perversion where nothing matters but pandering to his ego."

I don't know how to answer her frustration in any way other than my best attempt at a reassuring squeeze.

She lifts her head to meet my gaze, her chin steady. "It's all right. I knew whoever I married, it'd be a political match. The point is what we offer each other. It's only… I assumed there'd at least be a *chance* that some kind of love could grow out of it. I think Marclinus would laugh if I mentioned that hope to him. Maybe even slit my throat for suggesting getting groped and paraded at his side isn't enough."

It's not all right. She's strong and determined and unyielding, but anguish rings through her voice and shines in her eyes. More pain and anger than she's ever let me see before.

It feels like a gift. I have no idea how to repay it with anything that'd be remotely comforting.

If I could give her the hope she's talking about, I would. There's so much I'd want to say that I can't.

I'm just as trapped as she is.

My free hand sketches through the air with the best I can offer. *Nothing wrong with you. It's all him. You are wonderful.*

She understands well enough that a choked sort of laugh tumbles out of her. Her fingers curl into the front of my shirt. Her deep blue eyes meet mine with something that might be an invitation or a plea or maybe a mixture of both.

Great God help me, I can't do anything but answer it.

My mouth crashes into hers as if it couldn't belong anywhere else. Aurelia kisses me back hard.

Just like that, everything is her. Her warmth against my front, her breath tart with a trace of wine, her encouraging whimper working its way up her throat.

There's something fiercer about this collision than the ones before. Her fingernails graze my scalp; her teeth nick my lip.

I'm lost in the need to get closer, to take in more of her, as if I can meld myself to her so well I'll shield her from all the horrors of the world beyond this room.

My hands move of their own accord, sliding down to her thighs, lifting her onto the edge of the bare worktable. Her legs splay in my wake, the skirt of her dress riding up to her knees.

When I glide my fingers up her smooth calf, careful of the lingering scar from this morning's wounds, Aurelia lets out a soft little growl and yanks my mouth back to hers. Her arm slings around my shoulders as if to lock me there with her.

There's nowhere I'd rather be. I ease closer, my dick throbbing behind my trousers as I push against her bunched skirt.

I've had a tumble here and there—ladies of the court whose enjoyment of my music overrode my other deficits for the length of a brief fling. After the first few, my own enthusiasm waned when I realized they had no interest in anything other than how I played and how I could get them off.

It's never been like this, like it is with Aurelia. Never been a passion so consuming every part of me aches with it.

When I cup her breast, her breath stutters into my mouth. With the swivel of my palm, her entire body quivers.

I've never felt like this with anyone before her, and Marclinus has never made *her* feel half as good as I am now. Triumph flares amid my eagerness before desire swallows everything up again.

I need more.

I glide my fingers along the neckline of her dress, and Aurelia leans into my touch. Through kiss after kiss, I ease the fabric down over her shoulder.

My lips travel with it. I tease the edges of my teeth over the edge of her jaw, her gasp making me twice as hard, and brand every inch of her neck. Following the path of her collarbone, I scoop my hand under dress and chemise together and lift her bared breast to my mouth.

The moment my lips close around her stiffened nipple, Aurelia gives a cry she can only partly stifle. She clutches my shoulder and the short strands of my hair, the clamping of her fingers urging me onward.

I'm not sure I've ever missed the tongue I gave up quite as much as this moment, but I can do plenty without it. I suckle her down before trailing my teeth across the pebbled nub, and her hips rock toward me.

I meet the motion, unable to stop myself from grinding into her through our clothes. My cock feels ready to burst. I shift my head to nibble my way to her other breast—

And Aurelia nudges me backward.

It's not quite a push, but firm enough that there's no

mistaking her intent. My heart constricts and my groin aches, but I draw back a few inches.

Both of our chests are heaving. Aurelia reaches for her skewed bodice, and I tug it back into place with a twinge of loss.

"I'm sorry," she murmurs. "I—It's not that I don't want —To risk *everything*—"

I take her face between my hands and bow my head so our foreheads rest together.

I know. I know we shouldn't be doing this at all. I know the little of herself she's shared with me is already an unexpected prize.

How did this start with me simply wanting to ruin her, to have something Marclinus hadn't gotten to claim yet, to steal what wasn't rightfully mine the way Raul boasted about?

Maybe that desire isn't totally gone. Maybe part of the ache inside me is the longing to have her want me more than him so much that she'd throw caution to the wind.

But mostly I just want *her*. I want to believe with all I have that she could be something right in this place where so much has always been wrong.

Assuming that's true could be a mistake, though, couldn't it?

She'll never be mine. Not even here in this room where we're alone, where I had her clinging to me and crying out with pleasure. Marclinus is here too, in the press of her hand returning the distance between us.

No matter what else happens, if she survives the trials, she's going to marry him. She doesn't like the idea, but she'll do it for reasons beyond her own heart regardless. She's never once pretended otherwise.

And I'll have to watch her do it.

My emotions have tangled so much I don't know how to

pick them apart. Aurelia tilts her head to offer me one more kiss, but this one feels like an extension of her apology more than an act of passion.

She slides off the desk and reaches for the door. I let her go, not sure who I hate most for it.

Chapter Thirty-Two

Aurelia

I thought spring in Dariu was uncomfortably warm, but this afternoon is giving me my first taste of how sweltering the summer might become. The sun blazes down over the garden from the cloudless sky. Even in my airy Darium-style dress, sweat forms on my back after a few minutes under its rays.

The gentlemen and ladies of the court have resorted to gathering around the flowering trees and taller hedges where they can take shelter in the shade. The heat turns the usual floral aroma even more cloying. Many of the ladies have spread out embroidered sheets to sit on, far too fine to be used for picnicking, while most of the men insist on stoically standing.

I meander between the patches of shadow, always on the edges of the conversations. Several of the maids have come out with us to attend to their mistresses with beverages and fanning, but I made myself ask for Melisse to join me today so I don't appear to overly favor Rochelle. I couldn't have talked freely with the former lady in front of the court anyway.

How ridiculous is it that I find myself wishing someone would call us to a lawn game? We'd all melt from perspiration, but at least we'd have something to do other than chatter.

I pause beneath the arch of a vine-draped arbor, sipping the sweet but watery juice that Darium society apparently turns to on hotter days. Part of me is relieved not to have to face another trial just yet. Part of me wishes we could get the rest of them over with.

A twinge runs up my leg from my foot still recovering from yesterday's beating. I glance down—and my pulse lurches.

A black stain is spreading across my pale blue bodice, creeping even faster in the instant after it arrests my gaze. It looks as if I've been stabbed in the heart but the blood's coming out dark as tar.

My body stiffens, but I manage to clamp down on the shriek that hitches up my throat. Remain calm, stay centered, take stock—

A glimpse of flame-red hair at the edge of my vision douses my panic. I turn my head just enough to confirm that Fausta is sitting nearly out of view around the side of a nearby hedge sculpture, surrounded by her friends.

While I study her from the corner of my eye, her head ticks toward me as if she's surreptitiously checking my reaction.

The next time I glance down at my dress, the stain has vanished. The fabric beams as starkly white as ever.

She projected another illusion at me. A much briefer one

than before, but she wouldn't risk exhausting herself on a gamble when we have no idea when the next trial might begin.

She must have been hoping I'd make a fool of myself in front of the court—and Their Imperial Eminences, who are strolling the gardens too. Maybe even end up looking outright mad.

So sorry to disappoint her.

I doubt her gift is strong enough for her to want to extend it much more than she already has today, but I meander onward in the opposite direction. I'd rather not linger in hostile territory.

A slightly cooler breeze drifts over me from the largest of the garden's fountains. I head toward the marble fixture with its statue of Sabrelle the warrior godlen striking down a helmed man, and slow when I realize that the emperor has naturally picked the most refreshing spot in the garden for himself.

He's standing by a shaded bench with one of his chief advisors and a few other high-ranking members of his court. They appear deep in discussion—I catch enough words to gather a new iron mine has been established in Lavira.

Maybe they'll move on to a subject more useful to my purposes. I spot Giralda sitting with a few other ladies a little closer by and settle onto the edge of their sheet as if I have every right to be there. Which I suppose I do, although Giralda makes a quick grimace as if she's bitten into something sour.

Their murmured conversation continues next to me. I feel no need to insert myself into the debate on the merits of various types of belt fastenings.

Emperor Tarquin is saying something about the route the metals will be conveyed along to reach the sites where they're needed. "How many of the appropriate cargo ships do we have available for the lake crossing?"

His advisor dips her head. "I believe there are only a few not already assigned, but we could adjust the allotments as you see fit."

The emperor hums. "I want as much as possible moved before the summer storms."

A familiar terse tenor speaks up from a bench farther around the curve of the fountain. "You'd be able to move it more efficiently with a land-based route through Cotea."

Both my and the emperor's gazes jerk to the slim, auburn-haired figure whose head is still bent over the book open on his lap. Emperor Tarquin's eyes narrow just slightly.

"What was that, Your Highness?" he asks with a sharp undercurrent of warning.

I'm not sure Prince Bastien fully thought through his remark rather than responding to the topic automatically. His head comes up, and he blinks at the emperor as if he hadn't quite realized who he was talking to. Whose planned strategy he was criticizing openly in front of members of the court.

It's hard to say when he's already so pale, but I think even more color leaches from the prince's face. His body tenses with his hesitation.

The safe thing to do would be to retract, apologize, and flee the emperor's sight. But as I watch, Bastien's narrow jaw firms.

He holds Emperor Tarquin's gaze unflinching. "I said it'd be simpler to set a land-based route through Cotea, Your Imperial Majesty. Fewer concerns about the weight the boats can handle. Fewer delays from the storms. There's a good road straight from—"

The emperor cuts him off with a scoffing sound. "Your

intention couldn't be clearer. You're simply hoping to earn more profits for your own kingdom by having them host the caravan. You'll have to come up with a subtler gambit than that if you want to skew results to your benefit, young prince."

Bastien's mouth flattens. He doesn't look disappointed or abashed, only irritated.

That's all I need to convince me that it wasn't a gambit at all. He was offering Tarquin solid advice based on his knowledge, and the emperor has thrown it away because he didn't come up with the idea himself.

Perhaps because he already decided he'd rather take on more expense than see any economic benefit go to one of his conquered countries.

"My apologies for interrupting," Bastien says, and turns back to his book.

He must know his brief offer of regret is unlikely to be enough. His shoulders stay rigid.

Indeed, it's only a moment before Emperor Tarquin makes a thoughtful sound as if something has just occurred to him. "Since you're keen on 'educating' those around you today, Prince Bastien, why don't you put your familiarity with my library to some use. In the botanical section, there's a volume by Plinta Iviserra on the native flora of Dariu. Fetch it for me."

His tone makes it clear this is an order, not a request. Bastien accepts his punishment in silence, leaving his own book on the bench and setting off for the palace.

I expect that'll be the end of it. The ladies I'm sitting with paused their conversation to watch the altercation but now go back to their own concerns. Melisse comes by with a fresh glass of juice, and I accept it with a grateful smile.

It takes several minutes for Bastien to reach the palace,

get up to the second floor, locate the book, and return. He offers the massive text to the emperor, who motions for him to set it on the edge of one of the planters.

Tarquin sounds only bored now. "Never mind that. I wonder if the weather might shift—go to my chambers and have one of my staff retrieve my crested jacket for me so you can bring it back."

The request is obviously absurd. I doubt it'll be cool enough out here to warrant another layer of clothing even in the middle of the night.

Bastien's eyes flash, but he heads off again.

This trip takes him a little longer. When he arrives with the requested jacket heaped in his arms, his face is taut with tension. His voice carries a hint of a rasp when he displays the thick garment with its ornate detailing. "Your jacket, Your Imperial Majesty."

My throat constricts. Emperor Tarquin isn't simply giving him busy work and humbling him by treating him like a servant. He's purposefully pushing the prince's physical limits.

The imperial chambers are on the third floor of the palace. The vast staircases and heavy cargo of the two trips close together might have left *me* out of breath. For a man who's relying on only one lung…

The emperor flicks his hand, and one of his pages who could have carried out the errand in the first place collects the jacket.

"I have a mind to take a closer look at the birds nesting in our trees," he says. "Retrieve the spyglass from the observatory room for me. In its case with its various lenses. Quickly, please."

Bastien ducks his head and strides off again. My heart sinks.

The observatory room is on the third floor too, and gods only know how big this case is.

Is Tarquin going to keep at the prince until he outright collapses?

A flicker of anger guides my tongue. I lean closer to the other ladies, pitching my voice low as if sharing a confidence. "How unfortunate for the prince that His Imperial Majesty is so changeable in his desires. Of course, he must only be pretending to be so unfocused."

No one could accuse me of insulting the emperor. At face value, I'm applauding his sly strategy.

But as the ladies around me glance toward Tarquin, their expressions turn a bit curious.

I've also sown the idea that he *is* acting oddly unfocused.

No one else in the garden cares much about what happens to Bastien, though. I've gathered that Neven spends quite a bit of his days with tutors, and I haven't seen Raul or Lorenzo since breakfast either.

I sit back on my hands and pretend to be enjoying the breeze passing by the fountain. My innards knot tighter with every passing minute.

Finally, trudging footsteps approach from the palace. A moment later, I make out breaths broken into ragged hitches.

Bastien composes himself as well as he must be able to before he comes around the hedges that circle the fountain, but his forehead shines with sweat and his skin has taken on a sickly cast. He inhales and exhales through parted lips with a trace of a wheeze he can't suppress. His whole frame wobbles as he sets down the hefty wooden chest near the emperor.

Emperor Tarquin looks the prince up and down and clicks his tongue disapprovingly. "Your health seems to be particularly weak today, Prince Bastien. If you're in such a state, you'd better retire to your room."

I'd imagine the pointed comment strings, but Bastien simply bobs his head and stalks away. He's probably grateful to be released.

I have to hold my fingers back from clenching, willing my agitation not to touch my posture or my face. My mind whirls, the threads of my gift tingling through it.

No potion in the world could regrow a lung or expand the one remaining to match the full capacity of two. But there are ingredients that can soothe results of straining one's body that way. I have most of them in my tea box.

I asked Bastien for his help. The least I can do is offer my own in return.

To be sure I'm not obvious, I wait for a few excruciating minutes before I get up from the sheet and walk around the other side of the fountain. I wander on through the gardens with no sense of urgency, just happening to end up by the rows of herbs outside the kitchen door.

No members of the court have ventured this far from the others. I pluck up a few leaves and then continue on to one of the proper back entrances.

On my way to my bedroom, I catch a maid in the halls and ask her to bring me a pot of hot water. By the time she arrives, I've already mingled the herbs that revealed themselves to my mind's eye in the bottom of the teacup.

I pour the water over them and a brew for myself for focused calm before lifting the small tray. They'll steep on the way over.

I face the slight conundrum that I don't actually know where Prince Bastien's bedroom is. But it seems likely the emperor will have his foster sons roomed close together. I head toward the hall where I know both Raul and Lorenzo have their chambers, my steps soft and my ears pricked.

I'm three doors down from Lorenzo's room when I make out faint coughing filtering from the one next to me.

As soon as the fit has passed, I knock on the door. "Prince Bastien?"

There's a pause and then a creak of the floor. He opens the door a few inches and peers out at me, his face still sallow, his slender body rigid with tension.

I point my chin toward the tray I'm carrying before he has to waste breath asking me why I'm here. "I made you some tea that should help soothe your throat and lung. If you'll accept that kindness."

Bastien's jaw twitches. I don't think he likes the idea of being pitied any more than Lorenzo did. But considering that he's seen me laid low more than once, he must feel his pride can stand one turnabout.

He motions me inside with a jerk of his head.

Like Lorenzo's, the room is only perhaps two thirds the size of mine. The curtains have been drawn back from both of the tall windows, the panes raised to let in the afternoon light and as much breeze as the late spring day offers.

Between them and on either side stand floor-to-ceiling bookcases packed with texts—whether ones Bastien borrowed from the imperial library or his own collection, I can't tell. They stand in much more orderly fashion than Lorenzo's haphazard collection.

A few more books and a sheaf of papers sit in neat stacks on the desk next to the doorway to the bathing room. Nearby, a narrow sofa faces a small, low table. Across from them, a four-poster bed fills the rest of the space.

The room is a little cramped, but the atmosphere is calm and orderly, as if everything has a place and could be found in an instant. From what I've gotten to know of the prince of Cotea, I'm not surprised.

I bring the tray over to the table and sink onto one end of the sofa. Bastien takes the other end, muffling a few more coughs with the back of his hand against his mouth, and contemplates the tea.

The corner of my mouth quirks upward. "If you're concerned that I might have decided to repay you for your trick with the stew, I'll happily take the first sip."

His gaze darts to meet mine, accompanied by a swift grimace. "I wasn't thinking that," he says, a bit hoarsely. "I just wasn't expecting you to go out of your way…"

I wave off his objection and pick up my own cup. "This is what my gift is for. I'd rather make use of it to see you feeling better than offer my talent to most of my other company in the palace."

A hint of a smile crosses the prince's lips. He picks up the other cup without hesitation.

"It's good to inhale the steam as well as drinking the liquid," I tell him.

He takes a deep breath and a tentative swallow. Immediately, his shoulders come down. With his next sip, some of the rasp in his chest smooths out.

Bastien smiles at me a little wider, if crookedly. "It does feel as if it's loosening things up. I shouldn't have doubted after seeing you at work before."

I shrug, absorbing the comforting scent of my own tea. "I'm glad I could help somehow."

He looks down at his cup. "It was stupid, challenging him like that. But I'm so tired of keeping my mouth shut and kowtowing. Gods smite me, I'd have been making his goals *easier* and I was fine with that if he'd just listen to me."

"He doesn't give you much of anything to do, and you

obviously have a sharp mind. I can only imagine how stifled you feel."

Bastien rubs his temple. "I don't really want to assist him in anything that strengthens the empire. So it was doubly stupid. But I suppose I got a very concrete reminder of why."

Is this a glimpse into my future: always unheard, always ineffectual?

I squash down the flicker of despair. "How much longer do you have to remain here? I've gathered Emperor Tarquin doesn't plan to keep fostering the four of you for your entire lives."

"I believe the plan is that once our older siblings—the ones who inherited our kingdoms—have a second-born child of acceptable age, Tarquin will call them to court for fostering and send us home." Bastien sighs and leans back in the sofa. "My younger nephew is four. So I have three more years? But it's hard to look forward to leaving when it means him being dragged here in my place."

My heart squeezes at the thought. "Of course. I don't know what I'd do if he wanted the same from my sister."

Bastien lifts an eyebrow. "If you get what you want, she shouldn't have to worry about sending any of her children, should she? *You* won't be going back."

And I'll be giving Marclinus children myself, very directly. The reminder makes me queasy.

I wet my lips. "I can try to speak against the fostering in general—"

Bastien eases over to touch my arm. "You don't need to make me any promises. I know how hard it is to budge the emperor. And you must have plenty of more personal concerns."

He pauses, studying me for a moment. "For a long time, I was under the impression that the empire didn't meddle all that much with affairs on Accasy because of the distance. I've come to suspect that impression was misguided."

Ah. That explains some of the resentment the princes showed when I first arrived. I suppose it's not an unexpected assumption.

My mouth twists. "The distance has its upsides and downsides."

"How so?"

"Well… Because it's harder for us to offer Dariu resources or service, Tarquin extracts everything he can in taxes. There's little chance for any business or trade to flourish. The soldiers stationed within our borders are assigned to their posts for long stretches with fewer opportunities to visit home than I've heard is usual elsewhere, and they often take out their frustrations on our citizens. And…"

The memory wavers up of the men and women I've waved goodbye to, resisting the urge to wrench them from our overseers. My throat constricts.

I speak around the anguish. "To move the resources of ours that Emperor Tarquin wants brought to Dariu, it's a long, dangerous trek. He prefers to leave that mainly to my people rather than his own. I can't tell you how many I've seen conscribed to the transport missions who never return. That's not to mention those he forces into soldier garb in his endless attempts to regain the western half of the continent."

When I lapse into silence, Bastien winces. "I'm sorry. I didn't realize— There's so much they never enter into the records."

"I'm sure there's plenty I don't know about your own struggles. Accasy's geography has left us a little isolated from the rest of the continent in general." I hesitate, recalling one particular struggle Rochelle mentioned to me yesterday. "I heard about Neven's older brother. Prince Pavel? You two must have been close."

Bastien's hand drops from my arm, the other clenching around his cup. He takes another drink before answering, his gaze veering away from me.

"He was the first of us to arrive, the only other foster here when I was brought. It'd have been a lot more difficult for me to adjust if I hadn't had him to lean on. I don't know how he managed those first several months alone… Maybe that's part of why he ended up snapping."

I swallow hard. "It must have been awful losing him."

Bastien's eyes stay distant. "I didn't have any idea he was going to do it. Maybe *he* didn't even know he was going to do it until that moment…"

I want to ask what exactly happened, but it seems cruel to pry into those painful memories.

Perhaps Bastien must sense my curiosity regardless. He drags his gaze back to me. "He had a gift with fire. We were in a private meeting with the emperor, reporting on our progress in our studies—we'd do that once a week. Mostly Tarquin would pick at us and make us feel like idiots. He was just laying into Lorenzo about some minor inconsistency when Pavel suddenly threw himself forward with a blast of fire…"

The picture he's drawn in my mind makes my pulse hiccup. "And Tarquin survived the attack?"

"The flames never even reached him. None of us realized it before then, but he always has at least a few guards around, even if they're mostly out of sight, and they must have powerful gifts for sensing and repelling magic. They leapt in and deflected Pavel's gift, and Tarquin didn't have one hair on his head singed."

I've realized the emperor always keeps guards on hand,

but I hadn't known they could protect him quite that thoroughly. He'd never need to worry about magical assassination with gifts like that surrounding him.

Bastien hasn't returned to his original position on the sofa. I scoot even closer and take his hand in mine, remembering how he did the same when we spoke in the records room the other night. Imagining the man next to me at thirteen, watching his closest friend and confidante make a fatal mistake.

He considers our joined hands. His voice has turned rough again, but I don't think it has anything to do with his lung this time. "I've always wondered if there was something I could have said to stop him, if only I'd noticed just how angry he was getting…"

"It couldn't have been your fault. You were just a child still."

"So was he, really. Children making childish decisions."

Something about his tone makes me think there's more he's not saying.

Instead, he changes the subject, giving my hand a little squeeze. "None of it's your fault either. I've been so focused on keeping us safe every way I can—I didn't give you a chance to show me who you were before I'd already decided it. Every time you prove you're not our enemy at all, I feel more ashamed of how I treated you. You're… You're a remarkable woman, Aurelia."

A flutter passes through my chest, but I can't help teasing him a little. "So I shouldn't start shunning you to let you feel more justified after all?"

He shoots me a half-hearted glower and sets down his nearly empty teacup. "All I'm trying to say is that if I can make up for it, I will."

My smile softens. "Everything I've seen of you tells me you'll keep that promise."

Something in Bastien's face shifts. He stares at me for just a moment, his dark green eyes lit with a hunger I don't totally understand.

Then he cups my cheek and leans in to kiss me.

It's not at all like last night's fervid encounter with Lorenzo. Bastien's mouth moves against mine with a tender intensity, as if he's charting the texture of my lips, the hitch of my breath, the skip of my pulse—making a cartography of who I am and where I fit into his life.

And into his embrace. He lets go of my hand to slide that arm around my waist, tugging me closer.

Even as I kiss him back, guilt tickles through the heady rush of desire. I *was* just kissing Lorenzo last night. I let Raul kiss my neck the same afternoon.

What kind of wanton am I becoming?

It isn't as if these men could believe our encounters will lead anywhere meaningful, though, is it? They're not expecting any kind of commitment or exclusivity.

They all know why I'm here—they know the outcome of the trials. In the space of a week, I'll either be dead or married to Marclinus.

It's hard to think their interest is even all about me. I know how much they hate the imperial family. I've heard the way Raul compares what he can offer to Marclinus's groping.

If I'm getting some kind of momentary escape from my fate with them, they're getting the satisfaction of seducing their tormentor's bride-to-be at the same time. We're all pursuing something more than just attraction.

If they don't feel guilty about it, why should I?

My uncertainty dwindles, but it doesn't fade away

completely. My heart is still at risk, aching more with every ardent caress.

I can't tumble so far into this escape that I won't find my way back out to accomplish what I'm here to do.

I must tense up a bit, because Bastien eases back to meet my gaze. As much as I know I need to extricate myself, the thought of outright rejecting him sends an even sharper twinge through my chest.

I touch his face. "We'll just keep looking out for each other."

His flicker of a smile accepts both my boundary and my statement. "Then I'd better let you get back to the gardens before Marclinus wonders where you've disappeared to."

CHAPTER THIRTY-THREE

Aurelia

When Rochelle finds me on my way to luncheon, her hands fly straight to the ribbons at my waist for a hasty adjustment.

"What have you been doing?" she murmurs. "I had these tied perfectly before breakfast."

I restrain a grimace and pitch my voice even lower than hers. "His Imperial Highness had some fun teasing all 'his' ladies during this morning's activities. Thank you."

As she eases back, I shoot her a quick smile. "How have you been doing? Are you getting on in the servants' quarters all right?" We didn't have an opportunity to talk openly this morning because Melisse was seeing to my hair and powder while Rochelle sorted out my clothes.

Rochelle laughs softly. "I mean, it's certainly different from my usual chambers. But my father won't lower himself to coming there to speak to me, so at least I don't have to face his disappointment, as much larger as it must be now." Her own smile falters. "He probably wishes I'd died."

I give her arm a reassuring squeeze. "*I* certainly don't. He doesn't get any say in your life now. But I do. Hopefully more say soon enough. Are you decently comfortable? Have you run into any problems?"

A little amusement comes back into Rochelle's tone. "There were nights here and there at home when I ended up falling asleep in the stables, or out on the porch—a servant's bed is cozier than that. So I can't complain." She pauses. "I think Melisse is annoyed that you've taken on a second maid, though."

I frown. "Has she complained to you?"

"No, nothing direct. She just always seems irritable when she talks to me. Or she'll give me the cold shoulder… Maybe I'm only imagining it."

"I'll keep trying to make sure I'm still giving her plenty of work too."

As we reach the dining room, Rochelle hurries ahead of me to check with the other staff about where I should sit. I'm meandering after her when careful fingers graze my arm.

Bastien's voice reaches me from behind, dropped to a whisper. "I overheard the emperor talking to the kitchen staff a little before lunch. He was asking them to bring up a couple of extra crates of wine beyond the usual. I don't know if that's significant, but…"

As he trails off, dread pools in my gut. This is the second day since we ladies pleaded for Marclinus to let us continue the trials, and three since we last had a full test of our devotion.

I couldn't have expected the reprieve to last much longer.

I dip my head in thanks, not sure if the prince even sees

my acknowledgment before he ambles onward as if he was simply brushing past me.

Rochelle motions me over to the head table and pulls out my seat for me. Since two nights ago, Marclinus has moved his chair back to the foot of the table. I'm glad to see this time I'm not seated at the end next to him but vaguely middle-ish.

I end up in between Iseppa and Giralda, neither of whom are willing to chat much with me after Bianca's efforts at cooling the court's opinion, but neither of whom have ever been overtly hostile either. I keep a close eye on my food and my drink regardless—and only pretend to sip my wine.

If something important is going to happen with our beverages today, less intoxication is almost always safer than more.

Neither the emperor nor his heir make any unnerving moves during the meal. Tarquin keeps up a subdued conversation with the older members of court seated around him. Marclinus is his often-typical jovial self, laughing and teasing both those nearby and occasionally hollering quips to the nobles at other tables.

As the servers clear our dessert dishes, the emperor motions for those of us at the head table to stay in our seats. Other staff move into the center of the room, pushing back some of the furniture and arranging several chairs around a smaller, round table where they set out more than a dozen bottles of wine and a ring of goblets.

My pulse thuds faster in shaky anticipation. Some members of the court have drifted out of the room, but many linger around the edges, watching with open curiosity.

We're about to become another spectacle.

Marclinus gets to his feet and beckons us. "Ladies, join

me for an extra drink. You deserve a chance to relax after all your efforts."

Somehow I have trouble believing that the tableau he's creating has anything to do with us relaxing.

The six of us remaining move to the circle of chairs, Fausta striding ahead with a regal air though I can't see that any of the options gives an advantage over the others. At least with her seated first, I can ensure I'm not sitting next to her.

The imperial heir settles into the last of the chairs and snaps his fingers at the waiting server. She takes the first bottle and fills all of the goblets to the top. Emperor Tarquin positions himself beyond our ring, his piercing gaze traveling over each of us.

There are only six glasses, I can't help noticing as the server sets one right in front of me. Is Marclinus not partaking of this drinking session?

"Don't be shy," he says to us in a cheerful tone. "Drink up!"

I raise my goblet tentatively to my lips. The wine isn't one of the typical vintages we drink with meals but something sweeter, headier. It goes down smoothly, but I can tell it'll pack a punch.

Unfortunately, there's no option for moderation now. As I sip, Marclinus motions to us all with energetic impatience. "Come, now. Look how much we have to get through! You're not really celebrating until you're at least three glasses in."

Three goblets of this stuff and I might be on the floor.

I can't avoid his orders, though. By seating us at a new table with nothing else around, there are no napkins for me to spit into or dishes that might conceal an errant dribble.

What's he after with this trial? It doesn't seem like him or his father to put us through a repeat of our previous over-indulgent dinner, only with purely liquid this time. And there are no buckets to contain the results of a few drinks too many.

By the bottom of the second glass, my thoughts have taken on a fuzzy edge. By the third, I seem to lose my sense of balance for a moment here and there, leaving me swaying to one side and the other. From the giggles and wobbles around our table, I'm definitely not the only one so affected.

Marclinus offers us a pleased smile. "That's more like it. No need for nerves, no need for caution. You can say whatever you like to me without a single worry. Lady Leonette, how have you been enjoying these trials?"

The normally solemn woman now has a small, uneven smile curving across her dark face. "You've certainly given us a lot of variety and challenge."

"Indeed I have; indeed I have. Lady Giralda, I'd love to know—what about me do you find most obnoxious?"

A chill seeps through my tipsiness, but the other woman guffaws and then covers her mouth. "You're not at all obnoxious, Your Imperial Highness. You're just perfect."

"Wonderful." Marclinus taps his mouth by his scar and gestures to the server. "How about another round? Any objections?"

I'd like to make one, but I'm abruptly sure of the nature of this test. He's looking to get us drunk enough that we might let some supposedly traitorous thought slip out.

As if any of us should really be blamed for not appreciating every aspect of his personality and his ridiculous, sadistic trials.

Those are exactly the sorts of resentments he and his father are hoping we might reveal. I take a few slow breaths as the server refills our goblets, focusing my mind on the simplest, most positive ways I could view the situation we're in.

Keep those thoughts at the front of my mind. Shove the frustration and the horror so far down they can't spill out no matter how much the wine loosens my tongue.

Between swallows I pace as slowly as I feel I can get away with, Marclinus leans toward me. "And our lovely princess. Am I everything you expected?"

A giggle bursts out of me alongside a jolt of panic that I couldn't contain the sound. But it's funny partly because I can honestly say, "Oh, yes, absolutely."

Every bit the cruel, selfish prick I desperately hoped I'd be wrong about.

His eyes gleam with malicious mischief. "But if you could change just one thing…"

"We would already be married," I tell him, more emphatically than I'd have preferred, but it is also true without sounding like a real complaint.

Marclinus claps his hands in approval with a laugh of his own. "I'm sorry to have delayed that promised day. It shouldn't take much longer, if you prove yourself until the end."

Fausta speaks up abruptly, lifting her goblet as if she's calling for a toast. "You don't like having competition, wild princess. Don't like needing to prove yourself when you know we're better than you. When we've been nothing but welcoming."

Annoyance surges up inside me, but even in my increasingly blurry state, I recognize that she's goading me. She wants me to snap back at her about her abuse.

Why?

There are things Marclinus isn't supposed to know… about what she and Bianca have done… about how *I* recovered from it.

I'm already snorting at the absurdity of her statement.

"Welcoming? You've insulted me every chance you get, even when I've been perfectly nice to you. You ruined my dress. You—you—"

I shut my mouth through sheer force of will. I'm not going to talk about what happened in the woods.

It would get me in more trouble than her.

Fausta isn't willing to let the subject go. "I *what*, Princess Aurelia? I think you've just been careless, then trying to blame your faults on others."

My goblet wobbles in my hand. Yes, I carelessly walked into her fists and knees—not her fault at all she broke my bones—

No. Not that. "I'm going to win fairly instead of by tearing everyone else down," I announce. "You must be awfully afraid you're not good enough if you think you need to attack me to make it through."

The jab satisfies me without bringing back the panic that I've said too much.

Fausta growls and grabs one of the still-full wine bottles. "Let's have another drink just the two of us, Princess. *I* want to celebrate His Imperial Highness's generosity and cleverness to the fullest."

I can't restrain another snort, but at least it could sound like I'm mocking her desire to celebrate rather than the idea of Marclinus being generous. As she fills her glass herself and makes a grabbing gesture toward mine, he watches avidly.

What will he make of it if I refuse? Gritting my teeth, I shove the goblet across the table toward my rival. But I watch every move she makes for signs of sabotage.

I suspect she sloshes even more wine into my glass than her own, but she snatches up hers and throws it back before I can protest for a comparison. I clutch mine with an increasingly wobbly grasp and force myself to gulp.

My stomach turns. Before the end of this, Marclinus might wish he'd brought buckets after all.

He's still watching our standoff with interest, but his attention has shifted toward Fausta. "Why does Princess Aurelia bother you so much, Lady Fausta?"

Fausta points an accusing finger at me. "She doesn't belong here. She doesn't know Dariu, so she can't be everything you need."

"I'll learn," I retort before I can catch my mouth. My mind is absolutely reeling now. Shit.

"And surely our great country could become even greater with fresh perspectives," Marclinus suggests.

Fausta shakes her head and then looks slightly green from the motion. "No. No. It's perfect as it is. Just like you."

I think she might honestly believe that.

Marclinus's smile sharpens. "But you don't think I'm perfect. You think I was wrong to invite Princess Aurelia into this competition."

My heart skips a beat. For a second, it seems Fausta might have backed herself into a corner—that this might be her end.

I'm not even sure how I feel about that. As much as she's harassed me, would I cheer for her death?

But Fausta brushes off the imperial heir's accusation without a hint of concern. "You weren't wrong. You're reminding us all that we must always aspire to be better, or the outer domains might try to usurp us. We can't get con —complacent."

She smothers a hiccup.

Mollified, Marclinus turns to his next target. "How have you been enjoying the tasks I've set out for you, Lady Iseppa?"

I think Iseppa might have already gone through a couple

of glasses of wine during lunch. Her mouth is twisted as if she's fighting queasiness, and her gaze wanders aimlessly. "They're good," she mumbles. "Showing what we can do. Good."

"You don't sound all that sure about it."

Her lips part, and at first all that comes out is a thin wail. "Why are you bothering us? We're trying. I'm trying. It's hard."

Despite my hazy state, my body stiffens. That isn't the right answer.

The room goes utterly silent. Even Giralda's drunken snickers subside.

Marclinus fixes Iseppa with a piercing look. "Have I been too hard on you, Lady Iseppa?"

She stumbles over her words. "Yes—no—I don't know what you want me to say. Tell me… I can do this right… It's just too much."

"I'm sorry you feel that way."

He speaks without the slightest trace of compassion. I don't even see the gesture—perhaps Emperor Tarquin was the one to give the summons from beyond our circle.

A guard grabs Iseppa off her chair and yanks her away from the table. She only manages a whimper before I hear the gristly sound of severed flesh.

My shoulders slump. That means this trial is over, doesn't it? He's eliminated one. What more could he possibly want right now?

I should know that with Marclinus, there can always be more. As the guard hauls Iseppa's corpse away, the imperial heir nudges his chair back from us and beckons to someone beyond our circle.

Not someone—several someones. Perhaps a dozen of the

young men from the court step forward. My gaze snags on Prince Raul among them, but he isn't looking at me.

Marclinus's benevolent tone returns. "I'm not the only one who finds you quite pleasing, my ladies. Allow the esteemed men of my court to show you their fondness as well."

What in the realms is happening now?

Five of the men continue approaching. Raul goes to Leonette, right next to me, his gaze trained only on her. Another jolt of nausea ripples through me watching him stroke her smooth cheek as she stares back at him.

"I've always thought you were a beauty," he says in the cajoling voice I know well.

One of the noblemen pushes toward me, and I jerk my attention to him. My hand has clenched—I don't know if I want to punch Raul for talking that way to another woman in front of me or Leonette for receiving his flirtation.

I can't. Neither. This is the rest of the trial.

The man who fondles his lovers in front of us wants to make sure we're loyal only to him, I suppose. The fucking hypocrisy.

My would-be suitor taps my chin and offers a provocative smile. "I think you've been neglected during your time here, Princess Aurelia. None of the other ladies can hold a candle to you."

His even features and bright eyes would be handsome enough if I were making an objective assessment. I can barely focus on him with Raul murmuring husky promises to the woman just a couple of feet away from me.

My chest constricts. This is dangerous. All of it is dangerous: everything I'm feeling, everything I've felt.

If I lose too much of myself to the princes who've evolved from enemies to allies, I'll have prepared my own doom.

The nobleman whose name I don't know teases his fingers along my jaw. Anger vibrates through me—and I realize that now, just this once, I can let it out.

I can release the fury that's built up inside me over the past week and a half, even if I can't aim it at the right target.

I slap the man's hand away. "Don't touch me. I'm not here for you to play with."

As I wish I could have shouted at Marclinus all those times before. As I'd like to yell in his face now.

He'd kill me if he knew I meant these words for him, but he'd *want* me to lash out against a potential seduction from anyone else.

This sick, sick game…

The nobleman in front of me starts to stammer. "I only wanted to admire you up close. It's impossible not to be drawn to you—"

"You'll just have to figure out how," I break in, letting my rage sear through my words. "Get away from me. I don't want you anywhere near me. I didn't ask for this."

Someone in our audience lets out a low whistle. As the nobleman retreats, face blotchy with embarrassment, my listing gaze lands on Marclinus.

He's grinning at me. So triumphant in my supposed faithfulness.

But the anger I just unleashed has taken enough edge off my temper that I don't spit the same harsh words in his face. And then he turns, just as one of the other ladies sighs at her suitor's caress of her neck.

The man tenses and glances toward Marclinus. The imperial heir gives him an encouraging nod, though his smirk has hardened.

"Shall I go on?" the nobleman says to his target. "You've

always been the sweetest lady in the court. If I could kiss even your hand, it would leave my heart singing."

Her face flushes. She pulls her arm back when he tries to carry out his request, but her eyes sparkle as she looks up at him. A giddy smile crosses her lips.

Just like that, she consigns herself to execution.

Marclinus stretches out his legs. "I prefer the ladies who have eyes only for me. If all it takes is a few glasses of wine to let another turn your head…"

He flicks his fingers, and another guard steps forward.

At the hiss of the drawn blade, I allow my head to loll forward as if simply out of drunkenness. Once again, I hear but don't see the slice of the flesh, the thump of the body.

The sound rings on through my head alongside my jumbled thoughts.

Four left.

Any satisfaction I got from releasing a little misdirected anger sputters out.

It didn't get me anywhere. I'm still just as trapped as I was before.

And gods only know what misery our adoring husband-to-be will put us through next.

CHAPTER THIRTY-FOUR

Raul

I remember hearing Lorenzo play when we were kids, before he had any gift. The way he'd get caught up in the melodies he could create with his own two hands seemed like a little piece of freedom.

Now, as the court circulates in the hall of entertainments, the strains of music that wash over me sound even sweeter than they did back then. All the same, my stomach clenches tighter with each new song.

They've turned into a reminder of how the emperor will take anything we can do and twist it to his own advantage.

Lorenzo doesn't want to be playing for these pricks. He doesn't even *like* any of them.

But he's still going, song after song, because not capitulating would lead to something even worse.

Bastien comes up beside me where I'm standing by one of the tall windows, out of the way of the roving crowd. He considers Lorenzo's pose on the performer's platform several feet away and frowns. "It's been nearly two hours now, hasn't it?"

I nod, my teeth setting on edge. Tarquin set Lorenzo up with his vielle the moment we came here after dinner and hasn't given him more of a break than a minute to have a brief drink.

As we watch, Lorenzo's bow glides to the end of the current song. His arm wobbles as he lowers it. His face looks drawn.

He glances toward Tarquin, who's pontificating to his advisors and other high-ranking nobles by the front of the room. I can't make out much of the emperor, but I catch the quick wave of his hand: the universal gesture for *Keep going*.

Lorenzo's mouth tightens. As he raises the bow again, something about his posture makes my own body tense.

He strokes the bow across the strings, sending notes so bright they practically shimmer out into the room. The melody winds through the crowd.

And Lorenzo's knees buckle.

A shout of alarm breaks from my throat even as I launch myself toward him. Bastien dashes after me.

The collapse seems to slow through the blurring of my adrenaline, or maybe Lorenzo is still aware enough to catch his fall a little. But then his eyes roll up, the instrument tumbling from his fingers—

I dive forward just in time to shove my hand beneath his head so his skull smacks into my palm rather than the hard wooden platform. I barely register the twinge of pain.

"Lore!" I say, patting my other hand against his cheeks. "Hey! Can you hear me?"

His eyelids flutter. Bastien drops down beside us, his

expression taut. "He pushed his gift too far. He should see a medic."

Lorenzo reaches up to snag my arm with his fingers. He manages a firmer blink and then a shake of his head.

Ignoring him, I straighten up to scan the room for any of the imperial medics who might be in attendance. If there's one around, they should at least take a look at him.

Instead, my gaze stalls on our other foster brother. Neven's face has hardened into a mask of fury as he stares in our direction.

The kid's gaze jerks to the emperor, who's barely given Lorenzo a cursory glance after the fall. Neven is too far off amid the court nobles for me to hear his voice, but the movement of his lips is emphatic enough for me to decipher his words anyway: "Fucking bastard."

He hurtles toward Emperor Tarquin.

My heart lurches. "Neven," I hiss to Bastien, and jump off the platform, leaving him to help Lorenzo sit up.

The head of pale blond hair is weaving through the crowd at an aggressive pace. I'll have to shove my way through to reach him before he gets to Tarquin, and then it'd be a scene anyway.

But at least not a scene that would see Neven executed.

I'm shouldering between a couple of barons when an unexpected voice brings me to a halt.

"Prince Neven!" The chandelier light gleams off Aurelia's bronze-brown hair where she's moved to intercept the kid. Between the shifting bodies that block most of my view, I make out a swift flash of her smile. "I'm so glad our paths crossed. I was hoping you could lend me that book you mentioned from your recent studies before you turn in for the night."

What I can see of Neven's expression is utterly baffled, his confusion momentarily fracturing his vengeful rage. I don't know what answer stumbles out of him, but Aurelia gives an impressively easygoing laugh.

"It's all right. I'm sure you have a lot of responsibilities to keep track of. I could walk with you now—I was about to take my leave for the evening as it is."

She nudges him toward the doorway. Whatever Bastien said to calm his animosity toward the princess obviously sank in, because the kid doesn't try to bite her head off instead of Tarquin's. She manages to get him out the door without any blood spilled or even insults hurled.

I have to clamp my jaw to stop myself from gaping. That woman is nothing short of a force of nature.

Why did she even intervene? I can't believe Neven really did offer to lend her a book—or that anything from his studies would interest her when she has access to the entire imperial library.

Bastien and Lorenzo join me, Bastien still gripping Lorenzo's arm to steady him. They stare toward the doorway.

"I talked with her about Pavel," Bastien says quietly. "She'd already heard a little of the story… She knows how much it matters to us to make sure Neven doesn't get into trouble."

So she took it upon herself to step in when the rest of us were too distant. Simply because she could.

After everything I've seen of her, I shouldn't be surprised. Still, an ache expands through my chest from throat to gut, like nothing I've ever felt before.

I force myself to turn back to Lorenzo. "Are you all right? We can still demand a medic—"

Lorenzo makes a hasty gesture that amounts to, *I'm fine. Just need to rest.*

The regular court musicians are already assembling on

the platform, apparently directed there by Tarquin. So fatherly of him to show absolutely no concern for the foster son he pushed to the point of fainting. Much more important to make sure the nobles don't have to go without music for more than a minute.

I bite back my own rage and help Lorenzo out into the hallway.

After Bastien and I have escorted him to his bedroom and confirmed that he isn't going to crumple again, Bastien says goodnight with a grimace and trudges into his own chambers. I hesitate outside mine for a few seconds and then stride back the way I came.

My knock on the door to Aurelia's room brings no answer. Where else would she go?

I know she's ended up in the library before, but a glance into the maze of decaying paper reveals no sign of her. I'm wandering the halls, caught up in a restless tension I can't expel, when I glance out a window and spot her pale dress amid the garden hedges.

Of course. The princess of the wild north likes to roam— as far as our imperial jailers will let any of us wander, at least.

By the time I make it to the gardens myself, Aurelia has meandered past the fountains, hedges, and beds of flowers to the edge of the woods. She pauses there, considering them as if unsure whether she dares to venture into the thick shadows between the trees.

I can't blame her for hesitating after the violent reception that met her the last time she walked that far.

At the rasp of my steps over the path, her head jerks around. She turns to completely face me, the lavender silk of her dress swirling around her perfect curves.

Seeing her now after all I've watched her endure, it's hard to believe I ever thought she looked *soft*. The steel inside her shows in everything from the set of her eyes to the firming of her posture as she braces for my approach.

Why is she studying me so warily? I thought we'd parted on reasonably warm terms the last time we spoke. She welcomed my attentions, if only for a short time.

Of course, the last time she *saw* me, I was fawning over one of her competitors right next to her.

The memory turns my stomach, and not only because of the role I played in it. Watching her sway and slur her speech with the addling of the wine, her careful composure crumbling... It was almost as awful as when Marclinus literally stripped her bare of any possible defenses.

But she held on to her iron will throughout. Aimed her ire at the only safe targets she had and managed to play the eager fiancé to Marclinus.

Gods above, I'd have liked to punch his arrogant face in.

She shows no sign of drunkenness now. From what I noticed, she didn't touch the dinner wine.

Her voice is absolutely steady and clear, if quiet. "What do you want?"

There's no hostility to the question, but I can't say it's remotely friendly either.

I stop a few paces away and offer a crooked grin. "It's a lovely night. Who wouldn't want to take a turn in the gardens? It'd be even better with a little conversation."

Aurelia's eyebrows arch. "So you came over simply hoping to chat?"

Her tone remains impassive. She's definitely not *pleased* with me at the moment, whatever's going on in her head.

If we're going to hash out the problem, I'd rather move completely out of view of the palace. I motion toward the nearby trees. "Perhaps I could accompany you into the woods, since they've sometimes proven treacherous."

The corners of Aurelia's mouth tighten, whether because of my company or my reference to her beating, I can't tell. She whirls with another ripple of her airy dress and walks into the shadows without waiting for me to escort her.

I follow her in silence. The forest around us is still other than the occasional rustle of the leaves overhead and the buzz of passing insects.

When we've ventured far enough that I judge it safe to speak, I lift my voice just loud enough for her to hear. "Thank you for stepping in with Neven tonight."

Aurelia stops. "It looked like he was about to get himself into trouble he might not be able to get back out of. And I understood why he was angry." She glances at me. "Is Lorenzo all right?"

The concern in her voice is the first definite emotion she's shown. Jealousy I'm not sure I have any right to feel jabs through my chest and draws me closer to her. "Tarquin's been pushing him to use his gift too much, but he should be fine once he's had some rest. Neven wouldn't have been fine if he'd thrown a fit about it."

My lips curve into a softer grin. "I'm starting to think you're not so much a lamb as a shepherdess."

I was hoping to provoke a smile in return, but she only offers the same impenetrable expression. "I help where I can."

Anger prickles up alongside another wave of jealousy.

This is all Marclinus's fault. He ordered me to be a puppet in his psychotic trial; he humiliated both of us.

And he's going to be the one who has her in the end.

It isn't fucking *right*. After what he's put this woman through, the only thing he deserves is a knife in the gut.

I take another step toward Aurelia, reining in my roiling emotions as well as I can. "You know I didn't want to be a part of his idiotic test. I didn't want to be fawning over her with you right there."

Aurelia shrugs, but heat flashes in her eyes. "From what I've heard, you've fawned over plenty of ladies when I wasn't around. I'm not sure why my proximity should make a difference."

"None of that mattered. It was performing, just like you said."

"And what do you call what you've been doing with me?" she demands.

It isn't the same. I don't want the others. I've never wanted *any* of the simpering ladies of Tarquin's court the way I've been burning for this fierce and yet caring woman in front of me.

I saw the full depths of her strength when she fought her way through that wretched illness to cure herself. I knew she'd convinced even Bastien that she wanted to protect our countries as well as her own.

But nothing prepared me for watching her stand up to Marclinus the other night, utterly naked yet unshakably determined, risking her life to save a woman she met only weeks ago. Outmaneuvering the imperial heir in his own sick game.

When her spot remained empty at the breakfast table the next morning, when we realized Lady Fausta must have done something to her—the memory of the anguish that surged up inside me makes my gut shudder all over again.

None of the words I could use feel like enough to convey all that emotion. A strangled sound escapes me.

An urgency I can't contain—to show her how much she matters, to make her see—propels me forward.

Grasping her waist, I push her up against the nearest tree and plant my lips on hers.

Gods help me, this is a kiss worth all the waiting, all the sniping and sparring of our chaotic flirtation. Her mouth sears against mine, her lips parting like an inevitability. She clutches the collar of my shirt, but only to yank me closer.

I flick my tongue over the seam of her lips to coax them farther apart, and she opens to me. A whimper works from her throat that has me hard in an instant.

The things I want to do with this woman—the things I *could* do out here in the woods with no one to see—

Her hands ball against my chest, and then she's shoving me away.

I let go of her and back up a single pace, heat still flooding my body from our embrace. Even in the dimness, I can see the flush that's risen in Aurelia's cheeks, the hungry widening of her eyes.

With a quiver of my gift, I know just how damp her drawers are.

Why is she putting a halt to what we're both craving?

The words tumble out, harsher than I intend. "We're not done."

Aurelia crosses her arms in front of her. "You don't get to decide that. Not unless you think you're going to force the issue as Marclinus prefers to."

The comparison cools my lust while raising my hackles. I wave my hand toward her. "You *want* this. You're panting for it."

"It's been made very clear to me over the course of the past several days that what I want has little bearing on anything at all."

Her voice is tart, but the truth behind those words cuts right through the core of me. My anger dwindles too.

I meet her eyes in the darkness, searching for the gleam of defiance and passion I know she still has in her. "It matters to me. I mean that. Not as any kind of ploy, just because it's true. You deserve better than anything that prick can offer you. I'll still believe that even if you never kiss me again."

Her face tightens. "How can it matter when I can't choose anything else in the end anyway?"

The faintest quaver runs through the words, a hint of sadness that wrenches at my heart.

Before I can come up with an answer, Aurelia brushes past me and strides off toward the palace.

All I can do is stare after her, feeling more beaten than any opponent in the arena has ever left me.

CHAPTER THIRTY-FIVE

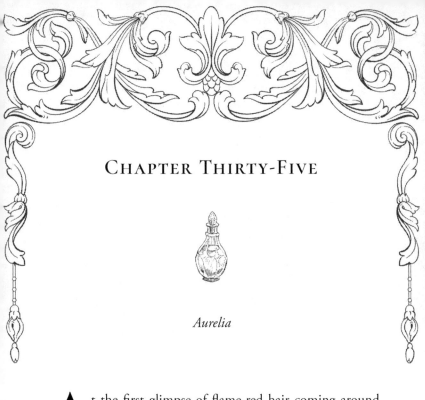

Aurelia

At the first glimpse of flame-red hair coming around the bend in the stairs below, I nearly halt in my tracks.

But why should I give ground to Fausta? As hazy as my memories of our drunken argument yesterday are, I know what I said was true.

She's harassed and attacked me because she recognizes that I'm a threat. She's afraid of me.

I'll be damned if I'm going to let her believe I'm at all scared of her.

I continue down toward the second floor, not planning on sparing her even a glance, though I'm monitoring her carefully at the edge of my vision. But Fausta stops, moving to the side as if she means to block my way.

I pause and peer down at her, unwilling to push for an altercation. "Excuse me."

Fausta meets my gaze unwaveringly, her bright green eyes as hard as the emeralds they resemble. "I don't think I will."

For the sake of all that's holy, will this woman never give up?

I hold in my exasperation. "I didn't set out to make you my enemy. I have nothing against you." Other than the injuries she's already dealt me. But it was Marclinus who put us at odds.

It doesn't appear my rival cares about that fact. She ascends another step. "You didn't need to come here at all. You have so much, *Princess*. This is my only chance to be something more than the wife of an ineffectual nobleman."

What does she think my other options would have been?

I swallow hard. "He asked for my hand. He invited me here."

Fausta scowls. "Do you even actually *want* him? I've known Marclinus since I was a toddler. I know exactly what he needs in a wife, and I'll enjoy offering it. All you see is his crown."

That isn't entirely accurate, but the kernel of truth in her words pricks at me.

She makes it sound so simple. She has no idea the responsibilities resting on my shoulders, the grief and suffering of an entire country I'm carrying with me.

Her comment about "ineffectual noblemen" proves that she wants to stand beside him for his power just as much as I do. How many people would that power benefit in her hands besides herself?

"There's only one imperial heir," I say, "and he'll decide what he wants for himself. How many marchions and viceroys could you have chosen from and still stayed right here in the palace?"

Fausta takes one more step up so she's just below me on

the staircase. "Why should I have to settle for anything less than you would? What makes you more deserving than I am? Because you happened to be lucky enough to be born a princess?"

The thread of pain in her voice sends a pang through me. Our respective titles *are* a mere matter of chance.

Before the brief flicker of compassion can fully take hold, Fausta rams her knee into my shin, just inches from where she fractured the bone three days ago.

I gasp, my leg buckling, but through the blaze of agony I manage to shove out before Fausta can land another blow. My push sends her stumbling across the stairs.

We glare at each other for several thuds of my heart, my hand clutching the railing and my weight shifted onto my better leg. My other arm rises defensively in case she launches herself at me again.

Fausta must judge it too great a risk to attack me when I'm prepared. She offers a sharp little smile and minces on up the stairs past me without a backward glance. "May the best of us win."

Her tone leaves no doubt about who she believes that would be.

Gritting my teeth, I test my battered leg. The pain left behind after the medic's attentions had mostly faded, but now it's searing all through my calf again.

For all I know, she's re-cracked the bone.

I limp slowly down to the second floor. By the time I reach the hall, it's clear there's no unbearable damage done. I can walk steadily as long as I don't try to hurry—and gird myself against the continued ache.

Straightening my spine, I walk on to the parlor where most of the court is currently gathered.

The moment I step through the doorway, my gaze lands on Bastien's slim form by the table laid with appetizers. The other three princes stand nearby, clustered together in conversation.

I yank my gaze away and head to the opposite side of the room.

I've made peace with them; I've earned their good will. That should be enough. That's all I *need* to count on their support.

And the things I've started to want could threaten my chances more than Lady Fausta ever has.

Gods only know what they might do if they found out she hurt me again right here in the palace.

I've only made it a few steps before a careful hand catches my elbow. "Princess," Rochelle murmurs at my side. "I need to, ah, consult with you about some new dresses."

That hardly sounds like an urgent conversation, but I let her usher me over to a couple of chairs in the corner with a little distance from the closest nobles. As I sink down, taking the weight off my injured leg, my stance relaxes with relief. "What's this about dresses?"

Rochelle's mouth twitches with a brief grimace. "Sorry. That was just an excuse to come in and talk to you. I saw you in the hall—it looked like you were favoring your leg more than this morning. Are you well?"

I wasn't able to put on quite as good an act as I hoped, at least not to someone who's familiar with my habits.

I let out a restrained sigh and rub my shin. "I had an unpleasant encounter with Lady Fausta in the stairwell. It might have set my healing back by a day or two. I have a salve in my chambers that'll help with any bruising. It'll be easier to walk all the way there after I've rested my leg a bit."

Rochelle sits up straighter, her voice darkening. "You'd think she'd be satisfied after everything she's already done. What a terror of an empress she'd be. Do you want me to fetch the salve for you?"

I shake my head, a smile crossing my lips at her fervor. "Thank you, but I wouldn't be able to put it on in here without being obvious about it anyway. The discomfort has already improved quite a bit; I'm sure I'll be fine in a few minutes."

Rochelle smiles back at me. "If you weren't a princess, you'd make an awfully good medic, you know. Obviously there's your gift, but you've also got such a calm, steady air about you... That's one of the things that made me notice Tevio too. The way he can always put whoever he's helping at ease."

I ignore the twinge that passes through my heart. "I'm glad you have a good man to count on."

"Hopefully." Rochelle laughs, twisting her hands on her lap, but her expression turns dreamy despite her brief show of nerves. "My little brother sprained his ankle a few days before Father and I made the trip here. Tevio had him fixed up and clambering around again right away. When I saw him out, he gave me a dried rose he'd saved for me... I left it in my bedroom at home. I thought it was safer there."

She's lost her title and possibly her family—but she still looks happy when she talks about the man she adores. An echo of that feeling reverberates through me, stirring an unwanted melancholy.

That sort of love isn't for me. It's not what I'm meant for.

The things I'll accomplish instead will be worth more than anything I'm missing.

And if reminding myself of that fact doesn't soothe the

ache in my chest quite as well as it has before, I won't acknowledge it.

"I'll let you know as soon as I hear anything from him," I assure Rochelle.

"I know." She glances around. "I should probably go before anyone thinks it's odd that we're talking for so long. I'll be ready if you need anything else."

After she's ducked out of the room, I wait for another couple of minutes before getting back to my feet. A renewed throbbing wakes up in my shin, but significantly dulled.

I figure I can stroll around the room a couple of times to show I've made an appearance and then slip away to my room without anyone wondering. As I'm passing the windows overlooking the gardens, a small group of nobles I think I recognize as all barons and baronissas approaches me.

I brace myself inwardly while keeping my expression mild. But even though I catch Bianca shooting a narrow glance our way from farther across the room, my five sudden companions all dip their heads to me and beam in a manner I can only describe as ingratiating.

"It's good to see you well, Your Highness," one of the baronissas simpers.

Is it? No one in the court has shown any concern for my well-being before.

I have to be gracious. "Thank you. It's a lovely day."

A baron puffs out his chest. "And lovely to have you among us for it. We hoped you might share your thoughts on the palace cuisine."

Another baronissa, possibly his wife, nods eagerly. "We were thinking it would be interesting if Their Imperial Eminences included more delicacies from Accasy in your honor."

An inkling of what their sudden interest might be about tickles through my head.

There are only four prospective brides left. I've handled myself at least decently well in every challenge so far.

Some of the nobles are hedging their bets. Predicting that I'll be the next empress and deciding it'll be to their advantage to be among the first to act more welcoming.

They don't really like me or care what I think. They don't *know* me.

It's just one more game I have to play along with.

My spirits sink lower, but I know I should make the best of the situation. It might win me points with the emperor and his heir if they notice that their court is starting to warm up to me, whatever the nobles' reasons.

I adjust my course to meander toward the far end of the room where Marclinus is in the middle of a lively debate. Emperor Tarquin looks on, sipping from a goblet.

"It's kind of you to want to try more of what Accasy has to offer," I say to my new "friends." "I'd be happy to make a few suggestions to the kitchen staff if Their Imperial Eminences request it. But I've been very pleased with the offerings so far. The cooks are impressively skilled."

Another baronissa pipes up with a glint in her eyes that's almost manic. "What's your favorite dish so far? I *adore* the crusted cod."

We had that for one of our courses at dinner a few nights ago. "It was quite good. I'm not sure I could pick a favorite when so much of it has been so delicious."

The baron beside her clears his throat. "I thought the creekvine wine was quite a unique addition to our first meal with you. Is it a very popular drink in Accasy?"

So we go on, with every answer I give met with hollow smiles and a hasty attempt to show their enthusiasm, however superficial. No one mentions any topic more thought-provoking than the contents of our meals. When I make a brief comment about my admiration of the people who work in our vineyards, my hangers-on murmur vague agreement and immediately move on to discussing the best sort of soup.

Is this a taste of what my life as empress would be like?

I run my thumb over the side of my ring, letting the rippled texture ground me.

I know why I came here. I know how much good I can do.

Fausta's right that I was born a princess through chance alone, and that's the lot I have in life, good and bad. This opportunity is what all my education and preparation has been leading toward.

It doesn't do anyone any good wishing for a different life.

But I do.

With a tremor of guilt, I squash down that selfish desire as far as I can. In my distraction, I almost miss the energetic swing of Marclinus's hand and the way Emperor Tarquin's arm twitches with a jolt of startled reflexes just as he's lifted his cup to his lips.

It must send an extra surge of liquid into his mouth. He sputters and coughs into his hand.

I knit my brow. "I hope Emperor Tarquin is all right."

The nobles around me pause. One of the baronissas speaks up tentatively. "I heard someone mention he's seemed a bit off lately…"

A baron jumps in with an anxious tick of his jaw. "I'm sure it's only a brief illness, obviously something mild. He's always had a very hardy constitution."

We make one more circuit of the room with another round of fawning and frivolous conversation. The ache in my shin starts to expand, telling me I'm going to need to get off that leg soon.

I smile at my companions with what I hope passes for gratitude. "Thank you for the delightful conversation. I'm going to retire to my room for a little while."

I walk to my chambers as quickly as I can without looking like I'm fleeing. My heart lifts at the sight of the door up ahead—and sinks when I step inside to find Melisse waiting for me.

The maid greets me with a wide grin. "Your Highness—I timed things well. I'll get everything ready for your usual bath."

She bustles into the bathing room with a swish of her fawn-brown bob.

This is good, I tell myself as water hisses into the tub. I already decided I needed to show her I still value her service as much as possible. I can accept a little more company and tend to my leg with the salve after the bath. A soak might do it some good as well.

I wait in my gown for Melisse to return. Looking pleased, she loosens the adjustments Rochelle made this morning and peels it off over my head.

"Did you have the chance to talk with His Imperial Highness today?" she asks. "I know you've made a good impression so far."

My stomach twists, but I brighten my voice. "Only a little, but I was glad to."

"Maybe there'll be more opportunity at dinner or after. Oh, I can't imagine what it must be like to have a man like him courting you."

I'm not sure anyone could say Marclinus is courting *me* —or his other potential brides—rather than very much the

other way around. And something about Melisse's tone
niggles at me.

She ushers me into the bathing room and folds my
undergarments as I remove them. "I suppose even so you
must miss your old home after being away for so long."

My uneasiness digs deeper. She's prying for information,
trying to judge how happy I am. Did Emperor Tarquin ask
her to prod me?

Easing into the warm water, I try not to think about all
the events I'll have missed. Are my sister and her husband
expecting their first child now? Has Lady Nica put on the
play she was planning to bring more laughter into the city?
Did Lady Cataline finally work up the courage to confess her
feelings to the lord she's been eyeing?

I push those questions aside. "Of course it's difficult not
seeing my family. But I'm so well taken care of here, it's hard
to be homesick."

Melisse leans over to pick up the sponge. "If you *are* ever
dissatisfied with anything, you can just let me know, and I'll
see that it's made better for you."

Or run straight to the emperor and tattle that I've dared
to complain.

All at once, my whole chest constricts. I don't know how
much more jostling from Tarquin's people I can take today
before I crack.

I firm my voice so it doesn't shake. "I don't think that will
be necessary. And I'm quite settled now, Melisse. I'd prefer to
bathe alone."

It's far from the first time I've made that request, but the
maid's face falls. She sets the sponge by my shoulder.

"If it was Rochelle attending…" she mutters under her
breath as she stalks out of the room.

I close my eyes against the pressure still welling up inside me.

Maybe I misjudged Melisse's intentions and she was only trying to be friendly? I might have just made Rochelle's new life here even more difficult.

And there's nothing I can do to take back that possible misstep now.

CHAPTER THIRTY-SIX

Aurelia

The letter from Medic Tevio in the town of Garince arrives on the tray Rochelle brings with the hot water for my morning tea. She doesn't comment on it as I set the leaves steeping, but her gaze keeps ticking toward it.

I'm not going to draw out her suspense. As soon as I've put away my tea box, I unseal the letter and scan the sparse contents inside.

Whatever he made of my careful letter to him, he obviously understood the need for discretion. He assures me that as far as he's concerned, "all is well" with my newly hired maid, and he has no apprehensions at all about the position she's taken. If I should want her health re-assessed, he'll be right there in Garince whenever we might stop by.

A clever man as well as a kind one. My friend has good taste.

When I look up at her, her freckled face is so lit with hopeful anticipation that any twinge of envy I might feel melts away beneath the joy I can share with her. "He's made it clear that his feelings for you remain the same and he'll wait until I can return you to Garince."

Rochelle's cheeks flush alongside her sigh of relief. "Thank the gods." She taps her fingers down her front to emphasize the remark of divine gratitude. "Knowing that, I can wait however long it takes too. I don't want to leave in any way that'll cause you trouble."

"I'm sure we can find a reasonable excuse. Once Marclinus is married, there'll necessarily be changes in the arrangement of the palace staff."

I just have to ensure I'm the one marrying him.

I arrive at breakfast holding tight to that goal and smile at the imperial heir as if I'm nothing but delighted to see him. He appears to be in one of his milder moods, offering chuckles rather than raucous laughter and often simply sitting back in his chair to observe the conversations around him.

When we retire to the hall of entertainments with a sudden rain shower pattering against the windows, he ambles over to observe *me* while flanking his father.

Emperor Tarquin studies me with his piercing gaze. "You had correspondence from Garince this morning, Princess Aurelia. I'm surprised you'd be familiar with anyone in that far-flung place."

Of course he's informed of every letter that passes in and out of the palace by official means. That's exactly why we had to be so cautious. I wouldn't be surprised if he read it himself and then resealed it.

I dip my head in respectful acknowledgment. "Since the former Lady Rochelle has never carried out maid duties before, I wanted to be sure she had no infirmities I should be aware of when assigning her responsibilities. It wouldn't do if she embarrassed me with a weakness I wasn't prepared for. She gave me the name of the medic who's attended to her family so I could request his opinion."

It should sound like a sensible enough story. There's no reason for Tarquin to suspect Rochelle of a romantic entanglement with the man.

He hums to himself thoughtfully. "How very thorough of you. Were you satisfied with his assessment?"

"Quite. It seems she has no previous issues with her health that should interfere with any work I might require of her."

"Excellent," Marclinus says. He's toying with his dagger again the way he sometimes likes to do, spinning it slowly between his fingers. The flash of the blade makes my throat tighten, even though he's never carried out any of his ladies' executions himself.

Emperor Tarquin lifts his voice as if he intends to draw the attention of others beyond our small conference. "You haven't had any missives from Accasy thus far."

Where is he going with that point—and why does he want to bring anyone else into the conversation? Several of the court nobles standing nearby glance up at his comment and drift closer to us to follow the discussion. Among them, Bianca offers me a typical smirk and rests her hand on Marclinus's arm.

The emperor stays focused on me. I'm not sure what response he's looking for, but honesty is always safest where possible. "It's a long journey from our capital. It's doubtful that my former maid has even reached my family to confirm my safe arrival yet. I look forward to writing to them to inform them of my happiness here once I've earned your and your son's full approval."

A glint of challenge lights in Marclinus's gray eyes. "You're sure that you will, it seems?"

I bob into a partial curtsy. "I can only endeavour to do my best. But I know this is where I'm meant to be. If I fail to prove that, I'll deserve my fate."

He lets out a short bark of laughter. "So very yielding."

His father's gaze turns more intent. "I wonder if we should thank your dedication to Elox for that part of your temperament, or if it's simply common for Accasians to take such a submissive attitude? I've heard that your people sometimes wander off into the woods when they feel unwell and let the wilderness take them as it will."

Bianca giggles as if this is the funniest idea she's ever heard.

I pretend not to notice the implied insult in the emperor's words. "That's an old tradition, mainly among those who are elderly and feel they've lived their full life already. It's not very common anymore."

In Accasy, it's seen as taking control of your fate rather than submitting to it—deciding that you're ready to go—but I doubt Tarquin will appreciate me contradicting his interpretation.

"It is fascinating to hear how things are done in other places," Marclinus says, although the laziness of his tone hardly gives the impression of avid interest. "I've been honored to know that Accasians include portraits of my father in your temples to pray to him alongside the gods."

Bianca isn't the only one who titters at that comment. I will my stance to stay relaxed despite a flare of irritation.

Some of our temples do hold an alcove dedicated to the current emperor—but only because the invading forces forced the change, insisting that we needed the additional reminder of who we should thank for our "acceptance" into the empire given our distance from its heart.

None of us prays to Tarquin's visage unless there's a soldier watching to take offense if we don't.

It would be deeply unwise to mention any of that. I keep my voice even. "Indeed, we have the utmost respect for our benefactors."

The emperor speaks up in his dry voice. "I've been surprised that for all your rugged landscapes, your workers haven't proven hardier. So many of them end up faltering in their jobs, at least under our watch. Perhaps their passive nature has left them without much ambition to strive to do their best."

With that outright attack on my people's character, I recognize what they're after. This is another small test, seeing whether they can provoke me into arguing on my country's behalf.

Confirming that I'll bow to their opinions even when it comes to the people who matter most to me.

As much as I want to retort that they push the workers they wrench from Accasy far harder than they do their own citizens, that so many of our ambitions are squashed by the empire's demands for money and manpower rather than any lack on our part, I can't. For the sake of those same people.

To serve them later, I have to denigrate them now.

My mouth tastes bitter, but I lower my eyes as if ashamed. "That could be so. We have tended to live fairly simple lives."

"I've been glad to see *you're* not so simple-minded," Marclinus remarks with another spin of his dagger. "That father of yours—we left him in charge of a straightforward bridge-building project, and he managed to ruin it in a matter of weeks. Not the brightest of kings, is he?"

I can't stop my teeth from setting on edge. The bridge in question was far from straightforward—I remember Father venting to Mother about the ridiculousness of the Darium representatives' demands, with no consideration for the practicalities of our landscape.

The project failed because of their own idiocy. Or perhaps they wanted it to fail so they could hold the fact over our heads for some other purpose.

And if I suggest as much, it might be the last thing I say before Marclinus's blade slashes through my flesh.

I hope I've smoothed enough of the strain out of my words for my audience to miss it. "He has never been called brilliant."

The imperial heir guffaws, and a ripple of laughter passes through the gathered nobles. I reach toward my inner calm.

The cool, still space in the center of me no longer feels quite so serene. I'm tarnishing the memories of the majestic forests and cozy hearths with every slight my hosts force me to agree with.

Will they not be satisfied until they've torn apart every bit of who I am?

The answer comes to me as instinctively as breathing.

No, they won't. What are the trials for if not to break us down until nothing remains but our dedication to serving the empire and its rulers?

But it does no one any good if I die for honesty, even if I'm dying inside at the lies.

After a couple more taunting remarks about my homeland, Marclinus appears to bore of the game and saunters away with Bianca hanging on to one arm and a marchionissa I don't know on the other. Emperor Tarquin lingers for a moment as if he's searching for the thoughts I'm hiding behind my carefully tranquil expression.

"One who knows her place will always find a good fit," he says.

He walks off in the opposite direction, leaving me wondering whether that was a compliment or a warning.

Behind my placid mask, my spirit has frayed. I exchange a few more nods and smiles and a warm greeting with one of the baronissas who strolled with me yesterday, but every gesture and word feels more brittle than the last.

I can't afford to snap. Not when I'm so close to my goal.

As soon as I'm sure my departure won't appear to be caused by the conversation about Accasy, I take my leave. To my relief, I find my bedroom empty. I've always told both Melisse and Rochelle that there's no need for them to attend to me between breakfast and lunch.

I flop down on the bed and squeeze my eyes shut against the burn of threatening tears.

I'm stronger than this. I know my purpose. I've already endured so much worse.

Yet every incident I've faced here has chipped away at my foundations before I've had time to re-fortify them, like Fausta bashing my not-quite-healed leg yesterday.

How much longer can I go on before the resolve that keeps me steady starts to disintegrate beneath me?

I've only taken a few deep breaths when a knock thumps against the door. My heart leaps and plummets with dread.

What now?

I force myself to get up and walk closer so my wary voice will be heard through the thick wood. "Who is it?"

There's no answer other than a lighter rap of knuckles against the surface. Abruptly, I can picture the figure on the other side.

I open the door to meet Prince Lorenzo's gaze, turned even darker than usual with worry. He makes a motion asking if he can come in.

My first impulse is to shake my head and close the door again. I've been keeping more distance from the princes since the last trial for good reason. I can't let them shake my focus or my conviction.

I won them over as allies for good reason as well, though. It wouldn't do to outright push them away now that they're on my side.

And, gods smite me, it'd be nice to speak to someone without having to pretend I'm happy here.

I step back to let him enter.

As soon as the door has swung shut, Lorenzo touches my cheek with a brief caress. The brush of his fingertips sends both a bloom of warmth and a shiver of uncertainty through my nerves.

His hands sketch through the air, drawing a clear enough picture of what he wants to convey. *I heard what the emperor and Marclinus said. It was awful. You shouldn't have to listen to them.*

My mouth twists. "But I do."

He frowns in return. *You're not okay.*

I splay my hands in a helpless gesture. "I'll get through it. I always have. It's not as if how I feel about the situation makes a difference."

I care. Lorenzo casts about before his gaze comes back to me. His frustration shows in the brusqueness of his next gestures. *But I can't protect you. What would help? Do you want to go outside?*

I shake my head. "I'd rather not be around anyone else right now. I mean, anyone I'd have to put on a false front with. I appreciate that you're trying."

You could talk. I'll listen.

"I don't know what else there is to say." I look down at my hands, my mouth twisting. "I just… I don't want to lose myself completely. And it's starting to feel like I'm coming so close to the edge."

Lorenzo touches my chin to bring my attention back to him. He turns his fingers in a motion I've come to recognize as meaning himself and the other princes. *My foster brothers and I stay strong by staying together. I'll stand with you too.*

I don't know how to answer the devotion in his message. I don't know how I've earned it.

The words blurt out of me unbidden. "You don't have to. I wouldn't have expected—"

He makes a rough sound and jerks his hand in an emphatic motion. *I'm here.*

He slips his fingers around my elbow and, when I don't resist, gathers me in a gentle embrace. I tip my head against his shoulder, fresh tears prickling at the backs of my eyes. His warm, tangy scent fills my lungs, reminding me of the summer breeze over the ocean back home.

The logical part of my mind tells me I should put a stop to this. I shouldn't toe the line of temptation any farther than I already have.

But the tenderness of Lorenzo's embrace smooths out the cracks that've formed in my center of peace. It's easier to feel like myself when I know at least one other person in this place sees me as I am.

As the ache of loss melts, sharper pang takes its place, running straight down my chest to spark heat between my thighs.

I'm so tired of all these games, of pretending I want what I don't and that I don't want what I do.

In a few days, I'll either be dead or chained to a man I

hate for the rest of my life. A man who was flaunting his lovers in front of me less than an hour ago.

How could anyone say it's wrong for me to pursue my own desires before I've even made a full commitment to him? This might be the last chance I ever get. A little taste of romance to carry me through the long years ahead.

It might be temporary, a sham of anything you could call a real relationship, but at least it'll be mine.

I ease back from Lorenzo just far enough to look up at him. He meets my gaze, teasing his fingers into my hair. Hunger smolders behind the concern in his eyes, but he doesn't lean in.

He's letting me make the choice of where I want this moment to lead. Somehow that makes me even surer.

I bob up on my toes and meld my mouth to his. With a hitch of breath, Lorenzo kisses me back hard.

The moment we've started, it's hard to imagine we could ever stop. Like I'm drunk on him and parched for more.

As one kiss blurs into the next, he strokes his fingers down the side of my neck, sparking tingles in their wake. There's nothing but confidence in the way he cups my breast now, drawing a gasp out of me with one firm swivel of his thumb.

My body sways toward him of its own accord. He trails his hand down to my waist and tugs my hips closer against his. His teeth nick my lower lip before grazing over my jaw and down my neck to follow the same path as his fingers.

Every inch of my skin has lit up. I grasp his hair, his shoulder, whimpering when he sucks hard on the crook of my neck. My legs tremble with the rush of sensation.

Lorenzo's hand teases down my thigh and back up again, and I clutch him harder through another tremor. Then he's lowering me onto the thick rug so we're kneeling together.

He kisses me on the mouth again, long and so intense my breath shakes when we part. A heated sort of determination solidifies in his expression.

He guides me back on my ass and slides his hand up my calf beneath the skirt of my gown. My pulse hiccups with a mix of excitement and fear.

Just how many lines am I going to cross this morning?

As he reaches my knee, my lips part with an instinctive protest—and Lorenzo raises his other hand. He holds my gaze firmly, spelling out his intentions with emphatic gestures.

Only for you. I'll make you feel good.

The promise reminds me of Raul offering to distract me from my pain here in this room just days ago. But Lorenzo doesn't look like he's trying to claim a prize or prove his superiority.

He wants to give me this one thing that he can.

I shift back on my hands, my heart beating fast. Giving him a chance to show exactly what he has in mind.

If I change my mind and tell him to stop, he will. I'm sure of that much.

Lorenzo smiles so brightly it sends a flutter through my chest. He strokes his fingers down to my ankle and up to my knee again. A giddy shiver races straight to my core in their wake.

I was about to slow him down, and now all I want is for him to get on with it.

Slowly, as if giving me plenty of time to reconsider, he eases my dress up to my thighs. As he bares my lower legs, he presses a kiss to my calf, to the side of my knee.

His hand travels higher, up over my outer thigh. When he reaches the edge of my drawers, he reverses the caress, back to my knee, then repeats it.

The silk of my skirt pools around my hips. Lorenzo skims his fingers over my thigh to the more sensitive inner flesh. Another wave of shivers shoots to my sex.

At his nudge, I let my knees splay. He must be able to see how damp my drawers are. His teasing fingers drift ever closer, until I can't restrain a whine of need.

As if in answer, Lorenzo leans over to claim my lips. While he kisses me, his hand moves to the crotch of my drawers.

With the first caress between my legs, I can't hold back a moan. Lorenzo absorbs it into the kiss and strokes me again.

Every caress of his fingers sets off a deeper pulse of pleasure—and need. I find myself pushing into his touch, throbbing for more.

He delves beneath my drawers to slide his fingers against my slick flesh skin to skin. I whimper, clinging to his shirt and rocking with his movements.

Lorenzo gives me one more mind-reeling kiss. Then he positions himself between my legs and lowers his whole head to the apex of my thighs.

He drags my drawers down just in time to press his mouth to my sex. Bliss sweeps through my body in a torrent.

My hand whips up to muffle my cry as well as I can. I sag back against the rug, boneless and writhing with every motion of the prince's lips against my flesh.

He focuses the attentions of his mouth on the most sensitive spot above my folds while his fingers dip into my opening. With each pump, they slide a little deeper.

Pleasure soars through my veins. I can barely feel the ground beneath me.

All of his bliss is only for me, just as he said. He hasn't removed a single piece of clothing, hasn't made any move to demand the same pleasure for himself.

Through the giddy haze, emotion swells around my heart.

We've come so far, but all at once, it doesn't feel like enough.

Fuck lines, fuck caution. Just one time, I'm not going to hold back.

I curl my fingers into Lorenzo's coarse hair. At my tug, he glances up at me with a look of such satisfaction a heady shudder passes through me.

I trail my fingers down his face. "I want all of you."

CHAPTER THIRTY-SEVEN

Aurelia

Crouched between my splayed legs, Lorenzo stares at me blankly for the space of a heartbeat. As my meaning must sink in, his eyes widen, his pupils dilating with desire.

But he hasn't moved yet.

I curl my fingers at the edge of his jaw and give the slightest tug. "Come with me."

With a strangled noise, the prince surges up over my body. His mouth crashes into mine. My musky flavor lingers there, strange but a reminder of the adoration he's already shown me.

His head bows over mine with a panted breath as he yanks at his trousers. I squirm completely free of my drawers with help from his guiding hand.

The head of his cock strokes from my clit to my slick opening, and a desperate growl reverberates from my throat.

As he lines himself up, Lorenzo braces himself on one elbow, gazing down at me. His handsome face has never looked more intense.

With his first press into me, his lips part with a stuttered breath. He eases himself into me inch by torturous inch, charting every flutter of my eyelids, every soft, needy sound that escapes me. A flush brings a russet hue to his dark cheeks.

It occurs to me that he must think this is my first time. That's why he's being so very careful when every particle of my body is clamoring for him to drive home, to fill me to the brim.

Maybe it's wisest not to challenge that assumption. Would he think differently of me if he knew how I once loved and lost before I ended up here?

I want to treasure every second of this encounter, not rush it toward its end.

When he's pushed all the way into me, the delicious stretch of penetration radiating bliss from my core, he simply holds there for a moment. A brilliant smile curves his lips, and my heart skips a beat in answer.

For just this instant, I am his and he is mine. It will always have been so, no matter what happens afterward.

No matter who else I have to give myself to.

I run my fingers over his hair, and he ducks his head to capture my mouth. Then, with a rasp of heated breath over my lips, he bucks even deeper into me.

Pleasure flares through my nerves all the way to the tips of my toes. I gasp and lift my knees to welcome him.

Lorenzo tucks one hand beneath my ass to help me arch into his movements. With each thrust, his mouth brands my cheek, my jaw, my neck. When I dig my fingers into his shoulder, a groan tumbles out of him.

His hard length strokes against a particularly delightful spot inside me, and I shudder with the impact. "Right there. So good."

At my encouragement, he picks up his pace, hitting his mark again and again. With each wave of pleasure, I clutch him harder. The urgent pant of his breaths makes me even giddier.

We rock together faster, wilder, his teeth grazing my shoulder, my fingernails nicking his back through his shirt. I curl up to meet him, seeking out his lips through the rush of bliss.

Our mouths scrape together, almost frantic. He plunges into me at just the right angle, squeezing my ass, and the building pressure bursts.

My head tips back, my vision blurring. The wave of ecstasy sweeps through me, shaking me down to my bones.

Lorenzo lets out another groan, his hips jerking. I feel the moment he joins me in release with the clamp of his arm hugging me to him and the ebbing of his thrusts.

We lie there entwined for several breaths, the prince's face tucked close to mine, every exhalation stirring the hair bunched by my neck. He kisses my cheek, ever so tenderly.

And I hear a resonant baritone voice as clearly as if it's speaking right into my ear. *"I wish we could have done this forever."*

I flinch in surprise. Lorenzo lifts his head, his hands against the sides of my face. *"It's all right, Aurelia. It's me."*

He's smiling at me, soft and secretive, but his mouth hasn't opened.

I stare at him, my mind whirling. "I—I don't understand—"

His lips move with his next words. *"Is it easier for you like this? It's my gift. I can conjure illusions—the impression of divinely impressive music, or a voice... or just about anything. To a limit."*

I realize I'm gaping and collect my jaw. "But the emperor —everyone—they all talk as if it's just the music."

Lorenzo's smile goes crooked before he speaks—no, *appears* to speak—again. *"No one knows except Bastien, Raul, and Neven. It's... better if nobody finds out how much I'm capable of."*

Despite my stunned state, that part of his explanation makes sense. I can only imagine how else Tarquin might exploit the supposedly mute prince if he knew.

Even Fausta with her much smaller gift with illusions was able to use it as a formidable weapon.

Something about the voice he's conjured isn't totally alien to me. A sense of recognition seeps through my mind. "I think... I think I heard you before, just for a moment or two, when I was sick."

"That's not totally surprising. I was so worried about you, I wasn't concentrating well. I don't normally speak this way to my foster brothers when anyone else is around, just in case my focus slips or one of Tarquin's guards notices I'm using magic."

I hesitate, dizzied by the shock and the surge of pleasure I'm still coming down from. "Why are you telling me now?"

Lorenzo lets out a choked sort of chuckle that I think is real and adjusts his position over me. With impressive grace, he sits up and scoops me onto his lap.

Wrapping his arms around me, he dips his head so his chin rests against my temple. *"There have been so many things I've wanted to say to you—properly, not with waves of my hands and a few words scrawled on a paper. You opened yourself up to me so much. I couldn't keep hiding this part of me from you."*

A lump fills my throat, awe and anguish combined. He's

trusting me with this immense secret, putting so much of his fate in my hands. Have I really offered him that much trust?

Can I ever?

The longing wells up inside me to tell him every trouble that's ever weighed on me. I swallow it down.

It's not just my fate that could hang in the balance but that of every person back in Accasy.

As the pieces of Lorenzo's story and my memories of what I've seen during my time in the palace gradually combine, a different realization hits me.

"No wonder it takes so much out of you, performing for the court. You're not using your gift on yourself to heighten your music. You have to cast the illusion over everyone in the room who's listening."

I feel Lorenzo's wince. *"It can be a strain."*

I turn my head to look up at him, struck by a sudden urgency. "When you're speaking to me, you can keep it to just a voice. You don't need to make it look as if you're actually talking. That must take more out of you."

Lorenzo's breath hitches, and then he's hugging me even tighter against him. *"Gods, every time I think I already know just how wonderful you are, you show me even more. How could I not fall in love with you?"*

My whole body goes still. His last words resonate through my body in time with the heady thumping of my pulse. "Lorenzo..."

"I know. I know it can't go anywhere beyond this. But it's true. You should know. You should hear it from someone who means it."

The tears that nipped at my eyes earlier spill over without warning. At my smothered sob, Lorenzo cups my face and peers into my eyes. *"I'm sorry. I wasn't trying to rub your situation in. If I could get you out of this—"*

"It's okay," I say, getting my emotions under control. I swipe at my eyes. He doesn't even really know why I'm crying.

My choices brought us here. I don't know if I've made everything even harder for myself or if this will be one glimmer of joy I can hold on to for strength through the days ahead.

"I won't be able to talk to you like this very often," Lorenzo says in an apologetic tone. *"Like I said, I avoid it when anyone else is around. And sometimes it's easier even in private to stick to gestures if I can. If I don't need to extend my gift."*

Because he never knows when Tarquin might decide to run him ragged. The image of him collapsing in the hall of entertainments the other night wavers through my head.

I lean closer to him again, soaking up the warmth of his muscular frame. "I understand. Thank you for sharing it with me at all." My mind keeps whirring, and another possibility occurs to me. "The other princes—their gifts—"

Lorenzo's conjured voice turns wry. *"I'll have to leave it up to them whether they want to share secrets of their own."*

"Fair enough." What else might Bastien be capable of beyond summoning and dismissing rain clouds? Can Raul see more than just what's within people's clothing?

Lorenzo's mind has turned to other relevant matters. *"I have a supply of mirewort—but I haven't been taking it myself. No need. I'll get it to you before there's any risk."*

Of pregnancy, he means. The herb can only act as a contraceptive for the man if it's taken before the act.

I nod, deciding it's better not to mention that I'm already taking regular doses. I have no intention of bearing Marclinus any children until I'm good and ready.

But that's hardly a typical attitude for any would-be-wife to take.

A sudden burst of laughter filters through the door. My head jerks toward it, my pulse stuttering.

We have much more immediate concerns.

I shift my weight on Lorenzo's lap reluctantly. "You should probably go as soon as the hall is clear. If one of my maids comes back early before luncheon..."

Lorenzo nuzzles my hair. *"We must have at least an hour before anyone even thinks of lunch."*

"But if anyone sees you..."

"We'll hear the lock." He pauses. *"I can go out the other way."*

The way the princes have stolen into my locked room more than once? I twist around to raise my eyebrows at him. "Are you going to reveal *that* secret?"

His pleased smile takes him from handsome to absolutely breathtaking. *"I suppose it's only fair. There are passages in the walls that connect the servants' area to a handful of the most prominent bedchambers in the palace—from some time ago when the highest ranking nobles wanted to be attended to as promptly and discreetly as possible. They were theoretically closed up before we ever arrived here, but we stumbled on one entrance in an unused bedroom down the hall from ours, found our way in, and made them our own."*

Lorenzo points to the wall next to my bed. *"The wallpaper blends in perfectly, but it's right there. If anyone comes, I'll vanish in an instant. If I absolutely have to, I can hide behind an illusion for additional cover."*

At his assurances, my stance relaxes. I narrow my eyes at him. "I would prefer if from now on you all at least knock before barging in."

"As you deserve. I'm sorry we invaded your privacy before."

"I think that's really more on Raul and Bastien to apologize for."

"And I look forward to hearing you tell them so." He strokes his thumb over my cheek, setting off new tingles that race through me. *"Do you want me to go, Rell?"*

Hearing him grant me that nickname gives me a thrill I hadn't anticipated. I can't deny the answer that clangs through every particle of my body. "No."

As I turn my face toward him again, he catches my chin and lowers his mouth to claim a kiss. It carries on, lingering and sweet, until I'm aching in all sorts of ways.

"What would you like, Princess?"

My mind is still rattled from everything that's happened today, but a longing rises up in me too swift and strong for me to ignore it.

Why not? Why deny myself anything from this moment now that I've embraced it?

I turn in Lorenzo's arms so I can kiss him more firmly. Then I say, my voice little more than a whisper, "I want you to take me to the bed, strip off all my clothes, and make love to me as if we're the ones getting married."

His face lights up with so much affection I lose my breath.

Taking my hand, he stands and draws me upright with him. My skirt falls back around my legs. My drawers lie in a puddle by my feet.

Lorenzo kicks his loosened trousers the rest of the way off. He walks me over to the bed, his eager gaze never leaving me.

When we've reached it, he peels my gown off over my head. He takes in my mostly bared body and pauses over my forearms.

Lifting my hand, he presses a gentle kiss to the smattering of purple scars below my wrist. *"You never need to hide these from me. They're as beautiful as the rest of you."*

He grasps my chemise next. I find that standing nude before him is a totally different experience from the nakedness Marclinus forced on me.

There's only one pair of eyes watching me now, with nothing but admiration.

I grip the hem of Lorenzo's shirt. His smile widens as we tug it off together.

Now it's my turn to admire his sculpted form, not as massive as Raul but impressive in his own right. In the middle of his chest, his brand of Inganne's sigil stands out slightly paler than his rich brown skin.

As I run my fingers down those muscular plains, Lorenzo closes his eyes with a shaky breath. Then he sweeps me off my feet and deposits me in the middle of the bed.

Clambering after me, he beams with fond amusement. *"Our wedding day, is it?"*

The room around me shimmers. Pale pink fabric drapes across the canopy frame—the color of Ardone, the godlen of love who oversees weddings. Matching roses, her symbolic flower, bloom along the head and footboard. The posts jut out into the shapes of elegant swans.

An awed giggle tumbles out of me. With his gift, he's painted a picture of a bedchamber decorated for an elaborate wedding celebration.

Lorenzo lowers his head to bring his lips to mine. As he caresses my body unhindered and I continue exploring his, a pinching sensation deep in my gut pierces through the dreaminess of the moment.

It *is* only a dream. Perhaps Marclinus will arrange a bedroom like this for our wedding night, should I make it that far, but there'll be nothing loving about the act we commit in it.

I may never again feel this cherished or so cherishing in return.

But I might have never gotten it at all. So I sink into the waves of affection and desire, bottling every sensation deep inside me.

I can lock away this new precious secret and keep it to the end of my days. It doesn't need to be more than one brilliant moment to still matter.

CHAPTER THIRTY-EIGHT

Aurelia

As the after-dinner revelries begin to break up, I slip away among the first members of court to depart. It seems as good a time as any to indulge the curiosity that's been niggling at me ever since Lorenzo shared his many revelations this morning.

After he left by my bedroom's regular door, I realized I hadn't gotten him to show me how to open the entrance to the hidden passage that connects some of the palace rooms. No amount of peering and prodding at the wall he pointed to revealed the means.

But he said that he and the other princes stumbled on another entrance in an unused room near their own chambers. If that one is obvious enough that you could find it by accident, I should be able to locate it knowing approximately what I'm looking for.

First, I have to determine which room it is.

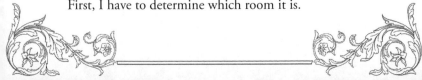

I pause in the hallway I know holds all of the princes' bedrooms. The doorframes look similarly ornate, but one toward the end has just a little more flourish to it, the carved vines with their gold sheen curving farther out from the edges.

Only the most honored of the palace's inhabitants had the benefit of such immediate access for their servants—while past emperors still considered that access a benefit rather than a threat to security.

I walk over to the door and test the knob. It turns without resistance.

A glance inside confirms that no one has slept in this room for a long time. The cleaning staff must come through periodically for a brief sweeping, because no dust lingers on the floor, but the furniture is draped with protective sheets.

I skirt the sprawling mound of the bed and study the wall to the right of it, the same area where Lorenzo said the entrance is in my room.

There must be some button or switch, perhaps enchanted in its function, to open the way to the passage behind. The servants would have needed to come and go without much fuss.

I simply have to find it.

Leaning closer to the wall, I notice a slight imperfection in the red-and-gold striped wallpaper. The outer layer has curled a bit with age—and perhaps with recent use.

My fingers skim a faintly rough line that I suspect is one edge of the door. It runs from the baseboard to a spot a few inches above my head.

All right. I've found the panel, but there's nothing to pry it open with—and prying hardly seems like a convenient technique. How is one supposed to release it?

I'm sliding my hand over the wall checking for any other

subtle protrusions or indentations when the regular door swings open behind me.

With a lurch of my heart, I spin around.

Raul and Bastien halt just over the threshold. The door thuds shut. We stare at each other for a few uneasy seconds.

Then Raul's mouth twists into a scowl. He strides forward, his pale eyes flaring. "It didn't take you long, did it?"

I blink at him, thrown by both his angry demeanor and his vague accusation.

I expected this might be an awkward conversation, but why is he so upset with me already? He's not even asking what I'm doing here.

Bastien trails behind him, his pace more hesitant but his expression hardening. "Did you think we wouldn't find out? We tell each other everything—everything important."

Now I'm even more lost. I step away from the wall, uneasy with the sense of being cornered. "Find out what? What do you think is going on here? Lorenzo mentioned the passages in the walls, and I wanted to—"

Raul's voice turns even harsher. "He 'mentioned' it because you fucked all the good sense out of his head. Did you just figure he was the easiest target? Seduce the one with the softest heart and then stomp all over it?"

Well, now I know what Lorenzo told *them*. My own irritation sparks. "I haven't stomped on anything or seduced anyone. If anything, it's been the other way around. Or have you forgotten how many attempts *you've* made at trying to entice me into bed?"

Raul stops a few paces away, glaring down at me from his full imposing height. "I haven't forgotten—I definitely haven't forgotten how you acted like you were offended by the thought. But Lorenzo was fair game, wasn't he? Get him head over heels for you so he'd spill all our secrets."

Understanding snaps into place, fueling my own anger.

I narrow my eyes at him. "You're pissed off because I gave him what you wanted. Does he know you think you're so much more deserving than he could possibly be?"

My gaze jerks to Bastien, who's still standing there stony-faced. "Is that what's eating at you too? I'm not allowed to dally with any of you unless I dally with *all* of you?"

He winces, but his expression doesn't soften. "You did dally with all of us, as far as I've gathered. But with the two of us, you were careful not to let it go beyond a kiss or two. It does seem rather strategic."

"Strategic?" I glare at both of them. "Do you seriously think I risked Emperor Tarquin's wrath to find out more about Lorenzo's gift and a few secret passages, neither of which I had any idea he *could* tell me about? How does any of that information help me at all with what I'm here to do? Is disappearing from my bedroom going to win the trials for me?"

Raul folds his arms over his chest. "You did come running straight here to investigate, it appears."

"Yes, straight here, several hours later." In which time, it appears my lover already found plenty of time to gossip about our interlude.

With a twinge of pain, I drop my gaze. "I don't suppose it occurred to you in all your strategic thinking that I might have felt more comfortable with Lorenzo because he's the only one who never hurt me? He never sabotaged me in the trials or stole from me or made me ill. Any idiot could see why I'd be more cautious getting close to the two of you. Although considering *he* apparently ran straight to you to brag about his victory, maybe I misjudged him too."

My retort seems to stun both men momentarily speechless.

Bastien lifts his voice first, still strained but without the hostility it held before. "He wasn't bragging. And he didn't come to tell us. He was practically radiating happiness all afternoon, and it took some badgering before he admitted why. And mainly then because he thought we should know what he told you."

"Ah." A thread of relief winds around my heart. I might still end up regretting this morning's fantasy of freedom, but I'd rather not. "That much is fair."

Raul has dropped his hands to his sides. "I haven't done anything to hurt you since you proved you were on our side."

"I don't know why I had to prove that in the first place, given our positions," I mutter.

"Well, if you dislike us so much for it, why toy with us at all? Why pretend you're tempted if you know you want nothing to do with us?"

"I didn't pretend—" I cut myself off with a growl, not sure what I can say that will actually soothe his temper.

I never thought that giving in to my feelings for Lorenzo might mean ruining whatever amity I've forged with his fellow princes. If Raul continues to think I've wronged him somehow, will he go telling stories to the emperor about my indiscretions?

If he knew the truth…

I pause over that thought, rubbing my hand over my face as if I can settle my mind that way. *I* don't even want to look at the full truth of the situation that's brought us here.

Maybe that's the only salve that can heal the wounds I've inadvertently dealt, though.

Raul and Bastien think I didn't trust them enough. It's made them believe they can't trust me after all. I could turn that assumption around with just a few dangerously honest words.

Raul told me I was more shepherdess than lamb, but every dedicat of Elox knows that sometimes vulnerability can win battles that a firm hand won't. My show of weakness when they stole my ring defused some of their hostility before I'd ever started to earn their loyalty.

I can play the lamb to win them back.

In my hesitation, Bastien clears his throat. "I never demanded anything from you. You kissed *me* first."

"I know." I gird myself and raise my head. A quaver ripples through my voice, and I let it stay. "Nothing intimate that's happened with any of you has been a gambit or a lie. I'm falling for Lorenzo, and I've been falling for both of you too. It's not how I set out to feel; it just is. And I don't know what to do about it. I've been trying to keep my heart safe, because I know nothing real can come of it, but I want so many things… If I've confused you, it's only because I'm confused too. I apologize for that."

By the end of my declaration, my throat has closed up.

I don't want it to be true. I don't want to care this much.

What's the good in it when I'll have to throw it all away in a matter of days regardless?

There's a moment of silence as both of the princes stare at me. Something warm and hungry dawns in Raul's eyes.

He steps toward me, the heat he's emanating not remotely angry now, and trails his hand down the side of my face. "Princess, you don't need to apologize for wanting me. I swear I'll never do anything to harm you again. The only gasps I want to hear from these lips are from pleasure, not pain. If you don't believe it yet, I'll just have to keep proving it to you."

A hot flush washes over me from head to toes. "Raul…"

He dips his head to mark the corner of my jaw with the slightest nibble, gentle but provocative enough to set off a quiver beneath my skin. His husky murmur tingles into my ear. "You tell me to stop when you feel like you need to stop. I'll just do my best to convince you that you're in good hands after all."

I *should* probably stop him, shouldn't I? I gave myself an out. I told them why I can't just hop into bed with all of them.

But gods help me, the press of his lips against my neck, the flick of his tongue over my skin, and those provocative words echoing through my mind do feel so incredibly good. If he needs this brief intimacy to believe what I said, wouldn't it be "strategic" to indulge both our desires?

Raul lifts his head to glance over his shoulder toward Bastien, who's standing stiffly watching us, his own face flushed. The bigger man shoots him a cocky grin. "Are you going to help me show her how well we can take care of her or not? We have a lot of mistakes to make up for."

Bastien's blush darkens, but he steps closer and catches my hand. A hint of determination sets his jaw.

As Raul returns his lips to my neck, Bastien cups my cheek at my other side and leans in to capture my mouth.

Gods above and below, I had no idea my body could light up like this, encompassed between two men at once. Every nerve sings with the heady thrill of it.

They haven't made their own confessions of deeper devotion. I'm not sure how much this encounter is about staking a claim for their egos rather than dedicating themselves to me. It's awfully hard to worry about it when Raul is sliding his hand around my waist, Bastien tangling his fingers in my hair to pull me even closer…

I sway between the two of them, clutching their shirts, so swept up in the moment that I don't hear the click of the door, only the rasp of startled breath that follows.

Bastien jerks away from me to whirl around. Raul draws back at a more measured pace, his hand lingering on me possessively, but his confident expression falters as we face the new arrival.

Lorenzo glares back at us, his hands clenching at his sides. His illusionary voice reverberates through my head. *"What the fuck is this?"*

I didn't tell him I'd been attracted to Raul and Bastien too. I assumed they all shared their stories of the conquest.

Apparently not. There's no mistaking the tremor of betrayal coloring his illusionary voice and passing over his face.

"Lorenzo," I say, pulling away from the other men. "I—"

His hand slices through the air in an emphatic gesture to stay away. The other hand jams into his belt-pouch and hurls a small paper packet in my direction. As it hits the floor, he spins on his heel and stalks out of the room without another word.

Bastien curses under his breath and rushes after his friend.

Raul glances from him to me, looking stricken. "We'll sort this out."

Then he's vanished into the hall too.

I exhale in a long, shuddering rush. My nerves are clanging with a mix of unfulfilled lust and bewildered guilt. It's a dizzying combination, and not in a good way.

How upset is Lorenzo with me? How upset *can* he be when he knows I was already planning on marrying another man—when he told me to my face that he understands?

Maybe being the only illicit affair in my life mattered to him. Maybe he thinks I've done much more with his foster brothers than I actually have.

I creep forward to pick up the packet he threw at me.

Before I've even finished opening the flap, the mildly bitter scent seeping out tells me it contains the mirewort he promised me.

Oh, Lorenzo...

I tuck it away and wait to see if the princes will return so we can hash out the answers to my uncertainties. When several minutes pass without any sign of them, I spare the wall one last look, but I've lost all enthusiasm for uncovering secret passages.

The hallway I slip out into is empty. I hustle back to my own bedroom, passing a few of the court nobles along the way but none of the princes I was so recently entwined with.

I gather myself even more before I open the door, expecting to find at least one of my maids inside. To my surprise, the knob turns at my touch before I've brought the key to it.

Didn't I lock it when I last left? Did Melisse or Rochelle forget to after a recent trip inside?

Apprehension prickles down my back. I nudge the door open without leaving the threshold.

The heavy curtains have been drawn shut, leaving the room dark. So the first thing that hits me is the smell.

A rancid odor wafts out to meet me, as if the kitchen waste buckets were emptied inside.

After a couple of tentative steps, I think that might be exactly what's happened. Decaying vegetable ends and slimy strips of gristle lie strewn across my bed covers, the rug, and the heap of dresses that've been yanked out of my wardrobe.

With another step and the stench thickening around me, I realize that's not the only damage. My new Darium-style gowns have been torn and gouged to tatters.

With a lurch of my heart, I dash to my trunks.

The one that holds my books, tea box, and other odds

and ends has obviously been rummaged through, with more refuse dappling the outsides and one of my teacups lying in shards. The trunk with my clothing is worse. It looks as if someone dug a blade through the layers of dresses and undergarments I brought from home, turning them into a slurry of shredded fabric and fetid food scraps.

A cry catches in my throat. I stagger backward, searching the room for answers.

The thought darts through my mind that one of the princes might have done this in vengeful anger. But I don't think Raul or Bastien was *that* furious until they stumbled on me trying to open the hidden passage, and there's hardly been time for them or Lorenzo to desecrate my room since he stormed off.

Besides, why would they specifically ruin my clothing over everything else? Any of the three men would know that out of the contents of this room, the tea box and my brewing apparatus are my most prized possessions, and those have barely been touched.

My gaze slides to the door. The door someone left unlocked.

Rochelle wouldn't have been that careless. But Melisse, who revealed how spurned she feels just yesterday…

It wouldn't have taken Fausta or Bianca much to bribe her into leaving the way open for them, would it? I can picture either of them—or perhaps both—tossing the contents of those buckets around the room, ripping through the layers of silk with gleeful ferocity.

My stomach turns, both from the stink and the viciousness of the assault. They couldn't destroy me, so they destroyed the next best thing.

And now I have to clean it up. Procure new dresses. Pretend this latest attack hasn't fazed me at all…

Footsteps patter down the hall outside, and I realize I left the door ajar. I hurry back over to it, not sure I'd want anyone else witnessing the disarray inside.

Rochelle stops when she sees me in the doorway, a tight smile springing to her face. "Good, you're here! Their Imperial Eminences want the last four potential brides to come straight to the grand hall. They're starting the next trial."

Chapter Thirty-Nine

Aurelia

When we reach the grand hall, it looks as if most of the court has already gathered around the edges of the expansive room, waiting for the latest spectacle. The crowd of nobles parts at my arrival, opening a path for Rochelle and me to venture deeper into the space.

Chandeliers beam overhead, lighting up both us and the enchanted paintings across the ceiling that swirl and shift before the eyes. I can't take the time to admire them.

Up ahead, a low platform, no more than half a foot high, has been constructed on the wooden floor. Its circular surface stretches perhaps twenty feet across, dappled with small tiles cut in irregular shapes of pale purple and yellow. Like an erratic mosaic that forms more the impression of a picture than anything identifiable.

Fausta and Giralda are already standing by the platform, their maids hovering nearby. The emperor and his heir sit on gilded chairs off to our right, placed on another platform that's nearly as tall as my shoulders.

Why do they feel they need such a lofty view of our performance here? What is any of this about?

As I approach, Fausta's gaze settles on me. A sharp little smile crosses her lips, so triumphant that any uncertainty I had about who vandalized my room vanishes.

I don't have much opportunity to gather my jangled nerves. Steady taps ring out as Leonette strides to join us, her dark face set in its usual serious expression. She nods to all of us as if to say, *Well, here we are.*

Emperor Tarquin claps his hands, and the murmurs that were passing through the crowd halt.

Marclinus grins down at us so eagerly the hairs on the back of my neck stand on end. "Maids, please assist your ladies by collecting their shoes and holding on to them for safe keeping."

Our shoes? I blink at him for a second and then bend over to peel the thin leather slippers off my feet. Nothing good ever comes from questioning His Imperial Highness.

Rochelle takes my shoes from me with a furtive squeeze of my hands. Clutching the slippers to her chest, she steps back a few paces to the inner edge of the crowd.

My competitors have similarly bared their feet. I'd feel glad that's the only part of us Marclinus is demanding go naked, except I'm sure there's much more to his challenge than this request.

His grin hasn't budged. "I need a wife who can keep up with me through any revelry, no matter the circumstances. Who can celebrate our union and our empire during times both joyful and dire. So let us see you dance for as long as your body will keep moving!"

He gives another extravagant swing of his arm. "Up onto your dance floor you go. Frolic until one of you proves too weak for the task. All you have to do is stay up there and cavort your hearts out."

His laugh peals off the high ceiling. Restraining a shudder, I step onto the low platform.

As soon as my bare feet touch the tiles, alarm jitters beneath my skin. The surface isn't as smooth as I was expecting. Some of the irregular edges prick at my soles.

There has to be a reason he set up this special setting for our dance rather than holding the trial in the ballroom.

Emperor Tarquin turns in his seat. "Prince Lorenzo? There you are. My heir and his potential brides deserve the liveliest melodies you can conjure. We have your instrument right here."

He motions to the base of his tall platform, where one of the pages is waiting with a lyre.

Lorenzo pushes through the crowd into view, his stance tense. He accepts the lyre, glances down at it, and then looks toward me.

His mouth twists. His dark eyes burn into me with as much anguish as I saw in them when he walked in on me with Bastien and Raul, but it's not all because of me now.

A crease forms in his brow. Then his jaw clenches as if he's gathering his resolve. His gaze flicks from the emperor above and back to me, his lips parting, and all at once I know down to my core that he's about to refuse. To rebel against the man who keeps him leashed.

For me. Because no matter what he thinks of me tonight, he doesn't want to play a part in tormenting me.

Panic jolts through my nerves. My hand twitches at my

side, a hasty gesture I hope he'll see without anyone else realizing it's more than anxious fidgeting. *Play.*

Lorenzo hesitates, the furrow in his forehead deepening. Tarquin glances down at him, probably wondering what's delaying his pet prince, and I twist my fingers in another swift gesture. *I'm all right.*

I don't know if it'll make this night better or worse to be dancing to the music of the man I trust most in this place, who might not trust me at all now, but I'll be damned if I let him get any more hurt because of me.

"Well?" the emperor says in an ominous tone, but Lorenzo is already bracing the instrument against his abdomen. He sets his fingers against the strings and draws out the first strains of a song.

I can't help thinking I pick up a faintly sad strain beneath the spirited tune that spills out into the air. My throat constricts.

There's nothing I can do but lift my arms and move my feet to follow the melody.

It only takes a few steps to confirm my fears. Giralda gasps, and Fausta's face tightens into a pale, fierce mask. Even Leonette can't suppress a quiver of her chin.

The uneven edges of the tiles scrape against the unprotected soles of our feet. They don't slice straight in—I suppose because then this trial would be over far faster than suits Marclinus's need for entertainment—but they pinch and nip and jab, sending slivers of pain up my legs with every movement.

Quivering through the bone in my shin that isn't quite finished mending. Waking up the dull ache that'd almost died down again after Fausta's latest attack.

I gird myself against the building pain, focusing my attention on the music instead. On the other sensations flowing through and over my body with the sway of my limbs. On the center of calm inside me—shrunken but still there.

Giralda shows the first evidence of actual injury. A whimper slips from her mouth, and a thin smear of blood marks the tiles with the next movement of her feet.

Marclinus, the sadistic prick, lets out an approving chuckle. Emperor Tarquin simply smiles.

The vibrant red stands out starkly against the pale flooring. No doubt that's why they picked the color scheme.

They want everyone to see how much we're enduring to appease them.

Giralda's face pales with each step in time with the rhythm. Every glimpse I get of her tugs at my heart more.

She hasn't stood up for me against Bianca and Fausta, but I can't blame her for that. She's never actually hurt me.

I sashay closer to her until I'm close enough to speak without Fausta overhearing. I have no intention of giving my most vicious rival the benefit of my advice.

"Always lift your feet a little off the floor," I murmur, following my instructions as I give them. "Don't slide them over the tiles at all. The rough edges will dig in less that way."

She gives the slightest nod, her eyes wide.

The strategy isn't enough to avoid injury completely. Step after rhythmic step, the thin ridges dig in more. My heel stings, and I bite my lip.

I'm not surprised to see smudges of red trailing after my feet as I dip and whirl.

With a stifled hiss here and a flinch there, more and more blood dapples the tiles. Fausta's eyes have gone vacant, as if she's retreated into her head as much as I'm trying to.

Little cuts throb all over my bare soles. I dig my fingers

into my palms as if I can offset the pain below with a distraction above.

"Look at the art they're making!" Marclinus calls out, sounding so jovial I'd like to shove my bleeding foot right down his throat. "But I think it's gotten a little boring. Let's speed up this dance, shall we?"

He shoots a pointed look at Lorenzo. The prince's arms tighten around the lyre, but he speeds up the tempo with a flick of his hand.

The quickening patter of my feet sends even more twinges racing up my legs. Giralda muffles a ragged groan, leaving behind whole blotches of crimson beneath her halting steps. Leonette has dug her fingers into the skirt of her dress, swishing it to add to her dance while gripping it as if clinging on for dear life.

Fausta's breath hitches through her teeth, but she prances on, smattering blood in her wake.

My gaze flits beyond the platform and collides with two pairs of staring eyes: one pale blue and blazing with fury, the other pine-green and horrified.

Raul and Bastien have advanced to the front of our audience. They track my movements across the platform, the muscles in Raul's shoulders taut, Bastien's mouth pressing ever flatter.

Are they still upset at me after everything that happened between us and Lorenzo today or is all their ire aimed at the men who set me on this bloody path? I suppose it doesn't really matter.

If they challenge the emperor, if they even reveal that they care what happens to me, my fate and theirs could become ten times worse.

Beyond them, the crowd shifts. I spot servants in the

imperial livery weaving between the nobles along the inner circle, handing each of them something from a box.

Oh, gods, what new chaos is Marclinus about to unleash on us?

At another jab, another shock of agony lances from the ball of my foot to my thigh. My knee wobbles, but I throw myself into a spin that tips my balance onto my other leg. Blood trails across the tiles in a smeared spiral.

The imperial heir gives a whoop of approval. "Such dedication! My ladies have proven they're up to an even greater challenge. Let's bring out their dancing partner."

At his beckoning motion, a page darts onto the platform between us and flips over a larger central tile about the width of his hand. A steel loop juts from its surface.

I peer at the metal ring in a haze of pain, confusion, and growing exhaustion. What in the realms is that—

A snarl cuts through the hush of the crowd. My veins turn to ice.

The nobles jostle away from another figure cutting through their swarm. This servant holds a long chain, the other end of which is attached to a collar on the neck of a huge, spotted panther.

A leather muzzle criss-crosses the beast's face, preventing it from doing more with its mouth than snarl and growl. Its keeper yanks on the chain to direct it up onto the platform with us and fixes the chain to the loop in the floor.

Then he detaches the muzzle with a jerk of his hand and dashes away with the leather straps in his grip.

All four of us have slowed despite the spirited tune lilting through the room. Giralda presses her hand to her mouth to muffle a faint shriek. Even Fausta is gaping at the immense wild cat, her skin turned outright sallow.

Emperor Tarquin gives his order with a note of warning. "Dance."

Lorenzo's playing has wavered. He looks as if he grits his teeth before digging back into the song.

I shuffle to one side and the other, rippling my skirt to make the movement look more artful. My attention stays glued to the most literal predator in our midst.

The panther prowls around the platform, its muscles flexing throughout its intimidating but graceful body. I edge away from it as well as I can while following the melody. The beast makes a harsh rumbling sound low in its throat, its amber gaze sweeping across all of us in turn.

The chain is just long enough to let it roam the platform freely but not venture beyond. Although I'd imagine Emperor Tarquin asked for his high vantage point to ensure his and his son's safety should the creature manage to break free.

The largest wild cats we have in Accasy are sturdy lynxes that stand no taller than my waist and flee at the sight of humans. I don't know what might provoke this animal or how to ward off an attack.

There usually seems to be strength in numbers. The more imposing we seem, the less likely it'll judge us to be easy prey.

I mince over to Leonette and urge Giralda to join us. "Dance close to each other. If it sees us together, we'll look harder to pick off."

Leonette's stern expression doesn't shift, but she takes a couple of steps toward me. Sweat has beaded along the roots of her chestnut hair, but her curvy yet athletic form emanates determined strength.

Giralda bobs and turns, veering in our direction. Before

she's made it very far, Bianca's arch voice pierces through the murmurs of the crowd.

"I hope none of you are stupid enough to fall for the wild princess's tricks. She'll lure you in like bait if you let her."

I'm too focused on avoiding the panther and willing away the pain in my feet to argue with her taunts. Giralda hesitates and then stays where she is, still several paces away from us.

"Go on," someone says behind me, and I find out what the nobles were given. Bits of meat and poultry bones fly through the air to fall at the panther's feet. One bloody scrap splats against my skirt.

The scent of flesh brings another snarl to the predator's lips. They curl back to reveal its fangs. When a bone strikes the panther's haunches, it whips its head around with a snap.

Now we have even more to dodge as our feet flit across our stage. My already raw heel comes down on a shard of bone, and a cry I can't catch breaks from my throat.

I haven't quite righted myself when Fausta's chin twitches toward me.

Whatever illusion she's cast with her gift, it's so concentrated only the panther must see it. But it's enough to enrage the beast.

It lunges around with a roar and hurls itself straight at me.

My pulse lurches. I mean to fling myself out of the way, but as I strain my feet to propel me, my sore leg gives.

I stumble, throwing out my hands to catch my fall. The uneven tiles scour my palms. The panther's hurtling paws pound toward me.

And with a choked gasp, a body hurtles into the space between the beast and me.

As I whip around, the panther crashes into the woman

who's jumped in front of me. Blond curls billow out around her freckled face. Claws rake through the maid uniform with a horrible tearing sound that's more than just fabric.

Rochelle crumples beneath the animal's charge. Blood spurts from the gouges across her chest and belly.

"No." The word lurches out of me, so hoarse it's little more than a rasp.

The panther catches one of Rochelle's arms in its jaws and wrenches it back and forth with a guttural growl. My friend whimpers with a sputter of scarlet liquid over her lips. Her breath is already fading into broken hitches.

I push myself toward her with some ridiculous idea that I could fight the beast off her, but it turns out I don't need to. The taste of blood and the sight of her limp form appears to mollify the huge cat.

It rips a chunk of flesh off her arm and backs away, gulping the mouthful down. Then one of the chunks of beef tossed onto the stage catches its attention.

I grasp Rochelle's shoulder, turn her toward me, and clamp my teeth against a yelp. The wreckage of her ravaged torso makes my stomach flip over.

Gods help me, what can I do? I reach toward my gift, but no images rise up.

There's nothing. Nothing at all.

Words spill out of me in a mumbled torrent. "What were you doing? You weren't supposed to— You shouldn't have—"

Rochelle gazes blearily at me, her lips curving into a shaky smile. "You saved me. I save you. Win it. You have to win…"

Her faint voice peters out. I snatch at the shreds of her dress, searching for some way to stem the bleeding.

It's too late. In the space of a few heartbeats, her eyes glaze over completely. The last bit of life drifts out of her slumped body, leaving her vacant against my clinging hands.

Marclinus's raucous laughter carries from the high platform. "Now that's a show! Where's our music? They're not done yet."

As Lorenzo resumes his faltered playing, I stare down at my savaged friend through a blurring of tears. Pulling myself upright takes an effort as if a mountain rests on my back.

Emperor Tarquin's cool voice breaks through the tumult of the crowd. "Princess Aurelia, are you so distressed over your maid?"

Because that's all Rochelle was supposed to be to me. Because if I lied about my reasons for saving her life before, then I'm a traitor.

In that moment, I'm not sure I really care what the emperor thinks of me. All that holds me upright is Rochelle's final words spinning in my head.

You have to win.

She gave her life so I could keep going. What kind of awful tribute would it be if I threw her sacrifice in her face?

I can't let her down. I can't let her die in vain.

I will back my tears and draw my posture straighter. The best answer I can summon seems to float up from somewhere deep and distant inside of me. "Not at all, Your Imperial Majesty. It's only a little overwhelming to see such a savage death happen right in front of me. I look forward to continuing this dance."

My response must not sound as hollow as it feels. Tarquin nods.

Fausta spins toward the high platform, but her gaze locks onto Marclinus rather than his father. Her words come out shrill. "The princess should have died! The beast was going to kill *her*. She lost. Call the guard."

When my head jerks toward my supposed betrothed, his eyes have narrowed. I don't know if he'd have accepted Fausta's appeal if she'd framed it in more cajoling terms, but the imperial heir mustn't like her tone.

"I'm the one who gives the orders," he says with chilly nonchalance. "We can't prove that Princess Aurelia would have succumbed to the beast's attack. She might have dodged or fended it off. She stays in… as long as she keeps dancing."

The other ladies who've stalled around me shudder back into motion. Every particle of my being wants to bow over Rochelle and weep and pray that her soul is at peace in the embrace of her chosen godlen.

But the emperor and his heir expect me to dance. If I don't, it'll be my corpse lying right next to hers.

You have to win.

As I curve my arms around my body, my chest feels utterly vacant. My legs sway under me out of time with the music, pulsing with agony.

I don't know how much longer I can keep going anyway, but I have to try. Otherwise, *he* wins.

This man I'm not sure I could hate more. This man I'm going through all this torture just to marry.

I shift my feet with the tune. Swing my arms around my hips. Let my head droop and toss it back.

I stay next to Rochelle's slack body, her cloud of blond curls always at the edge of my vision. Showing my allegiance in the only way I have left.

One step after another. Stay in motion. Keep following the melody.

The song quavers into another. The tempo winds around me, dizzyingly.

Rochelle's wisp of a voice echoes on within my skull.

You have to win. You have to win. You have to—

A yelp yanks my gaze across the platform.

Before my hazed vision, Giralda stumbles backward. The panther is stalking past her, and she's reeled out of the way instinctively.

Unfortunately, she'd already drawn close to the edge of the platform. Her scrambling, unsteady feet send her careening right over the rim.

She topples to the ground and doesn't even bother to lift her head. Her shoulders shake with whimpered sobs.

She left the platform. She already knows what's coming.

Is she terrified or grateful for the release from this misery?

Hasn't there already been enough death tonight? I can't stop a protest from bubbling up my throat. "Don't—"

My voice comes out too thin to be heard above the excited roar of our audience. I can't imagine what difference it would have made even if I'd bellowed from the depths of my lungs.

A guard stoops over Giralda and slices his sword through her throat.

Marclinus stands up in front of his chair, clapping vigorously. At his example, applause breaks out all around us.

His words ring out above the approving thunder. "Congratulations and well done to my three victorious ladies. The medics will see to your feet. Then you may retire and get some rest. The final trial commences the day after tomorrow."

Chapter Forty

Aurelia

I don't remember the walk back to my chambers. I look up, and there's my bedroom door in front of me, as if someone conjured it there the moment after the medic tended to my feet.

I think the medic must have put my shoes on me as well. Rochelle couldn't have. Rochelle—

Images flash through my mind: my friend's gouged body, the panther tearing into her arm, the bloody spittle flecking her lips.

The life in her eyes going out like a lantern snuffed.

How could it have vanished? She was so happy this morning, knowing her medic was waiting for her back in Garince.

I protected her, I circumvented the rules and prevented her execution—I wanted one person to come out of this charade with more joy than misery.

Maybe that was where I went wrong. I let myself start to hope again. I let myself imagine *I* could have joy and still do my duty.

I knew how that goes. She isn't the first person I've cared about that the empire ripped from my life.

I thought I'd learned my lesson well enough the first time. Now she's paid for it too.

I shouldn't have let myself be tempted. I should have kept all my attention trained on the narrow path ahead of me...

But then she'd have died days ago during the trial when Marclinus declared her a failure, wouldn't she? Would that really have been better?

My thoughts are too muddled for me to sort them out. The calm inside me has shattered, leaving only jabbing splinters. A dull but emphatic ache radiates from my chest into every other part of me.

I failed. I couldn't keep even one person safe.

Do I really stand any chance of defending my entire country in the face of these tyrants? Even if I win the trials, even if I stand next to Marclinus through the rest of my days, what are the chances I'll ever sway his mind so much as an inch?

Emperor Tarquin is a horror, but I'm starting to think his heir is even worse.

I could go through all this and yet accomplish nothing but my own suffering.

Voices farther down the hall prompt me into motion. My hand rises automatically to fish out my key and fit it into the doorknob.

The events of the incident before the trial have faded so far behind my anguish that in the first second, I'm startled by the stink that meets me. Then the rest of my memory clicks into place.

As I step into the defiled room, Melisse spins around where she's standing in the middle of the mess. She's lit a lantern that's sitting haphazardly on the vanity, and the yellowish glow turns her face a sickly shade.

Or maybe that's her reaction to the disarray, because her voice quavers with similar distress. "Your Highness… I'm so sorry. I thought—she said it would be some small prank—I never should have given her the chance. Please, if you report this to the emperor, I don't know how he'll punish me and my family. I'll do whatever I can to set it right."

I gaze at her blankly for a few heavy thuds of my pulse. I didn't trust her in the first place, and I have even less faith in her now. But the thought of seeing more blood spilled on my behalf makes my stomach churn.

I can't ask for another room without revealing what happened here. The fact that my maid turned against me enough to open me up to this vandalism might count as a strike against me as well as her.

What can I do but make the best of it?

The thought of anything about this situation being "best" brings a pained guffaw into my throat. I swallow it down and gesture vaguely toward the room's ruined contents.

My voice comes out as vacant as the aching hollow inside me. "Replace the bedclothes so I can sleep. Clean up the worst of the mess as well as you can in the next hour. We'll deal with the rest in the morning."

Melisse bobs her head, a trembling picture of deference now. "Yes, Your Highness. Thank you, Your Highness. I'll fix the bed right away."

As she hurries over and starts yanking off the covers, my gaze drifts to the heaps of shredded gowns. Some small practical part of my mind kicks into gear long enough for me to add, "I'll need new dresses first thing tomorrow. Whatever Madam Clea can supply that's reasonably close to my size."

A couple of sample gowns should be enough to hold me over until the final trial. The day after tomorrow, Marclinus said.

Three more competitors, two more days.

Then I'll be empress-to-be or dead. Either I can commission whatever replacement clothes I like or they can bury me as I fell.

Melisse dips her head even lower, bundling the sheets in her arms. "Of course, Your Highness. I'll speak to her the moment she wakes. I'll be back to do more cleaning in just a few minutes."

She scurries out of the room.

If I find myself empress-to-be, I reflect, I should also be able to pick whatever new staff I wish.

Briefly alone, I stare around me at the vast, desecrated room. The sour smell of kitchen refuse fills my nose.

My mind slips back to my bedroom at home in the castle at Costel—the bed heaped with the softest of blankets, the fire so often crackling merrily in the hearth, everything warm and familiar and safe.

Except it wasn't really safe, was it? From the moment I was born to a king and queen under the Darium empire's thumb, a king and queen who already had an heir, that castle wasn't truly mine. The place I thought of as home was always going to be taken away from me.

I assumed I could make a new home with new comforts wherever I ended up. It's hard to summon even a flicker of that kind of optimism now.

A wave of revulsion sweeps through me, every nerve recoiling from the idea of staying in this room while the maid who betrayed me scrubs, quivers, and fawns as if her life depends on it. It's not as if I can sleep yet.

Where *can* I go? What can I do?

What am I doing here at all, if this is what all my efforts have led me to? Have I gone so far astray I've lost the path without realizing it?

I turn and step out into the hall. My still-stinging feet carry me as if compelled—past the rows of doors, past the last stragglers from the court heading to their private rooms, down the stairs and on to the east end of the palace.

The arched doorway to the palace temple looms at the far end of the last hall I step into. I haven't ventured into it other than the second night of our starvation trial, haven't wanted to deal with clerics and devouts who must be more dedicated to their imperial overseers than the gods they worship.

But I need my godlen tonight, and I don't think I'm going to find the serenity to reach him in my sullied bedroom.

As temples go, the one attached to the side of the imperial palace like a small extra wing is modest in size if not in opulence. This space is meant to accommodate the spiritual needs of the emperor and his court alone, no one else. I caught a glimpse of the immense public temple in the middle of Vivencia on my journey through the city when I arrived.

Like that one, the emperor's private temple belongs to the All-Giver along with all the lesser gods. Walking into the domed space, I pay more attention to the details I was too weakened to appreciate last time.

Nine panes of color stretch across the ceiling overhead, swirling into a spiral of silver and gold at the very peak. Golden statues of each of the lesser gods stand in alcoves spaced an equal distance around the curving walls. Silk curtains in their associated colors frame each recess, with matching cushions on the marble-tiled floor.

A few lanterns beam along the edges of the ceiling, but I don't see anyone else inside at the moment. No doubt the imperial cleric and devouts have taken to their beds at this late hour.

So there's no one to watch as I cross the room to the statue of Elox within his draping of pure white.

I sink onto the white cushion and peer up at the statue some past emperor must have commissioned. My godlen's features look wrong sculpted out of the luxurious metal, a material I can't imagine him having any use for unless it's to pay to help those in need.

They've portrayed him with his typical flowing hair and beard, both reaching just below the level of his shoulders. In one hand, he holds a willow branch like a walking stick, curved at the top as if yielding to the wind. The other hand cups a real sprig of lavender that the temple staff must replace regularly.

His characteristically plain tunic and trousers contrast with the precious metal even more than his face. The gold is even etched with the lines of patches supposedly mended in the fabric.

He's gazing down fondly at the two sheep nestled at his feet. A dove perches on his shoulder.

Despite the contradiction between the expense of the sculpture and the figure it depicts, the sight of my godlen soothes my grief just a little.

I tip my head back, my eyelids sliding closed. The lantern light glows through them. I picture the figure before me as if he's made of that light rather than gold.

After tapping my fingers down my front, I press my knuckles against my godlen brand. Then my hands curl together in my lap, the sapphire on my ring pressing into the opposite palm. I let my stance sag as I give myself over to Elox's guidance, emptying myself of personal will.

Elox, my godlen, I fear I've lost my way. Is it truly your intention that I continue on this course amid so much violence and pain? How can I heal what's so very wounded? I would serve you, but I don't want to cause even more harm. What would you ask of me now?

For the first several slow breaths, nothing comes to me. Then a gentle pressure settles on my shoulders like my mother might have rested her hands there when reassuring me. As if to say, *I'm with you. I hear you.*

I sink deeper into my meditative state. My awareness of the room around me dwindles. Even the ache of loss and guilt fades away.

There's nothing but the steady rhythm of my breath and the thump of my pulse, on and on and—

A vision swims up from some place beyond consciousness.

A sheep stands in a field of grass. The blades around it shine verdantly green; the rest droop, dry and yellowed.

A knife that's little more than a glint of light slashes through the animal's plump body from chin to chest. The sheep's legs crumple into the gush of blood.

The crimson flood spreads out into the field—and new tufts of grass spring up in its wake, dappling the ailing areas with more and more vivid green while the creature deflates against the ground…

My eyes pop open. I stare up at the statue of Elox, a sharper pang resonating through my chest.

There's a parable Elox's devouts like to tell about a poor farming couple who begged for help against a band of raiders. Elox told them to slaughter their herd of sheep for the marauders.

"Surrender can be a weapon," the godlen said, so the tale claims. "Sometimes blood must be spilled to prepare the ground for peace."

My godlen believes I should shed even more blood than seeped from my feet tonight, however literally or metaphorically, before I've seen my duty through.

I can't say I'm even surprised by the answer. More unexpected is the image that passes before my eyes as I lower them.

Just for an instant, with a shift in the lantern light, a beam streaks across my cupped hands in the shape of a butcher's knife.

I peer at my hands for several heartbeats longer after the sign has vanished, as if I'll find a clearer answer written there. But really, that's as direct as the divine presences who watch over our world ever get.

The blade is in my grasp. It's my choice whether I go forward.

Elox can't force my hand.

Every cleric preaches that all people have free will regardless of what the gods might ask of us. But for whatever reason, my godlen felt the need to emphasize that point.

A choked laugh sputters out of me.

"Where else would I go?" I can't stop myself from asking out loud, peering up at the statue again. "What else could I do?"

I remain poised there on the cushion for several more minutes, but he offers no answers to those questions. It's my decision, and he's told me what *he* thinks would be best. If I want to strike off in some other direction, I'll have to figure that out for myself.

Here I am, then, with the cards I was dealt. I can throw them away and leave the empire's fate—and my kingdom's—to a woman like Fausta, or I can play the next rounds as well as I damn well can.

Gods help me, I might know how to surrender, but not to absolute oblivion.

I pick myself off the cushion, every inch of my body still filled with an unsettling combination of aches and numbness. As if every piece of me has hollowed out, leaving nothing behind but the lingering pain.

As I walk back through the halls, my mind has settled enough for me to take in the tapestries and paintings hanging on the halls. Around the bend from the temple, my feet jar to a halt in front of a particularly enormous gilded frame.

The painting encompassed in that frame stretches nearly to the ceiling and four times as wide as my arms can reach. I have to step back to the opposite wall to take it all in.

As soon as I do, I know why it caught my gaze.

Flames lick across a hilly landscape spotted with forests and towns. Trees have toppled, buildings have collapsed. Tiny figures flee in chaos across the terrain.

It's a depiction of the Great Retribution. The punishment our greatest god, the All-Giver, rained across the realms in response to terrifying acts of brutal magic as a scourge of twisted sorcerers attempted to raise themselves above any higher power.

In the aftermath, out of divine disappointment and offense, the Great God abandoned our continent to the care of the lesser gods who remained. But the painting isn't one of despair.

Right in the center of the epic masterpiece, a new city shimmers, sunlight catching off the spire of its temple and its silvery rooftops. There's no mistaking the intended symbolism.

Just as the cleric said that past evening, out of the ruin of the Great Retribution, Dariu recovered first. It was during those early days of recovery that an emperor saw the opportunity to bring the surrounding countries under his sway. His armies swept across the continent while the rest of us were still picking up the pieces of our livelihoods.

The painting might as well be gloating about their victory at our expense. Still, even as I grimace, a fire of my own flares up inside me to fill just a little of the emptiness.

Hundreds of years ago, after the worst destruction the continent has ever faced, Dariu rose from the ashes and turned itself into something even stronger than before.

Who's to say I can't do the same?

CHAPTER FORTY-ONE

Lorenzo

The sky above the trees is pitch black. I can barely see the strings of my lute in the faint illumination that seeps from the distant palace lanterns.

I ought to be in my bed. Weariness drags at my bones. I keep missing notes, stumbling over melodies I know.

The problem is that whenever I close my eyes, I see too much. Marclinus's ladies smearing blood beneath their feet as they dance to my music. The panther lunging among them.

Aurelia's grief-stricken face when the former Lady Rochelle lay crumpled in front of her.

Then the flush in her cheeks as she embraced Bastien and Raul together, so much like the rosy hue that came over her face as she gazed up at me in her bed.

My fingers trip over the strings again. I grimace at the instrument as if it's at fault rather than me.

The crunch of footsteps brings my head snapping up. If a

few restless nobles are wandering the forest looking to relieve their late-night boredom, I'd rather not become their target.

The forms that emerge from the darkness are more welcome, if not by much in my current state of mind.

Raul comes to a stop a few paces away, carrying a lantern set at a dim glow. Bastien draws up at his side.

The slimmer man's mouth twists with an uneven smile. "I figured if you weren't in your chambers, you'd be out here."

I don't feel like expending the energy to focus my gift if I don't have to. Gripping the lute's neck in one hand, I let my other dart through the air. *What do you want?*

My gesture must look as brusque as the question sounds in my head, because Bastien winces.

"You're obviously upset," he says. "We never had a chance to talk after— I'm sorry, Lore. It shouldn't have happened that way."

He isn't saying it shouldn't have happened at all. Does he have any idea just how forcefully that moment in the shuttered bedroom sent me ricocheting from one extreme of emotion to another?

I've never felt anywhere close to as happy as I did today, with Aurelia's caresses and eager words repeating in my memory. To know that she wanted me enough to offer up every part of herself, that she trusted me so much she didn't fear the consequences, that she wanted to dream of another reality where we might have been entwined for the rest of our lives…

Even the awful truth of her situation and who she'd have to marry dwindled to nothing but a faint sting in the midst of that giddy whirlwind.

But I don't have her even that much. She looked just as eager for my foster brothers' attentions as she did for mine. Just hours after we tumbled together…

Do I even still have the men I thought of as my closest friends? They noticed my good spirits, I revealed the reason to them with all due respect to the woman involved—and they immediately set out to have her for themselves.

I'm sure I've felt this low and lost before. When I first arrived at the palace. When Tarquin marched Pavel to his execution. But it's been years.

There hasn't been anything for me to feel this strongly about in all that time. Not until now, when I grasped joy close only to have it wrenched away by the only people I believed I could count on.

My hand clenches around the neck of the lute. I have the sudden, wild impulse to bash it against the nearest tree trunk, as if destroying something else I care about would sate the anguish inside for more than an instant.

Too much rancor has built up inside me for me to hold back my illusionary voice. *"It doesn't matter. To you or to her, obviously. I was being a fool, like you've always warned me."*

Raul grimaces and steps forward. "That's not true. She was very clear about how much she cares about you."

"Strange way of showing it."

"Lore." He lets out a growl of frustration. "You shouldn't blame her, not at all. It was our fault. When we heard how many secrets you spilled to her and realized she fucked you after she rebuffed our advances—we got suspicious."

Bastien shoots him a pointed look. "And *jealous.*"

Raul glowers at him. "I wasn't alone in that." He turns back to me. "We found her in the vacant room already trying to put the information you gave her to use. It looked bad. We laid into her, and she told us off—called us idiots for thinking she'd have been with you as some kind of scheme."

"She told us that she trusted you more than us," Bastien puts in. "That she's falling in love with you."

"And that she's falling for us too, even though we've been much bigger assholes to her." Raul swipes his hand over his face. "Hearing her say that—I got caught up. I wanted to test how true it was. It's not as if you weren't aware I've been pursuing her. I'm the one who suggested we should."

I can't deny that fact, even though remembering it sends an uncomfortable lump sinking into my gut. *You didn't say you'd gotten anywhere.*

"I hadn't really. I wasn't going to report all my failures. That's part of why I couldn't understand— But it makes sense. You were what she needed the most."

Bastien swallows audibly. "Barely anything had happened between me and her before that moment. I kissed her the other day and she stopped me. That's it. But it's hard not to appreciate her, isn't it? Seeing how deftly she's handled everything Tarquin and Marclinus have thrown at her, the fortitude she's shown through every setback… You know I didn't set out to care about her."

I do. And there's no mistaking the affection running through his voice as he speaks about her now.

Bastien isn't much for big emotional declarations. Him saying he appreciates and cares about her might as well be an announcement of utter devotion.

Can I really tell him that I'm more worthy of her?

I focus on Raul. *What about you? Is it all about having a tumble and being able to say you won her?*

His flinch answers my question before he even speaks. His voice comes out rough. "No. I've never craved anyone the way I want her, but it's not just— When I thought I didn't have any chance at all— She's an amazing woman. She should have so much more than that prick Marclinus would think to offer her, in *every* way."

We agree on that much.

I exhale slowly, the tension in my chest loosening but not leaving. Where do we go from here?

None of us can have her, not really. Maybe the worst part of this whole mess is how wrong that feels.

Even if I never got to touch Aurelia again, I'd rather see her in Bastien's or Raul's arms than Marclinus's.

Bastien takes in my stance and must judge that my temper has dwindled enough. He beckons to me. "This isn't something we can fully hash out without taking Aurelia into account. We made too many assumptions behind her back already. I doubt she's sleeping well after what happened tonight. Let's go to her, sort the rest out—and offer her whatever comfort we can, if she'll accept it."

A gleam lights in Raul's eyes that makes me want to punch him. I'm pretty sure Bastien, at least, means "comfort" in its least provocative sense.

"It sounds like we all owe her some apologies too," I say. *"Rather than immediately trying to sweep her up in some new seduction attempt."*

Raul's jaw ticks, but his expression turns chagrinned. "I can keep my dick in my pants."

"You haven't offered much proof of that claim so far."

Bastien sighs the way he always does when we squabble and waves us toward the palace more insistently. "Come on, before the sun's rising again."

It wouldn't be wise to march up to Aurelia's bedroom door and demand entrance in the middle of the night. We slip through the palace halls to the unused bedroom that's been our usual entry point, then weave through the narrow, stuffy passages to the one that ends at her chambers.

Raul moves to the front of our procession. After a brief pause by the hidden doorway, he nods. "There's no one else inside. She's lying on the bed. I can't tell if she's asleep." His forehead furrows. "Something about the room feels… strange."

My pulse stutters. *"Is she all right?"*

Bastien nudges us forward with renewed urgency. "We're here now. Let's see for ourselves."

The moment Raul eases open the hinged panel in the wall, a current of cooler air wafts into the stillness of the passage. Cooler and tainted with an odd sour smell like food that's gone off.

My nose wrinkles reflexively. Raul steps into the room with a mutter under his breath. "What the fuck…"

The curtains have been left open, letting in the faint glow of the outer lanterns and the night breeze. It isn't enough to wash away the fetid odor that seems to linger in the space.

In the dimness, my eyes pick out splotches on the floorboards and the rug where Aurelia and I came together so passionately this morning. Stains? And farther across the room, near her wardrobe—

Raul flicks a hasty glance toward Aurelia's form tucked beneath the covers. When she doesn't stir at our arrival, he strides over to the heaps of ragged cloth on the floor.

Bastien and I trail behind him. I notice more blotchy stains everywhere I look.

Raul bends over the heap and sucks in a sharp breath. He holds up the skirt of what's obviously a gown—or used to be. It's sliced and ripped into tatters—and mashed with shreds of muck that give off more of the putrid stink.

Bastien's face tightens. "What happened here?" he asks in a harsh whisper.

Raul sounds as if he's struggling to keep his voice low. "All her dresses." He paws through the heap. "Totally ruined." He glances up at us with narrowed eyes. "Didn't Fausta tear one of her gowns before?"

I swallow hard. *"None of this mess was here this morning."*

Sometime between now and then, a destructive force swept through Aurelia's chamber, through her things. When? Was she already grappling with this new assault when we found her in the other room? When she had to dance to the tune Tarquin ordered me to play?

I drift back toward the bed, seeking out Aurelia's shape. The bedspread looks unmarred—but it's a different color than the one we lay on this morning, isn't it? Blue rather than green.

It's a huge bed, befitting her station, and she's curled tight beneath the covers—knees drawn up, head ducked low so only her forehead and the splay of her hair across the pillow show. She isn't a small woman, but right now, in the middle of the expanse of the mattress, she looks outright tiny.

My stomach twists. Every day, she endures more trials than even we know about. She takes them on her shoulders without complaint.

Because she's so completely alone in this place that she doesn't feel she can turn to anyone.

Maybe she would have reached out to me if I hadn't stormed off on her this evening. We should have been here offering her comfort from the start, not skulking around stewing in wounded emotions.

How selfish would it be for me to resent her taking whatever joy she can find with my foster brothers as well as with me? Did I really think that with all the menaces she's faced in the place, I could be a sanctuary for her all on my own?

A pang in my heart draws me closer. Without thinking, simply propelled by the need to be there for her, I peel back the covers enough to slide under them and tuck myself carefully around her huddled body.

Despite my gentleness, Aurelia stirs. Her initial flinch sends a jab of guilt through my chest, but she relaxes a second later, turning her head toward me. Her voice sounds far too thin. "Lorenzo?"

"I'm sorry." The apology spills out of my mind in a rush. I hug her deeper into my embrace, bowing my head next to hers. *"I'm sorry I got angry. You didn't do anything wrong."*

"I should have told you… We should have talked about it first."

"This whole situation is a mess. None of us knows what we're doing. But I'm glad—I'm glad you have more than just me. You should have all the adoration you can get from people who see how wonderful you are."

I've let the illusion project far enough that my foster brothers will hear it too. They've come around the other side of the bed.

Bastien perches on the mattress and reaches over to stroke his fingers over Aurelia's hair. He bows his head. "I have to apologize too. For making the accusations at all—for getting jealous when I had no justification. I keep getting things wrong with you. We've had to be so wary for so long…"

"I know," she says softly.

Raul shifts his weight from one foot to the other, looking as if he's afraid to get any closer. His hands have clenched at his sides. "None of this is right. None of what they've done to you—to Lady Rochelle—what happened to your room— If *I've* pushed at you too much in any direction, I'm sorry. I promised you better than that."

Aurelia shifts around in my arms. She clasps Bastien's hand and peers at Raul through the darkness. "I could have stopped things sooner if I'd wanted to. It's not all on you."

He holds her gaze. "What do you need from us? How

can we make tomorrow and the next day better instead of worse? Who the fuck do I need to kill so you don't have to worry about finding your room in ruins again? Just say the word."

A quaver runs through Aurelia's next words. "I'd rather there was less killing instead of more. I don't think I'm going to get that, though."

Bastien squeezes her hand, but none of us knows what to say. We can't stand between the emperor's guards and whoever he directs them to murder without getting murdered ourselves.

I hug her tighter for a few aching thuds of my heart. Then I sit up, leaving my hand on her shoulder as I turn to my foster brothers. *"We should at least make sure no one can disturb her for the rest of the night. Let her get as much sleep as possible—she needs it."*

Bastien glances around and gets up. "Come on—we can push one of the trunks in front of the door. No one else will be coming in uninvited."

I leap up to help him shove the trunk into position. Raul paces beside the bed, the muscles in his shoulders flexing. "We can wait here in case anyone tries. Make that bitch wish she never—"

"No." Aurelia's voice clears with growing alertness.

She raises her head from the pillow, concern etched on her weary face. "You shouldn't stay. If anyone realizes you were in here with me at night— It means a lot that you want to protect me. But I'll feel better if I know you're all safe from sanction too."

With all the burdens she's carrying, she's still as worried about us as herself. My throat constricts. *"Aurelia…"*

She shakes her head. "I won't be able to sleep if I know

you could get caught. You need your rest too, so we can all face the next day stronger."

So we can help her if we do have the opportunity. My body balks, but I incline my head in understanding.

"We can't just *leave* when—" Raul starts.

Bastien prods his arm. "What were you just saying about pushing? She's told us very directly what she wants."

The larger man lets out a huff, but his stance deflates with resignation. He pauses by the bed once more. "We'll be watching over you, Shepherdess."

"And if you need to get away in a rush…" Bastien eases past him and points out the spot on the wall just behind the side table that triggers the hidden door. "Press it two times quickly and then once hard until it opens."

Aurelia watches him, her expression unreadable in the dimness. "Thank you."

I can't shake the feeling that there should be more I can do, more I can offer, but I have no idea what that would be. As Bastien and Raul step into the passage, I hesitate.

Aurelia catches my eyes and offers a gentle smile as if she knows what I'm thinking. As if I need reassurance more than she does.

My heart skips a beat. *"I love you,"* I say just for her— knowing it doesn't make a difference, needing her to hear it anyway—and follow my foster brothers into the wall.

As we creep through the passage back to our own chambers, a gnawing uncertainty follows at my heels. Would a braver man have insisted on being there for her no matter what she said?

CHAPTER FORTY-TWO

Aurelia

I'm not sure I've ever felt truly at ease among the imperial court nobles, but this morning my mask feels especially brittle.

I smile and swallow bite after bite of breakfast, all of it tasting like ash in my mouth. I don't show any hint of how Rochelle's death last night is still wrenching at me.

When Emperor Tarquin stands at the head of the table to command our attention, I push the corners of my mouth higher and try not to imagine my cheeks cracking with the effort.

He raises his glass in toast. "To the three talented women who've risen above the rest to earn my son's esteem."

I lift my goblet to clink it against my neighbors'. The tinkling of glass resonates throughout the dining room.

The imperial heir gets up next, his mouth curled into a smirk. "Today is a day of rest before the final challenge tomorrow, but it's also a chance for me and my potential brides to begin forging what may be a lifelong bond. I'll meet with each of my ladies in private so we can get to know each other better."

My skin creeps at the thought of what "getting to know" him might entail in his mind, but my smile stays plastered on my face.

My godlen's message was clear. I'm on the right path.

I simply have to keep going forward, and maybe something good will come of it in the end. Even if it's hard to imagine how any of my plans will make a difference even for myself, let alone all the people counting on me back in Accasy.

After the meal, we meander down to the gardens. Just outside the palace, Marclinus catches Leonette's lean arm and draws her away from the rest of us. They vanish down one of the paths between the hedges.

Are all of the private chats going to happen out here, or is he setting up something different for each of us?

The question gnaws at the edges of my mind as I pick up a glass of juice from one of the servants' trays. I need something to do with my hands.

I'm dreading more bland, fawning conversation from nobles hedging their bets and attempting to curry favor with a possible future empress, but the figure who drifts over to join me first provokes a different sort of apprehension.

Prince Neven ducks his white-blond head and then peers down at me with a slight grimace. "Good morning, Princess Aurelia."

Well, he's not insulting or glowering at me yet. I suppose that's a good sign. I haven't spoken to him since I cajoled him out of the hall of entertainments when he was on the verge of unleashing his anger on Emperor Tarquin.

That night, as soon as he realized I was just tricking him into leaving, he simply spat a few curses at me and stalked off.

"Good morning, Prince Neven," I say, matching his even tone. "No studies today?"

He shakes his head with a flick of a glance around the garden. "It's a day of rest for me too."

"I hope it proves invigorating."

His gaze slides back to me, a hint of a furrow forming between his eyebrows. His hands twitch at his sides as if he's resisting the urge to fidget.

Finally, he speaks again, a little rougher than before. "I'm sorry for how I spoke to you the other night. I know you were acting in my best interests. It's just not always easy to see what those are in the moment... sometimes not until other people point it out to you."

The corner of my mouth ticks upward with my first genuine smile of the day. "Your foster brothers had a few things to say, I gather."

He shrugs with a hint of adolescent defiance, his gaze sliding to where Bastien and Lorenzo are standing together by one of the hedge sculptures. "They don't need to fuss over me quite as much as they do. But that doesn't mean they're always wrong."

"They care about you a lot. It's nice to have that concern, even if it's sometimes annoying. Although I suppose three older brother figures is probably a little more stifling than the one older sister I have."

As the words leave my mouth, I realize I might have inadvertently prodded a sore spot. He lost an actual older brother to Emperor Tarquin's cruelty ten years ago.

Neven's expression tightens. "I have an older sister too.

Back home. But I only get to see her once a year, so she can't exactly get overbearing."

Before I can decide whether to mention his late brother, he gives me a quizzical look. "Had your sister eased back on the hovering by the time you were older?"

I suppose I haven't offended him, at least.

My last conversation with Soreena floats up from my memory, and my smile falters. I hope she's not still beating herself up over failing to shield me from this fate.

Gods only know what she'd feel if she realized what I've actually been through just to confirm my marriage.

"Maybe a little," I say. "I think she'll always want to protect me—she's simply had to recognize that there are times when she can't. But there are benefits to having older-sibling overseers too. The support and encouragement." I summon a quick grin to show I'm happy to take on that role as well, if he wants me to. "Good luck with your musician."

Neven's cheeks turn pink. He mumbles a "Thank you" before he moves on, but his posture looks more relaxed than it did when he approached me.

Perhaps I've given one person a little more peace than they had before.

He ambles toward his foster brothers, and I tamp down the urge to follow the same route. Last night's recriminations and expressions of devotion have tangled into a chaotic jumble. What if their feelings have shifted all over again?

I can't risk putting my muddled emotions on display in front of the entire court.

Instead, I wander toward a fountain with a sculpture of Prospira spilling a bounty of water and marble fruit from her extended hands. Maybe that was an unwise direction too, because looking up at the godlen of abundance reminds me of Rochelle's dedication brand.

Before I can settle on a new destination, the noble company I anticipated begins to cluster around me. This baroness wants to know what I think of the combination of colors in a nearby flowerbed. That marchioness compliments me on my dress, even though it's one from Madam Clea's untailored stock that Melisse had to spend half an hour pinning to make sure it fit properly enough to befit a princess.

One of the viceroys tells me I handled myself admirably with the panther last night, and I admirably resist the urge to throw my drink in his face.

None of my new hangers-on give any sign that they remember someone died last night—a woman who used to be a lady and their peer. They barely seem to recognize that *I* wasn't having the time of my life dancing on bleeding feet.

Possibly, as far as they're concerned, any task that could lead to marrying the imperial heir is an honor more than a trial.

After several minutes of painful conversation, Fausta minces around the fountain toward me with a couple of her friends in tow. I tense up automatically at the sight of her bright red hair, but my smile never budges.

She smiles back at me, so wide and unassuming I'm unnerved. "It's a lovely morning, isn't it, Your Highness?"

I fight to keep a dry edge of disbelief out of my voice. "Yes, quite lovely."

She adjusts the small hat perched on her head and gives the slightest of respectful curtsies. "There are so few of us left now… It wouldn't do for us to be at each other's throats, would it? What's done is done. Now the best woman will win by her own strengths, as you've always said."

I don't believe she really buys into that sentiment, not for a second. Does she think I'll lower my guard if she plays nice for a day? Or is there some trick embedded even in this sham of kindness?

My tone stays mild. "It would be wonderful if tomorrow's trial could be all about our personal abilities."

Fausta lets out a melodic giggle. "I know you'll give me a challenge. You've pushed me to be an even better match for His Imperial Highness than I was before. I should thank you for that."

"I'm glad my efforts have been appreciated."

She lingers through a turn about the garden and more aimless conversation before veering off to consult with Bianca when our group crosses paths with the vicerene. Bianca aims a narrow glance my way as if she's not even going to pretend to be on board with this supposed truce.

We move to the lawn for a series of games that are enjoyable only in that I know no one will be bleeding or dead at the end of them. I've just finished a round of tossing rings, which has seemed to be more about watching the ribbons twined around the silver hoops flutter in the breeze than landing them anywhere near the designated posts, when a footman approaches me.

"His Imperial Highness would see you now, Princess Aurelia."

My turn. I nod as if I'm grateful and follow him through the garden.

He leads me all the way to the edge of the woods, where I find Marclinus waiting in a typical casual pose but with his eyes unsettlingly alert.

He cocks his head, his small smile lifting the scar through his upper lip. "Since you've mentioned your fondness for forestland, I thought we could take a stroll through my personal woods together. I even brought an appropriate snack." He tosses a small silk bag in his hand. "Baked lacquernuts. Do you like them?"

They're a childhood favorite among almost all Accasians. Just hearing the name brings a smoky sweetness of remembered flavor onto my tongue.

I've never seen them in the imperial palace. Did he import some specially for this occasion?

What's *he* playing at?

I keep those questions to myself and amble over to join him. "I do, quite a bit. It's generous of you to have arranged something from my old home."

As I reach him, Marclinus sets off into the woods, clearly expecting me to keep pace. He pops one of the nuts into his mouth and offers them to me so I can pluck one out.

I suppose the fact that he's eating from the bag at random should reassure me that they're not doctored in any way. I force myself to select one without hesitation.

It does taste like home, the crisp yet creamy taste spreading through my mouth as I chew. Like winter nights by the big hearth in the castle's great hall, listening to the bards sing stories with my family and friends around me.

The imperial heir takes a rambling path, skirting patches of underbrush and turning his face to meet the gusts of breeze that ripple through his golden hair. But he spends at least as much time watching me as he does absorbing the atmosphere.

"What do you like about the woods?" he asks rather abruptly.

What would be the most appealing response to that question, as far as he's concerned? I pop another lacquernut into my mouth to buy me a little time.

If I let myself forget who I'm walking with for a moment, breathe in the fresh scents of the trees and listen to the chirps and scurrying of the wildlife we pass, it's easier to compose my words. "I think it reminds me that there are things bigger than myself, that I'm just a piece of a much larger picture, but that picture is vibrant and full of life—all the more, the more you look for it. And spending some time away from all other concerns is good for clearing my head so I can focus on what's most important."

Marclinus hums. "And what would that be, Your Highness? What's most important to you right now?"

I don't have to think about *that* answer. "Proving myself worthy of you, of course. That's all I've wanted since the moment I set out for Dariu."

"*All* you could possibly want?"

His tone is teasing but skeptical. I don't want to lay it on too thick.

I give a light laugh. "I suppose that's a bit of an exaggeration. I've wanted appropriate dresses to fit in at your court, and food as it's provided, and my afternoon baths. But in terms of importance, gaining your good opinion is certainly by far at the top of the list."

He considers my words for a few minutes of silence. I'm starting to wonder if I'm supposed to provide the next topic of conversation when he speaks again. "Not all of the court ladies have been welcoming to a newcomer from the north."

Oh, he's actually noticed that from his gilded seats, has he? I couldn't read concern or accusation in his tone.

I peek at him sideways, trying to judge his expression. "I'd imagine that's to be expected, especially when I've come from so far away. Most of them will never have met any Accasians at all. It's been delightful to see them warming up to me."

"You have no complaints to make about anyone in particular."

I suspect doing so would reflect worse on me than whoever I point my finger at. "No. I trust that all will work out in the end as it should. But of course I will keep my experiences in mind going forward."

To my surprise, the imperial heir chuckles. "Accepting and yet canny. An interesting combination. What would Elox say about holding grudges?"

I allow myself a little tartness. "They aren't grudges. It's useful information to guide me on the best course toward a peaceful and constructive existence."

"A very polite framing."

He grins at me, and just in that moment, I don't feel any malice in it. It's as if he honestly thinks we're sharing a joke— as if he *wants* to share the humor of the situation with me, rather than imposing some jape without a care what I make of it as long as I laugh on cue.

I do laugh, my mind whirling with uncertainty. Is he trying to disarm me so I'll give something away? Set me at ease so he can throw me off balance all over again?

Or is it possible that some small part of him might be open to listening to me occasionally after all?

Naturally, the next moment he douses my flicker of hope with a harsher laugh. "I am glad it wasn't you the panther sank its jaws into last night."

No condolences or expressions of sympathy. Because as soon as he dismissed Rochelle as a contender for his bride, she ceased to count as a person to him.

Probably she never did. I'm not sure I ever will, even if he takes me as his wife.

My whole body goes cold. I force another titter, as if the woman who did die doesn't matter to me either. "As am I, Your Imperial Highness."

The rest of what Marclinus asks me about my

observations of the woods and his court, I answer equally politely and mostly on instinct. Yesterday's numbness has come over me again, detaching me from the sounds entering my ears and the movements of my mouth.

At the ringing of the city bells to mark the hour, the imperial heir leads me back to the edge of the garden. Emperor Tarquin stands several paces away by one of the carved limestone planters, as if he just happened to have walked that way at this moment. But he's alone.

At least, he appears to be. Remembering Bastien's comments about his host of guards, I pick out a hint of movement by the nearby hedges.

Does he go undefended even in his own bedroom? Doubtful.

Marclinus nods to his father. "I'll see you at lunch," he says, perhaps to both of us, and saunters off toward his court nobles.

I move to follow him, but Tarquin holds up his sinewy hand to stop me. He motions me over until I'm standing just a couple of steps away and looks me up and down. His gaze is all assessing, none of the leer I'd expect from his son.

His eyes settle on my face, as keenly penetrating as always. "Our princess of the wild north. You've adapted to the change in expectations well."

So many of my expectations have been turned on their heads in the past two weeks that I'm not sure what he's referring to. A vague answer is all that's required anyway. "I came here to serve the imperial family as well as I'm able."

His next remark clarifies his meaning. "You thought you'd be greeted with a wedding rather than a series of trials. But you're close to that wedding now. I hope there's no resentment over the tests we've required or their lack of forewarning."

Resentment? Try bone-deep revulsion and seething rage.

I push my mouth into yet another false smile. "Your Imperial Eminences must evaluate who will make an ideal partner as you see fit. It's a relief to know that after the final trial, there should be no doubt of who that partner is."

"Indeed." Tarquin smiles back at me, but I don't feel any warmth from it. "You are well-spoken enough to sit beside my son's throne. I'm sure of that already."

He motions for me to continue through the gardens, so I go. My knotted stomach leaves no room for actual relief.

No matter how much of his approval I've earned, all it will take is one wrong step, and he'll throw me away. Even after Marclinus and I have said our vows.

Everything depends on how well I play this last stage of the game.

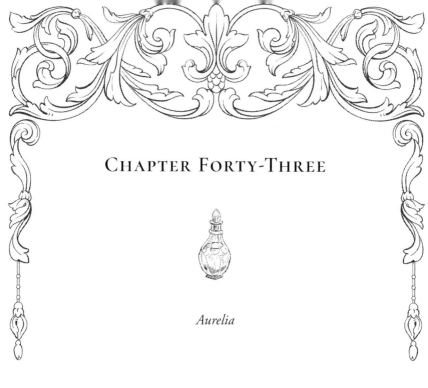

CHAPTER FORTY-THREE

Aurelia

By dinner, the imperial heir is back in one of his buoyantly irreverent moods. He seats Fausta and me at either side of his gilded chair at the foot of the table, and sometimes when he leans forward to snatch something off a platter or laugh at his own jokes, he slides one hand beneath the tabletop to caress my thigh.

I suspect he's doing the same to Fausta here and there. A hint of pink colors her porcelain complexion. When she's not aiming bright smiles of false friendship my way, she's gazing at him coyly through her eyelashes and tossing her hair flirtatiously over her shoulder.

I laugh and smile and lower my eyelashes too, aiming for a more modest version of her encouragement. I don't actually want him getting any bolder.

As if to make up for the attention he's offered us over his third prospective bride, Marclinus swoops in on Leonette as soon as the court has moved to the hall of entertainments. He guides her closer to the musicians with his hand lingering on her back, just above her ass.

Neven is already standing nearby, watching the performers avidly. I spot Bastien keeping an eye on him from one of the cards tables. Raul and Lorenzo, who Emperor Tarquin didn't order to perform tonight, have joined a game of darts.

I tug my gaze away as soon as I've noticed them, not wanting anyone else to notice *me* studying them. Which is a good thing, because my traveling gaze lands on Fausta just as she ducks out of the room.

Something about her stride strikes me as furtive. With a prickle of apprehension, I slip after her.

When I peek out into the hall, her petite form is just passing around the bend to my left. I hurry after her, my slippers nearly silent on the marble tiles.

As I come up on the bend, a faint murmur of voices reaches my ears. I ease my head around the corner, immediately grateful for the statue of some past emperor poised by the wall on the other side which offers me cover.

Halfway down the next hall, Fausta and Bianca have their heads bowed together in quiet conversation. I can't make out their voices, but Bianca passes something to Fausta, partly concealed by the fabric of the cloak she's wearing.

Did she go right out of the palace to get whatever item she's brought for her friend?

They share a sharp laugh. When Fausta turns toward my end of the hall, her expression is so smug you'd think she'd already been crowned empress.

A chill courses down my back. I knew she had to be up to something, that there was no way she'd truly be backing down from making this competition a fight, but I have no idea what to expect from her tomorrow.

I can't imagine what the final trial will even be, other than presumably it'll prove the grandest of them all. Was Bianca able to uncover details in advance like she has before?

How many opportunities will Fausta get to sabotage me? What is she planning that's left her so confident?

I can't linger to speculate while she ambles toward me. With my gut clenched, I hustle back to the hall of entertainments before my rival can realize I followed her.

Once I've entered, I stay near the doorway, watching it. Perhaps I can find an excuse to accost her and find out what Bianca handed over.

But Fausta doesn't appear. She must have headed to her chambers instead to secret the illicit item away.

I doubt she'll bring it into my presence until she's ready to use it. Presumably tomorrow, during the trials she may also know far more about than I do.

Standing in the midst of the throng of nobles, I feel abruptly adrift.

My one friend is gone, so utterly my entire chest aches to think of her. I certainly can't ask Melisse if she's heard any rumors among the palace staff.

The gentlemen and ladies who've flattered me in the past few days are looking forward to seeing me jump through whatever hoops Marclinus has in store. They wouldn't risk his wrath or the diminishing of their fun by helping me prepare.

My gaze catches on Bastien's auburn head again. He warned me of a coming trial once. Would he have already approached me if he'd stumbled on a clue?

Any of the princes might have seen or heard something that could help me get through tomorrow without them realizing the significance. They're the only allies I have left. I need to make use of them.

Even if I'm not completely certain where we stand after last night's fraught encounters.

I drift closer to the dart boards, pretending to be observing the games being played at nearby tables. When I see Lorenzo glance my way at the edge of my vision, I make a hasty twist of my hand.

You three meet me at my room.

The last part I can only convey with a brief jab in the direction of my chambers. Hopefully he understands.

I don't dare look at him directly to see how he reacts. I just meander away, weaving in the general direction of the door and then out into the hall.

I don't know how long it'll take Lorenzo to pass on the message to the other two princes and for them to discreetly leave. It seems safest to head straight to my bedroom. If anyone asks why I've left, I'll say that I want to get as much rest as possible before the final trial.

As it turns out, I don't pass anyone except for a couple of silent guards. In my chambers, I pace across the stained rug. Melisse spent most of the day scrubbing at the remaining residue from the refuse Fausta left strewn here, but despite that and the open windows, a trace of the sour smell lingers.

My rival has been able to break through my defenses so easily too many times.

I don't know how low she'll stoop now that the prize is inches from her grasp. I don't know what tactics she might turn to next.

The only thing I'm sure of is that she'll stop at nothing to be the one who wins tomorrow's trial and Marclinus's hand.

She was willing to break my bones and leave me to die in agony less than a week ago. How much worse can it get?

Gods help me, if I lose tomorrow, I want it to be because I wasn't up to the challenge, not because some vindictive noblewoman cheated me of the chance.

After several minutes, my restlessness and the unpleasant smell lead me to the wall next to my bed. The spot Bastien indicated last night has the slightest indent.

I press there three times as he instructed me, and a portion of the wall sighs open.

The reveal seems like magic even though I knew the hidden door was there. Perhaps there is a little enchantment in the wall, helping to conceal it from unknowing eyes.

I step into the small alcove on the other side. A cramped passage leads off to my right. There's definitely some permanent enchantment in here, because a dim glow wavers into being at my entrance, providing just enough light for me to make out the wooden boards that line the passage's floor, walls, and ceiling and the bits of cobweb that cling to them. The air that seeps into my lungs has a stale oaky scent laced with dust.

It's clearly been a long time since anyone used these inner hallways regularly. Does Emperor Tarquin even know they're here, or has mention of them been erased so thoroughly that even the owners of the palace have forgotten?

I don't expect Melisse to return tonight, but I find a button on the inside of the doorframe and push it to swing the panel closed, just in case.

It only takes a few minutes before the soft scuffing of footsteps reaches my ears. Lorenzo comes into view in the lead, his face tense with worry.

Our middle-of-the-night conversation feels more like a dream than an actual memory, but he doesn't look at all angry with me. Has he completely forgiven me for all of yesterday's confusion?

I turn toward him, and he wraps his arms around me automatically, ducking his head next to mine. As if there's nothing more natural than catching me in his embrace.

All the anxious thoughts that've been whirling through my head settle down, overwhelmed by the ache of longing that's washed over me.

I wish this *was* where I belonged.

Behind Lorenzo, Bastien clears his throat.

Raul lets out a soft huff. "She called for us too, you know." But his chiding sounds good-humored. His tone darkens as he shifts his focus to me. "What's wrong, Aurelia?"

I pitch my voice at a whisper, not sure how close we are to the other rooms around mine. "There's nothing immediate. I only wanted to ask, with the trial tomorrow— have any of you picked up on anything at all out of the ordinary happening around the palace? Or overheard any unusual conversations? If I had even a small idea of what I'll be facing…"

Lorenzo eases back and shakes his head with an apologetic grimace.

Raul frowns. "I can't think of anything. They kept all the past trials awfully quiet too."

I look past Lorenzo to Bastien, the one who's come through for me before. His brow has knit with concentration.

Then he shakes his head too. "I'm sorry. I've been wondering about it myself all day, so I'd imagine I'd have noticed if something had come up."

He doesn't need to apologize. He doesn't owe it to me to help me through this mess.

But all the same, the longing rises up to tell them my suspicions about Fausta, to implore them to keep an eye on her…

For what purpose? What could they do if she lashes out at me during the trial?

After all the turmoil we've been through, can I really ask any of them to step in and intervene directly if it comes to that? Why should they stick their necks out and risk their own safety?

Just yesterday they were all furious at me at one point or another. I can hardly expect our alliance to be secure, no matter how much I crave the certainty of knowing they have my back.

Bastien reaches out to grasp my hand. Raul peers past him, his gaze smoldering into mine with enough unspoken passion to send heat blooming over my skin.

When Lorenzo leans in to kiss my temple, a flare of inspiration lights inside me.

There might be a way to solidify whatever connection they feel to me. To ground the idea of us and the bonds we share in a totally concrete way, so they'll believe it's worth contributing everything they *can* safely offer.

It may not make enough of a difference, but at least I'll know I did everything I could.

And if my heart leaps a little too giddily at the possibility, I won't examine that fact. Why shouldn't I want more—want everything I can get while I still can?

It isn't as if they wouldn't get plenty of satisfaction out of the experience too.

Once the idea has taken hold, I can't shake it. It quivers through my nerves, and the next thing I know, my mouth is opening. "Is there a room we can reach through these passages where there's no chance we'll be disturbed? My chambers hardly feel secure now, and my maid always has access."

Bastien cocks his head in thought and then beckons to

me. He squeezes past Raul to take the lead in the opposite direction.

We wind through the narrow passages, around corners, up a few steps, down several more, through a few turns, and then descend a tight spiral of wooden stairs.

At the bottom, we emerge into a space that's totally dark other than the thinnest haze seeping from the staircase behind us. Bastien gropes through the blackness and flicks on a lantern.

The glow fills a cozy space where the furniture is draped with sheets. Unlike the unused bedroom above, it's clear no one has been keeping this room clean. Dust blankets the covers and the floor, with indents of footsteps where at least one of the princes must have ventured here sometime in the past.

"I think this used to be a sort of sitting room for servants who needed to be especially on-call." Bastien motions toward the doorway kitty-corner from the stairs. "It's totally blocked off from the inside now. No one will be coming in from the regular staff areas—no one should be close enough to even hear us."

Beyond the doorway lies an even smaller room. At the far end of that, strips of metal have been fastened across the wall from the floor to a couple of feet below the ceiling—forming a barrier where the main staff entrance to the passages must have been.

It does look secure enough, if not the cleanest of spaces. I tug tentatively at one of the sheets, which appears to be draped over an armchair.

Warmth fills my cheeks. "I'm not sure if this is the best setting…"

"For what?" Raul asks, arching his eyebrows.

They're all standing close enough to me that the heat of

their bodies envelops mine. I can't help thinking of the moment yesterday when both Bastien and Raul were caressing me with their hands and lips...

My blush deepens. For all the hungers stirring in me, for all the other reasons I have to want this, I'm hardly a practiced seductress.

I reach up to touch Lorenzo's jaw and press a light kiss to his mouth. As he loops his arm around my waist, I turn in his embrace to face the other two princes.

The man who's already been my lover shows no sign of disapproval when I tease my fingers up Bastien's arm. When I stroke them partway down Raul's chest.

I make myself meet their eyes one after the other, the desire gleaming there sparking more inside me, and lean into Lorenzo to show he's just as much a part of this conversation. "Tomorrow, my life as I know it is going to be over one way or another. I only have a little time left. I'd like... I'd like to know what it feels like to be as cherished as I can be, while I have the chance. While I can be with the men I actually want, no matter how briefly."

Bastien's eyes widen. Raul lets out a low growl and steps closer.

Lorenzo's arm tightens around me, but not to ward them away. His illusionary voice fills my head. *"You'll still have us. We'll be here, even if you have to marry him."*

I can tell from the tightening of the other men's expressions that he's extended his gift enough for them to hear too.

I swallow thickly. "I know you'll want to be. But if I make it through and become Marclinus's wife, I'll be guarded so much more closely. Everyone will be watching. I'll have to share my room with him... I don't want to put any of *you* in jeopardy. As anything more than acquaintances, the association between us will have to end tomorrow."

Raul makes a scoffing sound and cups my cheek. "We'll see about that, Princess. If you need us, I think we can find a way."

I rest my hand on his forearm. "I'd rather go without your attentions but still see that you're well than risk losing you completely. But tonight—tonight could be ours."

Maybe it's better if they believe something might continue between us even after the results of tomorrow's trial. More to fight for, more reason to champion me. But I'm not going to lie to them and pretend I think it's possible.

Tonight I can think of myself as well as my goals. After tomorrow, Princess Aurelia really will cease to exist. Everything I do will be in service of my country.

Which is all the more reason to make the most of this moment.

Bastien wets his lips and glances around the room. His stance tenses just slightly in a moment of hesitation.

His voice holds an uncertain note I don't totally understand. "I can give us a nicer venue." He lifts his chin with an aura of resolve. "Yes. It'll only take a minute."

Before I can ask what he means, the lean muscles in his shoulders flex, and a draft sweeps through the space.

Not just a draft—a gust of wind, tugging at my hair and dress as it passes me.

The current of air flicks the sheets off the furniture and blows them into the other room. It catches all the puffs of dust rising from the floor and sends them billowing after, wiping the floor clean.

In a matter of seconds, the lantern glow beams across a worn but clean rug on a smooth stone floor, two mismatched armchairs with a scuffed wooden table between them, and a faded settee by the wall.

My jaw has gone slack. I reel it back in, my gaze jerking to Bastien. "That—your gift—"

His smile looks pleased if a tad sheepish. "Lorenzo showed you his. You might as well know mine. I can manipulate air."

Understanding clicks in my head. "I heard you can send away rainclouds. That's how? You just *push* them with the wind…"

Gods, it's hard to imagine how much magic that must take—and how much else he might be able to do with a gift that strong.

But then, he did give up an entire lung for it. It isn't as if the sacrifice wasn't worthy.

"Show-off," Raul grumbles.

He scoops his hand through the air next to the chair we're standing near and lifts it with a strange object clenched in his fingers. It looks like a clump of dark, gauzy cloth standing erect, but somehow both filmier and denser in its darkness than actual cloth would be.

Then, as I watch, the edges of the shape ripple. It stretches out, thinning into a ribbon of the hazy material.

With a twist of his wrist, Raul slides the ribbon across my neck. It feels like a swath of mist, cool and tingling, grazing my skin.

With a squeeze of his fingers, the substance hardens. He traces it over my shoulder as if stroking me with a rod of smooth wood now.

A shiver travels through my nerves. "What *is* that?"

Raul grins. "A shadow. Mostly I can just sense what's in them—the shadows of pockets and pouches and what's under ladies' skirts."

He dips his head to brush his lips against the spot where the shadowy ribbon touched my neck. "But if I can touch part of a shadow, I can grab hold and shape it however I want. You can thank Kosmel for that."

I suppose the trickster godlen would be amused by the uses Raul typically puts his gift to.

As he slides his band of shadow over my hip and uses it to rustle the skirt of my gown, Bastien folds his arms over his chest. "Now who's showing off?"

Raul simply smirks at him and lets the shadow soften to lick across my shin.

Even in this isolated room, the peal of the hourly bell resonates faintly through the walls. Bastien glances toward the sealed doorway and back at me, hunger reigniting in his deep green gaze.

"There are only so many hours left in the night, and our princess needs her rest before tomorrow's trial. We can ensure that she's completely sated before she retires to bed, can't we?"

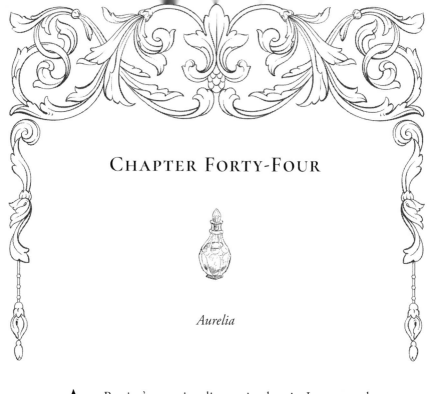

Chapter Forty-Four

Aurelia

As Bastien's question lingers in the air, Lorenzo takes my hand and raises it to his lips.

I meet his eyes with a skip of my pulse that's not only desire. "Are you okay with this? I never meant to mislead you…"

He draws my chin toward him. As his mouth melds against mine, his voice weaves through my thoughts. *"I made my own assumptions. If this is what you want… all I want is to see you happy. There's no one in the world other than these two I'd trust to look after you."*

When he pulls back, a sly smile crosses his lips. *"It'll be interesting to see how much pleasure we can offer you together."*

"Gods, yes." Raul guides my head around so he can claim my lips for himself.

His kiss is just as fierce and demanding as I remember, hot enough to make my head spin. I've barely caught my breath when a wisp of air tingles across my neck beneath my hair.

My eyes lock with Bastien's where he's still standing a couple of paces away in the small room. He doesn't move, but the breezy current trails down my skirt and wraps around my ankle. It gradually spirals higher, stroking around my bare calf to my knee like the lightest of fingers.

"Loosen her dress," he says in an even but firm tone that rings with understated authority.

Raul's grin widens. He follows his older foster brother's orders without complaint, working at the spots Melisse pinned the slightly over-large dress around my waist and bodice.

Lorenzo presses a kiss to the corner of my jaw and follows suit at my other side. As he fiddles with the fabric, he grazes the back of his knuckles against my breast, stirring more flickers of desire.

This is really happening. I *am* wanton, inviting three men to indulge in every carnal pleasure we can imagine.

Why should there be anything wrong with that? Why should my husband-to-be get to enjoy every woman who catches his eye while I wait patiently in the wings?

These three men and I understand each other as no other could. We're pampered pawns, bound to our duties on gilded leashes.

We can take what we need from each other and recognize how much it matters… and how much it can't.

As the gown slackens around my torso, Bastien steps forward. He teases his fingers along my jaw and kisses me with an intensity that feels more pensive than Raul's but just as potent.

Then he eases back half a step and flicks his hands upward.

Wind ripples under my skirt. It courses across my legs and lifts the dress with it.

I raise my arms instinctively, and the silk flows over my body as pliant as water. The gown floats up over my head and then drifts down into a puddle of cloth near the doorway.

A heady shiver races over every inch of my skin in the wake of the conjured breeze.

All of these men have seen me naked before, but I feel abruptly shy stripped down to my chemise and drawers. I grip the front of Lorenzo's shirt and tug, surest of the reaction I'll get from him. "If clothes are going to be flying, it'd better be more than just mine."

With a chuckle, he helps me peel off his shirt. Then he dives in for another kiss, wrapping his arms around my waist and hooking his fingers beneath the bottom of my chemise to trace my bare belly.

Raul hums low in his throat. "I like the way you think, Shepherdess."

He yanks his own shirt up over his head, ruffling his sleek ponytail. When Lorenzo releases me, I can't resist drinking in the larger man's uncovered form—all that massive muscular brawn on full display, even more impressive than when it's hidden beneath his clothes.

I reach toward Raul and glide my fingers across his chest, noting the paler lines that mar his tawny skin where weapons in the arena or perhaps elsewhere pierced his flesh around the sigil of Kosmel slanting over his sternum. He makes a rough sound and lowers his head to nip the shell of my ear.

One of his hands settles on the small of my back, the other cupping my breast. He squeezes the pliant flesh through my chemise and rolls the peak beneath his thumb to shock a gasp out of me.

His husky murmur tickles into my ear. "I've wanted to

attend to this perfect chest since the moment I saw it. So many possibilities in the right hands…"

He pinches my nipple to set off a spike of bliss. I can't hold back a whimper, my fingers digging in where I'm gripping his broad shoulder.

At my other side, Lorenzo leans in and nibbles a path down the side of my neck. He massages my other breast and then slides his fingers along the top of my chemise. When I turn my head to seek out another kiss, he drags the thin fabric down over my shoulder.

Our mouths meld together. His hand dips beneath the chemise to fondle my breast skin to skin, and my sigh mingles with his eager groan.

"Nothing has ever felt as good as touching you, Rell. Or as having you touch me."

With a quiver of pleasure, I tease my fingers over Lorenzo's scalp through his thick hair and glance toward Bastien. The eldest prince is watching his foster brothers from the same spot right in front of me.

He's barely touched me except with his gift-driven air currents, but then, we'd barely done anything intimate at all before now.

I reach out tentatively and grasp the front of Bastien's shirt, with a slight upward tug in question. His pupils dilate. He unfastens the buttons by the collar to open it and hauls it over his head with my assistance.

When he drops the shirt to the floor, he stares back at me with an expression that's almost defiant. Is he afraid of how I might judge him in comparison to his foster brothers?

It's true that his shorter, slimmer frame isn't as overtly impressive as Raul's or Lorenzo's. But the compact muscles that line his slender chest and arms look like they were carved out of marble. His pale skin shines in the lantern light, unblemished except for the sigil of Jurnus branded in the middle of his chest and the faint pink scar running over the edge of his ribs, where the cleric and the temple medics removed his lung.

He's absolutely gorgeous in his own way. I'd laugh at anyone who tried to say otherwise.

"Come here." Curling my fingers around the back of his neck, I pull him to me.

Bastien's mouth crashes into mine hard and hungry. He angles his head to deepen the kiss, and his tongue flicks between my lips to tangle with my own.

He's got no lack of confidence in claiming what he wants from a woman once he's sure of her interest—that's obvious.

It seems as though he likes to be in charge in all sorts of ways. When our lips part, he casts his gaze toward the men on either side of me. At the glint of promise in his eyes, a fresh wave of heat washes over my skin.

He inclines his head to Lorenzo. "Let's get her chemise off, Lore. Raul, put that mouth of yours to good use in something other than bragging."

With no sign of offense, Raul guffaws and helps Lorenzo strip my chest bare. The massive man wastes no time bending down so he can suck the tip of my breast into his mouth.

The first flick of his tongue shocks an embarrassing mewling sound out of me. More bliss pulses through my chest with each rhythmic swipe, sharpening with the graze of his teeth.

I tangle my fingers in his hair, loosening the dark brown strands from his ponytail. "Raul… Don't stop."

Not one of us is dedicated to Ardone in all her sensual glory, but I feel as if I owe the godlen of love several prayers of thank you for this divinely ecstatic encounter.

Smiling in approval, Bastien captures my mouth again.

His hand travels over my other breast with a swivel of his palm against my nipple to provoke a whimper, then on down my side to my hip and back up again.

Lorenzo fulfills the promise of that downward journey first. He trails kisses along my spine and the lower edge of my shoulder blade before slipping one hand around my thigh to test the aching dampness between my legs.

At the first delicate probe of his fingers against the crotch of my drawers, a moan tumbles out of me. Bastien breathes it in and kisses me harder.

"Fuck," Raul mutters against my breast.

Lorenzo teases his fingertips up and down over the silky fabric until I'm swaying to draw him closer. With a grin and a kiss to my shoulder, he draws a small, torturous circle around the neediest part of me. *"I love feeling you urge me on."*

Raul clicks his tongue at the other prince. "You shouldn't leave her wanting, Lore." He tucks his hand beneath the waist of my drawers—and all at once a velvety-soft pressure has formed against my skin all across my pelvis.

He's caught the shadow there. It undulates against my core and delves between my thighs, stroking every sensitive part of me at once.

The heady sensation leaves me quivering. "Oh, gods…"

Raul keeps his other hand against my back to hold me steady. "Take it in, Princess. Imagine how much I could do for you in a dark room where there's nothing but shadow to play with. Working over every slope and dip of your body at the same time…"

Bastien's authoritative voice comes out electrifyingly raw. "You're not the only one who can get her off. Make sure she's ready for me."

He sinks lower so he can close his mouth over the breast Raul abandoned.

Raul gives a mildly disgruntled sound, but the swath of shadows he's maneuvering firms. He eases it between my folds, part of it still rubbing against my clit.

I gasp, my grip on his hair tightening. He steals a kiss and rocks his shadowy toy deeper into me. "Oh, she's ready all right, Bas. Completely drenched for us."

Bastien tugs my nipple between his teeth to earn himself a gasp of his own and glances up at Lorenzo. "Get those drawers off her."

As I wriggle out of my last scrap of clothing with Lorenzo's aid, I trail my free hand down Bastien's chest again, all the way to the bulge behind his trousers. Touching his rigid length through his pants ignites a deeper flare of need between my legs.

My voice comes out more breathless than husky. "It feels like you're ready for me too."

Bastien's chest hitches, and he yanks at his trousers to unfasten them alongside me. With the rustle of his pants dropping, he spins me around between the other two men so my back is to him.

"Hold on to the chair," he says in a commanding tone, but his caress down my side to my ass is all tenderness. I'm not sure which turns me on more.

Raul jerks the chair around so I can brace both of my hands on its back. He sinks down beside me, dappling kisses across my hip. His fingers skim my inner thigh, nudging me higher. "Let's see you spread your legs for him, Princess."

As I push myself up on the balls of my feet, Bastien strokes his straining cock between my thighs from behind. The pressure of his hardness sliding over my slick folds propels another moan out of me.

Then he pushes inside, and all I can do is clutch on to the chair and pant for mercy.

Bastien grasps my hips, pulling me tight against him as he deepens his thrust. While the feeling of fullness radiates through me, Raul eases up again to return his attention to my breasts.

But his brief stint down below must have inspired Lorenzo. My first lover's eyes gleam avidly. He sinks to his knees and scoots between me and the chair.

I have no idea what he's up to before his mouth meets my clit, just above the place where Bastien and I are joined. A sharper cry breaks from my chest alongside the flare of bliss.

Bastien inhales raggedly and bucks into me, his breath searing my shoulder. Each rock of my body propels me into Lorenzo's eager mouth. I'm being stretched from within and savored from without, and nothing in my existence has ever felt so glorious.

Raul teases his tongue along my earlobe. "You love it, don't you, Princess? Being locked between them, letting them worship your body every way it needs. They're going to take you right over the edge, higher than you've ever flown before, and I'll be right here to catch you."

At his words, the pleasure building in my core spirals through me even faster.

Bastien picks up his rhythm, every slam of his cock into me setting off a surge of delight. "So good. So fucking good. Come for me, Aurelia. I want to feel that precious cunt clamping around my—"

Lorenzo flicks the edges of his teeth across my clit, and I careen over the edge.

Stars spark behind my eyes. I shake and cling to the chair, swept up in a rolling wave of pleasure.

Bastien groans, his hips stuttering against mine. With a hissed curse, he spills himself inside me.

While my legs are still trembling, he eases me around and combs his fingers into my hair. His mouth seeks out mine to offer the sweetest of kisses.

After, he stays close enough that our noses touch. "You're incredible, Aurelia. You deserve to be treated like it every fucking day for the rest of your life."

A pang peals through my chest. "*You're* incredible. All of you."

Before the ache of the knowledge that I won't be worshipped like this for all time—or probably ever again—can take hold, Raul draws me toward him. "We're not even done yet. I can offer you even more." His lips curl into a smirk. "But I've got a lot to handle, so I think I'll let you set the pace."

He guides me the few steps over to the settee, kicking aside his pants and drawers as we go.

He wasn't lying about having a lot to handle. When he sprawls out on the cushions, his thick erection juts into the air, as intimidating as the rest of him.

As Melisse suggested, nothing bulges beneath his cock other than a couple of slight protrusions that must be all that's left of his balls. But the absence only makes his member look even larger.

Raul guides me up to straddle him and slicks his thumb between my legs. "Gods be damned sure you're ready now. Fuck, you're so wet. Bastien used you well, didn't he?"

Something about his phrasing stings even though it could be said I'm using them too. Then Raul pushes the head of his cock up into me while massaging my clit, and the blissful burn sweeps every other thought from my mind.

The other princes have followed us to stand beside the

settee. As I ease down over Raul, Lorenzo strokes my face and kisses my forehead encouragingly. Bastien teases caresses up and down my sides and over my breasts.

Raul exhales in a rush and lifts his hips to fit us together more closely. One hand keeps strumming the sensitive spot above my entrance, but the other closes over one of the hands I've braced against his brawny chest.

"You can take it all, can't you?" he murmurs. "I knew it from the moment you threw my words in my face and refused to back down. Never needed a woman like I need you. That's right. Show me that wildness."

An embarrassingly desperate sound quavers up my throat. I've lost my capacity for actual words. Even after my orgasm, he's a tight fit, but with every fraction he slides deeper, my body craves more.

And not just of him. Where Lorenzo's standing, I can't ignore his neglected erection straining against his pants.

The memory of his lips working me over while Bastien pounded into me makes me shiver giddily. My mouth waters with the urge to return the favor.

Clutching Raul's fingers, I lift my other hand to tug at Lorenzo's pants. My appeal stumbles over my tongue. "You too."

The rough noise that escapes him tells me he's caught my meaning. As Raul rocks up into me, Lorenzo sheds his pants.

The moment he's freed his stiffened cock, I tilt forward to lap my tongue over the tip. The salty flavor laces my mouth, turned delicious by Lorenzo's urgent groan.

He steps closer, and I take him all the way into my mouth as I slide the last inch down onto Raul. The man beneath me gives a ragged laugh. "You're a fucking marvel. Ride me as hard as you like, Princess."

I rock up and down over him—at first only a little as I

find my rhythm, then rising up and dropping down more emphatically once I've steadied myself. With each pulse of Raul's cock inside me, I bob back and forth over Lorenzo's, swirling my tongue around his length, sucking on the head to hear his fragmenting breaths.

Raul slides his hand farther back to give my ass a light slap that sparks a strange mix of prickling pain and sparkling pleasure. He traces the cleft between my cheeks. "Someday, I'd like to see you take two of us this way. Maybe even all three. But we're not prepared for that yet."

The thought of what he might mean makes my face heat —and my sex dampen with even more arousal. The throbbing need for release is swelling inside me again even though I just climaxed a few minutes ago.

I chase the high, bucking harder over Raul until his breaths grow shaky too, sucking down Lorenzo's cock as deep as I can without choking.

Lorenzo clutches my hair, his hips jerking to meet my mouth. Even his illusionary voice has gone raw. *"You feel amazing, Rell. I don't think I can— I'm going to come."*

He moves as if to retreat, but I clamp my lips around him emphatically.

That's all it takes. The salty spurt of his release fills my mouth.

His frenzied mix of praise and curses stokes the flames inside me. As he eases back, I lean over Raul.

The massive prince pushes himself up on one elbow to meet me. Clamping his hand around my hip, he propels us together again and again with even more force. Our mouths crash together in a frantic kiss.

With one more flick of his thumb, my second orgasm sweeps through me, bowling me over with its force. I'm sagging into Raul and soaring away all at once.

He hisses through his clenched teeth through a few more thrusts that propel me even farther into ecstasy. I'm vaguely aware of the flood of heat inside me.

Our colliding bodies slow into a gentle rocking and then a slumped embrace. The other princes sink down next to us, Lorenzo tipping forward to claim a kiss.

Bastien rests his hand against my back. His smile has gone uncharacteristically dreamy. "You really are something, Aurelia. Was that everything you were wanting?"

I can't hold back a dazed giggle. "Very much so. I wish—"

I catch myself, an uneasy tremor penetrating the afterglow that's clouded my head. Some things will only be more painful if said aloud.

Perhaps the three princes understand me in that too. Raul tightens his embrace. Lorenzo's mouth twists.

And Bastien's eyes shimmer with unspoken emotion. "So do I."

I close my own eyes against a much less welcome sort of burn. The rest of what he said echoes through my head.

I certainly intend to really be something. And that means I can't forget why I came here.

CHAPTER FORTY-FIVE

Bastien

Looking up at Aurelia sprawled across Raul's body and dozing in the aftermath of our shared passion, I can't stop a pang of jealousy from rippling through my chest.

The passion *was* shared, so why should he have her nearly all to himself right now?

I know the thought isn't entirely fair, but I don't see anything wrong with reminding her just how much I'm still here with her too.

With a nudge of my gift, I will a wisp of a breeze to coil around her slack ankle and onward up her leg. I'm expecting to have to gather a thicker current before she realizes it's more than an errant draft, but after just a few seconds, she adjusts her head against Raul's chest so she can gaze over at me.

The fondness in her dark blue eyes and the little smile

that curves her lips, as if it's a secret just for us, wrap around my heart like a taut thread. As if she's stitched together with the core of my being as surely as the bound pages of a book.

My throat constricts. Everything that happened tonight was indescribably fantastic and yet also not. How can it even be *all right?*

We had this fleeting moment of cherishing her, as Aurelia so accurately put it, and tomorrow we send her to her doom, whether her death or consigning her to Marclinus's whims for the rest of her life.

It is what it is. It's why she traveled to Dariu in the first place.

But she couldn't have anticipated just how awful her betrothed would prove himself to be. I grew up with the prick, and even I wouldn't have imagined Marclinus would treat the ladies vying for his favor quite so sadistically.

It's clear Tarquin has raised his son to match him in cruelty.

I don't know if I can handle seeing Aurelia's resilience and spirit ground down until she's nothing but a shell of the woman she's meant to be. Until the earnest compassion that comes so naturally to her wilts on the barren ground he'll offer.

I won't be around to see most of it, of course. I'll get to return to Cotea within a few years, to find a match among the local nobles and set myself up in a position to provide some small help to my family and our kingdom closer at hand.

It seems ridiculous that I once resented the princess for the time she had before she was sent here. As if those early years of freedom will do anything but make the bars of her new, impenetrable cage glare more sharply.

The hopeless ache that's spreading through my chest

brings me back to the moments after Pavel exploded with fury, while Emperor Tarquin barked seething commands and the guards wrestled my foster brother into submission. While I stood by grasping out and finding only empty space, scrambling for something I could do or say that might save him.

Wondering what signs I missed, what mistakes I made that led to the catastrophe.

Am I going to simply watch while another person I care about is destroyed in front of me?

Aurelia shifts and starts to get up. Raul adjusts his position with her, keeping his arm around her waist as she sits next to him on the settee.

I automatically move to take a seat at her other side and slip my hand around her elbow. The smattering of purple scars stand out against the tanned skin of her forearm as a reminder that there's so much more to this remarkable woman than just a beautiful body.

Lorenzo looks perfectly content to remain on the floor, tipping his head against her knee. When she runs her fingers over his hair, his eyelids dip. You'd think he's about to purr like a cat.

But when our gazes lock, the same worries running through my mind shadow his dark brown eyes.

Aurelia reaches to twine her hand with mine while leaning against Raul's shoulder. There's a melancholy note in her voice that I'm not used to. "I'm glad we were able to have this."

Raul presses a kiss to the top of her head. "Don't assume we can't have it again."

As if that cocky statement will give her much comfort. Does he think a thorough fucking every few weeks will keep her safe from everything Marclinus will make her endure?

It seems Aurelia's concerns relate to events much closer at hand. Her gaze drops, and she lets out a hollow laugh. "If I'm even around for us to consider the possibilities. I saw Lady Fausta and Vicerine Bianca conspiring after dinner… Bianca brought her something secretly."

I sit up straighter with a jolt of apprehension. "You think it had to do with the last trial?"

"I don't know what it was, but I can't imagine Fausta *doesn't* have some kind of sabotage planned for tomorrow's trial. She's shown she'll do anything to ruin my chances. And this will be her last opportunity. She won't hold back."

Every particle of my body tenses in denial. "She won't get away with anything significant. Tarquin will have the trial set up so the court can watch—he always has so far."

Entertaining his nobles while he castigates them for their presumption. No one could ever accuse the emperor of failing to multi-task.

It does mean that the worst Fausta's attempted during a trial is caustic words Aurelia can shrug off.

The princess shrugs. "This time, she might not care if people see. She could gamble that Emperor Tarquin and Marclinus won't disqualify her for publicly harming me at this stage—or she might think the chance at taking me out of the game is worth any risk. Or whatever she's planning may be so stealthy she thinks she can accomplish it under their noses."

An edge of a growl creeps into Raul's voice. "She can't keep anything from me. We'll be in the audience—I'll check her for anything threatening she's hiding. We can intervene if we notice her about to go at you."

Lorenzo nods emphatically.

My own conviction grips me harder. "We'll make sure we notice. We'll watch her every move."

That vindictive shrew isn't harming one more hair on our princess's body.

Aurelia's fingers tighten around mine. "Thank you."

Her head has drooped against Raul again. My sense of the time prickles through my body. "We should get you back to your room. You'll need all the sleep you can get to be alert for tomorrow."

As do we, if we're going to defend her.

We pull on our clothes, Lorenzo moving to help Aurelia with her gown. Seeing the affection shining in his face as he sets his hands on her waist afterward, the unhampered joy with which he kisses her, I find myself smiling despite everything that's wrong.

She's brought a lot of rightness into our lives too. Started to mend the cracks that'd formed inside each of us.

We'd better be able to do the same for her.

We guide her through the hidden passages back to her room, where Raul extends his gift into the shadows to confirm that no one's arrived in her absence. Aurelia offers us all one more brief kiss before slipping away from us into the darkness of her chambers.

Silence hangs over us on our trek back to our own bedrooms. Even Raul, for all he got to show off his sensual prowess tonight, seems more brooding than triumphant.

I've had my conflicts with the prince of Lavira—the sense of unity between us fractured with Pavel's death, and I lost most of my patience for his posturing. I shouldn't have let our differing approaches distract me from the fact that we're all on the same side. All three of us still know what matters most.

When we emerge from the unused bedroom into the hall, my pulse stutters. Neven is standing outside the door to my chambers, his mouth slanted at an uneasy angle.

As we hurry over to him, he turns to meet us. Relief lights in his bright brown eyes but doesn't wash away the tension on his face.

"There you are." He drops his voice to a hush. "I saw something—I thought you might want to know."

My heart thumps faster. "What?"

He jerks his thumb toward the back end of the palace. "I took a run through the woods and then was walking back to cool off, and I saw a bunch of workers tramping out toward the wall with carts of stone and wood and who knows what else. What would they be building out there in the middle of the night?"

Raul scowls. "Something for the trial tomorrow."

I don't even need to think about it. I motion for the others to follow me. "We'd better take a look and figure out as much as we can."

Some of the nobles who don't have to worry about competing for their lives tomorrow are still enjoying themselves in the hall of entertainments. Music and laughter tinkles through the hallways as we make our way to the nearest staircase.

We amble out into the night as if we're simply taking a casual stroll. When we reach the edge of the woods, Raul peers into the darkness and sweeps his hand through the air.

The shadows thicken around us. We walk on, cloaked by his gift, even our footsteps muffled by a layer of condensed darkness.

Neven points us most of the way. I can tell when we're close enough to the workers for Raul to sense them because his expression tightens with concentration.

Voices start to reach us through the woods. It takes several more steps before we can make out the figures between the tree trunks.

At least a dozen workers bustle around by the high stone wall that surrounds the palace grounds, lit by a few lanterns resting on the ground nearby. They're definitely building something—they've already constructed part of what looks like a ramp veering up higher than the wall.

As I watch, one woman uses her gift to send a slab of metal flying up toward the top of the ramp, its edges gleaming wickedly in the lantern-light.

They aren't talking much, and when they do, they're mostly keeping their voices low. I only make out a phrase here and there:

"…make sure the angle…"

"…over by the river…"

"…careful of the edge…"

Nothing I overheard tells me the purpose of this structure or what else they might be planning to construct out here. I exchange glances with my foster brothers, but they look similarly puzzled.

Whatever task the emperor has set his people to, it must be part of tomorrow's trial. And it looks as if he and Marclinus are upping the ante by several measures.

Naturally they'd want an epic finale to their sick competition.

I ease a little closer, but the comments my ears catch are only focused on the immediate concerns of putting the structure together. No one remarks about what the ladies it's presumably for might have to do on it.

Or what it might do to them.

Apprehension congeals in my gut. I motion the others farther away until I'm sure we can speak unnoticed.

"Whatever they're planning, they obviously intend for it to be the biggest spectacle of all."

Lorenzo frowns and makes a rough motion with his hand. *And very bad for Aurelia.*

Raul bares his teeth around a snarl. "Haven't those psychopaths put her through enough already?"

I inhale slowly, gathering my thoughts. We know more than we did an hour ago. The trial is going to take place outside. It's going to bring the prospective brides all the way out here.

Amid the trees, there'll be so many places Lady Fausta might be able to launch a surreptitious attack. We'll have to keep our eyes on her, have our gifts ready to whip out the instant she acts—and make sure we're far enough away from Tarquin and his guards that no one will pick up on our magic.

Neven wasn't part of our earlier discussion. His tanned face has paled in the dimness. "Is there any way we can help her? I—"

He turns his head with an abashed expression. "Maybe it's stupid, but it feels like she's one of us. We should stick with her, shouldn't we? She's... she's part of our weird little family of people who don't belong here in Dariu but didn't have any choice about it."

Our family. His words hit me with more impact than he could have intended. My breath snags in my chest.

By almost every measure that counts, the three princes standing around me are more my family than my parents and brother back home could be.

It's the same for all of us, isn't it? Our parents might not have had much choice, but they let us go. They sent us off as playing chips in the game Tarquin and the emperors before him have been orchestrating for centuries.

We weren't first born, so we weren't worth fighting for.

Why should we keep imagining that one day we might

finally have the chance to fight for *them*? Why not take whatever chances we can to make the family we've formed here as strong as it could be?

Neven's right: Aurelia is one of us. She came from Accasy as an offering to appease the empire, a hostage to be used as a point of leverage. Even if she wins tomorrow…

As long as any of us dwell within these walls, we might as well be shackled to them.

The bits of conversation I overheard whirl through my mind. I suck in a startled breath. "They're taking the trial beyond the walls. The workers said something about the river."

Raul knits his brow at me. "So?"

I open my mouth and close it again, hesitation locking my jaw.

The proposal I want to make could be total insanity. It'd be throwing away everything we still have—

Except for each other. Don't all the things we stand to gain matter that much more?

I've spent so long encouraging caution. Sticking to the most practical path with whatever security it could offer.

What has that accomplished for us?

We never got to take the one gamble we sacrificed so much for. This could be our one chance to take another that would mean nearly as much—to us, if not to the rest of the empire.

The image of Pavel's struggling body passes through my mind again, and my tongue loosens.

"I have an idea that I think could help *all* of us…"

Chapter Forty-Six

Aurelia

I'm gazing a little aimlessly into my wardrobe, trying to decide which of my new, much smaller selection of dresses I should wear for the final trial, when Melisse bursts into the room.

Her bobbed hair swishes around her face with her urgency. "The emperor wants the trial to start as soon as possible. We need to get you ready!"

My pulse hiccups. Right now? Is the entire court foregoing breakfast?

Or perhaps they're all off in the dining room now, gorging themselves with advance notice before the main event begins.

I find it hard to summon much rancor even if that's the case. I'd rather get this sick game over with sooner rather than later.

Melisse's announcement at least makes my decision

simple. I point to the freshly laundered white dress I was wearing during Fausta's bout of destruction—the only remaining gown that's tailored to fit me.

Rochelle could have adjusted the fabric so it somehow set off my figure to even better effect, but it'll look perfectly fine as it is.

At the memory of the mornings when my friend assisted me with my dressing, my chest constricts. But even that pain feels dull and distant beyond the thumping of my heart.

Some part of me has already detached from the horrors that might await in the coming trial. I simply have to go through the motions and prepare for the final sacrifice, whatever that ends up being.

Last night's wanton indulgence might as well have been a good-bye not just to the possibility of love but to my entire life as it's been up until now. I got my final hurrah. Now it's time to face my fate.

Melisse slides the light silk over my head and ensures that it's settled right against the curves of my body. She pulls the brush through my hair with swift but careful strokes.

As soon as she's added a little powder to my face, I pull on my slippers and get to my feet. "Let's see what's in store for us today."

My maid fidgets with nerves enough for both of us as she leads me through the palace halls, down a staircase… and to the arching back doorway that leads out to the gardens.

A crowd of nobles has congregated at the far end of the broad stone path that stretches between the central flower beds. As we draw closer, I study the arching hedge that now stands between the tamer part of the grounds and the woods beyond. The court gathers on either side of it as if it's an entrance they're avoiding blocking.

That living arch wasn't here yesterday. The emperor must

have had someone with a gift for encouraging plant growth summon it overnight.

I halt several paces away, unsure of how to proceed. Emperor Tarquin and Marclinus are chatting with their subjects without any sign that they've noticed my arrival. Leonette stands on the path close to the hedge, her athletic form tensed and her gaze wary. It doesn't appear Fausta has found her way here yet.

But she already has friends in attendance. As Melisse scurries off to see if she has new orders, Bianca sashays toward me. Her fine black hair is coiled up in an even more elaborate style than usual, sleek braids weaving between broader whorls in a tapestry of texture.

She speaks in a low voice only I can hear. "I suppose today we'll see who truly knows what it takes to reign over Dariu. You're going to look like a fool in the end."

With everything else I have to consider, her barbed words barely nick me. I gaze into her pretty brown face with an unexpected sense of peace.

She's the one afraid of looking like a fool, of losing the man she's dallied with for so long in front of her own husband. But I've experienced pleasures beyond anything I can imagine ever enjoying with the man *she* covets.

What do I have to feel jealous about?

I offer her a reassuring smile. "I'm not going to stop you, you know."

Bianca blinks. "Stop me?"

I tip my head toward Marclinus. The sunlight glinting off his gold crown makes the golden-blond hair it's nestled on look tarnished. "From continuing whatever association you have with His Imperial Highness. If he wishes to enjoy your company after he's married and you wish to indulge him, that's between the two of you. An emperor-to-be should have everything he wants, shouldn't he?"

She's outright staring at me now. Her next words come out in a sputter. "You can't really mean— My sympathies aren't going to be swayed by frivolous lies."

With a rustle of her skirt, she spins on her heel and stalks away.

That's fine. I don't really care whether she believes me, and I'd rather not have to talk to her any longer than I already have.

My searching gaze catches on the rare cluster of welcome faces amid the nobles. The princes keep their expressions impassive, but Bastien tips his head in the slightest nod after his gaze catches mine.

They're here, watching over me, offering whatever protection they can. Gods above, let it be enough.

Footsteps rap against the smooth stone tiles, announcing Fausta's arrival. She's chosen a deep green gown that matches her eyes and sets off her flaming hair to even starker effect.

The embroidered pouch on the lustrous cord around her waist looks larger than what the women of the court typically use to hold their bedroom key and minor accessories. What is she carrying in there?

I'd see if I can contrive to get close enough to Raul to find out what his gift can tell him, but at that moment, Emperor Tarquin and Marclinus step in front of the arch. Tarquin claps his hands together for our attention.

As the crowd falls silent, the emperor pitches his voice to carry. "Today we will witness my son's prospective brides complete their final challenge and find out who is the most worthy of standing beside him. I hope we have all learned much from observing their trials and that there will be no further question of who deserves what. I look forward to welcoming the woman who earns Marclinus's approval into the family."

His piercing gaze sweeps over his audience, his tone dry but with an edge sharp as his guards' swords. He's reminding his court of the daughters he's taken from them as punishment for their presumption.

I don't even know how much Tarquin truly cared about judging us. Was the only real purpose of all this torment to carry out his ruthless vendetta?

His heir pipes up. "These three ladies have overcome many obstacles in their quest to prove themselves. For their last trial, they'll encounter many very literal obstacles. We will see who is the most committed to reaching me, with speed, agility, strength, and—most importantly—dedication. You may follow them all along the course. If you have a favorite, feel free to cheer them on."

He flashes a grin at all of us, as if he's ever so pleased with his brilliant test, before going on. "Ladies, I will take my leave of you so that I can be waiting at the end of the course. Make your way along the route as quickly as you're able to. The first of you to take my hand has won it."

He and his father stride off into the woods without another word, several guards flanking them.

One of the palace staff motions Leonette, Fausta, and me to the edge of the stone path, just before the hedge. Beyond the arch, which stretches a few feet into the woods, the underbrush has been cut back even more than usual to clear a wide track between the trees.

The watching nobles surge into the forest along our path, eager to watch us on our way with the best view possible.

The man who beckoned us lifts his hand, holding a large bell. "On my signal, you may run."

My mouth has gone dry as ash. I brace my legs instinctively.

At the resonant ding, all three of us spring forward.

As we hurtle beneath the hedge arch, a forceful current of air whips past us. Beside me, Fausta flinches and then yelps.

A second blast of wind hits her, and her pouch jerks right off her belt to career across the cleared earth.

Alarm clangs through me. That's no natural gust.

Bastien is using his gift to cast the pouch away from her —which means Raul must have sensed some kind of threat inside.

Fausta dives after her pouch, and I dodge out of her way. She manages to slam her heel back into my ankle. As I stumble to the side with a flare of pain, she snatches the pouch before it can blow any farther and wrenches out a small shiny object.

My rival whirls toward me, twitching her wrist to flick a small, hooked blade out of the steel handle she's holding. The honed surface gleams with an odd oily texture that makes my gift snap to attention with a shudder through my nerves. As if my magic is anticipating the need for a cure.

I'd be willing to bet all I have that there's poison lacing the blade. Fausta might not need to do more than prick me with it to cull me from the competition—and this world.

Catching my balance, I shove myself away and sprint the rest of the way past the arch.

Fausta's groping hand catches my skirt as it whips out behind me. She hauls me back toward her as she lunges forward. I heave to the side, spinning to try to fend her off—

And her face spasms, her eyes jittering as if tracking a peril I can't see.

An illusion aimed only at her?

Whatever Lorenzo must have conjured, it shocks a gasp

from Fausta's mouth and loosens her grip on the curved knife. I ram my elbow into her hand, and her fingers burst apart.

The knife falls. An instant before it hits the ground, a sharper current of wind hurls the weapon all the way between the trees. Another blast smacks into the backs of Fausta's knees, sending her tumbling to the ground.

With a hoarse breath, I dash farther into the woods, leaving her behind.

A mix of whoops and confused mutterings ring out when I race past the nearest nobles. "Princess of the wild north!" someone hollers, possibly meaning it as a compliment for once.

I have no idea what they made of my and Fausta's tussle, but no one appears to be inclined to intervene. Perhaps they see her attempted attack as a reasonable part of the challenge.

I don't think anyone's realized there was more to the fight than our own skills. I hear no shouts about unsanctioned magic.

Relief shudders through my lungs with my next breath.

My princes came through for me. They disarmed Fausta of the weapon she meant to murder me with. If they hadn't forced her hand, no doubt she'd have struck at some point when I was too distracted to defend myself.

I owe them my life.

I won't be able to thank them for their help unless I reach the end of this obstacle course first. I may have gotten a head start on Fausta, but Leonette has taken advantage of our scuffle to pull far into the lead. I spot her up ahead, her sky-blue dress rippling around her dark limbs.

Just as I push even more speed into my legs, she lurches to one side.

Sinuous shapes ripple across the dirt around her. She

scrambles this way and that, avoiding them as well as she can. The nobles who are just catching up holler with a mix of encouragement and derisive jeers.

Out of caution, I slow to a lope. As I close the distance, the snake-like obstructions come into clearer focus.

They're vines—thick cords of vegetation that are lashing back and forth across the cleared earth. Someone must be directing them with their gift.

And more of them stretch across our course as far as I can see into the fractured sunlight up ahead.

CHAPTER FORTY-SEVEN

Aurelia

I pause to observe the patterns of the vines' lashing movements, haphazard as they seem. I don't have much time before the thudding of footsteps behind me propels me forward.

Fausta didn't take long to recover from her stumble.

I leap over a few vines and dart from one side to the other, avoiding their twisting forms as well as I can. One hits the back of my calf. I heave forward a few steps, nearly tripping over another.

Only a few paces ahead of me now, Leonette's foot gets snagged. The vine flings her to her knees.

By the time she's scrambled up, we're neck and neck. Fausta mutters a curse right behind me, her shoes scuffing frantically across the dirt.

It's obvious this isn't going to be a simple sprint to the finish line.

As we jump and stagger around the writhing vines, more of the court nobles reach this part of the path, many of them venturing ahead of us.

"Look at them dance!" someone calls out, followed by a raucous laugh.

Bianca's arch voice quavers with worry as it carries through the din. "You can beat them, Fausta. Don't let anything slow you down!"

The cleared route through the woods veers to the left, and I spot the end of vine territory several paces away. Pushing myself onward with a frantic patter of my feet, I manage to draw ahead of Leonette.

I leap over the last few vines and dash across the apparently safe stretch of path.

It only takes a few steps to reveal my error. The dirt gives way abruptly beneath one of my feet.

I have just enough wherewithal to throw myself forward so my hands and knees take the brunt of the fall rather than my ankle.

Glancing back, I see my foot has broken open a pit in the path, several inches deep and the same around. More than enough to sprain an ankle or even break a few toes.

Leonette and Fausta were racing after me. Witnessing my tumble, they slow to scan the earth.

I shove myself back to my feet, restraining a wince at the stinging of my knees and palms. Brown smudges of dirt mar the white silk of my dress.

I can't make out any indication of where the rest of the path in front of us might be unstable. Whoever conjured the obstacles in this stretch of the trial laid their traps well.

"Go on, then," Fausta says in a sneering tone.

She wants me to uncover the pits by stumbling into them myself so she knows where it's safe to walk.

Before I can retort, Leonette strides ahead of us with an impervious air. She sets her feet swiftly but carefully—and hops to the side the moment another span of earth crumbles beneath her shoe.

I'm not going to look like a coward in front of the court. I hurry after her, imitating her method, narrowing all my attention on the feel of the earth under me.

If Raul and Bastien combined their talents again, perhaps they could crack some of the hidden pits to reveal them. But when my gaze darts over the crowd swarmed between the trees, I can't find their faces.

There's no sign of Lorenzo either. Did the princes decide they'd risked as much as they dared and leave rather than endure the rest of the trial's horrors from the sidelines?

A chilly twinge passes through my gut, but I grit my teeth against it and keep moving. I've always said I want to win the trials through my own merits. Why should I expect them to help beyond preventing outright sabotage?

I'll win through my own strength and perseverance as I always have before.

As I pull past Leonette again, a slight hitch beneath my toes gives me a warning. I shift my weight to my other foot and shove myself onward with only a brief wobble.

A moment later, Leonette crashes through a slightly larger pit, the ground swallowing her leg up to her lower calf. She pitches forward but keeps going with her mouth pressed tight. The hitch in her step suggests she's at least temporarily wounded.

"That's right!" one of the watching nobles hollers. "Stay on your feet for the emperor!"

We come around another shallow bend and find the terrain between the trees there is covered with a swath of jagged rocks. They jut up at different angles and sizes, some as large as my torso and others as small as my fist.

Fausta darts between me and Leonette, having dodged all the pits we knocked open. She clambers over the rocks, dipping here and there to catch her balance on the larger ones.

I rush after her and scramble over the uneven mess as quickly as I can. As I push from one flatter surface to another, avoiding the most precarious spots, my legs teeter under me.

It would really hurt to fall here—not just the risk of sprains, but the rough edges of the rock ready to scrape through our skin.

Fausta discovers that danger a moment after I think it, with the skidding of her shoe over a tilting stone. Her shin bangs another rock in front of her, and a breath hisses through her teeth.

She hurtles onward, a little shakier than before. Leonette and I both redouble our efforts to strip her of her momentary lead.

Whistles that sound more taunting than encouraging carry from the crowd. The energetic shouts of our audience are melding together into a blur of sound beneath the thudding of my pulse in my ears.

The rock-smothered path swerves once more, and all three of us falter at the sight of what lies ahead.

We've reached the outer walls of the palace grounds. The stone barrier looms up in some fifteen feet of layered blocks of limestone, unbroken other than a small doorway off to the side where palace staff are ushering the nobles farther along the course.

That's not what unnerves me. Our route itself soars right

up over the wall: a precipice of wood, stone, and glinting chunks of metal that rises twice as high as the wall itself.

We're meant to climb right over.

My jaw has gone slack, but I can't afford to let nerves take over for more than an instant. I charge toward the slope, already seeking out the handholds in the mottled surface.

I grasp one wooden protrusion and another, hauling myself up the steep incline. Then my hand starts to close around a spike of metal.

The sharp edge pricks my fingers. I jerk them away before the spike can pierce my flesh.

All right, I can't climb with absolutely reckless speed.

As I take a closer look at each outcropping before reaching out, Leonette hefts herself past me, her gaze intent on the top of our perilous bridge. Fausta clambers at her heels, but my quick peek her way shows her porcelain face has turned even more wan.

Is she tiring? My own lungs are burning from the strain of the race, and I have no idea how much more the emperor and his heir intend to put us through.

As we pull ourselves higher than the level of the treetops, a wind whips over us that feels totally natural. If Bastien is still watching after all, I can't imagine he'd think the warbling gust would help me.

I clutch the protrusions harder and keep heaving myself up. Fausta lets out a faint squeak beside me, her hair billowing with the breeze, but I don't even look at her.

As we come up on the peak, the gaps between the handholds lengthen. I have to stretch my arm to reach the next, my pulse hammering even harder.

Then, just inches from the wooden knob I'm gripping, a chunk falls out of the edge of the slope and plummets. A crash reaches my ears when it hits the ground.

Fuck. We're running out of time.

Leonette clambers even faster with a deftness I have to respect. As I scramble after her, I notice Fausta's arm shaking as she snatches at an outcropping over her head.

In her haste, she clamps her fingers around one of the sharp metal shards. A yelp breaks from her throat.

I can't help glancing over at my rival. Blood smears across the artificial slope as she scrabbles for other purchase.

Her pupils have blown wide with panic, her sallow forehead shining with sweat.

Leonette's blue-clothed form vanishes over the peak. Another piece of the precipice breaks away from the edge nearest to Fausta. I shove myself higher, my legs trembling with the effort.

Fausta's breaths follow me, turning more ragged by the second with a hint of a whimper.

Was she hurt that badly? She's never let much distress show before, even when we had to handle those scorching-hot serving dishes.

I grasp the top of the makeshift bridge. At a glimpse of the other side, my stomach lurches.

The structure descends just as steeply there, down toward the rocky terrain along the shore of the broad river.

I'm just swinging my leg over the peak, which is barely as wide as my palm, when the entire precipice shudders.

More chunks tumble away from the edges—including a slab of wood beneath one of Fausta's feet. She swings to the side with a shriek of pure terror.

I expect her to yank herself closer to the middle with her arms and the foot that's still braced on another protrusion, but she freezes in place. When I hesitate, peering down at her, her limbs look as if they've locked up against the steep slope.

Blood seeps from her cut hand over the stone knob it's wrapped around. Her eyes have squeezed closed, her breath coming in tiny hitches.

She *is* terrified.

Wouldn't it be quite the joke if the woman who's fought so hard to reach the loftiest position in the realms is afraid of heights?

It might be, but as I look at her, I can't find any humor in the thought. Nothing remains of the woman who challenged me so boldly in the hunched, quivering figure clinging to the precipice.

She *is* still just a woman. Just a human being caught up in the machinations of the court, in a world that told her she had to prove her worth with the connections she could forge and the favors she could curry.

She fought me to win. She fought me because the alternative was *death*. And the ones who threw us into this lethal conflict, the sadistic emperor and his equally merciless heir, are the only real villains.

No matter what Fausta's done to me in the past, nothing about this moment feels right. Tarquin has finally succeeded in knocking the fierceness out of her. He's found a way to break her just like he's broken so many others before, here and all across the continent.

With a rush of anguish, I extend my arm toward the other woman. "I'll help you away from the edge. You have to keep moving before it breaks more."

Fausta's eyes crack open to stare at me. She sputters a laugh, but it sounds more pathetic than mocking.

She hesitates for a few seconds, obviously reluctant to trust me. Whatever she sees in my face must convince her that I mean it.

Or maybe she realizes she can't get much worse off than she currently is.

She shifts her weight and leans toward me.

Our fingertips are just an inch apart when the slope lurches with another quake.

Fausta could still make it. One heave toward me, and I could grasp her arm, haul her out of the way.

But panic grips her with a flinch that sets her off-balance. She teeters and freezes up, her expression blanking and a whine spilling from her lips. Her other foot slips off into the air.

With the jerk of her full weight, her wounded hand slides from its blood-slick hold. She swings toward the edge. The snap of the impact shocks apart the fingers still clutching on.

Her fingernails rasp against the crumbling wood for an instant before her body tumbles away from me.

CHAPTER FORTY-EIGHT

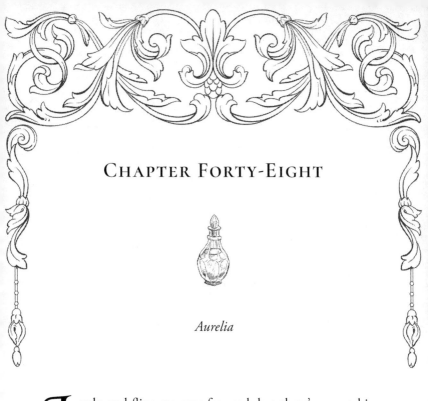

Aurelia

I yelp and fling my arm forward, but there's no catching
Fausta now. She plummets out of view with a warble of
her billowing gown.

For a fleeting moment, there's nothing but the distant
din of the watching court. Then the meaty crack of flesh and
bone shattering dispels any hope I might have that my rival
might survive the fall.

I close my eyes, and all I can see is her body slamming
into the edge of the wall right beneath us.

My stomach lurches, sending bile up my throat. The
wind wrenches at my dress.

The shouts of our audience keep drifting up, even more
avid than before.

I'm still not sure I won't vomit, but I force myself to
heave my other leg over the peak. To fumble down the far
side of the precipice, sliding from foothold to foothold.

I'm vaguely aware of Leonette descending below me: the rasps of her inhalations, the rustle of her clothes.

We're the only ones left. I have to catch up with her—I have to pass her.

Why?

The question resounds through my queasy daze so forcefully I almost lose my grip on the knobs I'm clutching.

I keep scrambling downward, flailing out with my feet for the next bit of solid ground, but it's as if my body is moving of its own accord. My mind is spiraling away.

Why am I putting myself through all this torture? To win a lifetime of more torment at Marclinus's side?

You have to win, Rochelle said to me. But my friend will still be dead either way. Reaching the finish line won't resurrect her.

So many women died so that I could still be here, banging my elbows and battering my knees while I clamber across an obstacle course designed for misery. Winning means seeing Leonette—a lady who's never done anything remotely spiteful to me, who's handled herself with absolute dignity through the entire competition—slaughtered in my place.

Can I really say I deserve to live more than she does?

Can I really say that I *want* to live more than I want to never have to look into Marclinus's maliciously arrogant face again?

Maybe that's the choice Elox indicated I have. I can escape, if only with my demise.

Gods smite me if that option doesn't feel awfully appealing in this moment.

Still, I keep moving. I keep stretching one foot beyond the other.

I have to stay in this race. I can't give up. I made so many promises and plans…

I'm just not sure I'll be disappointed if I watch Leonette dash to the finish line ahead of me.

The breeze continues lapping at my dress and hair as I skid on down the slope. I don't realize how close I've gotten to the bottom until my feet hit proper ground.

I spin around, reeling from fatigue and the horror welling up inside me, and see Leonette sprinting to the edge of the river.

I lope after her, my breath raw in my throat. A glance across the rippling greenish-gray water shows it's been divided into four paths, with wooden floats and billows of inflated cloth leading the way across them.

Nobles swarm the opposite bank, where it looks like they were ferried by the boats now docked alongside them. I can't help briefly searching for any of my princes among the crowd.

No. They're gone too. I gave them so much and still—

I yank my attention back to the course, clenching my jaw against a wobble.

Each of the paths looks different, but no features stand out as obviously better or worse. I hurry closer for a better look. Leonette is stalking along the bank, studying each of them in turn.

My gaze sweeps over the buoys again—and a voice, soft but clear, rings through my mind.

"Rell. Don't react, just listen."

Surprise jolts through my body. My face twitches, but I catch any larger response that might have been noticed by our audience.

I walk on, my eyes fixed on the lines of floats but my innards tensed with anticipation.

Lorenzo's conjured voice reaches me again, more urgently. *"Do everything exactly as I say. We have a way to get you out."*

The words repeat in my head like an echo, not quite sinking in. My pulse stutters.

What can he possibly mean?

His instructions come faster, with the same air of urgency. *"Take the route the farthest to your right. Move quickly so it looks like you're still completely invested in the trial."*

As I jog toward the path he indicated, the one the farthest along the river's current, he keeps speaking. *"We can take care of almost everything. You see the square raft about halfway across? When you get to that one, make yourself slip and fall into the water on the side away from the other floats. I'll conjure an illusion that will make everyone watching think you're struggling and then swept under. While I'm doing that, swim to the shore, aiming for the spot where the two pines stand behind the boulder. Bastien will direct the wind to help push the current that way. We're waiting for you there."*

They're waiting for me. They didn't leave after all.

They just rushed ahead of the main crowd to get themselves in place for this plan. To not just protect me from my rival but rescue me from every bit of my fate.

As I reach the start of my path, a lump fills my throat. I thought they were afraid to risk very much on my behalf, but they're committed so much more than I could ever have imagined.

Questions ricochet through my scattered mind. After I reach them, then what? How could this gambit possibly succeed? If they vanish from the palace at the same time as my supposed death, won't Emperor Tarquin realize the two events are connected?

Lorenzo knows me well enough to guess at my worries.

As I leap onto the first float, a triangle of wood that bobs unnervingly under my weight, his voice returns in a more reassuring tone. *"We've already set the stage here. By the time anyone notices we're gone and checks the area where we were last seen, they'll find signs of a struggle and a note indicating that we've been kidnapped by a coalition of rebel forces who are upset by our compliance. The distraction of the trial would make strategic sense. Then we simply disappear."*

A giddy laugh tickles at the base of my throat. They've set it all up so there'll be no backlash on our countries.

Tarquin can't blame my parents if he thinks I died in his own trials. No one knows about Lorenzo's gift with illusions, so why would they think a drowning they witnessed was anything but real?

It is believable that anti-imperial dissenters would hate and want to punish his foster sons, just like the princes hated me when I first arrived. The emperor has no idea how well they could defend themselves if they needed to either—no reason to question why they didn't overpower their attackers.

We've barely interacted in front of the court. No one would think we'd *want* to run off together, let alone had a chance to plan it.

Hope flares inside me like a candle wick that's just caught flame. They care about me—about being *with* me—so much that they'd risk everything.

Lorenzo said he loved me, but I didn't quite accept it until this moment. I don't even know what to call this level of devotion from them.

What we forged together was real after all.

As I sway on the buoy, I suppress the smile that's tugging at my lips. Steadying myself, I leap to the next with my newfound elation lightening my feet.

This float is made of fabric. It billows around me, my feet

sinking into the water. With a hitch of my pulse, I shove through the bulges of airy cloth and fling myself toward the next wooden platform.

Almost there. So close to them.

"It would be a simple life," Lorenzo says, as if keeping me company through my trek. *"But we have our gifts to help us get by and stay unnoticed. And we'd be together, supporting each other… Our families threw us away to appease the empire. We can take our lives back and build a new family that's our choice. I know we can look after you the way you deserve, no matter where we are."*

As his words sink in, my heart starts to sink too. The flame inside me wavers.

I know why he believes all that—why he believes I'll want to hear those sentiments. I've fed into the idea that I'm here as nothing but a pawn, that I'd want a life of my own.

But my family didn't throw me away. I came here for so much more than to simply appease the men who hold this half of the continent in their brutal fists.

As I approach a wheel of spinning blades that slice through the water, my chest wrenches. What am I supposed to do?

The viciously gleaming spokes smack the river's surface. Around and around, from the start through to the end and repeating again.

Like chair legs smashed into puddles of creekvine wine on the tavern floors in Accasy's cities and towns. Like the breamwood logs tossed into our northern rivers, over and over with more Accasian lives following them.

Like the bloody corpses of our compelled soldiers tumbling into the Seafell Channel in yet another vain battle against the western continent.

A tendril of resolve unfurls through my turmoil.

The men offering to free me *did* hate me on first sight. In all of two weeks, I've won them over so thoroughly that they're committing to throwing away all they've ever known for my sake.

If I could accomplish that… how can I doubt that I might eventually sway Marclinus? How can I abandon my entire kingdom for my own selfishness when there's still a chance so solid I can taste it?

How can I take a leap that promises only my own happiness when I might be able to bring so much relief to all the people I came here for—not just mine, but Lorenzo's and Bastien's, Raul's and Neven's too?

I spring between the wheel's jutting blades and crash onto the platform beyond it on my knees. But not a single sharp edge has nicked my skin.

The boards beneath me immediately dip below the surface and keep dropping. I jump onto a narrow cushioned float that tilts upward as if to throw me off until I scramble into the middle.

I'm strong enough to see my purpose through to the end. All my determination is still there inside me, as much as it's been buried by grief and doubt.

I'm more than a pawn. I shouldn't have had to shoulder this burden… but no one else could have done it.

It doesn't matter whether it's fair. Even with the choice that's just been placed in my hands, I know what I have to do.

Not because anyone ordered me to, not because of any divine message, but because I believe I can finally heal the immense wound that's plagued these realms for centuries.

The square raft Lorenzo mentioned lies right in front of me. I swallow thickly.

The princes are going to hate me again for this. They're going to think nothing I said meant anything, that I seduced them for their protection until I didn't need it anymore.

But I've endured their hate before. I don't think I could endure my own shame if I let my spirits crumble the way they almost did minutes ago.

You aren't the first men I ever loved, I think into the ether, knowing Lorenzo can't hear me. *But the first one died, maybe because of my selfishness. It's better for you if I don't drag you down the same way.*

I leap onto the raft and catch my balance, my hands splaying at my sides. Then, quickly but deliberately so there can be no doubt about whether I understood their plan, I flick the fingers closest to the two pines in one of the first signs Lorenzo ever taught me. *No.*

With the finality of that answer, something cracks inside me. The fire of my renewed resolve melds me back together enough for me to gulp down a breath.

I fling myself onto the next float and slide across its slippery surface. Just before I end up toppling into the water, I lunge toward the next.

A hundred barbs scratch at the soles of my soaked shoes and dig into my dress. They cling to the damp silk, but I tear it from their grasp and charge onward.

I won't think about the princes who touched me so passionately watching me hurtle on toward the man they tried to rescue me from. I won't focus on anything except reaching that end, whatever will come with it.

If there are tears in my eyes, it's nothing more than the spray of the river.

As I spring onto the last float I can see, the interlocking boards split apart beneath my feet. I assumed there were more floats partly beneath the water, but all I can make out from my fracturing vantage point is an open stretch of water, some thirty feet between me and the patch of sandy shore along the bank.

Nothing for it, then. I plunge into the water in a dive.

It's been a while since I had to swim. The lessons one of the royal tutors gave me and my sister in the Muran River back in Accasy rise up as if they were only yesterday. My arms sweep through the current; my legs plow through the water with forceful kicks.

I could have made it to the pines farther down even without Bastien's help, but that's not where I need to go.

The current drags at my dress, and I'm more grateful than ever for the airiness of the fabric that only weighs down my limbs a little. Strands of something farther below snatch at my ankles, but I kick them away.

My lungs ache, and my muscles throb.

Almost there. Fifteen more feet. Ten.

Five, and my shoes hit the murky bottom.

I shove myself upright and slosh through the shallows to the narrow beach.

I haven't had any attention to spare my remaining competitor. Now, I notice Leonette surging out of the river just paces away.

I haven't won yet.

A wider path lies ahead of us, the reddish-brown dirt split by darker lines. Gold gleams at the far end: a dais where Marclinus is standing, watching us approach.

Victory is in sight.

For both of us. Leonette dashes toward the path at the same instant I do—and draws up short at a sudden whoosh of fire.

Very real flames spurt from the lines drawn in the dirt,

searing up to lick at the air above our heads. Their scorching heat prickles over my face.

Leonette is closer to the left and notices the gap there first. Yanking up her sopping skirts so they don't hinder her legs, she dashes around the wall of fire.

I race after her, veering sharply to the right in the face of another crackling wall. The roar fills my ears from all around me.

Leonette has already gotten the lead. If we have to keep weaving back and forth so narrowly to avoid being burned, I can't see how I'll pull ahead of her.

With our next sharp turn, a dribble of water from my drenched hair streaks a line across my cheek. It cuts cool through the burning heat.

My breath catches in my throat. If I'm brave enough to walk into the fire…

Certainty condenses around my heart.

I duck my head so the wet strands fall forward to shield my face. My hand sketches hastily down my front in divine appeal.

Elox protect me, so I might do your will when this is done.

Wrapping my hands in the folds of my soaked shirt, I pull deep into the center of calm inside me.

Then I run.

I sprint in a straight line, directly toward my goal. One wall of flame and another hisses with the droplets of water that fly off my clothes and hair.

Searing heat and open air, searing heat and open air. The sweltering warble floods my head.

Patches of my sleeves start to sizzle with a biting sting. I hold myself distant from the pain, pushing my feet harder. The sodden silk slaps against my legs—

And I burst out of the last wall of fire onto firmer ground.

Marclinus stares down at me from the dais, his lips parted with what looks like shock. As I dash the last few steps to reach him, his eyebrows arch.

A typical chuckle is already tumbling from his lips as I hop onto the platform and grasp his hand.

His fingers tighten their grip as he turns toward me. With my free hand, I rake my still-damp hair away from my face.

The imperial heir's gray eyes glint down at me. "So you're willing to set yourself on fire just to have me, Princess Aurelia?"

The scalded spots on my arms throb, but I barely notice over the thrum of my pulse.

I did it. I'm here. I won the man I crossed the empire to marry.

The thought of all the corpses strewn in my wake, the dreams I shattered just minutes ago, turns my smile achingly bittersweet. But Marclinus won't be able to tell.

I beam up at him with all the resolve I have in me. "I'm willing to do anything for you, Your Imperial Highness."

Emperor Tarquin begins to clap, his smile nothing but self-satisfaction. The audience I barely noticed around the glade takes up the applause.

Marclinus grins and tugs my chin up to claim a kiss.

The brazen press of his lips leaves me cold, but I kiss him back all the same.

This is what I asked for, what I traded love and freedom for. I'm going to make everything I can of the chance.

As we break apart, Leonette staggers to a halt at the end of the trail of fire. She gapes at me in a daze, despair dawning on her face.

I don't have time to so much as twitch an apologetic grimace her way before one of the guards plunges his sword through her neck.

Marclinus doesn't even glance toward his last murdered potential bride. He lifts my hand in the air, his gaze still fixed on me, his grin sharpening into a smirk. "Tell the Cleric Pomia that it's time I take this besotted woman as my wife."

CHAPTER FORTY-NINE

Aurelia

The palace temple is smothered in pink.

The swaths of silk form a rosy haze at the edges of my vision as I gaze up at my soon-to-be husband. Everything about the past few hours feels similarly foggy—a blur of medics applying their gifts to my trial-induced wounds and attendants preparing my body for the wedding.

I've been bathed and dressed, powdered and perfumed, and now we stand here before the most prominent cleric of Ardone in Dariu.

I keep my hands loose and relaxed at my sides. The small weight of my sapphire ring provides a fragment of comfort.

It's the only article on me that actually belongs to me. I asked to wear it with my wedding attire as a symbol of this deeper union of Accasy with the empire as well as me with the imperial heir, and that one request was granted.

I can't risk looking away from Marclinus. The one time I did, to take in the swarm of nobles packed into the temple around us, my gaze caught on four faces I wasn't sure I'd ever see again.

The princes could have fled on their own as they'd planned. They didn't need me with them for their gambit to work perfectly well for their own escape.

But they're here, standing amid the crowd to my left, their stances tense and their faces taut with emotions I can't afford to dwell on.

The cleric finishes intoning her prayer for the godlen of love's divine blessing on our partnership. She wraps a strip of pink silk around my palm and then Marclinus's, literally binding us together in the Darium way.

I knew the expected words by heart before I ever left Accasy. "I swear before all the gods to love and honor you from now until my last breath leaves me."

Marclinus repeats the vow to me, his careless grin invalidating the promise in the statement.

Cleric Pomia slides a thin gold band over my other hand and activates the embedded enchantment. The metal contracts around my wrist, not tight enough to pinch but fitted so it could never be removed naturally. I look down at it as she does the same for the imperial heir.

It feels like a gilded manacle.

"Let it be seen that these two are married!" she calls out.

The court cheers. Marclinus bows down to kiss me soundly. The strip of silk falls away, and he grasps my fingers to lead me to dinner.

It's done. I'm his.

After he's licked the last icing from our wedding dessert off his fork, Marclinus raises his wine goblet toward me. "Was that not a most satisfying feast, wife?"

I widen the smile that's been molded to my face since the moment I joined him on the dais this morning and clink my glass to his. "The best I've ever had, husband."

My gaze slides away from him over the nobles assembled in the dining room before us. For our wedding banquet, we newlyweds took the head table all for ourselves, other than Emperor Tarquin watching us from his usual throne-like chair at one end. Platters holding more food than I could eat in a week are laid out all around us.

The feasting nobles chatter at a more subdued tone than usual, with regular glances shot our way. They're evaluating their new empress-to-be. Considering how they can best position themselves to benefit from this shift in power.

Possibly wondering how they might begin to ingratiate themselves into my favor after the chilly initial reception most of them offered.

I skim my eyes more swiftly over the four princes seated next to each other at the nearest table. I still catch a glimpse of Raul's scowl, Lorenzo's drawn expression, Bastien's glare, and Neven's braced stance.

Why didn't they take the chance they had and leave?

Perhaps it didn't seem worth the gamble when they couldn't know if I'd reveal their lies.

Perhaps they wanted to be here simply to ensure I realize how furious they are with me.

From their hostile glowers, we might as well have tumbled back in time to my very first day when this wedding should have taken place, with all of the intimacies we shared wiped away.

Marclinus squeezes my thigh beneath the table. The sight

of his pale hand against the pale pink of my wedding gown makes my stomach lurch.

Why did I make that remark to Lorenzo about marrying *him*? Every time I take in my bridal finery, the illusion the prince conjured around my bed during that brief spell of joy comes back to me with a pang through my heart.

My actual husband takes my hand and gets to his feet, drawing me with him. With a skip of my pulse, I realize we're about to move into the most important part of the night.

The part where I take my first step toward fulfilling all the silent promises I made to the people I left behind.

Marclinus's jovial voice rings through the dining room. "Let us all move to the ballroom to continue our celebration with much merriment and music!"

Once we've reached the hall, he releases my hand. The highest ranking nobles hustle out around us, a few of them diverting the imperial heir's attention with congratulations and promises of wedding gifts they've procured.

While he's laughing with them, someone gives my elbow a tentative tap.

My head snaps around with a hitch in my chest, half-expecting to encounter the bitter gaze of one of the princes up close. It's hard to say whether I'm relieved or disappointed to discover Bianca has come up beside me instead.

The vicerine peers into my face, her own expression inscrutable. Whatever her near-black eyes are searching for, I can't tell if she finds it.

"You stopped when you were going over the wall and reached toward Lady Fausta," she says in a similarly opaque voice. "Why? You were already ahead of her. You let Leonette get a larger lead."

My throat closes up at the reminder of my brief moment of compassion—and the agony I couldn't prevent.

I don't know how to answer other than with the truth. "It seemed like an awful way to die. I didn't think it should have to be that way."

I can't say that I don't believe *any* of my rivals for Marclinus's hand should have been executed. But at least most of their deaths were quick and clean.

Bianca's mouth tightens. I can't tell whether she's upset by my answer or simply agrees with my implied regret. She dips her head and falls back into the crowd around us.

Once we reach the ballroom, Emperor Tarquin glances around. "Prince Lorenzo, let's have your gift bless the dancing tonight."

My smile remains fixed in place. Of course. Why wouldn't the emperor want the most talented musician in the palace providing the music for his son's wedding festivities?

I fix my gaze on Marclinus as we take our places in the middle of the room, not wanting to see what shadows might have crossed my former lover's face. Will this performance be more agonizing for him than when he played as my feet bled, or less because he no longer has any reason to care what happens to me?

The prince strikes up a tune as beautiful as any I've ever heard from his vielle. Marclinus sets one hand on my waist, grasps my fingers, and whirls me around.

For the first minute or so, it's only us dancing while the rest of the court watches, leaving a circle of open floor for us to claim. A sly spark lights in the imperial heir's eyes. His hand drifts down to give my ass a teasing squeeze. When he spins me around again, he lets his fingers trail over my chest.

It doesn't matter that my skin recoils. I just keep beaming at him.

It's almost time.

After our initial display of marital union, other couples pick up the melody alongside us. Soon, most of the court is dipping and turning beneath the sparkling glow of the crystal chandeliers.

In the brief lull between the first song and the next, Marclinus eases back from me and glances toward his father, who's approaching through the crowd of nobles.

Emperor Tarquin nods to me with a smug smile of his own. "Let me say again how pleased I am that you've so thoroughly proven yourself a worthy partner, Aurelia. It's our tradition in Dariu that as emperor I have the honor of the second dance at any palace wedding."

As I already knew. I dip into a slight curtsy and lift my left hand for him to display me to our audience, flicking my thumb over the side of my rippled ring as I do. A subtle gesture, nothing anyone should make note of.

Emperor Tarquin raises my arm higher as he turns me toward the watching nobles, our fingers sliding briefly together. When he releases my hand so we can take our dancing positions, I stroke my ring once more.

The emperor might not be quite as energetic as his son, but he's still sprightly enough that I have to focus on matching his pace. Which is good, because it means I can't wallow in a single other worry. My pulse pounds faster with every emphatic tap of our feet.

At least Tarquin has no interest in groping me. Once the second song ends, he nudges me back toward my husband, whose grin has definitely become more of a leer.

Marclinus trails his fingers down my side before clasping my waist again. "I'd say we give it ten songs total, and then we can respectably depart for our chambers. We can christen your new bedroom first, my wild princess."

The nickname Fausta gave me prickles through my nerves.

Seven more dances after this one. I can agree to that timeline.

I peer at him coyly through my eyelashes the way my rival might have. "I look forward to it."

Even on his wedding day, it's expected that the imperial heir will spread the celebration around. While he dotes on one of the marchionissas, I find myself in the sweaty-palmed grip of her marchion. Then back to Marclinus.

Then he moves to entertain one of his father's advisors, and a slim but firm hand clamps around mine.

My gaze darts over to meet Bastien's dark green eyes.

I catch myself on the verge of wincing. My smile turns carefully polite. I accept his distant embrace, staying equally distant behind the disaffected mask I've put in place.

The prince's stare remains as penetrating as always, if much colder than I've experienced in the recent past. I have the impression he's trying to stab straight through my skull into my thoughts.

His jaw works. "You've had quite a day, Your Imperial Highness."

There's a cutting edge to his voice when he says my new title. I pretend I don't notice his rancor, pretend I don't remember how the hands now chastely placed once roamed over my naked body.

No one who observes our dance can witness so much as a twitch of emotion in my face or my stance. Bastien thinks he knows what's riding on his silence, but he truly has no idea.

"It has been rather a lot," I say carefully. "I'm grateful it's ended so well."

There's no way to play the devoted bride without driving the knife in deeper.

The prince looks as if he's gritted his teeth. "You have everything you wanted, then?"

My smile has never felt stiffer. "Oh, yes. I couldn't be happier."

He lapses into a chilly silence. My pulse thuds on, painfully heavy.

I can't imagine he'd reveal our secret encounters now, not when I know far more of his secrets than he does mine. We'll all just live in the misery we've made for ourselves.

Bastien's lips part as if he's going to say something else—and a sudden thump sends a flurry of gasps through the crowd. The music cuts out.

With a lurch of my heart, I spin around. My surprise isn't totally feigned.

I didn't know exactly how long the concoction would need to take hold in a man. I only ever tested it on animals back in Accasy.

Emperor Tarquin lies sprawled on the floor on his side, his limbs twitching, his face contorted. I let out a gasp of my own and rush toward my father-by-marriage.

Shouts ring out through the ballroom—"The emperor's ill!" "Get the medics!"—with a current of murmurs underneath.

"He has seemed shaky recently."

"That coughing fit the other day…"

"Sometimes the body goes swiftly after the first signs."

The offhand remarks I crafted have stuck in their heads and rippled through the court. Let them see nothing but an old man finally faltering with age.

The dancers pull back around the fallen emperor. Both Tarquin's face and body have gone rigid as the initial paralysis takes hold.

Three of his guards stand over him, their gazes sweeping

across his crumpled form and the mass of nobles around us, searching for any sign of malicious magic. But there's none to be found.

I worked my gift before I ever arrived in Dariu, over and over, until I had just the right mixture to cure the empire of its greatest menace.

I draw up short before I reach Tarquin and hold up my hands to the guards appeasingly. "The medics aren't here yet. Let me see if my gift can find a way to help him?"

They know I deal in potions for healing. One of them accepts my offer with a jerk of his hand.

I drop to my knees beside the emperor's prone body. His eyelids are frozen at half-mast, his pale gray eyes staring straight at me from beneath them, but there's still a glimmer of life in their helpless depths.

Good. I want him to know who dealt his final blow.

Let him die regretting every vicious choice he's made in the past two weeks.

I lower my head. "I think he's trying to say something!"

Leaning my ear close to Emperor Tarquin's mouth, I aim a whisper at the floor that only he will be able to decipher. "It's too bad you won't get to see what I do with your empire."

As I straighten up, the slightest tic quivers through the emperor's face, as if he's attempting one last struggle to break through the bonds of the drug. A thin breath rattles from his throat.

His eyes dim.

Two medics fling themselves through the crowd toward us. I scramble backward to give them room, pulling myself up onto legs I don't have to pretend are wobbly. Adrenaline races through my veins and churns in my gut.

One of the principles that I used to guide my gift was

that the potion should leave no unnatural trace. If Elox's blessing failed me…

The medics press their hands to Tarquin's body, their voices frantic. "His heart's stopped."

"The other organs— I'll try, but I'm not sure—"

My jangling nerves settle into a clammy queasiness.

It's done. I really did it.

I killed a man. But gods smite me, if any man deserved it, it was this one.

Sometimes blood must be spilled to prepare the ground for peace.

Marclinus comes to a halt beside me, gaping down at his father with utter shock. His hands flex at his sides as if searching for something to grasp hold of.

I reach out and twine my fingers with his as a devoted wife should, just as the head medic raises his head toward us with a grim expression.

"I'm sorry, Your Imperial Eminences. There's nothing we can do. It must have been a sudden fit, a severe one… He's gone to his godlen."

The imperial heir stands nearly as rigid as his father's corpse. He draws his chin up, but a tiny tremor passes from his hand into mine.

He's Emperor Marclinus now.

And I'm his empress.

If I can sway him toward compassion and peace, there's no one left to stand in our way.

No one with authority over us, at least.

I lift my eyes from Tarquin's body, and my gaze collides with an icy blue one just across from me. Raul's searing stare chills me straight through to my bones.

He's looking at me as if he's just seen me for the very first time. As if he knows exactly what I did.

What was going through Bastien's head when he and the other princes confronted Aurelia during her illness—and when he realized how sick she actually was? Find out in a bonus scene from his POV by going to this URL or using the QR code below: https://BookHip.com/DMDPLVH

The Gods of the Abandoned Realms

THE ALL-GIVER (the Great God, the One) - overseer of all
existence, creator of the godlen

THE GODLEN OF THE SKY

Estera - wisdom, knowledge, and education

Inganne - creativity, play, childhood, and dreams

Kosmel - luck, trickery, and rebellion

THE GODLEN OF THE EARTH

Creaden - royalty, leadership, justice, and construction

Prospira - fertility, wealth, harvest, and parenthood

Sabrelle - warfare, sports, and hunting

THE GODLEN OF THE SEA

Ardone - love, beauty, and bodily pleasures

Elox - health, medicine, and peace

Jurnus - communication, travel, and weather

ABOUT THE AUTHOR

Eva Chase lives in Canada with her family. She loves stories both swoony and supernatural, and strong women and the men who appreciate them.

Along with the Royal Spares series, she is the author of the Rites of Possession series, the Shadowblood Souls series, the Heart of a Monster series, the Gang of Ghouls series, the Bound to the Fae series, the Flirting with Monsters series, the Cursed Studies trilogy, the Royals of Villain Academy series, the Moriarty's Men series, the Looking Glass Curse trilogy, the Their Dark Valkyrie series, the Witch's Consorts series, the Dragon Shifter's Mates series, the Demons of Fame series, and the Legends Reborn trilogy.

Connect with Eva online:
www.evachase.com
eva@evachase.com

Made in United States
Orlando, FL
04 October 2024